WOLVES AND THE RIVER OF STONE

ERIC R. ASHER

www.daysgonebad.com

Produced by ReAnimus Press
www.ReAnimus.com

Edited by Laura Matheson
www.plainstext.com

Copy edited by Ashley's Freelance Editing
freelance.mcconnell05.com

Cover typography by Bookish Brunette Designs
brunettedesigns.wordpress.com/

Cover design © Phatpuppyart.com – Claudia McKinney

ISBN-13: 978-1492992899

First print edition: October, 2013

10 9 8 7 6 5 4 3 2 1

For that single word. Loathed by some, loved by many. Bacon.

Acknowledgements

A special thanks to everyone who spares an encouraging word for the creative people in their lives.

An enthusiastic thank you goes to my beta readers: Amy Cameron, Jason Cameron, Angela Shafer, and Ron Asher.

Thanks to the Critters.org workshop and their superb critiques.

Thank you so very much to everyone who has taken the time to read Vesik, The Series, and even deeper thanks to those of you that have become The Patrons of Death's Door.

Thank you to my editor, Laura Matheson, whose wise words saved me from more than one terrible, and sometimes amusing, misstep.

CHAPTER 1

Mname is Damian Valdis Vesik. I am a necromancer. The dismembered limbs littering the soft grass at my feet used to be a pair of zombies. The small man with terror in his eyes, shaking between the supports of a rusty old bridge is Lewis Hood, servant of Philip Pinkerton, one time love of my master, Zola.

I eased the bullets into my six-barreled pepperbox one at a time, forgoing the speed loader in the name of intimidation. Lewis's eyes went wide and locked onto the gun.

"Where is she?" I said. I took a deep breath, the Missouri River beside us masking every other scent aside from the decay of the blasted zombies. The shadowed tree lines hid us from the nearby population of Saint Charles.

Lewis shook his head.

Two days ago we learned Philip was still alive. Yesterday his servants kidnapped Zola. I didn't know why they took her, but she didn't go quietly. The Watchers would be using a spatula to clean out the alley where she was taken.

"You sicced your zombies on us?" I said. "A fairy and a necromancer?" The zombies had gone down fast with help from a demon staff inlaid with decorative, and functional, silverwork. I glared at Lewis. "I find myself ... irritated."

Lewis held up his hand and started to speak.

I holstered the pepperbox under my arm and wrapped my hand around the shield rune on my staff. A flowing glass surface sprang to life as a thread of power wound into the wood and metal.

"Don't even think about it," I said.

Despair washed over Lewis's face. He was breaking, and I could see it.

I leaned the staff against the bridge support opposite Lewis and re-leased my grip on the silver rune. The shield around me dissipated and I had a short, clear path to him. My pepperbox hissed as I drew it from the shoulder holster and leveled it at Lewis.

"N-No, no!"

"Where's Zola?" I said, my voice flat, but beginning to snarl.

"No!" he said.

Thunder and flame roared from one of the six barrels as Lewis's kneecap burst into a fine mist.

He screamed and fell into the mud. I won't deny the glimmer of satisfaction in my gut.

"Get away!" he whimpered hysterically.

"Thug to beggar in sixty seconds," I said as I moved my finger to the second trigger on my pistol. The second trigger was fairy work, capable of firing all six barrels at once—or the five chambered rounds, in this case. "Where's Zola?"

His eyes were wide. I could see the whites around his irises as they flicked from his knee to my gun and up to my eyes. "Please don't."

I moved my finger back to the first trigger. "Tell me where she is or I blow out the other one." I shifted my aim from his head to his good knee.

He grimaced and his head sagged. "Zion," he said as he gasped for air, "Mount Zion Church ... Hallsville."

I nodded and holstered the pistol. Relief spread across Lewis's face a moment before a sword sprang from his neck. The fairy oozed out of the shadows behind him, a savage grin split his pointed features as he jerked his sword down and back. Lewis's body fell forward be-tween me and the seven-foot fairy, a look of confusion etched across the corpse's forehead.

"What if he was lying, Foster?" I said as I cocked an eyebrow.

"Then you can raise him and I'll kill him again, put that necro-mancy to good use." Foster casually wiped his sword off with a swatch of Lewis's white shirt, flexing his black-and-white wings as he bent down. "That was too fast."

I shook my head and muttered, "Fairies." Fairies are one of the most merciless races I've ever met. You screw with their friends or family, and they'll tear you into pieces. Very small pieces. I've heard some of the old gods are more severe, but I've yet to meet any.

"Where's Hallsville?" Foster said.

I shrugged. "Oh, I don't know. Let's ask." I toed Lewis's head and spoke slowly. "Do you have a map to Hallsville, Lewis? Lewis? Are you okay?"

"Shut up, Damian." Foster's wings twitched as he sheathed his sword.

"We need to get rid of the body," I said with a broad grin as I slapped Foster on the shoulder.

He sighed and rolled his eyes. "Stand back a second." I stepped away as Foster drew a circle in the mud around Lewis and the zombie parts. "Hand me your staff."

Reluctantly, I handed my staff over. "You know, your mom will kill you if you hurt my staff."

"At least she'll kill you too." Foster smiled and turned his head back to the corpse. He whispered "*Somes reverto terra*" and brought the ferrule of the staff down hard in the center of the circle. He quickly stepped away as a murky grayish light ran from the staff and flared to the edges of the circle. The earth churned and swallowed the bodies in a quiet rumble as the scent of tilled soil and river water reached my nose.

The riverfront fell into silence again. Foster tossed my staff to me. It smacked against my palm as I caught it, and he snapped into his smaller form in a dim flash of white light.

"Let's get Zola," he said.

CHAPTER 2

Frank was working the shop for me. I was tempted to stop by just to see if my sister, Sam, was hanging around. I hadn't heard from her as much since she'd gotten more serious with Frank. Sam and Frank, if ever there was a sign of impending apocalypse, but there were bigger things to worry about at that moment. I knew Sam was worried about Zola too, but Foster had more productive ideas to fill our evening than catching up with the family. He was positive Carter would know how to get to the church in Hallsville without consulting the web. After our last online map sent us a hundred miles south of our intended destination, I wasn't arguing.

We set off for Carter's house without delay so I could meet my first werewolf. Poor Vicky—my custom '32 Ford, complete with flames. Nervous energy had me drumming her steering wheel into submission. Foster camped out in my oversized electric coffee mug, which happened to be filled with water and soap suds at the moment, and was plugged in to a retrofitted cigarette lighter on Vicky's dashboard.

"Damn, I love this mug," Foster said.

I glanced at his black-and-white butterfly wings, drooping over the edge of the steaming cup, and grimaced as we rumbled down the cobblestone street. "I will never be able to drink out of that again."

I heard a splash as Foster said, "You don't know the half of it. The other night Aideen–"

My eyes widened and I hurried to say, "Stop, stop now, for god's sake. How do we get to Carter's again?"

Foster laughed and sighed as he sank down to his chin. "Just take Fifth Street north. He's a few lights up. It's not far."

We left the cobblestone streets of Saint Charles and pulled onto blessedly modern asphalt. The scenery changed quickly from old world brick construction to not-quite-so old suburbia. In fact, the thought of a werewolf lurking in the area seemed asinine. It seemed even more so as I stood on the curb and stared at Carter's house five minutes later. "You sure this is the right place?"

"Oh yeah, check out the welcome mat."

I crossed over the white picket fence, passed the pristine lawn, and started up the tulip-lined walk to Carter's front door. The welcome mat, in front of the small white house with black shutters and a black door, was a cartoon wolf's head with the tag line, "*My, what big teeth you have.*" I stared at Foster for a minute as he squeezed the last bits of moisture out of the bottom of his wings and wrinkled his nose.

"He's definitely here. I could smell him from Cleveland."

A deep, rumbling laugh rattled the door a second before it opened to reveal an average man with sandy blond hair. "And I could hear the annoying squeak of a fairy in my yard over the stereo." I looked down on Carter—although being six foot five, I look down on most people—and guessed he was no more than five eight or nine. He had a light beard covering a strong chin. His eyes were profound, with a huge sunburst iris rimmed in black. His voice was deep as hell and just as intimidating.

Foster grinned and fluttered up to Carter's shoulder. "Hey Carter, this is Damian. I think you met him once at his shop on Main Street, The Double D?"

"It's good to see you again, Damian." Carter extended his hand and nonchalantly crushed every bone in mine.

"You too, Carter," I said, though I honestly couldn't remember his face.

"So what brings you two here?"

"We're in a rush and need to get to Hallsville. Damian still hasn't sprung for a GPS and his master's been taken by her old lover and is probably in deep shit at this point." Foster revealed all this in the span of one second.

I blinked and Carter nodded.

"You could have called me."

"Oh, but I don't have your number," Foster said.

Carter smiled a gentle smile. "Don't worry about it. You and your friends are always welcome. It may be wise to make sure it's not a full house in the future." He looked up at me. "Sorry to hear about Zola."

He stood aside and opened the door a little wider for us as we crossed into the werewolf's den. I was trying to be wary of the wolf, but I already liked him.

Carter's home was quaint, with a large dining room off to the right of the entry way. Judging by the glimpses I caught of the small living room and bedroom, the dining room was by far the largest room. I eyed the flat television mounted on the wall of the living room with a passing interest. The walls themselves were a subtle green color with white crown molding and beige furniture.

The only thing in the house that wasn't immaculate was the hard-wood floor. There were about a bajillion scrapes and gouges all across it. Apparently werewolves were really good at distressing wood. I caught a glimpse of myself in the entry way mirror, mud caked along the sleeve of my black bomber jacket and jeans. There was even some brown mixed into my black hair, causing it to stick out at odd angles over my left ear. My eyes looked tired, dim gray lights perched over the sharp edges of my cheekbones. I stroked the point of my chin and more mud flaked off. Watching it fall, I realized I had mud all over my shoes too. I sighed, pulled my shoes off, and set them outside while Carter just smiled.

Carter's wife really threw me for a loop as she came around the half wall of the kitchen and thrust a platter of crispy rice squares under my nose.

"Glorious, glorious rice squares!" Foster said as he pounced on the platter.

Carter laughed as bits of cereal pattered onto the floor and said, "This is my wife, Maggie."

She was a petite woman with platinum blonde hair and green wolf eyes. She looked almost fragile next to Carter, and I had a hard time registering the fact she could shift and tear my arms off if she felt like it. I smiled and nodded at Maggie and said, "Thanks" as I picked up a square of marshmallow-and-puffed-rice goodness.

"You are welcome in our home, until I say otherwise, necromancer." Her smile had all the warmth of a dynamite plunger.

My teeth stopped halfway through the rice square and my eyebrows rose as I looked at Maggie again. Her smile warmed a bit, so I nodded and finished biting a piece off the rice square. I glanced at Carter and he was glaring at his wife. I hid a smile behind a cough.

"These are fantastic!" I said as I shook the rice square in the air.

"Let's get your map," Carter said, his voice utterly flat.

Maggie smiled sweetly as we walked past her, through the living room, down a short hallway and into a den. The furniture was all leather and dark wood. The far wall held two huge barrister bookcases, stretching from floor to ceiling and wall-to-wall, with about four inches of space between them.

"I grew up in rural Missouri," Carter said as he reached in and pulled out one of the leather tomes. "I know the state better than most. I keep a few maps around just in case." He set the tome on the desk with a thump and cracked it open to reveal dozens of pockets stuffed with a mass of maps.

"Just in case?" I asked.

"Wow," Foster said. "You have maps for the whole country in there?"

"Just Missouri," Carter said as he thumbed through a few leaflets. "I used to get lost when I was a kid. I started picking up maps." He glanced at the bookcases. "It may have gotten a bit out of hand." He pulled out a small rectangle of folded paper. "Here we go. It's a little old, but it has the church on it." He unfolded the map as he spoke and laid it across the desk. "You know how to get to Columbia?"

I nodded. It was a straight shot out Highway 70.

"Good, once you're there, take 63 North. You'll see an exit for Hallsville a couple miles down the road." His finger traced the route as he spoke. "From there you should be able to follow the dead."

"What?" I said.

"It's an old battlefield and there's a decent-sized graveyard by the church."

"Battlefield ..." I started and my face hardened in anger. "Civil War battlefield?"

Carter nodded and watched me with narrowed eyes.

"That's why Philip has her there, Foster. Something's there. One of the artifacts, a Guardian, something."

"I don't like Zola's taste in men," Foster said.

I laughed, but it was empty. "Can we borrow this, Carter?"

"Of course, of course. It shows you the lay of the land pretty well, should help you plan an approach," he said as he folded the map up and handed it over.

"You want to come with us?" Foster said.

Carter shook his head. "I can't be involved in a fight between necromancers. It would cause too much tension in the pack. I am sorry."

Foster nodded without remark.

"Thank you, Carter," I said. "We have to go."

He walked us to the door and saw us out. We didn't see Maggie, but she'd left a small bundle of crispy rice squares on Vicky's front seat for us, with a note that said, "Good luck. We're always watching." I shivered.

"She's, uh, kind of creepy, Damian." Foster bit into another chunk of marshmallow as we traveled down Fifth Street to Highway 70.

"Yeah, I noticed. What was that all about?"

"She's probably caught up in the old ways."

"Old ways?" I glanced at Foster and he was staring at me with his eyebrows raised. "What?"

"Aideen told you all about werewolves. Did you not listen to her at *all*?"

"Sure I did. I just don't remember that part."

Foster snorted and it sounded like the puff of a nasal spray as we pulled onto the highway. "Yeah, you were so smashed you slept with Mary and let her munch on you."

Actually we'd gone out drinking with my sister Sam, Vik, Foster, Aideen, and a couple of girls from the vampire Pit. The Pit is Sam's vampire family. Fairies generally stay far away from vampires, but Aideen and Foster had grown fond of Vik, and were even tolerant of Sam's Pit, in general. Sometime in the evening, or early morning, Aideen had regaled me with the rich history of the Wolves of War. The night was fuzzy as hell, but I do vaguely remember doing things that ought not be done with the beautiful, irritating, and undead

Mary, and waking up with vampire bites in the morning. Apparently necromancers are a tasty snack.

I glanced out the driver's window in a failing effort to hide a grin as little flashes of the night came back to me. Vampires can get a little intoxicated by drinking alcohol, but drinking blood from an intoxicated human will get them flat drunk.

I scratched my head and looked at Foster. He was practically vibrating from all the sugar he'd been eating. "You were saying?"

"I was saying, werewolves used to kill necromancers on sight."

"Bah, what's new? Everyone used to kill necromancers on sight."

"Yes," Foster said, dragging the word out like he was talking to a toddler, "but werewolves are stuck in the past, bound to tradition even more so than some religious zealots."

My smile faltered a little as Foster's words hit home. Vicky bounced as I failed to dodge a pothole. "So some of them may want to dismember me on general principle?"

"Thoroughly, and violently."

"Awesome," I muttered.

CHAPTER 3

It turned out Hallsville wasn't all that far from us, but I was ready to pull out a flyswatter by the time we reached the area. Foster had shoveled down almost half of a crispy rice square and was flitting around the car like a gerbil on crack. I choked the steering wheel and steeled myself against my impulse to swat.

I ground my teeth and growled, "Why don't you sit down, Foster?" He responded, but his words blurred together so fast, and at such a high pitch, I couldn't make sense out of them. I sighed as I rolled down the window, threw out the crispy rice square remnants, and opened the console to reveal my fairy emergency kit. It consisted of a small plastic cup and a flask of Bushmills Irish Whiskey. I poured out a tiny measure and said, "Drink it, or you're going out the window next."

A swooping blur diminished the thimble-sized puddle of whiskey to nothing in a few seconds. Moments later, Foster was laid out on the dashboard with a ridiculous grin on his face. He drummed his fingers in a slow rhythm on the sword pommel slung across his hip and dragged his words out with a sigh. "Oh, yeah, that's good."

I feigned shock, raising my eyebrows. "Holy crap, you speak English!"

"For crispy rice squares, I'll do worse than that." He winked and pretended to shoot me with his thumb and index finger.

"God help us." I turned my head to hide a smile as I pulled off Highway 63. The tree line crept up close to the road as we continued north.

"So what's the deal with Carter? Are all the werewolves as nice as he is? You know, except for the whole killing necromancers thing?"

Foster stared at me for a minute, as if waiting for a punch line. "You bloody wish they were all like him. Most of them are like twenty four hour 'roid rage."

I shook my head. "No way, come on. You've got to be exaggerating. Carter seems laid back and in control."

"No shit, genius." Foster laughed. "Carter's the Alpha around here. His presence has to be calming to the rest of the pack or they'd wipe themselves out, not to mention everyone else."

I glanced at Foster as he jumped off the dashboard and down to the console. I squinted as the sun flashed off his golden armor. "You're not kidding, are you?" I said.

"No, I'm not," he said as he pulled his sword from its sheath.

"He's a werewolf. He's an Alpha. And he has a white picket fence." I shook my head and laughed.

Foster didn't respond. He stared out the windshield and then turned to look at me. "Do you feel it?"

My eyes flicked to the surrounding woods. "Yes." I'd felt it for a while. The horror and anxiety was building around us as we grew closer to the battlefield—it was as if I was diving to the bottom of a deep pool. The dead pushed on the edges of my aura like several feet of water. There was something else out there besides the fallen soldiers. It felt wrong, and angry. "We're close. Do you feel the ..." I paused, searching for the right word, "darkness?"

Foster's mouth flattened into a grim line and he nodded sharply. "Let's pull off the road. Hide the car."

I slowed, the tires crunching on the gravel shoulder, and watched Foster for a moment before I nodded. His gaze never broke from the small rise to the east. We'd been on Mount Zion Church Road for a few minutes when we pulled into an abandoned filling station with real, live gasohol pumps. I parked Vicky behind the rickety structure, grabbed my staff and my focus, and we struck out across the small road.

"I can't believe the road was named Mount Zion Church."

"Follow me," Foster said as a tiny smile curled his lips.

We moved through the woods quickly. Daylight vanished into the permanent twilight of the forest. Twigs and branches caught at my clothes as leaves crumbled, whispering around my feet. I held my staff in front of my face to deflect the worst of the low hanging branches. Foster fluttered nimbly between the leaves, leading us closer to the church. The dead were all around us now. I knew if I looked, I'd see the first signs of soldiers staring blankly at us from their gray bodies and ancient uniforms, surrounded by the calm flow of black, white, and dead auras. I crushed a small patch of honeysuckle as we hurried through a sunny clearing, the sweet smells of the plant an anathema to the tightening of my gut.

There was a flash of white and an explosion of fairy dust in front of me an instant before I walked into Foster's seven-foot-tall back with a grunt. It was a damn good thing I'd remembered my allergy medicine that morning. It's hard to be stealthy in the middle of a sneezing fit. Foster took in my scowl and shot me a grin, shrugging as if to say *sorry about that*. He pointed to the southeast. I followed the direction he indicated and could just make out the white church and the small graveyard beside it.

We shifted to the northeast and settled in the woods beyond the graves before a flash of color caught my eye. From our new vantage point, I could make out a man's silhouette near the edge of the church. I could see the close-cropped full beard on his round face. A bowler was perched over his formidable forehead and crooked nose. I couldn't see his eyes, but I knew they were small, black, and beady. The instant after I recognized Philip, I realized the crumpled form on the ground was Zola, her head leaning against a weathered and mossy headstone. Another figure had its foot propped against her neck.

It took everything I had not to run at them with guns blazing. I looked at Foster and saw the rage creasing his forehead, a mirror of my own. His hand had turned white where he held the hilt of his sword in a death grip.

"We kill that one and Philip kills Zola before we get out there," I whispered.

Foster nodded. "Kill Philip, and the other one kills her. Shit. Let's see if they shift positions."

Philip's voice rose and we could both hear his words clearly. "Tell me where she is or I'll leave you here in pieces." He pushed off the wall with his hands and casually kicked Zola in the ribs. She flexed in pain. Philip's partner stepped down harder until Zola was gasping for air. Philip grabbed Zola's hair, pushed the other person away, and dragged my master to her feet. She wobbled, but stood fast.

"Tell me where she is." He shook her head as he spoke.

Zola, true to form, spit a bucket's worth of blood across his face.

I could hear the impact as Pinkerton's partner hit Zola in the back of the head with the butt of a rifle. Zola went down hard. As she hit the ground, I got my first clear look at the accomplice: a middle-aged blonde woman with a glare that could keep a demon at bay. She laughed as Zola moaned. Philip looked at the woman, then back to Zola, without any hint of emotion.

Foster touched my shoulder. When I looked up, he drew a finger across his neck and then pointed at the other woman. He motioned to my staff and I handed it over. I nodded and shifted my weight forward as he moved silently through the graveyard and into the woods on the other side. They were causing too much damage to Zola for us to wait much longer. It was time to return the favor.

Philip crossed his arms behind his back and paced down the side of the small church, beneath the thin gothic windows adorning the building. I took that moment to move forward. "It's over, Philip. Let her go." I spoke loudly, projecting my voice as best I could as I struck out between the church and the graveyard with a loping stride.

His head snapped around and stared at me before a small smile lifted his face. "Ah, perfect. Just the inspiration she needs." He took a step toward me. "I'll pull you apart into manageable pieces until she talks. Dismantle her favorite son." His smile turned wicked, and the fire in his eyes was well beyond sane.

"No, let me kill him."

Philip stopped and turned to the woman holding Zola. He shrugged and waved his hand dismissively. "Fine."

My left hand itched to grab the silver inlays on my staff, the staff I had given to Foster. One grab of the right rune would call a shield around me in a split second, faster than I could speak the incantation.

Instead, my fingers traced the hilt of the focus tucked beneath my belt. It was the plain, leather-wrapped, silver and gray Magrasnetto hilt of an old Scottish claymore. Dime-sized holes spiraled up the grip at regular intervals, and channels ran down the sloping arms to the quatrefoil pattern at the ends. A wide hole gaped where the blade would normally be. An idea crept into my head and I looked around for Foster. He was nowhere to be seen. I cursed and turned my attention back to the woman holding Zola. Foster was going to get her the staff so she could shield herself from Philip; all I had to do was get her the focus.

The blonde met my gaze. "I am Agnes Smythe. I am your death." Her voice was almost peppy and it threw me off for a moment.

A small laugh made me glance at Philip. The smirk on his face lit fantasies of eviscerating him and feeding him whatever fell out.

I was about to fire off a witty retort, but Agnes elbowed Zola in the mouth with a vicious strike. Zola's head snapped back and I could hear the crack of bone from fifteen feet away. She crumpled to the ground in a heap. Through the rage in my gut I still felt a hint of relief as her hands moved to cover her face when Agnes put her foot back on Zola's neck.

With that, Foster had seen enough. The seven-foot fairy dropped silently out of the tree behind them, swinging my staff on a downward angle. He connected with Agnes's head. The crack was sickening. She jerked violently to one side and her foot fell away from Zola. Agnes staggered forward before flailing to the ground.

"Zola!" I said as I stepped forward, pulled my right arm back, and whipped the focus at her. It spiraled toward her on an almost perfect angle and the handle made a loud snap as she caught it.

Blood coursed over Zola's teeth as she stood up and smiled a death's head grin. Her right hand wrapped around the staff as Foster let go and the hilt of the focus was in her left. She pointed the hilt at the base of Agnes's neck and grabbed the rune near the top ferrule on the staff. Zola's body stiffened as her aura was forced through the focus and honed into a deep red aural blade, wrapped in a cacophony of blue, gold, and silver filaments. Agnes didn't even get to scream before the vibrating blade relieved her shoulders of their heavy burden. The ground beneath her hissed and popped as the blade shot home and Zola wrenched it to the side.

Philip stared at the decapitated body for a moment, then slowly raised his eyes to Zola. "That was wasteful."

A tinge of ozone reached my nostrils as I ran to stand beside Zola.

"Now, Philip," she said as she wiped her sleeve across her bloody mouth. "We finish this."

Philip made a fist and snarled, "*Pulsatto!*" A wave of force erupted from his incantation. Zola's hand moved to the shield rune and a flowing shell sprang up around us, dissipating the force of the attack. Philip took a step backwards, his brows drawn together, and then he turned to run.

I was sure I could see relief on Zola's face as Philip made his escape. "Let him leave." Her words were thick, like she had a jaw-breaker tucked in the side of her mouth. She fell to her knees and hung her head as she let out a long sigh.

Foster made a frustrated noise. "We should kill him now."

Zola squeezed her eyes closed and then looked up at Foster. Her old world New Orleans accent was more profound in her weakened state. "No, there are worse things to deal with first." She raised her hand to her cheek and winced. "We have to destroy the artifact here. It binds the demon Tessrian to our plane, and she is not to be trifled with."

Foster glared at Zola for a moment, but his expression softened an instant later. "Fine, but we're not doing anything until we patch you up a bit."

Foster looked over Zola's wounds while I considered her words. I wondered if the demon was really more important than Philip, or if Zola was just having a hard time deciding to kill her one time lover. I stared at my master and rage boiled up anew as I took in her wounds.

"Your face is broken," I growled.

"Yes, boy, it certainly feels that way." Zola's lips flicked into a tiny, swollen smile.

"It's not funny," Foster said. "You have a few fractured bones ... it's going to hurt when I heal you."

"Heal me," she said simply.

Foster let her braided hair swing back across the cuts on her face and nodded. He took a deep breath and closed his eyes before meeting Zola's gaze, pushing his hands forward, and speaking the words, "*Socius Sanation!*"

White light traced the wounds across Zola's face as her body went rigid. If she was fighting not to scream, she lost, and I held her head off the ground as she seized with the pain of Foster's healing. It was over in seconds, but left her gasping for breath.

"Thank you," she whispered.

Foster grimaced and began looking her over again.

Zola winced once or twice, but eventually she batted the fairy away. "Ah want waffles."

Foster and I burst into laughter.

Zola's face curled into a faint, wrinkled smile. "We need the artifact." She took a deep breath and concentrated on her words. "Thomas Anderson's headstone has a hollow recess." She closed her eyes and leaned back against a headstone. "Knock it over and reach inside the hole. It's still there."

I nodded and walked between the gravestones. Well-tended grass bordered the mossy markers. Thin rocks carved with the names of dozens of soldiers flanked the edges of the yard. Thomas Anderson was in the very back, at the edge of the woods. His stone was shorter than the others. Bone white and weather worn, it took some rocking to loosen the earth's hold on it. I laid the stone on its side, scattering a small group of beetles and pill bugs.

Reaching into a dark hole with bare hands is generally not advisable. My hand bumped into several small ledges inside the stone. Something raced over my knuckles and I ground my teeth together. Relief was welcome when my hands wrapped around a brittle leather cloth and pulled it out of the recess without getting bit. The leather crumbled. Exposure to air and dirt did nothing for its longevity. The artifact was a heavy crystal; its shape reminded me of quartz, but dark green with flecks and streaks the color of blood. I replaced the tombstone and walked back to Zola.

"Got it," I said.

Zola nodded and turned the focus in her hands as she stood up and we started back to the car. "Damian, Ah have a friend in great need of this focus. Would you lend it to him, Ah wonder?"

I shrugged. "How long?"

"Not long. Just a few days."

"Sure, I don't see a problem with that. Who is he?"

"Just an old mage. If he can use your focus, maybe we can convince the Fae to make him one of their own."

"Just an old mage, huh?" I pushed a few branches out of the way with my staff and let Zola duck through in front of me. "Why do I have a feeling that's not the whole story?"

"Whatever do you mean, boy?" she said as she tucked the focus into her cloak.

Foster flashed into his small form and fluttered ahead of us, gliding into Vicky through an open window.

I turned to Zola, placed my hands on top of my staff, and rested my chin on them. "Are you okay, master?"

She laughed weakly and held my gaze for a moment as wetness gathered in her eyes. "Damian, you need not call me master."

CHAPTER 4

We stopped at the Waffle House off Highway 70 in Columbia. There is something fantastic about walking into the sizzling sounds of bacon and the smell of eggs, pancakes, and grease. The server behind the counter eyeballed Zola and me before approaching our booth. I guess the Waffle House employees had seen stranger things than an eighty-something woman with a smear of dried blood across her chin and a muddy necromancer trailing behind her, because they didn't say a word.

Foster sat down on the table and leaned against a bottle of ketchup. We placed our order and were dining on pancakes, omelets, and hash browns in minutes. Foster glared at us. He generally didn't eat in public restaurants because food floating around in midair and disappearing in fairy-sized bites was generally disturbing to the other guests.

Zola was the first to break the relative silence of our feeding frenzy. "Philip didn't run because we scared him." She squeezed her right hand into a fist, leaned back in the small booth, and ran her fingers through her braids. "He ran because he wants you alive."

"What?" I asked, perplexed.

Zola took a bite of waffle and almost purred as she finished chewing. She set her fork down and rested her chin on the knuckles of her left hand. "Agnes talked too much when Philip wasn't around. Ah learned things, about Philip, and his *cult*." She almost spat the word and her lips curled into a snarl.

"*Cult*," Foster said. "He'd be so pissed if he heard you call his army a cult." He pulled a piece of shredded cheese off my omelet and started eating it from the end.

Zola nodded and turned her attention back to me. "He gave Devon the power to control other vampires. That's why Azzazoth seemed to have so many followers."

"What?" I said.

"It's a dark art. It bestows the vampire control almost equal to a necromancer. Think of the pranks you used to play on Sam."

Foster laughed and a smile curled my lips. I remembered when she was a new vampire. Though I didn't have absolute control over her, I could still flex my necromancy because she'd fed on my blood and could end an argument by making Sam tell me how great I was. Foster had witnessed it a few times.

"Now, think if you used that control to have Sam tear out her own heart, or wound herself gravely enough for a demon to take over her aura."

My smile died.

Zola nodded. "Perhaps worse, Philip thinks you're the key to unlocking Prosperine."

I narrowed my eyes. "Prosperine? The Destroyer? She died ages ago. She's as much a myth as some of the dormant old gods."

"No, she still lives." Her eyes closed and she took a deep breath. "You are the key because ..." She stopped and stared at me for a while. "Ah have kept things from you Damian. Ah thought to protect you, but Ah fear it was a mistake."

Zola looked unsettled, which was unsettling in itself. Anxiety twisted my throat and I swallowed the knot down hard. "It's okay. I know you were always looking out for me. Just tell me," I said in a carefully controlled voice.

At first I didn't think she was going to say anything because her face closed down. What she did say, I never saw coming. "Ah knew your grandfather in the war."

"What?" I said as my eyes widened.

"Ah never told you because ..." she grimaced and clenched her hands into fists again, "because he died to seal Prosperine away at the Battle of Stones River." She pounded her fist on the table. "It was my fault." Her lips twisted into a snarl.

Foster fluttered over to Zola and slapped her in the face with a wet napkin. "That's crap and you damn well know it." He pointed at her as she stared at him with wide eyes. "You didn't know enough back then. You were the student. You've told me this story before. You know as well as I do it's not your fault."

I gaped at Foster, then at Zola, and then Foster again. "You knew?"

Foster shrugged. "She just wanted someone else to know in case she didn't get a chance to tell you herself. Obviously your master is an excellent judge of character." Foster locked his thumbs in the edge of his cuirass, bowed, and smirked as Zola let out a tiny chuckle.

"Tell me what happened," I said.

Zola met my eyes and I thought she looked relieved. Maybe she thought I'd flip out when I found out she'd known an ancestor of mine I'd never met—an ancestor who had died well over a century before I was born.

"It was toward the end of the first day when she rose." A shudder rattled the spoon in Zola's coffee mug. "Gravemakers were being born out of the carnage at a rate Ah hadn't seen since Shiloh and wouldn't see again until Gettysburg and Chickamauga. We didn't know—we couldn't have known—she was fueling them. Men died from gunfire and cannonballs, yes, but many more were struck down by gravemakers. And Prosperine, by the gods, on New Year's Day 1863, Prosperine raised the dead rebs and yanks and marched them through both lines. They killed their own, and it was ... it was horrible.

"We were across the river near McFadden's Ford when we first saw her. She came out of the river and floated across the battlefield. Ah remember she was beautiful at first, like a raven-haired goddess, but her image stuttered on our plane. You'd see a flash of decaying tentacles and beaks wrapped in a mass to resemble a human body.

"One boy ..." she sighed and closed her eyes. "Ah remember a young boy, a Union boy of maybe fifteen that had the gift, he had the Sight. We were going to help him, train him if we could. He tried to run from the Gravemakers, but when he saw Prosperine he ate his gun. Didn't even sit down to do it, just put the rifle to his chin mid-stride and he was gone." Zola's voice grew strained and she started talking faster.

"Only he wasn't gone. Prosperine grabbed his soul and reanimated his body with it. He wasn't alive, he wasn't dead, and he was controlled by that demon. He was her tool. He killed dozens for her. Union boys, Confederate boys, it didn't matter to him or to her."

Zola shook her head slowly and her voice was smaller as she said, "Ah still wake up to that monster in my nightmares. The screaming. The blood." She closed her eyes and took a deep breath.

"Hinrik, your great-grandfather, Ah suppose? Watching that broken child pushed him over the edge. Ah remember his face. Ah always thought it was how a Viking should look, all hair and rage." She smiled and laughed an empty laugh. "He screamed for me to hide the artifact when he was done. Ah didn't realize what he meant to do. Ah thought he had some way to trap her. Ah suppose he did, but it cost him his life. Bound that monster into a bloodstone. We'd had our differences. He was a dark necromancer, Damian, but he was a good man, in the end."

I couldn't keep the shock from my face and my voice fell to a whisper. "He was a necromancer? A *dark* necromancer?"

Zola nodded.

Dark necromancers were abominations, blights walking the earth. They dove into taboo and truly evil practices like most people breathe air. If an incantation called for the sacrifice of a child, not only would they not hesitate, they were likely to use two, just to be safe. I shivered as I considered the fact one of my ancestors, one of the people I inherited my gift from, was dark.

"Do my parents know?"

"They knew he was gifted, but no, they don't know what he was."

"I pray I never fall that far," I said.

"You won't," Zola and Foster said simultaneously. Foster laughed and leaned against the ketchup bottle, with his arms crossed and his scabbard swinging at his side.

I sighed and glanced between my friends. Most of the supernatural community would consider Zola a dark necromancer for her past deeds, no matter how justified. She'd been a slave once. When she escaped with Philip, they'd taken their vengeance on the slavers that abused them. Philip had been a stable boy, beaten almost as regularly as the slaves. Zola took eight lives in a hideous ritual of torture and flames, and for her atrocity, she would live eight lifetimes. She still bore the scars on her back from the whips and flails. The raised skin on her wrists was still slick where shackles had torn them open again and again. She had been sixteen when she was beaten into slavery. Hideous ritual or not, the slavers deserved worse.

"Am I really the key to Prosperine?"

"Your bloodline, yes, and you are the only necromancer left in the line. Even if Sam had the gift, her vampire blood won't open a gate now that she is a vampire. Essentially, you are the key."

"Maybe we should just kill you," Foster said. "Save us some headaches."

I'd like to think he was joking.

"Even dead, his blood could still be used," Zola said.

"Guys, I'm right here."

"So torch him," Foster said with a snappy *isn't it obvious* tone of voice.

Zola casually rolled up her menu and whacked him into the next booth. I heard a tiny "Ouch" muttered from behind us and couldn't help but laugh.

"We need to destroy Prosperine's tie to our plane." Zola leaned forward. "We aren't strong enough to kill her outright. Not even with a key of the dead."

Foster fluttered down to the table again and said, "I don't know, you have a pretty good backhand."

I grinned and pushed my pancake remnants over to the fairy. His eyes widened as he just barely resisted diving into the pool of syrup. Aideen would kill him if she had to chip dried syrup out of his armor ever again.

"She can be banished with a blood rite and the thorough destruction of the artifact," the fairy said around a mouthful of pancake.

"Ugh." My stomach wanted to heave. "I hate blood rites."

"Yeah, especially when it's your blood," he said as he pulled off a tacky handful of pancake. I looked around for the servers and cooks to be sure they wouldn't see a floating crumb, but they were otherwise occupied.

"Ah'll need to research it," Zola said. "Take me to the Pit tonight and Ah'll check their elder works."

I cocked an eyebrow. "They're trusting you with the old books now, huh?"

She nodded.

"I'm impressed." The Pit was almost psychotically protective of the old books and grimoires they'd amassed through the centuries. It was unusual for them to let anyone see them, especially a human, given their greasy paw prints. "I guess you'll be needing some gloves then?"

"Vik already bought me some," Zola said. "Ah have a whole box in the archive."

"Wow, did you hand feed him a ferret or something?" Foster asked.

"Vik doesn't do much for anyone since the Devon ordeal," I said as I glanced at Foster. Devon was Vik's ex-girlfriend. She'd come frighteningly close to killing me last year with the help of her pet demon. I'd killed her spectacularly with fifty pounds of dynamite. Oddly enough, no one had been stupid enough to mess with my sister since Devon went to her maker in pieces.

"Ah have only provided him with a friendly ear, nothing more."

"Well, I guess that'll do it for some vampires," I said as Foster's shrill voice screamed, "I love pancakes!"

Zola laughed, pushed his right wing away from a mess of syrup, and wiped the pool up with a moist napkin. "Yes, for him, it is all he needed."

"So, who was Agnes?"

"A worthless Sunday soldier, but she truly doesn't matter now. That son of a bitch isn't acting alone. Philip's followers are loyal, and Ah'm sure the reasons why are atrocities in themselves." She pushed a pair of braids behind her neck. "Ah learned the names of two more of his cult while Ah was with them. One is Zachariah, a sadist and assassin of great skill. The other is Ezekiel." She paused and watched Foster as he stumbled back to his spot by the ketchup bottle. "Ezekiel is a monster. He is a practitioner of the Black Arts. Ah knew him before he was completely taken by the darkness. Ah watched him summon a demon to save a little boy, drowning in a flash flood. When the demon complained about his task after rescuing the boy, Ezekiel killed him. A minor demon, but a demon still. He is powerful, and ruthless, and I have no idea how Philip controls him."

"Fantastic," I muttered.

"If Philip has the power to control him, then he has become stronger than Ah ever imagined he could."

"Oh god, I'm dying," Foster groaned. He took a shallow breath and blew out a puff of air.

I laughed despite myself. Zola smiled and said, "Let's go home."

CHAPTER 5

Foster had a massive sugar crash on the way back to Saint Charles. His upper body was hanging out of Zola's jacket pocket, with arms limp beside his wings while he snored like a chainsaw the rest of the way home. I unlocked the front door to the shop and let Zola carry him inside. A small but sharp intake of breath drew my eyes to Aideen as she landed on Zola's shoulder. I offered up a lopsided grin to Foster's wife.

"Is he ..." she started to say.

"Asleep," I said.

"Oh, thank the bloody stars. Carter told us you went to rescue Zola. We didn't know what happened. We were going to come after you." It was then I realized Aideen was fully armored. A long and infinitely fine chain mail vest fell from her shoulders and was cinched with a belt to give her legs a full range of movement. Peeking out above her shoulders were the plain golden hilts of two Fae blades. Clad in a matching coif, greaves, and vambraces, she looked ready to kill.

Zola laid Foster on the counter. He grunted once and started snoring again.

"Was it really Philip?" Aideen said.

Zola only nodded.

Aideen exploded in a cloud of fairy dust and threw her arms around the old Cajun. "I'm so sorry." She squeezed Zola for a moment before she said, "I'm so glad you're back."

Zola laughed quietly and patted the coif around Aideen's head. "Ah'm glad to be back."

Aideen's eyes wandered back down to Foster as she reached out and squeezed my shoulder. "What happened?" she said as she took in Foster's condition.

"Ah, well," I said as I scratched the back of my head. "Pancakes."

"Damian Valdis Vesik, I thought you had more respect for my son than to get him blasted on sugar."

I turned to find a Cara hovering a few feet away. She too was draped in golden armor, but void of any swords, which made me very happy. "Sorry, Mom. We had a rough night, and he really wanted pancakes. They were ... celebratory pancakes."

Cara smiled and shook her head. "I'll let it slide this time, boy. It's good to see you safe, Zola."

Zola chuckled and I had a feeling it was because Cara called me 'boy.' It was one of Zola's favorite terms of endearment, or harassment, depending on your point of view.

"If you wish to talk, I'm always here."

Zola gave a brief shake of her head. "Thank you, but Ah just need to think."

Aideen looked at Foster again and then gestured to the back room. "Could you just put him in the clock for me?"

"You'll notice there's no syrup in his armor this time," I said.

"Don't you dare tell him I said this, but I'm just glad he's safe." Aideen glared at me in warning while Zola carried Foster through the saloon-style doors, into the back room, and to the large grandfather clock the fairies called home.

"Sorry about Foster, Aideen," I said as I almost bowed to her.

Cara laughed as Zola started back into the front of the shop. "Damian, Frank purchased a book he thought you'd be interested in."

I walked up to the counter and looked at the solid black tome. It looked thin and was very light when I picked it up.

"What is it?" I said.

"Some old witch's book of shadows."

I frowned and cracked it open. It smelled old, but the pages looked almost new. "Why would I want a book of shadows?"

"Well, for one it's an antique, and for another it's from the Salem witch trials."

My eyes widened. "Really?"

"Yes, really."

"Wow, I'll have to thank Frank." I didn't have any interest in a normal book of shadows, but one from an actual witch at the Salem witch trials? Oh yes, definitely.

We said our goodbyes for the night before Zola and I waved to Cara as I locked the shop behind us. I sighed and opened the passenger door for her.

"Thank you, boy," Zola said as I closed the door.

I climbed in the driver's side. "Alright, let's get you to the houseful of vampires."

Zola smiled as we drove down the cobblestone street.

***

It was a twenty-minute drive to the Pit's impressive home in Town and Country.

"These poor people have no idea there are vampires nearby," I said, for probably the thousandth time, as we drove through the neighborhood. A miasma of flowers, mature trees, and pristine landscaping decorated the well maintained road, driveways, and homes. A healthy sampling of evergreens would give the area a little color in winter.

Zola watched the nighttime scenery roll by.

"What do you think Philip will do next?" I said.

She stayed silent for a while. "Ah'm not sure. Ah'll think on it while Ah research."

"You doing alright?"

The metal in her braids tinkled together as she turned to look at me. "Ah will be, boy. Ah will be."

I pulled into the u-shaped drive a few minutes later.

"Are you going to come in and see Sam?"

"Nah, I need some sleep," I said. "I'll give her a call tomorrow."

She nodded and stepped out of the car. Before she walked to the front door, she leaned in and said, "Damian?"

"Yeah?"

"Thank you."

I grinned as she closed the door, walked to the enclosed porch behind the four enormous pillars, and knocked on the Pit's opulent black door. I could see Vik's outline as Zola walked in. He waved briefly before closing the door.

"Let's go home," I said to Vicky.

Unfortunately my apartment was right back the way we'd come. We made it to Saint Charles and eventually out to the edge of civilization. I groaned as I stood up and closed the car door. The night was dead quiet and my footsteps sounded like hammer strikes as I climbed the wooden steps. If it hadn't been so quiet, I may not have heard my intruders.

My heart rate spiked when I heard a scuffing sound and muffled voices as I topped the stairs to my apartment. I thought about knocking politely just to be a smartass, but opted for kicking the door in like a crazy person. With the knob turned just enough so I wouldn't break the door frame, I grasped my staff in my left hand, the pepperbox in my right, and kicked the door in, screaming, "You picked the wrong night you son of a–"

"*Damian!*" Sam shrieked.

It took me a horrified moment to realize it was my half-naked sister nuzzled up to a half-naked Frank on my now-violated, battered leather couch. It took a much longer moment not to pull the trigger just to change the scene that was quickly imprinting itself on my brain.

Sam zipped across the room, suddenly clothed again, and crushed me in a vampire hug. Bear hugs have got nothing on vampires. Her words came out in a rush, lost in the folds of the old leather jacket I was wearing, where her face was planted. "Thank god you're okay. Carter told Aideen what you were doing and Aideen told me. We were really getting worried."

"Why are you here?" I squeaked out.

"Frank's in-laws are at his place. Vassili has a bunch of out-of-town vamps at the Pit. I had a key." She grinned at me, flashing her fangs a half inch from my face. "We were worried."

When she released me and I could breathe again, I pushed back on her shoulders. "We're fine. We got Zola back."

"Thank god," Sam said as she stepped back.

"Hey, Damian," came Frank's voice in an uncharacteristically sheepish tone.

I cocked an eyebrow and said, "Thanks for watching over ... things. Now please make with the clothes. I don't want to be pulling back-hair out of my couch for the next month."

Frank laughed and picked up his green knit shirt.

"Christ, Frank. You been working out?" I was somewhat shocked to notice most of his gut was gone. His arms were even showing some light definition.

He popped his head through his shirt and grinned. "Yes. Have to look good for your sister."

I held my hand up and smiled. "You can stop there."

"Where's Zola?" Sam said as she gripped my shoulder.

"She's at the Pit."

"Research?"

I nodded. "Well kids, I need to get a few hours' sleep before work in the morning."

"You opening the shop?" Frank said.

"Yeah, so feel free to sleep in. If I have to leave early, I may give you a call if you're up for it."

Frank nodded and wrapped his arm around Sam's waist. Sam grinned and her eyes lit up.

I groaned and pushed them both out of my apartment. "Spare me the googly eyes."

"Talk to you soon, Demon," Sam said as she laughed.

"You bet." I waved to Frank as he did the same.

When they were gone, I closed the door and threw the deadbolts home with a metallic smack. I walked across the Berber carpet in the living room and paused on my way to the kitchen. The heavy oak coffee table was several feet out of its normal position, with fresh scorch marks across the carpet. I was really going to have to replace that old carpet.

I grabbed a cold slice of barbeque chicken pizza from my vintage green refrigerator. I turned off the ancient black floor lamp and end table combo beside my old leather couch as I tore off another chunk of pizza. I don't know why I even bothered with the floor lamp considering it did little to light the dark wood paneling adorning the walls and, yes, the ceiling.

I finished the pizza, brushed my teeth, and double checked my alarm clock. Three-and-a-half hours of sleep before I had to think about demons, werewolves, and dark necromancers. I sighed, killed the lights in the bedroom, and enjoyed my extended nap.

CHAPTER 6

I found a package of Frank's homemade beef jerky on my kitchen table in the morning. Frank made jerky with the intent to melt your eyeballs. Disturbingly, I'd acquired a taste for it over the past few months. "Oh, hell yeah," I said as I scooped up the jerky, grabbed two Frappuccinos, and pounded down the stairs to Vicky.

My brain was rattling across the cobblestones in no time as I crossed Main Street and pulled in behind the shop. The lower deadbolt screamed, "Don't do it!" as I kicked him in the face. The unfortunate Fae-turned-deadbolt opened with a groan as I unlocked the top deadbolt, and cracked open the door.

"It's Damian," I said before stepping inside. I was careful not to surprise the fairies after Aideen had almost gutted me a couple months back when I came in through the back door. The door was mostly open before it exploded out of my hand, the deadbolt lamenting its existence as it smacked into the doorstop. I had time to mutter, "Crap," before two waist-high yapping balls of green fur plowed me into the ground.

A chorus of laughing fairies joined the flurry of tongues and nails as Bubbles and Peanut fought to lick my face first. Bubbles clawed her way on top of my chest and was heavy enough I couldn't sit up. "What are you feeding these things, Foster?" My complaints were cut short as Bubbles's tongue found its mark. "Yearrgh!" I squawked as cu sith drool slid down my cheeks.

"Bubbles, Peanut, home," Aideen said as she pointed to the door.

The cu siths vanished into the shop.

Foster and Aideen swore to me the claims that cu siths were bred to drag fertile human women into fairy mounds to become providers for the Fae were gross exaggerations. Cu siths are supposedly the best guard dogs in history, or so my boarders keep telling me. All the cu siths really seem to guard against is my ability to enter my own store unmolested.

I wiped my face off on my sleeve and pushed off the ground. Foster and Cara were still laughing when I walked through the back door. Foster was perched on top of the center peak of the ancient grandfather clock the fairies called home, and Cara was laid out on the old Formica table, gasping for breath with her hands on her stomach.

"Good to see you, too," I muttered as I dropped the bag of jerky on the table, tripped on the old green cot setup beside the table for god knows what reason, and headed toward the front of the shop to flip the open sign. After unlocking the door and changing the sign, Death's Door was open for business, and it was open five minutes early for a change.

Death's Door is the name of my shop, though most of the locals call it the Double D. It's in one of my favorite areas in Saint Louis — Main Street, Saint Charles. There's an old world, small town feel in the air, with cobblestone streets, rows of historical buildings, and small shops of every kind of miscellany. The old brick storefront wasn't in the main strip; it was actually on the far northern end of Main Street. The shop was within walking distance of the Missouri River, a plethora of restaurants, and a fantastic fudge shop.

My master had given me the shop as a graduation present of sorts when she left on a mission of her own in years past. She didn't tell me what she was doing or where she was going, and it was years before I even learned she was still alive. Death's Door is set up to cater to a mixture of sorcerers, Wiccans, and even a smattering of tourists — carrying everything from texts to spellcraft supplies to crystals and antiquated artifacts.

My boots thunked on the ancient hardwood floors as I walked down the right aisle on my way back to the register. The aisle was stocked with bundles of feathers, dried plants, cauldrons, and other occult artifacts. The laptop Sam had talked me into getting for the shop sat beside the old register, which sat on a glass counter that doubled as a display case for some of the more expensive items. Old

Native American pipes and arrowheads were displayed with a mixture of raw, gray Magrasnetto on display. The Fae knew how to build wards into Magrasnetto, making it invaluable and dangerous. Heated by a summoned flame, Magrasnetto would turn to slag and take on the properties of metal; however, it would still retain the working laid upon it as a stone, creating a nearly unbreakable ward in its new form. I wasn't supposed to know all the details, but the fairies had told me all about it one night after a bit too much fudge.

A few of the arrowheads littering the display case were obsidian, made by the Paiute in the Great Basin in northern California. What made them unique were the runes, which closely resembled Nordic runes, etched onto the sides. I only recognized a handful of the archaic symbols.

Frank was constantly adding a few choice pieces of amber to the case, with prices that boggled my mind. What boggled my mind even more was how regularly they sold. Frank had done some really good things for our sales since he'd been working for me.

I sat down on the stool behind the counter and pulled out a box of hand-dipped candles. They were slightly uneven and made by a local Wiccan priestess, my customer and friend Ashley. She ground anise seed and blessed thistle into the deep red wax, creating a formidable foundation for a protection spell. I put the candles into overdrive by carving a ring of runes around the base, including Algiz, Gifu, and Uruz. The series of runes repeated twice. I then worked the edge of an athame into the wax to form the inverted peace sign symbol of Algiz, the x-shape of Gifu, and the slanted n of Uruz. The athame was actually a sliver of a broken sword, given to me by Cara. It was a Fae blade, entirely worked of Magrasnetto, which gave it far more power than a standard athame, even splintered into shards.

After carving three pairs of candles, I scooped them up and walked over to the far aisle. At the end of the aisle, up against the wall, was a tall display case of crystals and stones filled with aventurine, coral, brown jasper, obsidian, and several drawers of amber. I walked past the case to a section of candles and hung the latest batch over the dwindling rack with a sign that read "Protection." They were beside the rack holding black candles with a sign for "Curses and Destruction." Of course, unbeknownst to most of my customers, the "Curses and Destruction" candles were made with red and brown food coloring instead of blood, and had nonsensical runes carved into them. In fact, the runes were more likely to get up and dance than proliferate any kind of curse. It was an amusing inside joke between me and Ashley.

"Good morning, Damian." The voice reminded me of the soft echoes of a wood flute.

I looked up and my heart skipped a beat as Foster's distant cousin Nixie walked into the room. "I, uh, thought you had to head back to the sea or something, no?"

She ran her hands through the wavy cascade of nearly-white hair that fell to her waist. "It's not the same anymore. It's much more difficult to call sailors and pirates into the rocks with all this ... technology about. And without shipwrecks ..." she shrugged. "I was only thinking there may be more trouble to be had on land." Her smile broadened as I fought to keep my gaze on her face, and not the outrageously sheer nightgown she was wearing. In an obvious effort to help, she leaned forward on the display cabinet with her arms crossed beneath her breasts.

"Oh," I said.

Cara coughed as she landed beside the laptop and I tore my gaze away from Nixie's pale flesh. "Girl, put something decent on," she said.

Nixie pouted and her sheer nightgown grew more opaque until it verged on modest. Barely.

"Well, boy, I hope you don't *mind*," Cara said as she rolled her eyes, "but Nixie is going to stay with us for a while."

"In the shop?" I asked. "Oh, the cot."

Cara nodded.

I glanced at Nixie, and before I could think it through, I said, "You want to grab dinner sometime?"

"Yes, yes I do," Nixie said as a smile curled her lips.

"Nudd save us," Cara said under her breath. "Safe to say he's fine with you staying here, girl."

"You have customers coming," Nixie said. "I need to change." She smiled and slipped through the saloon-style doors. I thought I heard the back door open and drop closed, but I wasn't sure why Nixie would have been going outside.

The bell on the front door jingled as I finished hanging the candles on the rack by their wicks. I turned to find Carter walking in and waved before three morose looking men followed him. They were all bigger than Carter, dressed in Saint Louis Rams sweatpants and plain gray sweatshirts. The first was a black man built like a brick wall. He smiled and nodded to me once. The man behind him was a pasty blond youth who just glared at me. I noticed the third man was Native American, but my attention trailed back to the blond youth as he cracked his neck without breaking eye contact.

I raised my eyebrows as Carter sat a plate of crispy rice squares on the counter behind me.

"From the wife," he said as he brushed a crumb off his sweatshirt.

"Thanks." The pleasantries didn't go much further before the pasty one broke the mood.

"You're the piece of shit who dared trespass in the Alpha's home."

"Trespass?" I said. I glanced to my left as the cu siths came tearing into the front room, barking like rabid wolves. My heart sank when they stopped running and started backing away slowly. What the hell had Carter brought into my shop?

The pasty man blurred from across the aisle and suddenly had his hands twisted up in my shirt. His breath was rank. I could see a smattering of acne across his pale right cheek and the throbbing veins in his neck and head as I slowly raised my eyes to his. "Shit," I muttered as I saw the sunburst gray iris within the black ring of his eye.

The werewolf opened his mouth to speak again, but Carter was on him before he could issue so much as a grunt. Carter tore the other wolf's hands away from my shirt and punched him hard enough in the face to floor him.

"Alan, hold him down," Carter said.

The black mountain moved forward and placed one foot on the downed wolf. He was casual about it. "Got him," he said once it was obvious the kid was pinned.

I finally got a good look at the third man. He had the calm façade of a Native American elder, much like that of an Illiniwek elder I'd once met, one of Zola's old, old friends I'd been introduced to years ago. The man in my shop crossed his arms over his chest and nodded once, his motions slow and precise.

I nodded back and turned to Carter. I pointed at the werewolf beneath Alan's foot. "Did you try to bring the biggest jackass in the pack?"

Carter laughed and ran his hand through his hair. "No, Damian, I brought the friendliest wolves in the pack."

"Great," I said as I looked at the rage in the trapped wolf's face. "That's phenomenal." I gestured back to the counter. "At least you came bearing crispy rice squares. Otherwise I might be annoyed."

I saw the Native American's face twitch as he fought a smile. The other two looked none too happy.

"Well, what'd you need? You want a drink or anything?" I said as I turned to walk behind the register and get closer to my demon staff. Foster, Cara, and Aideen were camped out on the display case with swords drawn. They were still small, but I knew how fast they could morph and eviscerate the wolves.

"No, thank you," Carter said. His eyes were locked on the fairies as I made my way around the counter. He looked like he was wound up tight, and if he snapped, the whole situation was going to hell real quick.

"Crispy rice squares?" Foster said.

"Don't even think about it." I jabbed an index finger at him and said, "I don't need a psychotic blur in here right now."

I heard a deep laugh and looked up to find the last wolf walking up to the register with an easy stride. "I see you have befriended the protectors of the Piasa Bird." His voice held almost no trace of accent and his smile was warm.

"The who of the what?" I asked.

He gestured at each of the fairies. "The Fae warriors. I am honored, friends."

"Dominus Lupus," Cara said as she sheathed her swords across her back and bowed deeply to the werewolf.

He held out his hand and I watched in disbelief as Aideen sheathed her own blades and fluttered over to him. "It has been many moons since I have seen such warriors," he said, staring at Aideen as she also bowed deeply. "To keep such company, the necromancer cannot be evil. Carter, my friend, I believe your judgment has been proven keen once more."

Carter's shoulders relaxed and he rolled back onto his heels.

I glanced at the werewolf on the floor. He was now bright red and trying to squirm away from Alan. "I'm Damian," I said as I extended my hand to the Native American wolf.

"Hugh," he said as he extended his own hand. Aideen fluttered back to the counter as he moved. I raised an eyebrow and he smiled broadly. "It is short for Hohnihohkaiyohos."

I furrowed my eyebrows, debating on whether or not I should try to pronounce his name. Etiquette won. "Ah, Hugh it is." I nodded to him and glanced back at Carter.

"Yes, you've met Hugh, Jimmy is on the floor, and, as I said before, this is Alan," Carter said.

Alan nodded in a curt motion and pulled his foot off Jimmy. "Sorry about Jimmy," he said as he stepped over Jimmy and shook my hand. "Not the most forward thinking of us."

Jimmy dragged himself to his feet and dusted off his sweatpants as he grumbled. "This place is a dump."

I let it slide. I'm a perfectly reasonable person. After all, it would be impolite to cut him into pieces and feed him to the cu siths. Wouldn't it?

"I don't like Jimmy," Foster said.

I screwed up my face and coughed in an effort to hide my laughter. Hugh just sighed as Alan and Carter laughed outright.

The bell jingled again and I watched Nixie slink through the door. Despite the four werewolves in the room, I couldn't take my eyes off her. Some disengaged part of my brain wondered why she'd come through the front door, but I didn't put much thought into it. Her hair trailed to her hips, which were swaying suggestively below a small waist. She ran her fingertips down her throat and played with the aquamarine pendant hanging at the peak of her cleavage. Nixie smiled at me as she raised her left hand and quickly traced Hugh's jaw. My own jaw slackened at what she said next.

"Hello, Hohnihohkaiyohos."

Hugh pushed her hand away and nodded once. "Water witch."

Nixie's laugh was musical as she made her way around the counter. "My, but you have some guests, Damian. I need to speak with you again, but for now I'll wait in the back."

I smiled like an idiot. "That's fine. I'll be there in a minute." I watched her ass as it swayed into the back room again and I sighed as she vanished through the doorway. I turned back to the wolves and found them all staring at me. *"What?"* I snapped.

"She's beautiful," Jimmy whispered.

Hugh pointed at the back room and I heard a tiny crack of anger in his voice. "Do you have *any* idea what *that* is?"

"She is Foster's cousin to some removed degree, she is a water witch, an undine, and her name is Nixie."

Foster laughed and finally sheathed his own sword. "Damian's got a thing for her." He scratched his chin and said, "Actually, she has a thing for him, too. I thought she would have tried to drown him by now."

"Hey, I never said I had a thing for her." I narrowed my eyes at the fairy.

"Please," Foster said as he blew out a short puff of air. "You've asked about her five times in the past month."

"He does have a point, Damian," Cara said as she leapt from the glass counter and glided to the back room.

"And she has a thing for me?" I said as Foster's words sank in.

Hugh blinked and lowered his arm. "You, you're insane, necromancer." He crossed his arms and shook his head. "The story our Alpha told us is beginning to make sense."

I raised my eyebrows and looked at Carter.

"I told the pack you're not here to hunt the wolves," Carter said with a shrug. "You're out to stop the men who are."

"Hunt the wolves?" I said.

Carter's eyes widened. "Zola didn't tell you?"

"Tell me what?"

Carter took a deep breath. "I don't know if I'm really the one to tell you this, but werewolves don't hate necromancers just because they're necromancers."

"Then why?" I said. "Family feud?"

Foster snickered and then coughed to cover it up as Aideen slugged him in the arm.

"In days long past," Carter said, "necromancers raised zombie hordes and sent them after us. They saw *us* as the abominations, never mind the fact they were raising the dead to kill us. A few packs survived the cleansings. Some of the wolves, like Hugh here, destroyed unknowable numbers of zombies and gave birth to some very nasty legends."

Something clicked in my brain and I said, "Skinwalkers?"

Hugh shook his head and his mouth formed a tight line. "I am no skinwalker." He almost spat the word onto the wood floor.

Carter nodded and went on without further explanation of Hugh's disgust. "You see the three of us here today because a necromancer is hunting wolves again. Someone Zola knows."

I felt my face flush as my hands curled into fists. "Philip."

"And his cult," Carter said.

"Why?"

"Fun? Blood? Tradition?" Carter shrugged. "I don't know, but his group has killed dozens of werewolves in the past year."

I closed my eyes and took a few deep breaths before I opened them and met Carter's gaze. "Yes, my friends, I am here to help kill that wretched piece of shit and anyone dumb enough to follow him."

"But, he's just like you!" Jimmy said.

I'd almost forgotten the young werewolf was still there. I stared at him with an expression almost as flat as my voice until he fidgeted. "I am nothing like Philip Pinkerton."

Hugh glanced at Jimmy. "Yes, I am sure Philip Pinkerton is much too sane to pursue a water witch."

I heard a tinkling laughter echo through the back room.

He turned his attention back to me as he spoke. "I will trust the necromancer, as our Alpha has requested, until he provides a reason not to trust him."

"As will I," Alan said. He kept his eyes locked on Jimmy as he spoke.

Jimmy blew out a breath, but gave in to peer pressure. "Fine, but I still think it's stupid." Hugh and Carter both ignored the young wolf.

Hugh crouched down and stared at the display filled with Native American artifacts. "Those arrowheads, are they Paiute?" he said.

I nodded and pulled out the small cotton-lined tray with six of the arrowheads on it.

"May I?" he asked as he reached out.

"Sure."

He picked up the smallest arrowhead, studied the upright side, and then flipped it between his thumb and forefinger. His index finger ran along the edge and came away bloody. "Incredible," he whispered. I watched in amazement as the tiny wound closed. It vanished as Hugh rubbed the blood off on his sweatpants. His eyes swept across the row of rune-carved heads. "These are treasures. Truly incredible. Do you know how old they are?"

"Not exactly. I was guessing a couple thousand years since the runes are similar to Nordic runes, but I don't really know. I can't find those exact patterns in any of my books."

Hugh closed his fist around the arrowhead and smiled. "Tens of thousands, Damian. These runes have not been used in tens of thousands of years. They are from long before the time men thought to record their history. I thought they'd all been lost. My ancestors told stories of these weapons. They would never dull, never break, never miss." He shook his head and handed the arrowhead back to me. "How much must I pay you to acquire these?"

I smiled and laid the arrowhead back on the cotton lined tray. I turned the tray sideways and spun all six arrowheads into a protective cotton roll. Hugh looked confused until I held the ball of cotton out to him. "Consider them a gift from someone looking to win your favor."

Hugh's eyes widened and he stared at me. He raised his hands with his palms toward me, bowed his head, and slowly lowered his hands to curve below the roll of cotton. "Thank you, Damian." He held the roll to his chest and met my eyes. "Thank you."

"I will help you in any way I can if it means Philip Pinkerton and his followers are dead and buried," I said.

Alan nodded. "As will we."

Carter nodded to Foster and Aideen as he turned and left the shop with all three wolves in tow. I listened to the bell jingle as the four werewolves walked out onto Main Street.

Bubbles and Peanut tore through the shop in a clatter of toenails and started barking at the front door.

"Guard dogs, huh?" I said with a glance at Foster.

He shrugged. "I never said anything about werewolves."

"No, I suppose you didn't." I laughed as Aideen fluttered toward the front door to reprimand the cu siths.

***

I found Nixie sitting on the old green cot below the grandfather clock. It then clicked as to why the cot was unfolded in the middle of the back room.

"Hey Nix, what's up?" I said while I pulled out a chair at the old table and sat down.

"Is Zola here?"

"No, she's out with the vampires."

Nixie nodded. "I spent the last few months visiting the clans. Most of our race is worried about Philip."

"Why?"

Nixie glanced toward the front room as the fairies chased the cu siths around the aisles and she smiled. "His cult, they are trying to raise the Destroyer." She turned back to me. "The Destroyer is a real threat to my people. A dire threat, Damian. She's killed entire families, entire clans, in a span of hours. Our queen, our house, has been at war with her as long as our memory serves."

I grimaced and looked away.

"I think you and Zola and your friends should be made our allies. You are all so young, and yet you banished Azzazoth. A chief, a corruptor, banished by your own hand!"

"And lots of dynamite," I said.

Nixie smiled and brushed her hair behind her ear. "Your grandfather, Damian. He has given us over a century of peace through his sacrifice. Even if it wasn't intended as a sacrifice for us, it has created change in our people. We are struck by sympathy, and the elders see it as a dangerous change, a malignant change that will destroy us all."

"What do you mean?" I said.

She sat in silence for a moment and knuckled her eyes before she looked up again. "I think I like the old wolf." She stared at me, her pale brows drawn in confusion.

"I like him too. There's something peaceful about him. How did you know his name?"

Her lips quirked. "I met him along your river many years ago."

"Really?"

"Yes, his son fell in a flash flood and was swept away. He asked the river spirits to watch over his child, but I heard his call instead." Her eyes unfocused as she spoke. "The cub was still alive, but I knew he would be dead soon. The waters tell me much. I thought I wanted him to die, but the old wolf's words broke something in me." She rubbed her right hand on her breastbone. "The child was clinging to an old pier when I found him, just an old decaying log, barely sticking above the surface." She laughed softly and ran her fingers through her hair. "I think he knew what I was, because his face changed from resolve to terror. And it ... it hurt." She paused and looked away. "Such a young child. Once perhaps, but now I could never hurt someone so young, not even a wolf."

"You saved him?"

"Yes." Nixie looked away and frowned. "I shouldn't like were-wolves, Damian. It is not our way."

"Pfff," I waved my hand around in dismissal. "Apparently I should be sending zombies after them and eating their furry hides for dinner because I'm a necromancer. Werewolf chimichangas. It could happen." I shook my head. "Really, though, Carter and Hugh? They seem like good people."

Nixie nodded and leaned back against the clock. "Hohnihohkaiyo-hos is a very good person. Honorable to a fault, the kind of man I loved to drag beneath the seas."

I cringed at the vision my mind conjured up. Hugh below the water, dying, with Nixie laughing all the while. I looked away from Nixie and took a deep breath before meeting her gaze.

She smiled briefly, and then her smile faltered. There were tears in her eyes when she looked at me again. "I don't want to kill anymore."

I pushed my chair back and stood up. Two steps took me to the flimsy cot where I sat down beside Nixie and put my arm around her. "You don't have to, Nix. No one can tell you what you're supposed to be."

She leaned into me. "We are not allowed change. There are beings ..."

"I'll kill them." And I knew I would as I felt her warmth pressed against me. Even if we were only ever friends, I'd kill anyone forcing a friend to murder.

Nixie shook her head on my shoulder and put her arm across my stomach. "So much killing. Sometimes it seems like the only thing left in the world."

My heart rate spiked as I took a deep breath and filled my lungs with an ocean breeze. "Not the only thing," I said as I pulled her chin up and kissed her.

CHAPTER 7

I was walking on air when my alarm went off the next morning at 5:00 AM. I didn't even think about sending the giant red numbers into sparking ruin. I'd only had two hours of sleep, but I had some getting ready to do before evening rolled around. I picked up my phone and dialed Sam.

"This is Vesik," said my vampire sister.

"Yes, it is," I said.

Sam snorted. "Hey, Damian, what's up?"

"I've got a date with an undine and wanted to run an idea by you."

"As long as this isn't an excuse to leave me emotionally scarred."

"*Me?* I would never."

"Riiiiight. Well, if you ask me, it's about time you two went out. Maybe it will stop your babbling." Sam paused and I heard her fingernail click rapidly on the side of her phone. "So what are you thinking?"

"I'm going to call Ashley this morning. She has some blue-tinted obsidian that I think Nixie would like."

"Jewelry?" Sam asked. "You think that may be a little heavy handed? Too much, too fast?"

"Well, last night we–"

"Stop! No emotional scarring, dammit!"

I laughed. "Kissed, Sam, just kissed. Besides, the jewelry's not expensive or anything."

"Alright, just don't get her a necklace or a pendant. From what Aideen was telling me, that aquamarine Nixie's always wearing is very special to her."

My eyes widened. "Crap, I didn't even think about it. Thanks for that."

"What are sisters for?" Sam paused before she said, "Don't answer that."

A chorus of laughter broke through in the background noise. "Are you at the Pit?"

"No, we're down at the Blackthorne Pub. Chuck's doing vampire hour."

"Oh god, that sounds good." Chuck managed the pub. A vampire from Sam's extended family, with the benefits of being a manager, he opened up once a week for vampire hour. The hour was complete with ridiculous deals on pizza, toppings that would make a mortal gag, and complimentary, umm, beverages. No mortals allowed, except for the drinks. Last time I went with Sam, Chuck still served me a monstrous Chicago-style deep dish pepperoni.

"You still there, Damian?"

I swallowed and laughed. "Yeah, just thinking about that pizza Chuck gave me last time."

"Some things never change," Sam said with a sigh. "Did you need anything else? I'd like to get back to my food."

"Did you see Zola?" I said.

"Yeah, last time I saw her she was still in the archive with Vik. They've been doing some seriously heavy research."

"I figured. I haven't heard from her for a while. I'll go see Ashley and then swing by the Pit."

"Aren't you going to sleep tonight?"

"Already did."

Sam went silent, and I guess she was checking the time, because she said, "It's only five in the morning."

"Yeah, there's shopping to be done."

"You're a nutcase, Demon."

"Thanks!" I said cheerfully. "Talk to you soon."

"Later," she said as the line went dead.

***

I drove to Ashley's and knocked on her front door. She only lived a few miles from the shop, so it wouldn't take me much longer than usual to get to the Pit when I left. Her carport was empty, so I parked Vicky on the street and sat down on the old porch swing. She pulled in about five minutes later in her green Prius, back from whatever witchy stuff she'd been up to the night before.

Ashley's eyes widened like saucers when she saw me. She tapped her wrist to indicate the hour before she hefted a duffle bag with her left hand. She was strawberry blonde, short, and a little pudgy, but had the most incredible green eyes I'd ever seen, always kind and shining like glass. Her nose turned up just a little at the tip and I'm sure she got very tired of hearing how cute she was. A black robe hung from her shoulders, with her ever-present silver pentagram hanging across the front. I couldn't resist asking, "You wearing any underwear with that?" When she turned ten shades of red, I was fairly sure of the answer. I laughed and stood up.

"What are you doing here?" She grinned nervously and brushed her hair behind her ears.

"I have a date."

She looked at me and waited. When the silence started to get un-comfortable she said, "And?"

"I was wondering if you still had any of that blue obsidian you showed me last year. You're still selling your handmade charms and jewelry, right?"

"Oh," Ashley said as she nodded enthusiastically and walked to the front door. "Yes, yes, come on in. Let me change into something more ..." She glanced down at her robes and shook her head. "Some-thing more appropriate."

Ashley's house always feels homey and welcoming, even when I drop by unannounced at the crack of dawn. Her living room was just to the right, through a small archway with a half wall on either side. Both half walls were covered in snow globes. The priestess had deco-rated the small abode with a mixture of bric-a-brac, wicker crafts, and Wiccan symbols. Dried herbs hung beside the large front window and filled the room with subtle scents of spring. It was all tasteful, except maybe the snow globes. I thought the decorations went well with the traditional furniture and pale blue walls.

I sat down on the old corduroy couch against the far wall and picked up the framed photo of her coven from the end table. The coven had grown since the last time I'd seen a picture of the group. Everyone was wearing their robes, with hoods pulled over their foreheads. Ashley was front and center, with a chalice in one outstretched hand and a massive crystal in the other. My eyes widened as I looked at the crystal. It was larger than a baseball.

Ashley walked into the living room carrying a large black chest with both hands. She was wearing flannel pajamas, covered in Paul Frank monkeys. I was always a bit more of a Scurvy fan myself.

"Nice PJs," I said.

"I like monkeys."

"And snow globes," I said.

Ashley glanced at the rows of snow globes and laughed lightly as she sat the chest down on her coffee table. The table had a subtle pentagram worked into the layout of the wood surface, which I admired as Ashley fumbled with the latches and opened the chest. It was one of those old telescoping chests with five or six layers that opened as you moved the lid. Each layer had two dozen or more compartments filled with custom jewelry and loose stones. I recognized several pieces of amber she'd bought from the shop, now worked into bracelets and earrings and pendants.

"Oh, wow," I said as I picked up an ice cube-sized spiky crystal from the bottom of the chest. "It looks like the one in your photo, only smaller." The crystals were incredibly clear with a little frosting at the tips. It almost looked like someone had gone crazy with some quartz and a glue stick, except for the fact it was seamless.

Ashley glanced at the photo of the coven and nodded. "James got the one you're holding for me before he died, somewhere in Kirksville." She hadn't talked about her kid brother much since he passed away in a car wreck on his way to school three years ago. I had taken Ashley to speak to him once, at her request. From what I had seen of his ghost, he seemed like a nice kid. After I touched his ghost with my necromancy, I knew what a loss to the world he'd been. I don't think Ashley realized just how corporeal he would be when I helped her talk to him. He told her to move on, not to forget, just to move on, because he was fine and she would be too. She had thanked me, but she never mentioned it again. I'll never forget the flare of her aura when he reached out and hugged his sister as she broke down.

I gently laid the crystal into the chest again. "It's beautiful."

"Thanks," she said. She flipped a piece of velvet off the third shelf to reveal a plethora of obsidian jewelry.

There were several pendants, one of which I would have bought in a heartbeat, and that made me very glad Sam had mentioned Nixie's aquamarine pendant. I looked over the earrings for a while and then laughed.

"What?"

"I don't know if she has pierced ears. Hell, I don't know if her ears *can* be pierced."

"Well, I have some clip-ons, but I really don't like the things. Too easy to lose and they hurt if you wear them too long."

I nodded and lifted a heavy bracelet out of the corner slot. My eyes widened as the light from the ceiling fixture hit it. The blue obsidian was thin enough to let light through, but it didn't feel fragile. A ring of discs made up the bracelet, woven together with a fine silver chain. Each disc had four eighth-inch notches that allowed the chain to be wrapped repeatedly until it formed a square across the front of each. I glanced up at Ashley. "How much?"

She smiled and adjusted her monkeys. "For you? And the convenient hours you call?"

I snorted a laugh and nodded.

"Just make it fifty bucks."

"Seriously?"

"Yes, seriously, especially if you'll leave, so I can sleep."

I had a feeling she was cutting me a serious deal. "Fair enough, oh priestess."

She smacked my arm hard as she stood up and closed the chest with a smile.

"Where did you get these stones? I've never seen anything like them."

She glanced at the front wall which had a neat row of photos hanging vertically between the window and the half wall. "Oh, I was visiting my relatives in Germany. I try to go once every ten years or so. When the Rhine River was low, we found a cache of them buried with some broken pottery in the river bottom." She took the bracelet out of my hand and rubbed her thumbs over the discs. "They were close to Thurnberg. I don't know if we were actually supposed to be there, but ..." she shrugged and smiled.

"Close to what?" I said.

"Thurnberg, it's sometimes called Maus Castle. It's along the Rhine, pretty close to Rheinfels Castle. Well, it's across the river, anyway."

"Never been there."

"Have you even been to Germany?"

"Nope."

Ashley rolled her eyes. "A lot of people haven't been there, but it's a beautiful place."

I stood up and took the bracelet as Ashley handed it back to me. I handed her fifty dollars.

She walked over to the desk in the corner and pulled out a small cardboard box. "It should fit in here."

"Perfect. Thanks," I said as we both walked to the door.

"I'm sure I'll see you around the shop sometime soon," she said.

"Sounds good. You should get some sleep."

She gave me a lopsided grin as she closed the door behind me.

CHAPTER 8

It took almost an hour to get to the Pit from Ashley's house. Considering I'm usually comatose at this hour, I had no idea how much construction went on in the dead of morning. It was enough to have me cursing at everything as I made my way past the final flagman.

Highway 270 was blessedly clear and I was speeding a little too much in celebration. It was only a few minutes before I passed under the decorative overpass at Olive, which boasts more landscaping than my apartment complex, before I got off at Ladue. I took a few more twists and turns until I finally arrived at the U-shaped drive in front of the Pit.

I tucked Nixie's bracelet into the glove box and locked Vicky's doors before I walked up to the black front doors, with six decorative panels embedded in each. I glanced up and shook my head at the enormous chandelier hanging above the porch. It was dripping with antique bronze chains, which matched the core of the chandelier and stretched to the wall and the pillars at the front of the porch.

I used my secret knock, which involved pressing the doorbell over and over and over until an irritated vampire opened the door. Footsteps sounded behind the door, and quickly turned into irritated stomping. The door whipped open to reveal Vik, who had an impressive scowl etched across his face. It was an intimidating look, with his sharp nose and cheekbones. He had on an unremarkable white button-down shirt and olive slacks, but his raven-black hair was trimmed to a quarter inch, with a lengthier stripe down the middle. It wasn't his usual style, but he hadn't been himself for a while.

I stared at the stripe for a moment, until Vik slowly raised one eyebrow.

"Hi!" I said with as much teenage-style perk as I could muster.

"Vesik," he grumbled and nodded. "I assume you are looking for Zola?"

"Yeah."

"She is still in the archives. I will take you in."

My eyes widened. "Really? You don't usually let me in."

"You need to see what she has found."

I beat the mixture of excitement and dread back with a bat and said, "Okay."

I glanced at the cherry bench on the right side of the entryway as we walked by. It was my usual waiting place while vampires milled around me, but today there wasn't another vampire in sight. The Pit's house was beautiful, and my curiosity about our lack of company quickly vanished as my eyes wandered over the entryway. A vaulted ceiling spread out from the front door and over a magnificent wooden staircase, with a path to the basement in the center and two sides that flared out and met on the second floor. We started up the right side and I got a good look at the ancient coat of arms hanging above the stairs to the basement. The swords had been cleaned and oiled again since their use in last year's battle. We continued on to the second floor and Vik turned left down the empty, wainscoted hallway.

"Where is everyone?" I said.

"The sun is rising, so most are already downstairs."

"Oh yeah, it's morning." I laughed. "I'm not usually up this early, much less here."

Vik nodded and continued his steady stride toward the archive.

Almost all of the vampires I knew were paranoia in motion. Sunlight wouldn't kill them; it would only weaken them to near-human levels of strength. They didn't burst into flames or anything, at least not without help. Only the young ones, who've yet to reach their full paranoia potential, prowl the daytime streets. Most vampires avoid daylight because they don't trust other vampires not to kill them in their weakened state, never mind the fact the other vampires would be just as weak. Ah, the gift of paranoia.

My escort stopped at the end of the second story hallway. The door was titanium, painted to look like wood. I'd rarely seen the other side. You drop one little four hundred year old tome ...

I smiled at the memory and looked at Vik. He was almost as tall as me, and I stand about six five, but his shoulders had a slight slump to them, giving away more than he probably realized about his mental state after Devon's betrayal last year. Getting over your ex-girlfriend become a demon-worshipping warlock before trying to kill you and all your friends is something I hope I never have to relate to. "How're you doing Vik?"

He paused and met my eyes. "I am better, Damian. Thank you." He smiled a little as he turned around and unlocked the door to the archives with his thumb print. The locks disengaged with a muted click.

As he pulled the door open, he said, "Try not to drop anything."

"That was an accident!" I said. "You know I love old books."

I caught a hint of a true smile as he closed the door behind me in silence and left me to the archive.

For a few minutes, I just stared. Row upon row of brushed metal shelving ran from the floor to the twelve-foot ceiling on either side of the entryway. The shelves were so packed there was hardly space to add anything more. The outer walls were lined with floor-to-ceiling display cases filled with antiques and memorabilia the vampires had collected over hundreds of years. The windows had been bricked over to prevent UV damage to the antiques and books, some of which were thousands of years old. You couldn't see the bricks from the outside; the windows just looked like curtains from the street. The archive took up the entire south wing of the second floor, which was no small thing.

"Shit," I whispered as I shook my head and walked toward the reading nook. It was in the back row, all the way to the right. I had always thought I had a lot of books on the second floor of the shop, but this was something else entirely.

Zola was there, hunched over with her nose about three inches from a yellowed monstrosity of a tome. As I got closer I could see the brittle parchment was hand written and still legible. Even with her nose literally buried in a book, Zola has an intense presence. Her braids fell to either side of her head as her white gloved fingers danced down the pages. Tiny bits of iron and Magrasnetto tinkled as she glanced at me. Her eyes were bright and slightly sunken below her forehead, hidden among her distinguished wrinkles. Zola leaned back into her deep gray cloak and squeezed the bridge of her nose.

She sighed, looked up again, and gestured to the mesh seat beside her. "Pull up a chair, boy." Her old world New Orleans accent was heavy when she was tired, and now it was very heavy indeed.

I looked at the display case in the corner as I pulled out the chair. One of the vampires—I think Sam said it was Vassili—was a gun nut. He'd amassed an astounding collection of engraved rifles, ancient hand cannons, and pistols. I recognized a few, like a Colt Dragoon, and an 1851 Colt engraved Navy revolver, but there were far more obscure weapons like a harmonica pistol in the case too. Perhaps most impressive were the rows and rows of dueling pistols, many of which purportedly participated in some monumental and infamous conflicts. I sat down and turned my attention back to Zola.

"Vik said you found something."

"Ah suppose you could say that," she said as her eyes rolled back down to the open book. "Vik does like to oversimplify." Zola paged back and forth in the book and sighed. "Ah believe Philip could resurrect Prosperine without your blood."

"How?" I said.

"By using a soulstone." She turned the book so I could read the page.

I stared at the words for a moment. "What language is that?"

"A dead one. Older than Sumerian, and Camazotz believes it is over 10,000 years dead. We don't know how old the writing is."

"You can read it?"

"No." Her voice was small and her eyes flicked across the room.

"Meaning?"

"Ah called in a favor from Ronwe."

I blinked a few times. "You called in a favor to a demon? How in hell does a *demon* owe *you* a favor?" I held up my hand and said, "Actually, never mind. I'd rather not know."

Zola's lips quirked up just a little. "That is wise of you." She nodded and pointed to some of the illustrations on the page. "These give you the basics." She turned to the next page and I did a double take. It had a drawing of a crystal almost identical to one I'd seen very recently.

"The one in the corner looks like the artifact Tessrian is bound in."

"Yes, it does. The book calls it a bloodstone. From what Ah can tell, it is much like a soulstone, only formed on the battlefields of demons, not men."

"It traps a demon's soul?"

"Not a soul, no. It absorbs fragments of the demons themselves as they're obliterated."

"So is the crystal with Tessrian in it just a fragment of a demon, or is it actually Tessrian?"

"Oh, it is Tessrian." Zola chuckled and flashed a wicked grin. "Ah put the bitch down myself."

I stifled a shiver at the gleam in Zola's eyes. "Does it say how to destroy it?" She nodded and my excitement died almost as fast as it was born. "And you didn't tell me this already because of *what* terrible portent of doom?"

"You're getting wise in your old age, boy."

I sagged back in the mesh chair, staring at the taupe ceiling for a moment before I blew out a breath. "Hit me with it."

Zola's finger followed along the page as she said, "To destroy a bloodstone one must fuse it to a soulstone in the Devil's Forge and smash it with the Smith's Hammer. What truly worries me, is the chance Philip has to release the demon trapped in a bloodstone. He may only need a soulstone, or the right soulart." She pinched the bridge of her nose. "Ah think we need to destroy Tessrian's stone."

My face curled into a frown and I said, "That doesn't sound too bad."

She chuckled and rested her chin on her knuckles with her elbows on the dark wooden table. "Really? If Ah didn't know better Ah would assume you have no idea what either the Devil's Forge or the Smith's Hammer is."

"I may be a bit rusty on the topic," I said as I scratched my head. "How hard is it to find a blacksmith's hammer?"

Zola laughed outright. "*The* Smith's Hammer, Damian. Some legends place the hammer in Vulcan's forge. Others label it the cause for

Vesuvius's eruption and the destruction of Herculaneum and Pompeii in 79. That is 79 AD."

I stared at Zola in disbelief.

"It is *the* Smith's Hammer, Damian, not *a* smith's hammer."

"Where the hell do you find something like that?"

"Ah know people," she said with a smirk as she closed the book. I was surprised to see the runes for preservation and longevity carved into the back cover. I reached a hand out to the cover and Zola slapped it away.

"Respect the archive's rules. No gloves, no touch. Ah don't care if the book's warded to survive an open flame. Put the gloves on."

I chuckled and put my hands under the table. "How old are those?"

"Older than they should be. These runes shouldn't have existed 10,000 years ago." Zola frowned. "Ah've never seen Magrasnetto worked into a cover to build a ward before. It is brilliant. The book is nearly indestructible."

"But I can't touch it?"

Zola raised an eyebrow and glared at me. "No matter how indestructible something is, you seem quite capable of making bad things happen to it."

"I do alright with the shop, and my library."

"Other peoples' things," Zola said, half question, half statement.

I shrugged. "So what is the Devil's Forge?"

"It is a place of great geologic power and fire. The forge can be found many places on earth."

I raised my eyebrows. "A volcano?" She nodded and I squeaked, "A *volcano*!?"

"Finding a volcano is easy enough, but Ah must consult with Aeros about the hammer."

"Aeros would know?"

"If he's been honest with me, he had it in his possession once."

"I think I'm done. My head's starting to hurt. Let's get some lunch before we go to the shop."

"That is an excellent idea, boy." She smiled as she stood up, grabbed her knobby old cane, and led me to the archive's door. "There is still the other fact Ah learned in the book."

"What's that?" I said as we walked down the aisle of ancient litera-ture.

"Philip may not need you to resurrect Prosperine."

"Oh, right. Happy days."

"Ah found a passage detailing the use of a soulstone to release a demon into our plane."

"Is that something Philip would know?"

"Ah don't think so, because Ah didn't know it ... but it is always possible. Philip has always been more interested in the Black Arts, and this skill is questionable at best. He could use you as a distrac-tion."

"A decoy," I said.

"Yes, to keep our attention away from his true goal. Ah don't think that's the case, but we should be wary. Do you want to know what is truly frightening?"

"Sure, why not, I get too much sleep as it is." I stopped with my hand on the door to the archive.

Zola glanced up at me. "The book says that with a large enough soulstone you can awaken an old god onto our plane."

"Are you serious?"

"Yes, and it is a simple process."

"Someone would have to be completely insane to do that. The wrong god could tear our planet in half and devour the sun."

"Some of the old gods could devour the galaxy, Damian."

I shuddered and opened the door. We walked out of the archive and down the hallway. The locks clicked home behind us.

Vik was sitting on the bench when we descended the stairs to the entryway. "Did you tell him?"

Zola nodded and Vik visibly relaxed.

"Why wouldn't you have told me?"

"He knows you don't like hearing about Camazotz and demons. He was worried Ah'd keep it from you." She patted my cheek and said, "Have to protect those delicate sensibilities."

I quirked an eyebrow as Vik laughed and turned to me.

"I have no wish to keep secrets from you. You ..." he looked away for a moment, "I trust you, Damian. I want you to do the same."

"I do Vik, even if I didn't know you, you have Sam's stamp of approval and she's a real bitch about shit like that."

Zola snorted a laugh and gave Vik a hug before we left.

"Let me know what you're doing?" he said.

"We will," Zola said.

"Good, I wish to help in any way I can. Vassili knows we owe you a debt for last year."

"Eh, what's one dead demon?" I said. "It's no problem."

Vik smiled, and it was the first full smile I'd seen on his face since Devon tried to kill everyone he knew.

CHAPTER 9

I opened Zola's door for her when we got to the driveway. The sun was much higher and the morning dew that had covered everything when I'd arrived was almost gone. I had to squint in the burst of daylight. Zola climbed in and closed the door while I made my way around Vicky on the asphalt drive. I noticed a smattering of sap across the roof from the nearby evergreens and grumbled about needing to wash the car again.

"Open up the glove box and tell me what you think," I said as we pulled onto the road. "I picked something up for Nixie."

"You're smitten with a water witch. Unbelievable." I caught a smile out of the corner of my eye as she opened the glove box and pulled out the small package.

"I got it from Ashley this morning."

She slid the top off and I heard a sharp intake of breath. "Oh, Damian. This must have cost a fortune."

"Really?" I said, sincerely curious.

"I've never seen blue obsidian so thin and clear before." She pushed on the center of one disc a little with her thumb. "It feels heavy, very strong, but very clear." She turned the bracelet through her hands and shook her head. "It's a beautiful gift."

"You don't think it's overkill?" I said.

"Perhaps, but you are taking a water witch to dinner. She is likely accustomed to sunken ships and drowned men on a first date."

"When you put it like that," I said with a grimace.

Zola laughed as she put the bracelet away. "Ah don't know of any etiquette when it comes to gifts for a water witch. Ah would be surprised if Nixie didn't appreciate the gesture."

I tried hard to wipe the stupid grin off my face, but it was stuck for the rest of the drive to Saint Charles.

***

We came to a grinding halt on the cobblestones of Main Street behind an enormous string of traffic. I groaned and bashed my head on the steering wheel. "What the hell is *this* mess?"

"It's Saturday morning."

I turned my head without lifting it from the steering wheel and said, "It is? Crap, you're right." Saturdays saw Main Street transformed into a throng of tourists and shoppers. With stop signs on every block and a sea of pedestrians, the mass of cars and SUVs slowed to a crawl. My gaze traveled past Zola and honed in on the fudge shop. "Ooo, breakfast."

"What?" She turned her head toward the storefronts. "Aideen will kill you if you get fudge for Foster."

"Not if I get her Irish crème fudge too." I pulled the car a little closer to the curb, not close enough to actually be parked, and leapt out to the sounds of shoppers, cars, and the faint smell of the Missouri River on the breeze. No customers were in the shop and the clerk's eyes widened when I shouted out my order, slapped some money on the counter, and ran back out the door the instant she handed me a three-pound bag. I heard a faint "Thank you," as the door closed behind me and I waved the bag in the air.

I slammed the car door and pulled right back into the traffic I'd just left. "Hold on, I'm going to take the back way." We pulled left at the stop sign and cut across Second Street to the alley that ran straight to the parking lot behind the shop.

"That was certainly faster than waiting," Zola said. "If Ah didn't know better, Ah'd think you drove into traffic just to get fudge." Zola raised her eyebrows, wrinkling her forehead, and stared at me.

"I'm just not a morning person, that's all," I said as I turned the car off and opened the door. "I wasn't thinking straight."

"Whatever you say, boy." She closed the car door and walked up to the back of the shop.

I unlocked the door set in the expanse of brickwork with a key and a swift kick to the second lock's gargoyle-like face, and cracked it open. "It's Damian and Zola!" I shouted before I stepped inside.

"You can never be too careful with fairies around," Zola said.

"And cu siths," I complained without any real conviction. A moment later a black nose attached to a green blur muscled its way through the door, almost knocking me down in the process.

Zola's voice took on the baby talk tone some people get around pets as she crouched down and ruffled the fur of Peanut's back. Bubbles came bounding out to join them. Peanut rewarded her with a facial exfoliation by tongue. Zola was smiling when she stood up, dripping slobber.

"Would you like a towel?" I said a split second before Bubbles yipped and launched herself at my chest. I stumbled and fell backwards into the shop, never relinquishing my hold on the fudge, as the sizable cu sith bounded off my chest and over me before I'd settled on the ground. "Ow," I muttered with my head on the floor.

I heard hysterical fairy laughter mixed with a more melodic sound. I rolled my eyes up and found Nixie smirking at me. She wore a miniskirt that barely peeked out beyond the edge of her hair and a summer sweater with a plunging neckline. My eyes trailed from her hair to her legs before Foster cleared his throat, which made for an odd sound while he was still laughing.

Peanut walked in casually, leading Zola. I was impressed and appreciative of the fact he took care not to step on me. Zola was smiling when she offered me a hand and pulled me off the ground. "Thanks."

I turned back around and held up the bag. "Hey Foster, I got you some peanut butter fudge."

"Oh, god. Fudge!" He jumped off the table and flew around the bag as I set it down.

Aideen shook her head and said, "Damian, I cannot believe you bought him fudge again when-"

I reached in the bag and pulled out the block of Irish crème fudge for Aideen and set it in front of her.

"Oh, god. Fudge!" she clapped her hands together and sliced the cellophane open with her sword even faster than Foster. "I'll let it go this once," she said in a small voice.

"Check this out, Mom," I said as I set a small block of Irish whiskey fudge in front of Cara.

"Fudge and whiskey," she said. "Someone is a genius in that shop. Thank you."

I pulled out a block of chocolate caramel fudge for Zola and me to share. Zola snatched it up and started unwrapping it as soon as it hit the table.

"I've never had fudge," Nixie said.

Foster's forehead wrinkled as his eyes widened, his mouth falling open in horror. "*Never?*"

She shook her head. "I had chocolate once, I think. That's what a cocoa bean is, right? I didn't like it very much, too bitter and grainy." She ran her tongue over her teeth like she was trying to spit out a bad taste.

"Nixie," Zola said. She waited for the water witch to look at her. "Are you telling us you've never had chocolate?"

She shrugged like it was no big thing.

"Cut a piece of that off for her," I said.

Zola ran a white plastic knife down the edge of the block and handed the resulting sliver to me. Bubbles gave me a forlorn look, tracking the fudge as it moved from Zola to me. I broke off a little edge and tasted it. It was a great batch, smooth and creamy with some slightly hardened caramel. "Taste this."

Nixie sniffed the sliver of fudge, jerked it away from her nose, and stared at it. "That smells good." She took a bite and her eyes widened. She crammed the rest into her mouth at once with a slurp and her shoulders sagged. "Oh, oh my." She closed her eyes and put a hand over her stomach as she melted into a chair. Her eyes opened slowly before she said, "I understand now. That *is* better than sex, Aideen!"

"Well then, no more fudge for you," I said.

Nixie and the fairies laughed as Zola slapped my arm. "You're terrible, boy."

"Only on weekends." I grinned as I swiped the slice of fudge Zola was cutting and handed half to Nixie.

She nibbled the second piece slowly, making all kinds of noise as she whittled it down.

"Better than sex?" Foster said to Aideen as he cut off a chunk as big as his head.

She took a slow bite and gave him a wicked grin.

I finally held up my hand before he took another bite. "Whoa now, we need to talk before you go crazy on me."

He nodded and took a bite of peanut butter fudge. "We should probably talk soon then."

I shook my head and pulled out a chair at the Formica table. Nixie took the seat closest to the back door, I took the chair closest to the front, and Zola sat between us with her back to the grandfather clock. The fairies each sat down, legs folded beside their blocks of fudge. As soon as I sat down, I jumped back to my feet.

"Maybe I should open the shop, huh?"

"Maybe you should," Foster said. "All those people pounding on the door might break it down."

"Ha ha ha," I said as I ran to the front, changed the sign to open, and unlocked the door. I flipped the lights on for the front of the shop as I walked past the switch by the back room's door.

Bubbles jumped and landed on my lap the instant I sat down again. "Oof!" I was instantly engaged in battle with the ten-foot tongue from hell. "It's good to see you too, girl." The cu sith poked her wet nose under my shirt and I yelped.

"I think she wants fudge," Cara said as she took a bite out of the fist-sized chunk in her hand.

"Bubbles, down," Nixie said. Everyone in the room stopped and stared as Bubbles jumped off my lap. "Now sit down and behave." Bubbles plopped her rear right down and wagged her tail.

"Holy crap!" Foster said.

"Hell has officially frozen over," Aideen said as she stared at the cu sith. "Why won't you do that for me?"

Bubbles sucked her tongue in and cocked her head to the side before letting her tongue roll back to the floor with a wet smack.

Zola shook her head and said, "Enough. Let us discuss our problem."

"Problem?" I said. "Just one?"

Foster hit me in the face with a wild toss of fudge. I laughed as it bounced off my cheek and disappeared before it hit the ground. I barely even saw Bubbles's tongue move when it snapped out to catch the rogue fudge.

Nixie narrowed her eyes. "I think she's part frog."

Foster and Aideen giggled.

Zola sighed, muttered something about all Fae being the same no matter what bloody part of the world they're from, and then said, "Fine, problems. Namely, Philip and his cult." She twisted a pair of beads in one of her longer braids. "Secondly, the bloodstones and how to destroy them."

Cara's head snapped up. "Tell me you didn't say bloodstones."

"What's a bloodstone?" Aideen said as she turned to Foster. "Do you know?" He shook his head.

"The book we read in the archive said they're like a soulstone, only formed from demons," I said. "Instead of trapping human soul fragments, it absorbs pieces of destroyed demons."

Nixie nodded and I glanced in her direction.

"You've heard of them?" I said.

"Yes, they're often red and quite beautiful, but they are cursed things. Most Fae won't touch one since we are more sensitive to bloodstones than humans."

"What do they do to you?" Zola said.

"They feel," she paused to think, "alive. As if they're trying to escape your grasp even though they are lifeless."

I shuddered and thought of Zola's demon dolls. Nasty, nasty, things.

Cara nodded. "It is also said they bring a curse against any Fae who is bold enough to touch them. It would curse you with misfortune far worse than you can imagine. Of course, it does not last long in the stories, as such a streak of misfortune tends to end in death."

"But for humans?" I said.

"I've never heard of a human being cursed by one. For a Fae, though, the only way to stop the curse is to destroy the bloodstone."

"Ah," I said, "and that is no easy task."

Zola gave me a sideways look with a small grin as I stole her words.

"Indeed, most of the damned end up dead before they can destroy the stone." She paused and looked at Zola. "There hasn't been a bloodstone recorded in decades. Where did you find it?"

"Ah made it," Zola said without emotion.

Cara's head jerked up. "How is that possible?"

Zola rubbed her cheek. "It is something of a long story."

"Just give us the short version," Foster said.

Aideen punched his arm and growled. "Respect, Foster. The fudge goes straight to your brain."

Foster grinned.

"That is not a bad idea, Foster," Zola said. "It was toward the end of the Civil War. A dark necromancer started a ritual to summon Tessrian to our plane. We came too late to break it. Now, though, Ah have to wonder if it was Philip that summoned the beast. Ah tried to warn Edgar and the Watchers about Philip's cult, but they're as thick-headed as Aeros." Zola sighed and squeezed the bridge of her nose. "Never you mind that now. Tessrian though, Ah trapped her in a solitary crystal, a small soulstone."

"I see," Cara said. "So the demon itself, not merely a gathering of its remnants, was trapped in the soulstone. That would create a bloodstone instantly."

Zola nodded. "Yes, but to destroy her bond to our plane, we have to destroy the bloodstone. And to destroy the bloodstone, we need a soulstone, the Devil's Forge, and the Smith's Hammer."

Cara sat in silence for a moment. "It would make sense, binding a soulstone to the bloodstone in the Devil's Forge, and using the Smith's Hammer to destroy them both." Her hand swept toward Foster and Aideen. "None of us can survive the heat of a volcano."

"Nor would I ask you to try," Zola said.

"I can," Nixie said.

I raised my eyes to her as everyone else turned their heads. She was scratching Bubbles's chin while she said, "I like the Devil's Forge. The hot springs are always nice."

"How can you possibly survive being close to the magma?" Cara said.

Nixie stopped playing with Bubbles and sat up straight. She looked between the fairies for a moment before speaking. "I like you all. And ... I trust you. I am a water witch, but that is a misleading name, and a name I dislike. I would like to share something with you, but it is not for the ears of others."

"You have our confidence," Aideen said.

"If you can't trust your cousin, who can you trust?" Foster said around a mouthful of fudge.

Nixie smiled and nodded to herself. "Most of my people spend their lives in the water, that much is true, but there are many of us living below the surface of the earth. Our entire family is resistant to heat. That is an ... understatement," she paused and smiled, seemingly amused by the word. "Some of our family lives in magma like others live in water."

"How is that possible?" Zola said.

Nixie shrugged. "I don't know, but I am also resistant to the heat of the Devil's Forge."

"I think I know," Aideen said as she glanced at Cara. "It's a story you used to tell us years ago."

Cara frowned and shook her head. "I don't remember."

"Gaia's children."

Cara's eyes widened. "No, that is a myth, nothing more."

"What are Gaia's children?" I said.

"In our stories, much like human fairy tales, forgive the pun, Gaia's children were the offspring of elementals and Fae." Cara looked back at Nixie and said, "The only problem is, no one I've met has seen an elemental, or knows if they even exist."

I shook my head and said, "I thought all the Fae were considered elementals, no?"

Foster laughed. "No. The elementals Mom is talking about would eat demons for breakfast and give the worst of the old gods a run for their money."

"As impressive, or maybe horrifying is a better word," I said. "Yeah, as horrifying as that sounds, I guess it doesn't matter right now." I turned to my potentially half-elemental date for the evening. "Could you really survive contact with a river of lava, Nixie?"

She nodded. "Oh yes, I would not mention it if I wasn't sure."

"So, we just need a volcano," Foster said.

"Oh, good, then I'm glad were in the middle of the Great Plains," I muttered.

Nixie's eyebrows furrowed as she said, "Why are you glad of that?"

Zola and the fairies laughed.

"He was being sarcastic," Zola said.

Nixie nodded and reached for a piece of fudge.

"The fastest path will be the Warded Ways," Cara said. "There aren't any open vents close to us."

"Even better," I said with a grimace. The Warded Ways are like terrestrial wormholes. Wormholes from hell. I remembered a few years ago when Cara regaled us with a story about a Fae king who had the ability to create wormholes at will. The only problem was, the damn things were permanent and began to tear the world apart. It eventually led to the Wandering War and the death of the great king when he refused to stop making wormholes. In fact, it was Glenn who killed the king. After the war, Glenn used wards to seal as many of the wormholes as he could find. The Fae can open them when they need to and the world stopped falling apart, held together with magical duct tape. For his troubles, Glenn became the great and feared Lord of the Dead, Gwynn ap Nudd.

"Ah'll speak with Aeros about the Smith's Hammer while you two are at dinner," Zola said. "If Nixie is still hungry after all the fudge, that is. Ah want to stop by the Pit and visit the archive again too. Cara, if you could find the nearest Warded Way to visit a volcano, Ah would appreciate it greatly."

"That shouldn't be difficult." Her wings opened wide and closed slowly as she spoke.

"How are you getting to Elephant Rock?" I said.

"Ah'm not," Zola said. "Ah don't need to be there to talk to Aeros. We had to go there to get the artifact, but his own body is not so limited. Ah'll call him from here."

"Maybe I'll put a sign out front and sell tickets."

Zola snorted. "Yes, you do that."

"Can I talk to him too?" Foster said. "I haven't seen the old rock pile in years."

Zola nodded.

Our conversation drifted away from demons and dark necromancers and focused more on fudge and all the other kinds of chocolate Nixie hadn't tried. A few customers came in throughout our conversation, but no one needed much. I turned around an hour later as the bell on the front door jingled again and found Sam walking in with Frank in tow.

I smiled and hopped up out of my chair. "Hey sis!"

"I hear you have a date."

I stopped with my arms halfway to Sam for a hug and raised an eyebrow. "Yes, I do, and please remember she's in the back room and can hear everything you say." I heard a lot of muffled laughter from the back.

Sam scowled and addressed the doorway. "I wasn't going to say anything bad!"

Foster fluttered to the register and looked at Sam. "Uh huh, that's like the sun deciding not to shine for a day."

"It could happen," she said sheepishly. She chuckled and gave me a hug.

I couldn't help but watch her aura when she hugged me. It was so similar, but so different from the human aura she'd been born with. It had black and deep reds like a demon's aura, but still retained the yellow and green pulses I remembered from when we were kids. She had always been a fighter, always adapting to whatever came her way. Becoming a vampire hadn't changed that at all.

Frank waved as he walked toward the back room and then came to a screeching halt about two feet from the door. I saw his eyes widened and his jaw worked to speak. "H ... Hi."

"Hello, journeyman," said a soft voice.

I laughed. "Her name's Nixie, Frank. Just say, 'Hi, Nixie.'"

"Oh good, god," Sam said as she took a few quick steps and gently smacked Frank's head into the wall. A nice hollow thump echoed through the room.

Foster and Zola laughed as Frank rubbed his forehead. He turned around, blushing, and walked to the display case in the corner.

Sam sighed, shook her head, and said, "So, what are you up to?"

"Didn't Vik tell you?" Zola said as she walked up beside the counter.

"A bit, but he's still a little distant." Sam's eyes trailed to the back room. "He's getting better, but he really took Devon's betrayal hard."

"Come on in and have some fudge. I'll fill you in." I turned toward Frank and said, "You can have some too if you stop ogling my date."

"I wasn't ogling," Frank muttered.

Sam laughed, grabbed Frank's arm, and dragged him into the back room. "Come on, I still love you."

"Gag me with a shotgun," I said as I followed them.

"Me first!" Foster said as he zipped through the door ahead of me.

We spent the next hour filling Sam and Frank in on everything we knew about the bloodstones, the Smith's Hammer, Philip, and our pending travel to the Devil's Forge.

"You don't mind taking Zola back to the Pit?" I said.

Sam shook her head, "Not at all." She took a bite of peanut butter fudge and turned to look at Zola. "You're welcome to stay the night again if you like."

Zola smiled, "It is much more pleasant than a hotel, and infinitely more pleasant than Damian's couch."

I coughed to hide a laugh.

"Good, let's regroup in the morning," Cara said.

"Frank's taking me out for lunch," Sam said. "So we probably won't be here."

"Going to snack on him in public?" I asked.

She narrowed her eyes at me, and Frank struggled not to laugh.

"No?" I said.

"No," she said as everyone burst into laughter.

Finally, it was time for dinner.

CHAPTER 10

We said our goodbyes and I walked Nixie out to the car for our trip to the restaurant. I opened the door for her and waited to be sure she had all of her hair safely tucked into the seat behind her.

"I'm out of harm's way," she said as I closed the door. I couldn't help but smile.

We rode in silence to Highway 70 until Nixie said, "Where are we going for dinner?"

"I figured I'd take you out for fish food."

"You figured *what?*" she said with a scowl on her face.

"I was kidding," I said with a chuckle. "Sushi. Do you like sushi?"

"Actually yes, I do," she said as her expression softened. "I find it difficult to follow you at times, Damian, as I am somewhat new to your humor."

"Sarcasm," I nodded. "Well, between me, and Foster, and Zola, you should pick it up pretty quick."

"Yes, I've noticed. My cousin also has a talent for being difficult."

I laughed as we merged onto Highway 270 south. Traffic was light, but I turned my signal on anyway. Olive was only a few exits away, up the ramp to an ostentatious overpass. I was pretty sure it was a memorial to someone, but I couldn't remember who as we drove past the flowered landscaping and decorative concrete.

"This is an odd expanse of road," Nixie said. "Are those stone flower pots?"

I glanced at the huge concrete pots filled with flowers. "I think so." Each was decorated with a broken heart.

"It is ... attractive for such bleak stonework."

"I suppose it is," I said as we turned onto Olive and passed a series of strip malls and a movie theater. We drove the last few minutes in silence, and I was happy to find it remained a comfortable silence. I turned into one of the strip malls and, though it didn't look any different from the others at first glance, it did hold an excellent sushi bar.

Nixie's eyes wandered around the mall with a disdainful look on her face.

"Well, it's not a fresh shipwreck, but hopefully you'll enjoy it."

Her lips curled up in a smile. "There is some truth in your sarcasm." She pulled her fingers through the incredibly pale hair draped across her lap and said, "I'm sure it will be fine, Damian."

I nodded and looked at the front of the restaurant. "Tachibana. I ate my first spider roll here."

Nixie looked at me in horror. "I thought this was seafood?!"

I laughed. "It's just their name for soft shell crab."

She looked back at the restaurant with a bit of a frown playing across her lips. "That's a silly term. And disgusting."

I shrugged and leaned across Nixie to the glove box. She smelled like clean seawater and soap and I fought back the embarrassing urge to sniff her. "I got you a present." She started to reach for the box and I snatched it away. "After dinner."

She pouted and my heart flip flopped. I'm pretty sure she noticed, because a huge grin lit her face.

"Yes, well, let me get the door for you," I said.

She waited until I opened her door and took my arm when I offered it. It felt natural walking beside her, and I hoped she felt the same.

Tachibana greeted us with the smells of sake, kelp, and sashimi. Paper lanterns decorated the ceiling above a sushi chef prepping rolls like a mad butcher in the dim light behind the bar to the left. A young, friendly Japanese hostess took us to a corner booth. It was away from the sushi bar, on the opposite side of the restaurant, but had a much more private feel to it, with shoji screens surrounding the sides of the booth. The wide, deep benches formed a U around the table. Nixie and I both adjusted the small square cushions as we sat down.

When the server left to get us drinks, Nixie scooted around to sit closer to me. I was a bit surprised, but I certainly wasn't complaining.

"So, what's in the box?" she asked as she stared down at the little package sitting to my left.

"It's a surprise, and I'm not giving you a hint. You'll just have to wait."

She pouted again and narrowed her eyes. I could only describe it as smoldering.

Before I could put a filter on the brain-to-mouth connection, I blurted out, "You're very beautiful." I wanted to smack my head on the table as soon as I'd said it. I saw Nixie's eyes widen before I started staring at the shoji screen across the booth.

"Thank you." She smiled, squeezed my hand once, and then put both her hands beneath the table. "What's good here?" she said as she pushed her menu away and leaned over to look at mine.

I choked back a sigh as my moment of idiocy rolled past without further comment. "I love their Diamond Beef. It's not sushi, but do you want to try it? We can split that and a couple rolls."

She nodded and said, "Let's get a spider roll and some tekka don. I love tuna." Her eyes wandered over the menu until she said, "Oh, they have Sapporo!"

"You like Japanese beer?"

She nodded. "Yes, we recovered several cases from shipwrecks."

"Does all of your new and interesting food come from ship-wrecks?"

"Not fudge," she said with a small smile.

We both ordered beer when the server came back.

A large shadow loomed over our table as soon as the server left. I expected to look up and find another server, or perhaps a manager making sure the guests were happy, but instead I saw Nixie look up and say, "Hohnihohkaiyohos!"

I looked up to find Hugh standing at our table shaking his head. "Please, call me Hugh. Damian, if I didn't know better, I'd think you were on a date with the water witch."

Before I could answer or even figure out how I should feel about Hugh's comment, Nixie said, "I'll call you Hugh if you call me Nixie. I don't like being called a water witch."

Hugh raised an eyebrow in what I believe was surprise. "Very well, Nixie." He nodded his head and continued, "I want you to know, I meant no disrespect by the name."

Nixie smiled. "I didn't think you did."

Hugh rubbed his chin and glanced between us. "You seem ... different, Nixie. You never smiled when you saved my son."

Nixie looked away and nodded.

Hugh inclined his head. "I apologize. I am intruding. There is only one more thing," he said with a smile. As Nixie looked back up at Hugh, he turned and beckoned to a young man sitting at a table on the other side of the restaurant. He had Hugh's dark skin and black hair and was wearing a brown leather bomber jacket despite the warm weather. He walked between the tables with a distinct slouch.

When he got close enough, he nodded to me and Nixie, smiled, and said, "What'd you need Dad?"

Nixie's eyes widened and her hand scrambled onto my knee. I grunted and gritted my teeth in an effort not to yelp from the suddenly excruciating pressure on my leg.

"You okay?" I said as quietly as I could.

She nodded quickly and stared at the young man.

"Stand up straight." Hugh pulled back on the young man's shoulders and smiled when the boy rolled his eyes and straightened up. "This is Honiahaka, my son."

I held out my hand awkwardly, since Nixie still had a death grip on my leg, and shook Honiahaka's hand. "It's good to meet you. I'm Damian, and this is Nixie."

"Call me Haka, and it's good to meet you too."

"Honiahaka, you met Nixie once before."

Haka glanced at his father and then back at Nixie. "No, I'd remember her." He looked embarrassed after he had a moment to think about what he'd said. I could relate.

Hugh laughed. "You were very young when she saved you. Not far from here, in the fury of the river floods."

Haka jerked his head and stared at his father. "What? I thought you made that up. It was just a story to teach a lesson or entertain, like the water witches you used to tell us about." Haka turned away from Hugh and stared at Nixie.

"May I tell him, Nixie?"

She nodded twice, in quick succession.

Hugh put his hand on his son's shoulder and said, "Nixie is a water witch. She is the water witch that saved you. Her action has inclined me to believe all her kind are not evil."

Haka fidgeted and then stared at Nixie. He said, "Thank you," and nodded to Nixie again.

The older wolf smiled and put his arm around Haka. His son looked mortified. Hugh laughed. "We will leave you in peace. I only wanted to give you my greetings and let Honiahaka meet you both."

I traded grips with Hugh and Haka while Nixie just nodded from the back of the booth.

Hugh said, "Be well," as they turned and left.

Nixie watched them leave and sighed as they walked outside. Her shoulders relaxed once we were alone again and the crushing pressure on my leg dissipated.

As the wolves left, the server came back and set down two bowls of miso soup and two Sapporos. Nixie dragged her soup closer with two fingers, picked up the bowl, and breathed in the steam.

"This smells delicious."

I tasted a spoonful and nodded. It had a subtle kelp flavor with green onions, salt, and tofu. "I really like their soup."

Nixie smiled as she slurped down a spoonful.

"Nix," I waited for her to look up before I asked, "How old is Honiahaka?"

She tapped her index finger on the edge of her spoon. "He would have to be close to sixty now."

I leaned out of the booth to get a glimpse of Hugh and Haka talking out in the parking lot near a trailer with a pair of kayaks. "Sixty? He looks twenty! I guess he's aging gracefully."

Nixie laughed so hard she snorted, and it made me laugh in turn. I worked hard not to stare when she leaned forward, showing me more cleavage as she laughed. I'd consider my effort not to stare a moderate success.

"Have you found anything new you like?" I asked.

"Like what?"

"You know, human things, since you've been mingling with us lesser beings."

She shrugged and stirred the remnants of her soup a bit. "I like movies."

"Really? Movies? What about TV?"

"Is there a difference?" Nixie said.

I laughed. "A bit. Have you actually been to a movie theater?"

She shook her head. "I've only seen movies on the television. Foster told me about movie theaters, they sound much like the amphitheaters we once watched plays in."

"Yeah, except they have air conditioning, snack bars, and speakers now." I drained my soup and adjusted my seat cushion. "I'll have to take you to the movies sometime."

"I'd like that."

The server came back again and laid down a plate of Diamond Beef, tekka don, and a sliced up tube of kelp. The tube of kelp was actually the spider roll, with a flurry of soft shell crab legs sticking out of either end.

Nixie leaned over the tekka don, took a deep breath, and smiled. "This was an excellent idea." After eyeing the sizable chunk of wasabi on the plate, I decided not to take a deep breath. I mixed a little into a dish of soy sauce and dipped a piece of the reddish tuna while Nixie ate hers straight up. It was fresh, smooth, and tasted nothing like a fish smells.

"I think I like it more with the scales on it, but this is still really good." Her chopsticks shot out and grabbed another piece of tuna.

I was left to tend to the Diamond Beef, which was alright with me. It was a delicious sirloin cut into strips and served in teriyaki mushroom sauce. I held a piece out for Nixie between my chopsticks, and despite the frown on her face, she reluctantly leaned over and tasted it. The fact she ate off my chopsticks made me smile, and about then I realized I was hopeless.

She chewed it for a minute and her face changed from a frown, to indifference, and then she swallowed it. "That's not bad. It's not fish, but it's not bad. I think it would be better raw."

I pushed the beef around my plate and said, "You let me know how that works out."

She laughed and picked up a center piece of the spider roll. I guess even a water witch can be unnerved by too many legs at the dinner table. We ate in silence for a few minutes, and again I found myself enthralled by the comfortable silence. Nixie glanced at me over her beer and smiled as she finished the tekka don. I ate one end of the spider roll and then pointed at the other.

"That one's yours, Nix."

"I don't really–"

"Nope, you're not getting out of it." I jabbed at the box to my left and said, "If you want the box, you eat the legs."

She scowled at me, but reached out with her chopsticks anyway. Nixie almost growled as she stared down the explosion of crab legs sticking out of the spider roll. She sighed and then stuffed the whole section in her mouth at once. Her cheeks puffed out while she chewed the mass of fried crab, rice, cucumber, and kelp. I couldn't help but laugh at the crunching sounds filling our booth.

Nixie swallowed, took a drink of beer, and stared at me. "Give me the box." I slid the small square box over to her, which she immediately picked up and shook.

"Oh, you're one of them, huh?"

"One of whom?"

"Whom?" I chuckled. "One of those people who always guess what their presents are?"

"Sometimes," she said as she smirked and untied the blue ribbon around the box. Nixie's eyes widened as she pulled the top off and removed the thin layer of cotton. "Oh, Damian," she said as she pulled the bracelet out of the box and rubbed the tips of her index and middle fingers on the discs. "Where did you find Wasser-Münzen?" The dim light of the paper lanterns made the blue obsidian look even darker than I'd seen it before.

"Actually, a friend of mine found the discs in Germany. Ashley, one of my customers—I don't think you've met her. I just thought you'd like something in blue obsidian." I scratched the back of my head and smiled. "What is Wasser-Münzen?"

"Currency ... money." She held out the bracelet to me. "These were used as coins by the undines centuries ago. Many ages ago, from before I was born."

I narrowly, but tactfully, avoided asking how old she was.

She held out her hand and I took the bracelet from her. "Help me put it on, would you?"

I smiled and slid the deep blue obsidian and silver chain bracelet over her left wrist. She ran her fingers over the discs a few more times and looked up at me. Her eyes were the clear, crystalline blues and greens of a brilliant ocean.

"Thank you," she said as she leaned forward.

My heart pounded as she came closer and a small smile lifted the corners of her mouth. I hadn't noticed just how red her lips were against her skin and how soft her lips looked until she closed her eyes and kissed me, slowly, and so very softly. She was warm and her kiss felt so good. It was natural to put my right arm around her and pull her close. Her thigh bumped against mine as our kiss grew and a wave of lust rolled over us. I wanted her then and there, sprawled across the table, nude.

I pulled away and stared at her. She leaned back and did the same, casually pulling her sweater down until her cleavage was impossible to ignore.

"I like my bracelet," she whispered in an utterly sultry voice. "We should go."

I nodded and flagged the server down, handing her my card before she had a chance to print out the receipt.

Nixie leaned against me as we walked out to the car. I opened the door for her and kissed her on the cheek before she climbed in. I put some serious effort into not running around the car and driving back to my apartment like a suicidal lemming.

About halfway home she undid her seatbelt and slid across the bench seat. She sat there with her head on my shoulder until we pulled into the darkening parking lot ten minutes later. As soon as I turned the car off her hand moved down and massaged my groin. "Let's go inside," she whispered.

"No drowning," I said with a grin.

"No promises," she said as she batted her eyelashes.

"That's the best I'm going to get?"

"Oh no, definitely not." She leaned in and kissed me again.

"Oh hell, let's go," I said as my jeans grew uncomfortably tight.

We were out of the car and clattering up the wooden steps in seconds. I fumbled with the keys while Nixie leaned against my back, sighed, and wrapped her arms around me. The door opened with a quiet squeak, and by the time I closed it, threw the deadbolt, and turned back to Nixie, her sweater was on the ground. She had her hair piled over her breasts in two thin ropes.

I kicked off my shoes and grabbed her hand, leading her to the bedroom. I was very glad I'd washed the sheets just a couple days ago. I turned back to Nixie as we reached the bed. She pushed against my chest to sit me down, and then she stepped back a bit. I watched her bend down and peel her miniskirt off as she stayed concealed behind a cascade of nearly-white hair.

She smiled as she stood up, green hues lancing through her aura in the dark light. As she straightened, she pushed her hair behind her and revealed her body. She was gorgeous—all pale porcelain skin darkened only by the shadows of her nipples. My eyes trailed down to the thin wedge of hair on her groin and back up to her crystalline eyes.

"You're beautiful, Nix."

She smiled and pushed me flat on the bed. Her hands undid the button and zipper on my jeans before she slid them off, fingers dancing back up to my thighs. As she moved, her mouth wrapped around me and I shuddered at the sudden warmth. Her head rose and fell briefly before she raised her face to show me a devious grin.

Nixie ran her hands under my shirt as she climbed onto the bed and kissed me hard. Her groin rubbed against my erection as we shifted higher on the bed. I could feel the heat and tension pulsing off of her. She leaned back, grabbed me in her right hand, and lowered herself slowly.

Nixie moaned as she started to push herself up and down and I wrapped my hands around her thighs. Her hands moved up to my chest and she dug her nails in as she kissed me, without losing her rhythm. Her breathing increased and I started to get an odd sensation, as if her every touch sent sparks of power through my skin. My entire body shivered as she moved. My hands moved to Nixie's waist and I was surprised when it had more give to it than I'd expected, but the surprise was lost in another wave of pleasure. She leaned down and kissed me again—her lips were wet, soaking wet and warm.

"I'm going to do something," she whispered. "Don't worry, it's normal."

"Normal," I said with a chuckle, but I didn't really care at the moment.

She smiled as she leaned back again and stopped moving. My hands felt her change. Her body became more and more pliable as she sat there, except I could feel her moving again. Her body looked perfectly still, but I could feel her pulsing up and down, her breathing increasing as the pace quickened. She smiled and groaned as an alien presence burst into my head. My eyes widened as she shuddered and I could feel everything, feel our bodies together at once. She tightened in an orgasm and I lost control in a spasm of ecstasy.

I stared at her in astonishment until our bodies stopped twitching.

Nixie laughed and kissed me again, her lips slippery and hot. "Was that okay? I don't usually let go like that. I didn't mean to push it all onto you."

"That," I said before I swallowed hard, "was bloody amazing."

"Oh good, because we're not done." She grinned as her hand grew translucent and flowed around my groin, more liquid than solid as we started all over again.

***

I woke up with a water witch in my arms, and couldn't remember the last time I'd felt so content. The morning sun seemed awfully bright at the corners of the dark drapes. I glanced at the oversized red digits of my alarm clock and muttered, "Oh, crap."

I gently shook Nixie's shoulder until her eyes opened. "Good morning."

She grinned, and gave me a quick kiss. She screwed up her mouth and said, "That must be morning breath."

"Better than fish breath," I said as I gave her another quick kiss and started to disentangle myself from her hair, which was wrapped around me and the pillows, and draped onto the floor. "We're going to be late. We're supposed to meet Zola at ten."

"Let's go then. I'm hungry." She gave her hair a quick yank and it pulled away from everything effortlessly. She threw the plaid comforter off to the side of the bed, stood up, and stretched her back with her arms over her head. I stared at her breasts shamelessly before I jumped up, grabbed her, and threw her back on the still-warm bed.

"Maybe we have time for a quickie."

She giggled and we managed to make ourselves another twenty minutes late.

CHAPTER 11

Istumbled through the front door of the shop with Nixie laughing at my elbow. A pair of white and black wings swooped past us and Foster landed on the shelf beside us.

"Weren't you wearing that yesterday, cousin?" he said.

Nixie shrugged. "I've been busy. Besides, all my clothes are here."

"I bet," Foster said. "Can't you change your clothes at will?"

Nixie narrowed her eyes at the fairy.

Foster grinned. "Glad to see you're still breathing, Damian." He glanced at the back room. "Company." As he spoke, a deep rolling laugh echoed up from the back.

"Who *is* that?" I said as I moved toward the back. Nixie's heels clacked on the wood floors behind me and I had my answer as I got close to the door. Hugh was sitting with his back to the grandfather clock, dressed in black slacks and a green button down, with Carter to his left, facing the doorway. Carter adjusted his jeans and rolled his eyes. Zola was shaking her head back and forth and laughing. She had her back to us.

Carter raised his hand and smiled. "Damian, Nixie."

"Why do I have a sneaking suspicion I don't want to know what's so funny."

Zola turned her body around and rested her left hand on the top of her knobby old cane. "Aeros suggested we invite the wolves."

"Any particular reason why?" I said.

Hugh nodded once and spoke. "The fact you would ask says much for your intuition. Most werewolves' auras are well balanced with the natural world. A dark necromancer is a greedy being, and their aura's no different." He paused and shifted his eyes to the left for a moment.

"Like a hyena gifted with the hunt, not stopping until he is starved, for he has killed all his food, and must now eat his fallen brothers."

I cocked an eyebrow. "Umm, I don't quite follow."

Nixie squeezed my arm and walked around me to stand between Hugh and Carter. "Hugh is saying the werewolves' auras will interfere with the Black Arts."

Zola nodded. "But there are ways around it. Philip will know of them."

"It may not stop an incantation completely, but the presence of a balanced aura should damage the efforts of almost any Black Art," Nixie said as she frowned. "It is difficult to explain, but it is good to have the werewolves on our side."

Hugh considered Nixie for a moment and then looked back to me. "Though I find it odd, I agree with Nixie."

Carter's head jerked toward Hugh and his eyes were wide. "You agree with a water witch? Truly?"

"Yes, Carter, I agree with *Nixie*." Hugh flashed Nixie a quick grin and she returned it. "I trust her. I think we must if we hope to succeed in pursuing the necromancer."

"So do I, I just ... " Carter shrugged, "it seems unlike you."

Hugh laughed, and I knew it was his laughter I'd heard from the front of the shop. "Even an old wolf can change his mind."

"Is that the only reason Aeros suggested the wolves?" I said.

"No," Zola said. "Ah think Aeros would like to see the wolves tear through Philip's cult with a black flag. The old rock has befriended the little ghost that Happy guards." She looked away and her eyebrows drew down at a sharp angle as her voice hardened. "She told him there was another man who abused her while she was alive. Someone in Philip's cult, but she didn't tell Aeros his name. Or she didn't know his name. Ah'm not sure which."

Foster cursed as he flashed into his full seven-foot height. His fist put a round hole through the wall beside the light switch. "Does it *never* end?!" Cara and Aideen flew out of the grandfather clock with their swords drawn.

I knew Foster's rage. I remembered the van full of body parts and the tiny hand he found in the mass of severed limbs. I remembered the little ghost girl dancing around the flames Foster had summoned to consume that abomination. I remembered the vampire Foster cut in half and the soul he trapped in a dark bottle. And I knew the rage was all the worse for the sister he lost to the monsters.

We thought there may have been more than just the one vampire responsible for killing the little girl and all those people, and now we knew. Not even God Almighty would be able to save the poor bastard when we found out who he was.

I put my hand on Foster's shoulder and felt the tension shaking his body. "We'll find them. It's alright. We'll find them. She's safe with Happy now."

Foster closed his eyes and whispered, "It will never be alright."

"The girl is blessed to be with Happy and Aeros," Cara said. "I know you wish you could have done more for her. I know it hurt you after what happened to your sister." Her voice grew quiet. "Your sister is in a better place, son."

"My sister?" he said as he glanced at her, and then away. "She killed herself. She left us by her own hand. She should have killed our father instead."

"Nudd be damned!" Cara shouted. "I strangled the worthless git with his own entrails! I should've done it sooner, I know, but we move on son." Her voice fell to a whisper, "We have to."

Foster closed his eyes and took a few deep breaths before he nodded to Cara. "I know. I'm sorry."

I squeezed Foster's arm as Nixie came around and hugged him from behind. He rarely spoke of his sister, many years gone, but I knew he still missed her dearly.

Zola sighed and turned to Carter. "Are we agreed, Alpha?"

He nodded and glanced at Foster again. "Yes, we'll speak with the Voice of the packs we know. Find out if anyone has encountered the Black Arts recently."

"What's a Voice?" Nixie said as she leaned against the wall.

"Usually a wolf who likes to talk too much," Hugh said.

Carter laughed. "That's the truth. Voices are wolves that are more social than the rest of the pack, namely wolves who don't mind talking to wolves outside their own pack. Maybe we'll get a lead, but I really don't know, Zola. I think we'll be more help locally, as our pack is not small. We'll stay spread out around the city to keep an eye on things here."

"Good, we will keep you abreast of our own movement." Zola stood up, held her hand out and shook Carter's even as Carter said farewell to Cara. Hugh extended his hand as well.

I raised my eyebrows when Nixie batted his hand away and hugged the wolf goodbye. A small smile lifted his mouth, but his eyes were sad when he looked toward Foster, the fairy's head resting on the wall beside the grandfather clock.

Carter gave Foster a wide berth as he moved toward the front door. Hugh did not. He reached out and grasped the fairy's upper arm. "You're an honorable friend, Foster. I am proud to know you and your family." Hugh nodded to me as he left. The bell jingled when the door closed behind the two wolves.

Once they were gone, a golden swirl swept up from the floor behind Foster. Aideen was suddenly there, over six feet tall, resting her head on the back of Foster's neck. He shuddered and his shoulders sagged.

Zola's gaze travelled away from the couple, and back to Cara as Zola sat down again. "Ah have other news from Aeros."

I nodded but no one else said a word.

"About the Smith's Hammer."

At that, Foster turned around slowly, sliding his arm around Aideen as he faced Zola. Cara rearranged her wings and sat down with her legs crossed. Nixie and I slid into the empty chairs.

"Tell us," Cara said.

"It is in the possession of a fallen demon. He is not far from here. Ah hope you enjoy Renaissance Faires."

I stared at Zola and said, "A demon at a *what?*"

CHAPTER 12

The faire was in Wentzville, about forty minutes west of Saint Louis.

"Is this the right way?" I said as I looked around and saw nothing but subdivisions, fields, and a huge water tower. Across the intersection, the road collapsed into two lanes and the asphalt was patched like an old pair of jeans.

"Yep," Foster said from the dashboard. "The water tower says Rotary Park."

"There's the sign, boy," Zola said a minute later.

I turned into Rotary Park and followed the narrow road around a bend and passed a large pond off to the west. "It doesn't seem very crowded," I said as we started around another bend to the north. As the field came into view, flooded with cars, vans, and RVs as far as the eye could see, I said, "Oh."

People were trickling toward the far end of the parking lot, some in plain clothes and others wearing plumage that would put a peacock to shame.

Aideen pointed to one group as we pulled off the road and bounced onto the grassy field serving as a parking lot. "That poor woman is going to bake in this heat." She had a black corset tied firmly around her chest and abdomen, trailing a blood red velvet skirt and matching sleeves.

"Yes, she is, but she'll look great doing it," Foster said as the car came to a halt.

Aideen smacked him in the back of the head, but she was wearing a smile of her own.

"Ready Nix?" I said as I looked in the rearview mirror.

Nixie shimmered and was suddenly enveloped by a tremendous red and white ball gown. She had to gather a pile of material into her lap before she could drag herself out of the car.

"Heavens, child," Zola said as she gaped at Nixie's overdone ensemble.

"She has never been much for subtlety," Cara said.

"I think it's beautiful," Nixie said as she turned in a half circle to twirl the hem of the gown. I caught a glimpse of her leather ankle boots, folded and fastened with a silver brooch of some sort. "You should have worn something more appropriate, Damian."

I raised my eyebrows. "It was kind of short notice, and I can't just ..." I waved my hand in useless circles, "make new clothes materialize. Zola's not wearing a costume either."

Nixie tapped her chin and glanced at Zola. "Yes, but she has character."

Zola coughed to stifle a chuckle and looked away, leaning forward on her cane.

We followed Nixie as she started skipping between the cars, trailing the sparse crowd of tourists and regulars. She stopped to pet a pair of enormous Alaskan malamutes, their heads hanging over a bowl of water beside a beige van. The old woman complimented Nixie's gown before turning to Zola.

"You look like an old wizard in that cloak, dear," she said as she gave one of the dogs a gruff scratching.

Zola glanced down at her old cloak and ran her fingers across the braided rope at her waist. Her face cracked into a wrinkly smile as she thanked the other woman.

"See," Nixie said as we walked away. "Character."

We crossed a short steel bridge as wooden planks thunked under our feet. Nixie took a deep breath over the creek, rushing from the recent rains. The frogs on the bank were drowned out by the drone of cicadas and the scent of rain still filled the air. Past the entrance we could see bright triangular flags rippling in the breeze, shaded by the surrounding forest, as costumed knights, princesses, and kings in full regalia traveled up and down the gentle hill beyond.

I paid the admission for Zola, Nixie, and myself before we headed up to the gate. It wasn't really a gate, just a wooden podium centered between the two open air ticket booths.

"Fairies enter free," said a small man with a graying beard, a knowing smile, and a glorious wide-brimmed leather hat.

"You can see us?" Foster said.

"Yes, master fairy. I see all three of you." He turned his gaze to Zola. "Addanaya," he said as he looked her up and down, "you haven't aged a day."

"Nor you Cornelius," Zola said as she embraced the man.

"One of the few good things that came from my old life," he said with a small smile.

"I have to go now," Nixie said.

I started to respond, but just smiled as she bounded off from performer to shop and back again. She spoke with a perfect English accent to noblemen and noblewomen of all shapes and sizes.

"Sometimes that girl is too happy," Zola said.

Cornelius laughed. "Take care inside, Zola. There are demons among us."

"That Ah know." She smiled as Cornelius stamped our hands and we started up the gravel path.

Cara chuckled as we trailed after the fairies, heading in Nixie's general direction. "My niece is refreshing," she said as she hovered between me and Zola. "Most of the water witches I've known have been dreary, awful things." I heard the first metallic ringing of a smith at work as we passed an axe throwing booth. A stage full of musicians sat off to the left, surrounded by benches with a cadre of laughing onlookers.

"So who's Cornelius?" I said.

Zola glanced up at me and then turned her attention to a small shop filled with handmade instruments and woodburnings.

We finally caught up with Nixie a few minutes later. She was crouched down between two young girls with fairy wings strapped to their back. I heard her say, "You're the most beautiful fairies I've ever seen and your wings are so shiny." She batted at the wings as the girls giggled. I could see their mother a little ways off, dressed in a spectacular royal blue gown with silver lace, smiling when Nixie waved at her and said, "They're adorable." I couldn't hear the mother's reply, but she was wearing a broad smile.

"Hey, Nix." I shouted. "Are you liking the faire?"

She wandered back to us slowly, pausing at a storefront filled with glass trinkets. A friendly woman sat out front with a torch and worked a series of glass rods into animals of all shapes and sizes as she talked to the onlookers. I came up behind Nixie and squeezed her arm.

"So, do you like it?"

She nodded. "Yes, but I still think you should have worn a costume." She frowned as her eyes wandered down my black t-shirt and dark jeans.

I sighed and rubbed my cheek. "Alright, let's go see the demon and then we'll look for a costume."

Nixie's eyes lit up. "I get to pick!"

"Hell. No."

She frowned. "I'll help."

Zola chuckled behind me. I flashed her a smile and walked back onto the gravel path with Nixie.

We followed the echoing clang of metal on metal to the crest of the hill, gravel crunching underfoot beneath the constant chatter of showmen and bartering merchants. Off to the left, the shouts and cheers of a joust rolled out from an open field. A large tented clothier boasted every medieval garment I'd ever so much as imagined, from corsets to codpieces, and my eyes widened as I saw the sign behind that shop.

"Turkey legs," Foster and I said in unison before we burst into laughter.

Aideen snorted a laugh while Cara and Zola just shook their heads.

"I've never had a turkey leg," Nixie said, a small frown still etched across on her face.

"You'll have one today," Foster said. "I think it's a rule."

"Did you see that lute?" Nixie asked. "I'll catch up." She hurried down the road that led past the clothier.

A hammer strike pulled my attention back to our purpose. My eyes swept to the right and found the blacksmith. Shadowed beneath the roof of an old structure, his forge glowed behind him, casting his slightly hunched form into shadow as his thick arm raised a hammer and struck again. With every blow, a small burst of sparks leapt from the red hot metal trapped on the anvil's surface.

Zola walked up to the counter a few feet away from the smith. Meant to keep the crowd safe, the counter was up to my waist and the wooden shingled roof came down close to my head. It would also be hard for anyone to strike the smith physically while he stood within the shop. He noticed me looking and gave a quick nod before plunging the metal back into the fires and pumping the huge bellows alone.

When the smith's eyes locked onto Foster, Cara, and Aideen in turn, I knew he at least had the Sight. He turned his attention back to the glowing strip of metal he'd just pulled from the brick forge until Zola said, "Hello, demon."

The smith landed another blow before he stood up straight, and it was only then I realized how big he was, at least as tall as Foster, with muscles like the werewolves and a close cropped layer of black hair. He had a barrel chest and massive arms with blackened hands. He started to laugh, hit the glowing rod one more time, and dunked it into a barrel of water. Over the hissing, and through the cloud of steam, he said, "Call me Mike, Adannaya."

"*Mike?* Mike the Demon?" I blurted out.

Zola sighed and shook her head.

"I take it he's the apprentice and you're the wise master," Mike said.

Zola smiled and nodded once. "Thank you for not calling me the *old* master, although Ah suppose it would be apt."

"You are a young thing to my ancient eyes."

Zola's smile widened just a bit more. "Aeros speaks highly of you."

Mike hung his hammer and tongs on a shelf that housed two dozen different implements along the brick forge. The fairies landed on a precarious pile of wooden display cases. Inside the cases were a variety of knives, belt buckles, brutal looking foot-long spikes of metal, and an overwhelming array of constructs I didn't recognize. My eyes fell on a knife, the entire thing, from blade to hilt, formed from a single piece of black metal. The hilt looked as though its metal had been braided, and only close inspection showed me the design that had been painstakingly hammered into it up to the point the cutting surface began.

"You made that?" I said as I pointed to the blade.

Mike the Demon nodded as he wiped his hands on a towel. "Everything you see. I do rather like those knives."

"It's fantastic." I said.

"It'll hold an edge better than any mortal blade."

"Better than a Ginsu blade?" Foster said with a smirk as he and Aideen glided over to the anvil.

Mike chuckled and rolled his eyes. It was disarming. I almost forgot I was talking to a demon.

"I'll be right back." He held up his index finger as he walked into the deeper shadow behind the forge. I heard a grunt and Mike came waddling back with an ancient, pitted anvil. It looked like it should be melted down into something useful. "Look out," he said with a strained voice. He dropped it on top of his good anvil with a solid crunch as the fairies scattered. He wiped his hands off and said, "This is it."

Foster and Aideen landed on the counter beside Zola.

"What *is* that?" Aideen said. "The power coming off it is so dark." Foster's hand moved toward his sword, stopped, and curled into a fist.

Cara's eyes moved from the anvil to Mike the Demon. She didn't seem frightened at all.

"You've seen this incantation before, haven't you?" Mike said as he gestured at the old anvil.

Cara nodded, but didn't speak.

I concentrated on the pitted chunk of metal and my Sight snapped into focus. Waves of black force were leaking off of it and running across the ground until they suddenly broke into rolling granules and dissipated. Mixed amongst the blackness were deep red highlights. "You masked it," I said.

Mike the Demon raised his eyebrows and pursed his lips. "There's a bit more to you than I expected." He laughed and held his hands out over anvil. "Am I clear, Adannaya?"

Zola glanced around us before nodding.

What I thought was dust and debris blackening Mike's hands surged forward and covered the anvil, leaving a saggy web between the demon's hands and the metal. I took a step back in surprise.

Bits of pitted metal and rust and iron surged toward Mike. A river of metal began flowing over his hands, and disappeared up his sleeves. He winced as his hands thinned and contorted into shaking claws. A curved bronze handle etched with hundreds, if not thousands of runes emerged where the striking surface of the anvil had been a moment before. The vanishing metal revealed more of the hammer every passing second until the head of the hammer was uncovered, etched with a solitary rune. One small, straight scratch in the striking surface. Isa. Power. Smoke rose from Mike's hands as he relaxed and took a deep breath.

"Ouch," he said as his hands began to pale slightly and the near-skeletal fingers began to look normal once again. He reached out and grabbed the handle, raising it close to his face. His eyes lit over the hammer, its head weighted toward the front of the handle. Mike examined every inch in great detail before he looked up at Cara again. "It's clean."

"That is truly the Smith's Hammer?" Cara said.

Mike the Demon flipped the handle and caught the spinning tool as if it weighed nothing. "Looks like a fancy cutler's hammer, doesn't it?" He spun the hammer sideways in his hand and smacked it against the remaining anvil. My body vibrated with the thunder erupting from the blow and I saw some of the crowd look up, as if expecting to see thunderheads in the sky. "Doesn't sound like one though, does it? I tried making a sword with it once, but the hammer made a bit much noise." Mike laughed and handed the hammer to Zola. "Take good care of that. It's a legend, to be sure. You should see it in action." He shrugged his shoulders in a circular motion and rolled his neck.

"Thank you," Zola said.

"Don't thank me. I owe Aeros. I owe him a lot, and he asked me to give it to you. I can't say no to the old bastard. Mind you, one good smack with that hammer would take care of him, but ..." he shrugged again and said, "I like the old bastard."

I took a wad of bills out of my pocket and set fifty dollars on the counter for Mike.

"What's this for?" he said as he picked it up.

"The knife."

The demon smiled and popped open the display case. He handed me the blade hilt first. It was heavy, but well balanced. He handed me a thin sheath that I snapped around the blade, and then slid into my pocket.

"Gut a fish with it, or stop a sword with it. The edge will hold."

"Hopefully I won't have to try either of those things," I said as I smiled and met his eyes. I was almost surprised to find a normal hazel color in their depths. "Thanks."

"Thank you, Damian Valdis Vesik. If it ever dulls, bring it back to me."

I raised an eyebrow at my full name.

"Aeros," Mike said as his lips curled up into small smile. "He likes to talk, and you're one of the more interesting things he's met recently."

Zola chuckled and fingered the hammer. Nixie walked up beside her and looked closely at the Smith's Hammer.

Mike almost jumped out of his skin. "A water witch?! What are you doing here?" He reached backwards and his hand wrapped around a hammer.

"Searching for the Smith's Hammer, of course," Nixie said. She straightened the shoulders of her gown and flashed a dazzling smile.

Mike's forehead creased as he let go of the hammer and rubbed his arms. When his hands pushed his sleeves higher I could see the black rivers and ash across his skin where he'd absorbed the anvil. It looked like abstract sleeve tattoos on both arms. "You're helping them?" he said.

She nodded.

Mike shook his head. "This world is not the one I knew. So much changes so fast." Mike gestured to me and Zola. "There was a time you two would have been killed by your own kind for not killing her."

"I am not so easy to kill." Nixie's face hardened and Mike's eyes widened as he took a step back. I don't know what he saw, but he seemed anxious as hell and ready to bolt.

I heard Foster whisper, "Let's go. This is getting weird."

"Getting?" I said.

I nodded to Mike and he returned the gesture as our group walked away from his forge. Nixie smiled and wrapped her arm through mine.

"What was that about?" I said as she steered me toward the clothing store.

"Mike is a fire demon," Nixie said.

Cara and Zola burst into laughter.

"Of course," Aideen said as she bounced in the air in front of us. "Being a water witch, you could kill him."

"Yes, I could." Her voice was cold and it made me look at her again.

"You okay, Nix?"

Nixie took a deep breath and nodded. "I don't like demons. They used to kill my sisters for sport, until one of us discovered fire demons can drown."

I bit my tongue just in time, almost having pointed out the fact water witches hunted humans in much the same way. Instead, I just nodded and thanked myself for the rapid use of my brain-mouth filter.

***

Call it destiny, call it an accident, but as I tripped up the stairs to the clothing store, my hand flashed out and landed on a rack of codpieces. Thankfully, empty codpieces.

"Oh, I agree," Nixie said. "You definitely have to get one of those."

Foster was in hysterics twenty minutes later as I handed the clerk more money than I thought you could spend at a Renaissance Faire. I glanced down at myself and blew out a breath. A forest green doublet with nickel buttons was fastened over a light linen shirt, and I had to admit it went well with my black jeans. Although I was still not sure what to say about the matching codpiece, tied to a thick leather belt.

"You look lovely," Nixie said as she slid her arm around mine.

Foster burst out laughing anew.

"Let's eat," I said as I ignored the fairy and led Nixie down the stairs. We only had to walk around the corner to find one of the many outdoor pubs at the faire. I placed an order while the others found a seat.

Zola came over to help me carry the food back to the picnic table.

"That was quite a bit of money to impress a girl, boy."

I shot her a glance and smiled. "That obvious, huh?"

She glanced at my crotch and chortled. "Well, Ah certainly wouldn't say it's subtle."

I felt my face flush, and not from the heat. "Yeah, yeah, you can give me shit later."

She laughed again as she started passing the food around.

We gorged on a round of turkey legs and some mad concoction known as a pizza bratwurst. Probably not authentic period food, but it sure as hell tasted good. The three fairies took a little bit off each of our plates.

"It's not chocolate, but I could eat another one," Nixie said as she licked the grease off her fingers.

"You ate the whole thing," Cara said. Her voice a mixture of awe and disgust.

Nixie paused with her pinkie in her mouth before she finished cleaning it off with a small pop. "Yes, it was good."

Foster was sprawled out on his back, his hands over his stomach. "I'm gonna die."

"Promises, promises," Aideen said as she leaned over his face and took a huge bite of pizza brat. "Mmm, that's good. The grease just runs right down your throat."

Foster put his hand over his mouth. "I'm gonna hurl. Bloody hell, I'm gonna hurl."

Aideen laughed and rocked backwards on her heels, balancing herself on outstretched wings.

We finished a few minutes later, water bottles and plates empty. I tossed the pile in the trash and we started walking back to the entrance. We had a few detours along the way. Cara was fascinated by a booth selling wooden roses. I shelled out a few more dollars to take a couple home for her. Nixie got distracted by a camel. Or as she called it, "A magical beast able to survive without water!" Foster and Aideen raided a sample of ice cream left unattended and eventually Zola stopped to say goodbye to Cornelius.

"Who is he?" I said when we had crossed the bridge and entered the sparsely populated grassy parking lot.

"Retired," Zola said with a snap.

"Retired what?" I said innocently.

She sighed and pinched the bridge of her nose before shooting me a sidelong glance with a small smile. "You're not going to stop are you?"

I raised my eyebrows and frowned just a little. "Stop what? We're necromancers consorting with a demon. What could be worse than that?"

"Take care in your questions," Cara said as she fluttered between me and Zola. "You may as well tell him. He does have a valid point."

"It's not that Ah don't trust you, boy," Zola said. "Ah promised Cornelius Ah wouldn't tell anyone about his past."

"Just a little?" I said.

"Give it up, Zola," Foster said. "You know he's as persistent as he is stubborn."

"Fine, fine," she said. "This goes nowhere. Cornelius is a blood mage."

I gaped at my master. A blood mage. I'd met a bloody blood mage. They'd warred with the old gods. They lost in the end, yes, but they wielded enough power to carry the war on for almost five centuries. They were referenced in some of my books. There were practitioners and even some Fae that theorized the blood mages influenced the strongest bloodlines. It was possible their meddling gave rise to the spike in powerful human mages over the past few centuries.

"Retired!" she said vehemently.

"I thought they were all dead. How old is he?"

"Old. Things have a way of surviving, as do some people."

"That they do," I said. "That they do."

We walked across the field in silence for a minute. Nixie led the way with the fairies fluttering around her head. I pondered the existence of a blood mage and wondered if Aeros would tell me more than Zola had. Or maybe Zola would open up if I pestered her about it. I smiled as my feet slid through the damp grass, wind whistling through the woods beside us.

"Can you believe this, Damian?" Zola loosed the Smith's Hammer from her belt and held it up in her right hand as her left shifted her cane. "Ah wonder what Mike could have done to earn Aeros's trust. The Smith's Hammer is a true power. Why didn't the demon use it?" She turned the hammer in her hand and then slid it back through the braided belt at her waist as Nixie and the fairies fell back beside us.

I shifted my codpiece and grunted. Nixie snickered.

"Mike told us he tried," Aideen said. "Maybe he succeeded and we just don't know."

"It is ... possible." Zola nodded as her cane clacked against the asphalt of the path running alongside the parking lot. "Damian, Ah need to get back to the Pit. They have a list of protected soulstones in the archive. We need a minor stone to destroy Tessrian's artifact."

"What's a minor stone?" Nixie said. "Is it a weak stone?"

Zola shook her head. "No, weak stones aren't classified. They're generally bad for a necromancer's art. Minor stones are powerful, but they are shadowed by major stones."

"Are major stones the strongest?" Nixie said.

"No, child. Pravus stones are the strongest."

"Pravus stones are abominations," Cara said. "They hold the remnants of thousands of souls. Only a few have existed, and all led to great times of darkness."

"But major stones and pravus stones are capable of great acts of benevolence," Aideen said. "All soulstones are, it just depends who is using them."

Zola nodded and tapped the head of her cane as we walked back onto the grass and up to the car. "And for some godforsaken reason, dark necromancers can sense the bloody things. A gift no Fae and no neutral necromancer can claim."

I unlocked the door to Vicky and said, "Sounds like they're meant to do harm."

Zola grimaced. "Ah've heard more people than you say that, boy."

"With a name like pravus, no atrocity would be surprising," Cara said.

"Would you like the front seat, Zola?" Nixie said, completely pulling our attention away from the darkening conversation.

"No, that's alright. Sit with the boy."

I smiled as Zola climbed in the back seat with the fairies and Nixie sat beside me. I tossed my bag full of street clothes onto the floorboards behind the seat. As I settled in, ripples ran through Nixie's gown and it was suddenly replaced with jeans and a black t-shirt.

"Are you trying to be funny?" I said.

"Whatever do you mean?" Nixie said in a musical voice.

"You know what, Damian?" Foster said. "I think Nixie looks better in jeans than you do."

"Well, so do I, but thanks for pointing it out." I laughed and shook my head. "Alright, to the Pit. Again." I pulled out of the parking space. "I think I've been in the vampires' house more than my own lately."

"Yeah, I'm sure you're really missing your crap shack," Foster said.

Aideen slapped him, but couldn't hide her own grin.

I sighed and said, "Bloody fairies."

Nixie and Cara exchanged amused glances before Zola burst into laughter. They were still chuckling as we pulled onto Highway 70 a few minutes later.

CHAPTER 13

No one wanted to be dropped off as we passed the Fifth Street exit that led to the shop, so we continued on toward the Pit. It didn't take too long to get all the way down to Town and Country, drop Zola off, and drive right back up to the shop. The sun was still bright, and I was looking forward to relaxing for a while.

Main Street was packed, so we parked behind the building. I could hear the cu siths barking before I even had the key in the door and my foot on the deadbolt.

"Aw, they missed us," Aideen said.

I laughed and braced myself for imminent attack as I pushed the door open. Bubbles and Peanut charged Nixie and Cara instead. They barely clipped my legs as they ran past.

"Hello, Bubbles," Cara said as she landed on the cu sith's head and began scratching her ears. Bubbles's tongue whipped out and hit Cara's hands with a wet smack. Cara laughed and wiped her hands through the cu sith's coarse fur before the fairy jumped off. Bubbles raced back into the shop. Cara landed on the floorboards and began trying to wring the slobber out of her wings.

Peanut was on his hind legs with his front paws on Nixie's waist. "Who's a good boy? Who's a good boy?" She was in total baby speak mode and Peanut's tail was just a blur.

Foster wore a proud smile. "And they make the best guard dogs, don't-"

Before Foster finished speaking, Bubbles bounded out the door again. Her tongue shot out, wrapped around the fairy, and he disappeared into her mouth with a squeak. She darted back inside, leaving the rest of us to stare at the empty doorway.

Horror gripped me before Cara began laughing hysterically. Then confusion gripped me.

"Shouldn't you be upset?" I said as I made exaggerated gestures at the door. "Your son just got eaten in front of us!"

Cara shook her head and wiped a tear away. "She didn't swallow, and-" she broke down laughing again before she could finish as Aideen said, "Spit that out!"

Aideen flashed into a six-foot-plus valkyrie and ran through the door, trailing a spray of fairy dust. "Bubbles! Spit that out right now!" She grabbed the cu sith by the scruff of her neck and boxed her ear.

I sneezed in the plume of dust as we followed Aideen into the shop, my allergy medicine unable to keep up with the direct onslaught. Peanut was glued to Nixie's legs. I closed the door behind the group.

I swear Bubbles smiled before her tongue rolled out and delivered Foster onto the wood floor in a puddle of slobber. He groaned, stretched out on his back, and wiped the drool off his face. "Oh god, what happened?"

"Your guard dog tried to eat you," I said.

Foster sat up. "That explains this ... mess," he said as he tugged at his drool-soaked armor.

Aideen bent down and picked Foster up. "That's going to take hours to clean." She sighed and tossed Foster casually into the grandfather clock. I heard a cry before he landed with a crash and much cursing ensued. Aideen blushed. "Sorry," she said toward the clock. "I forgot you can't fly yet." She lowered her voice and looked at me. "I'd better go check on him." Aideen flashed into her normal stature and fluttered into the clock.

"I suppose I'll help clean up his armor," Cara said. She laughed and then took a deep breath. "It's worth it though, just for the laugh."

Nixie and I looked at each other when the fairies were gone. A broad smile crept across her face before we both burst into laughter.

"Alright, let's open the shop up for the afternoon." I paused before I walked into the front room. "You guys want some pizza?" I heard a resounding yes from the grandfather clock. With the pizza ordered and the sign flipped to open, I set about showing Nixie how to work a cash register.

"So I just type in the numbers on the tag?"

"Yep."

"And hit the total button?"

"Yep."

"This is easy."

"Yep."

Nixie looked up and smiled at me. She turned back to the register, typed in the dollars and cents listed on small piece of amber and hit the total button. The register dinged and Nixie said, "Now what?"

"Well, if they're paying with cash, hit cash, and if they're paying with a card, hit the credit button and swipe their card. If it's debit, it will prompt them for a pin."

"That's it?"

"Pretty much."

"You don't seem to get a lot of customers in here, Damian."

"Pff," I said as I blew out a breath. "You should have seen it before Frank turned it around."

"It was *worse?*" Nixie said.

I nodded. "Ever since I put Frank in charge of ordering, we've been making a lot more money. The books have always done well, but keeping them hidden from the tourists is a priority. Frank wants to launch some huge Internet campaign to draw more business in for the books." I shrugged. "It could be worth a try. I'll let him run with it. As long as I can pay the bills, and Frank, I'm happy. And speaking of bills-"

The bells jingled on the front door as the pizza delivery man walked in. "Watch the store for a minute Nix?" She nodded and sat down on the stool behind the counter.

I paid the delivery driver in cash, although he probably wouldn't have known if I paid him in manure, because he was staring at Nixie the whole time. I laughed as he left and then I walked to the back with a large onion, pineapple, barbeque, and anchovy pizza for the fairies. I still don't know how they ate the damn things. Nasty.

The fairies descended on the pizza like a plague of locusts. Foster was wrapped in what looked like a toga and I tried not to laugh at him as he settled himself on the corner of the pizza box. The bell on the front door jingled as I walked back to the front room. I recognized the strawberry blonde hair in a heartbeat.

"Hey Ashley."

"Damian! Oh, thank the stars you're open today. I ran out of protection candles and need to buy some for a ritual this afternoon." She glanced at her watch and grimaced. "It's in an hour, and it's a thirty minute drive from here!" She rubbed her face and hurried toward the candles.

"How many do you need?"

"Four, I think." She paused and nodded. "Yes, four."

"Take 'em, no charge."

"What?" She gathered two pairs into her hands and walked toward the register. "I can't do that." Her eyes moved to Nixie and she stopped dead. "Oh, hello, I didn't see you there."

"This is Nixie," I said. I reached out, grabbed Nixie's arm, and raised it so Ashley could see the bracelet. "The candles are on the house."

"You make beautiful jewelry," Nixie said.

Ashley smiled, nodded, and said, "Thank you, and it's nice to meet you. I always hoped Damian would end up with a nice girl."

"Keep hoping," I said.

Nixie elbowed me in the gut and Ashley laughed.

"It's nice to meet you too, priestess," Nixie said.

Ashley crinkled her eyebrows at Nixie's words. Her face relaxed a moment later and she stuffed the candles into her voluminous purse. She turned back to me and froze with her hand in her purse. "Goddess's light, what are you wearing?"

"We went to a Renaissance Faire," I said.

Ashley glanced at Nixie, still wearing her skintight jeans and black t-shirt. "And you didn't have time to change?"

I wiped my hand down my face and laughed. "Long story. You want some pizza?"

"No thanks, I really have to run. It was good to meet you Nixie."

"You too," Nixie said as she waved.

The bell jingled again as Ashley bustled out of the shop at a near run.

Nixie smiled and reached out for the pizza box. "I like her. She's funny, and truly gifted."

"What do you mean?"

"I think she knew I was an undine, or at least not human."

"Really?" I stared out the windows and wondered what that could mean. I took a deep breath and said, "You ever had barbeque chicken pizza, Nix?"

"No, but it smells wonderful."

"That would be because it *is* wonderful."

***

We were enjoying our pizza as the late afternoon sun lit the buildings on the other side of Main Street, until a screaming man joined us. The body smashed through one of the shop's front windows, bounced off the wood floor, and crashed into a display of candle holders. The wooden, bronze, and silver candlesticks rang and twirled as they bounced off the ground, several coming to a rest below the candles at the far side of the store. I knew the man wasn't human when the cu siths ran into the front room, barked like it was Armageddon, and then started backing away from the unmoving body.

The crumpled form began to shimmer and pop a moment later. I felt power surge past my aura and it didn't take much to realize it was racing to the man on the floor. Black fur flowed around the man in the aisle before he rose up on his legs in a hunched, defensive posture. There was no four-footed wolf in the wake of that transformation. He had become something else—a living nightmare with long, clawed fingers, bulky arms, and a narrow snout. The werewolf leapt through the hole where my window used to be.

Nixie stared at me and blinked a few times.

I finished the last two bites of pizza I was holding, cursed, and grabbed my staff. I half jogged up the aisle to check out the scene. Sure, I was a necromancer, but my experience with werewolves up until the past few days had pretty much been "They don't live here, why worry about them?" Having one fly into the Double D should have shocked the hell out of me, but I'd just finished consorting with a demon, met a living blood mage, and still had a codpiece strapped to my groin. It was just one of those days.

"Why do they have to turn into giant, muscled wolf-men?" I said under my breath. "Can't they just turn into nice, friendly dogs?" I grumbled some more as Nixie ran up behind me.

"They're werewolves, not shapeshifters," she said, as if it was the most obvious thing in the world.

I pushed my way out the front door to the jingle of the small bell and stepped into a scene out of a nightmare. I had a pretty good guess who the bulky, khaki-colored wolf-man on the cobblestone street was outside my shop as soon as I laid eyes on him.

"Carter!" I yelled.

His eyes flicked up to me, followed by one pointed ear, then both flicked back to the werewolf I'd watched shift a minute earlier. Carter moved to the side and I could see a streak of blood along his left arm, with more in the street beside him and along the side of a smashed up SUV.

Carter growled something like, "Stay back," as he launched himself at the other werewolf. And I do mean launched. He went from a crouch to a furry missile faster than I could blink.

Carter's arm punched through the other wolf-man's neck in a spray of gore. The horrific crunch of cartilage and tearing of flesh were nauseating. I wasn't sure how much damage the wolf could take, but when Carter twisted violently to the side and the other wolf-man's head came off with a meaty snap, I was pretty sure it was dead.

Carter threw back his head and roared. The remaining windows shook on the front of the shop. He dropped the head in the gutter and crushed it beneath his huge paw. He jumped in front of me, movements verging on vampiric speed, and locked his clawed hands on my shoulders before I even realized what was happening,

It took everything I had not to crap myself. Carter's face had elongated along with his teeth. He had a narrow, wolfish snout, and walked hunched over. The muscles in his arms looked like furry bowling balls and there was nothing human left in his eyes. They retained their color, but I knew the man before me was more wolf than anything else.

"Who are they, Damian." Carter's voice was a gravel-filled growl.

I swallowed. "Uh, who?"

I heard swords being unsheathed and caught a flash of white out of the corner of my eye. A moment later I heard Foster when he said, "Carter?"

The wolf's ears flicked toward Foster's voice as he nodded slowly.

"Carter, there are too many commoners here, come inside," Cara said.

The claws relaxed their grip a little as I became aware of a swarm of screaming, terrified, tourists.

"They almost killed her," Carter growled. "They asked for you and your master, Damian."

"Maggie?" I said, stunned.

The wolf growled in affirmation as he pushed me into the brick wall and walked into the shop.

Carter's claws cut furrows into the hardwood floors as he paced to the back room. I stood in the doorway and stared at the wolf-man before he began to shimmer and pop. Power burned against my aura as Carter shifted back to a human form, his transformation giving off waves of force. His muscles shook and flattened out over his arms as his back straightened. His fur just fell off. Carter was looking at the ceiling as he rolled his neck and stretched his back.

I stared at the pile of khaki fur and said, "You're worse than my mother's old malamute." I toed the bed of fur and said, "Damn."

Carter didn't laugh.

"Oh, Carter!" Aideen said. She flashed a bright white as she morphed into her full height. She reached out for Carter's left arm and he winced when she touched it. "You're not healing ... why?" Her eyes widened and she whipped her hands away from the wolf like she'd been burned.

Carter balled his hand into a fist and grimaced when the muscles in his arm contracted. "I don't know. One of the necromancers ... Zack, or Zachary. He hit me with something." He rolled his arm to the right a little and I got a good look at the damage. The wolf wasn't healing at all. A deep red and black bruise was expanding near his wrist as we watched.

"Had to be Zachariah," I said. My eyes wandered over his arm. "That's broken, Carter."

"Look closer, Damian," Cara said. She sounded sick, and for the first time I was worried more about Carter than I was about what he might do to me.

I nodded and focused my Sight. Then I saw it. A pulsing blob of black and bloody red was burrowing into the werewolf's arm. "Holy fucking, fuck me, what *is* that?"

"We have to get it out of him," Aideen said. "Now."

Carter paled. "Get what out?"

We all ignored him. "What the hell is it?" I said.

Cara flashed, grabbed Carter's wrist, and pulled his arm out straight despite the pain on his face. She got close to the pulsing blob and cursed. "We used to call them demon worms. Dark necromancers use them to turn a person into a vessel."

"For what?"

Cara rolled her eyes up to me and blinked twice in quick succession. "For demons, boy, for demons. It would explain the vampiric zombies last spring. We should have seen it." She bit the words off.

"The what?" Carter said.

"Shit, later Carter," I said. "What do we do now?"

"Cut it off," Foster said as he drew his sword.

Carter's eyes went wide. "Are you kidding?"

"Stop, Foster," Cara said. "Damian, you have to tear it out of his arm. It's stealing his ability to heal as it feeds. Purge it and Foster's sword will be able to kill it and Carter should be able to heal. Or he'll die along with it, but I think we're early enough to avoid that."

"Do it," Carter said. His mouth flattened into a tight line.

"How?"

Cara looked at me. "Like you fought the demon last year."

"With dynamite?"

She gave me a flat look. "No, grab onto the aura, and then ... and then I don't know."

"That will have to be good enough," I said. I took a deep breath and reached out with my necromancy to the demonic worm feasting on Carter's body. I cursed as my power latched onto the worm's sickly aura. At first I was relieved I didn't get a burst of memories or visions from the thing, but my relief was short lived as the worm began to move. It felt greasy and warm and wriggly and wrong. I flexed my right hand into a claw, tightening my hold on the thing as I started pulling on it with my necromancy. My skin crawled as the feel of that greasy aura swam over my body.

I was aware, on some level, of Carter's screams and agony. I was also aware that, if this was anything like the godforsaken dolls Zola had trained me to fight demons with, I'd better not lose my focus.

The worm stretched and wriggled as it tore through Carter's skin, trying to escape my grip. Carter's flesh began to tear open along his forearm. Cara's words were all I had to go on. I focused everything on the parasite, extending my power as blades and lances, curving around the black and red abomination until my will held it motionless. And then I purged it.

"Modus vectigalia!"

The blades of power spun around the worm, snapping it out of Carter's body as the incantation sliced it away from his flesh. I screamed as its head turned toward me. A beak filled with sawblade teeth sprang from its eyeless, maggot-like face. It wriggled and scythed with that beak, trying to latch onto my aura. I couldn't even stand as I batted the writhing monstrosity away with a surge of power. The floor was hard and unforgiving when my knees slammed into it and my throat was raw with my screams. I forced my aura over the worm, pinning it to the floor as the thing continued to bite at the concentrated aura between my hands.

There was a flash of gray as Foster's sword impaled the demon worm and sunk into the floor below it. The worm vanished with a hiss and a few tiny curls of smoky power. The pain stopped and my hands shook while I stayed on the floor panting. Foster squeezed my shoulder, but no one else said a word. I knew why when I struggled back to my feet.

Aideen's voice registered, and I realized I'd been hearing it since I started battling the slug. She'd been trying to heal Carter since it started.

"Socius Sanation!" Aideen said. Her face was pale and sweat poured from her forehead.

A fraction of Carter's arm closed up, but there was still a gaping wound where I'd cut the demon out. Blood flowed in pulsing streams. He was unconscious and paler than the fairy. And the blood. Gods, the blood was everywhere.

"Let me help," Nixie said.

Aideen turned to Nixie with wide eyes. "Yes, of course. Yes."

Nixie closed her eyes and pulled her hands together in a steady, practiced motion. Her hands were flat and she formed a triangle between her waist and both arms. I saw a tremor run through her body an instant before I felt an alien power flood the room. Her eyes swept to Aideen and she nodded. I raised my Sight again and the disorientation almost put me back on the floor. It felt like I was watching things through the surface of a pool. Waves of power distorted everything around us.

And then Aideen spoke.

I never heard her voice, but the room pulsed with warmth and light. I could see the tiny white trail of the healing incantation within the maelstrom of Nixie's power. It snaked from Aideen's hand to Carter's arm, growing with every heartbeat in size and intensity. It slithered into the werewolf's arm and the room went white.

Everyone stumbled when the power surrounding us dissipated in a snap. I heard the cu siths whimpering in the silence that followed, and I was pretty sure I knew exactly how they felt.

Foster and Aideen returned to their normal size and hugged each other on the Formica table. Cara stayed so she could shift Carter's bulk and look him over repeatedly.

The werewolf was sprawled across the floor, his eyes covered by the inside of his elbow. His breathing was ragged, but steady. As he lowered his arm and closed his eyes I could see the tiny scar where I'd torn the worm from him.

"Get the poor man a towel, Damian," Cara said. "He's quite naked."

And he was. I swallowed hard and took a deep breath. "Yeah, and get me a shot of whiskey." I nodded to Cara and stepped carefully over Carter on my way to the closet. I pulled out an old blanket when I couldn't find a towel. I turned around to find Nixie staring at Carter for a moment before she giggled. I felt an irrational surge of jealousy, which vanished as soon as she put her arm around my waist.

I could just hear her whisper, "You did good."

Carter dragged himself to his feet, glanced down at his starkness, and turned toward me with a blush growing on his face. I tossed him the blanket.

"Thanks," he said.

"Get him water, would you?" Cara said.

I pulled open the fridge and grabbed the filtered water pitcher. Nixie pulled a glass off the shelf beside the closet and set it next to Carter. I filled the glass and left the pitcher. Carter sucked the liquid down in two quick gulps.

"There's lots more, if you want it," I said.

"No, thank you, I'm alright. Or at least I will be." He stared at his shaking hands and shook his head. "I need to tell you what's going on."

"We're listening," Foster said. His voice held a hint of ice and I glanced at the fairy before returning my attention to Carter.

"We have friends in the east. Two Taverns, Pennsylvania. It's practically within walking distance of Gettysburg."

Though he didn't pause, the name hung in the air and time seemed to slow. The moment passed as Carter went on.

"Well, not really walking distance, but it's damn close." Carter poured another glass of water and drank. "Their pack is small, but the wolves are resourceful. Their Alpha called us today. Dark necromancers have been found around Gettysburg and the pack wants to know why. Some of the necromancers were already dead, torn in half, missing arms, shredded," Carter shook his head. "God knows what did it to them."

"Gravemakers," I said.

Carter shrugged. "Maybe. It's one theory. There's also talk of rival cults attacking each other, although Two Taverns says two of the cults were organized. Too organized to be a cult. More like a militia. All the Alpha seemed sure of is the fact the necromancers are hunting for soulstones."

"How does he know that?" Cara said. "More importantly, why? What do they need the soulstones for?"

"I don't know," Carter said as he sat down. "Apparently another Alpha has moved in on the Two Taverns pack. He's trying to split them down the middle." Carter laughed without humor. "Good luck with that, idiot. Two Taverns is closer knit than most families I know. But a hostile Alpha, that's a problem I know too well.

"The Saint Louis pack is not as tight knit as Two Taverns. Another Alpha has moved into our territory too. He's peeling wolves away from us. I think I've already lost ten." Carter closed his eyes and sighed. "Some of the pack thinks I'm weak because I don't treat humans like fodder. And now," he paused and clenched his jaw, "now we have some serious troublemakers knocking on our door about *you.*"

"Oh," I said loquaciously.

Carter laughed lightly and shook his head. "I like you Damian. What you and your friends just did for me, I don't have the words, but I can't abide a threat to the pack. We'll have to remove you from the city if you won't leave of your own free will."

I gawked at Carter for a moment, speechless. "You think this shit will just disappear if you 'remove' me?"

Before Carter could respond, Cara said, "Nudd be damned, wolf. You're buried in crap up to your eyeballs and getting rid of one bucket," she slapped me on the shoulder, "isn't going to help."

"Um, thanks?" I said.

Carter's confident air cracked. His head sagged and he ran his hand through his hair. "It's all I can do. They attacked Maggie because I defended Damian to the Watchers. If Cassie hadn't been there, she'd be gone. The other wolves think we're in league with a dark necromancer. It's all I can do."

"No, it's not," Cara said. "You will join us."

I was still looking at Carter, wondering just what in the hell he was talking about.

Carter pulled the blanket tighter and looked at Cara, drawing his eyebrows down.

She didn't miss a beat. "In exchange for our help with the deserters, you'll help us destroy the dark necromancers and assassins pursuing Damian and Zola."

He smiled and shook his head. "No, I can't put the pack at risk like that."

"If you don't," Aideen said, "you'll die along with everyone else when Philip unleashes an arch-demon onto our plane."

Carter's eyes widened. "What?"

"His group plans to revive Prosperine, the Destroyer, with Damian's blood," Foster said. Not the entire story, but I think it got the point across. "You really think if they fail to bring Prosperine into our plane they'll stop?" He shook his head.

Cara placed her hand gently on Carter's cheek. "Child, if we do not destroy the necromancer and his cult, they will destroy us all."

Carter stared at her for a while and Cara's gaze never wavered. "You stand with him," Carter said as he nodded toward me.

Cara smiled. "As if he was my son."

"As if he was my brother," Foster said.

"Because he's our friend," Aideen said.

My eyes started to burn, so I bit my tongue, hard. I'll be damned if was going to tear up in front of a werewolf. Nixie squeezed my arm.

Carter sighed and stood up as he looked me up and down. "You have the backing of three Fae, Vesik –"

"Four," Nixie said.

"That ... well, it says something." A dark smile curled his lips. "I will talk with the pack. Some of them are going to think I'm insane, but if it helps keep them safe and keeps the other Alpha out of our territory, they can think whatever they want."

I nodded and extended my hand. Carter shook it and said, "We are bound in death, Vesik. I hope one day we are not."

"As do I, noble wolf," Cara said as she put her hand on Carter's shoulder. "As do we all."

"Ah'm afraid now is not the best time for us to pursue Tessrian's demise, Damian."

I looked up and met Zola's gaze.

"Why don't you put this away for safekeeping," she said. "Ah think you know a place it will be safe." Zola untied a small pouch from her braided belt and handed it to me. "Now," she said.

I grabbed the pouch and squeezed around Carter as I headed for the stairs. Zola's favorite place to hide something was in my reading nook. I crouched down behind the overstuffed leather chair on the left and grabbed the nearest handle of an old trunk. It was a couple feet wide and maybe a foot deep.

The trunk was set into the wall, but it slid out easily. It had been a gift from an old friend, a celebration of Zola gaining the right to vote. The man, known only as Ward, had given it to her, and wards were what he did. My hand trailed along the gouges in the wood and the old iron that formed the corners and the metalwork of the latch.

The contents of the trunk were hidden from the world. Zola said nothing inside it could be tracked, and no one could even see the trunk without permission. The wards formed a permanent misdirection spell.

The hinges were whisper quiet as I opened the trunk. There were a few old keepsakes tucked away inside, along with some of our most dangerous manuscripts. I opened the pouch and briefly looked at the bloodstone. It looked like a plain stone to the untrained eye. I frowned, closed the pouch again, and placed it inside before I slid the trunk back into its nook.

I was halfway down the stairs, looking up toward the front of the store when the cu siths ran into the front of the shop. I heard someone clear their throat when Bubbles and Peanut started growling.

"What now?" I said as I jogged back into the front room, weaving past Zola and Carter. My stomach flip flopped a few times when I saw Edgar, one of our local Watchers, letting Bubbles and Peanut sniff his hand by the register.

I cleared my own throat and waited for Eddie to look up.

CHAPTER 14

"Ah, Vesik. It feels like I was just here." He hooked his thumb toward the front window. "You seem to have a bit of a mess out front." He pulled a small spiral pad out of his pocket and flipped the cover open with his index finger. "Looks like you're going into another bracket, Vesik." He shook his head. "I don't envy you the fines from this one."

I caught Nixie staring at his bowler. It was a pretty cool hat.

I blew out a breath and walked toward Edgar. "Come *on* Eddie! I didn't have anything to do with *that!*" I pointed through my broken window at the curious people surrounding the decapitated werewolf corpse. "Why don't you go investigate the dark necromancers parading around the country?"

"Please, don't forget who you're talking to, son. We see everything."

I rolled my eyes. "Oh sure, play it by the rules, but I wasn't even out there!"

"He's telling the truth," Carter said. I glanced over my shoulder to find him leaning against the doorframe with the blanket pulled around him. Cara and Aideen were hovering beside him. Probably making sure he wasn't going to fall over.

"I killed that wolf," Carter said, "and you know it."

I heard Foster muttering something over by the register. I was pretty sure it involved someone eating their own hat.

Edgar sighed and rubbed his face hard. "Never mind, Vesik. I don't want to argue about this. There are so many dead werewolves to clean up, it's ridiculous. I'll just clean up this disaster and fine the wolves."

Hallelujah! I thought my fines would have had another zero or three added to them. "Thanks, Eddie."

Edgar narrowed his eyes before he turned toward the front door with his shoulders slightly slumped. "Do you realize how many memories I'm going to have to alter? There are going to be some strange birthmarks in the morning."

The Watchers' memory charms would leave scars behind. When they were complex enough, they would sometimes leave tattoos instead.

I scratched my neck and raised an eyebrow. The shop's phone rang as Edgar walked outside. I answered it, "Double D."

"Damian, is Carter there? He is not answering his phone."

"Hugh, is that you? Hey, that rhymes." I heard Hugh sigh on the other end of the line. "Sorry, yeah, he's here."

"I need to speak to him, please. It's urgent my friend."

I held the phone out to Carter. "It's Hugh and it's important."

Carter took the phone and placed it between his shoulder and his ear while he adjusted the blanket. I could still hear the voice on the other end of the line, though it was a metallic whisper from a distance. "Three dead wolves, Carter. It was the same group that hit your house."

"Where, where are they?"

"Alan caught up with them off Highway 40, near the island."

"How many are left?" Carter said.

"Three. They're in a black van with red stripes down the side. Haka killed one. Alan got another."

"I'm on my way." Carter snapped the phone closed and looked up at me. I was surprised he didn't ask who had died before he hung up the phone. "My car is in the shop, but I have a rental out front. Are you with me?"

"Oh yes." A chance to strike at anyone who was associated with Philip's cult wasn't a chance I was likely to miss. And Zachariah ... Zola had mentioned that name. "Mom, can you handle Edgar?"

Cara nodded and said, "Aideen, Nixie, help me with Edgar. Foster, go with Damian and Carter. They may need you to track the necromancers."

Foster was out the window before Carter and I had taken a step.

Nixie kissed me on the cheek as I left. Before I'd made it out the door I heard her say, "My, Edgar. Do you work out?" I couldn't help but laugh. Edgar didn't stand a chance.

***

Foster was already in the backseat, ready for battle with his sword sheath laid across his lap and his head bumping the roof when Carter and I made it to the rental. I didn't see a five pound bag of fairy dust exploded all over the rental, so I was pretty sure Foster had changed outdoors.

"Fancy," I said as I climbed into Carter's black rental SUV. The tires squealed as Carter slammed the SUV into drive and tore off across the cobblestones. I scrambled for my seat belt as twilight began burning the sky. "Shit, Carter. I'd hate to die before the necromancers got a chance to kill me."

"Sorry," Carter said through a hollow laugh.

"Where are we headed?" Foster said.

"South." Carter turned the fan up on the air conditioner. "I'm hoping to head them off somewhere between Clayton Road and 44."

"Black van with red stripes," I said. "Can't be too many of those around."

"Sure, but what are our chances of finding them?" Foster said.

"With Hugh and his son giving us info? Real good. Real damn good."

We traveled down Highway 70 to Highway 270 in relative silence. Carter had the speedometer straining around ninety and it earned us some nasty looks from the traffic around us.

I heard a bell ringing as we passed below the Olive Boulevard overpass. I wondered what it was until Carter reached into his shirt pocket and pushed a button on his phone. "Carter here."

A throaty voice came onto the car's speakers. "They're heading down Manchester. We lost them in Ballwin."

It was hard to hear Carter's voice over the roar of the air rattling the speeding SUV. "How fast, Haka?"

"Fifty or Sixty. Caused a pileup and we lost them."

Carter nodded. "Get there as soon as you can. We'll try to head them off." Carter hung up his phone and dropped it into one of the SUVs many cup holders.

"They're on Manchester, coming up on 270. If we hurry, we might catch them." It wasn't even a full minute before Manchester came into view.

"There! Foster said as he pointed toward the right edge of the windshield.

"Son of bitch," Carter said. "There's no way in hell we're catching that van."

Sure enough, a black van with red stripes was rocketing toward the overpass. A wicked grin cracked my face as I watched the van. "Think you could toss me up there, Foster?"

His eyes glanced at the fast approaching bridge and the van moving toward it. He nodded once. "Carter, keep us steady."

"What?!"

Instead of answering, Foster clicked the button to open the sunroof. He frowned at the slow-moving glass and punched the sunroof out of the rental instead. Carter yelped and focused on keeping us straight in the lane as the sunroof shattered on the pavement behind us.

"The Watchers are going to be pissed," Foster said as he glanced at the overpass. "Speed up!"

Carter ran the SUV up to ninety-five.

I climbed through the missing roof and laughed as the air tore through my hair. "This is nuts." I crouched with my hands on the luggage rack, one foot braced on the back of the roof's opening. "Fire when ready, fairy boy."

"Jerk," Foster muttered, but I could hear the grin in his voice. "Put your feet together. Good." He picked me up, pulled back, and launched me into the air.

I cursed and laughed like a maniac as I passed over the traffic below. My arms were crossed in front of my chest and my knees were pulled up like a cannonball. I enjoyed the wind snapping around me for the split second before I realized how fast the side of the van was coming up to greet me. A moment later, I screamed *Impadda!* and smashed through it. The metal screeched as it was torn apart by my shield to form dozens of razor sharp petals. The impact sliced the werewolf in the back of the van to pieces. Tires squealed and metal groaned as my shield slammed into the other side of the van. I dropped it as late as possible and spread out my arms and legs so I didn't fly through the other side. I only knew the dead guy had been a werewolf because there was fur and blood *everywhere*.

The impact wasn't pleasant. I was pretty sure my nose was broken and possibly a rib or three, but it didn't stop the growl in my throat as I screamed, "*Zachariah!*" I turned to the right as something moved beside me. I found a short blond necromancer about to leap out the back of the van. A swift kick booted him out before he was ready. There was a short scream. I heard him say "*Impadd–*" before a wet impact cut him off as a black sedan tried to swerve, but ran over his neck instead.

"Michael, jump!" Zachariah yelled to the passenger as he jumped out the driver's door. A shield sparked as he hit the ground and rolled onto Manchester Road. I caught a glimpse of his dark hair, pointed ear, and weak chin before he leapt. The necromancer in the passenger seat flung his door open and followed suit.

"Son of a bitch!" I jumped into the driver's seat and grabbed the steering wheel. I slammed on the brakes and put the van in park. The door opened with a swift kick and I hit the pavement running.

I couldn't see Michael, but Zachariah stuck out as he ran toward the Village Bar across the street. He was still close enough. I took a deep breath and screamed, "*Veratto!*" A surge of electric blue energy burned through my aura from the nearby ley lines and lashed out at Zachariah.

Zachariah's legs were ripped out from under him and he hit the road face first. He rolled over and held something in my direction. I didn't wait to see what he was going to attack me with. "*Minas Opprimotto!*"

An invisible anvil of force crushed the air out of Zachariah's lungs. His nose was bent, and by the time he got his breath back, I was already on top of him. He was cut and bloody from my attacks, especially from sliding across the asphalt on his face. I twisted his tattered white button-down up in my fist and said, "Where's the rest?"

I didn't give him a chance to answer. I punched his already lacerated face. The bastard still wore a smug expression. "Where the fuck is Philip?" Another rabbit punch to his broken nose sent more blood cascading down his chin. Foster swooped down beside us and landed by Zachariah's head. "You tell us, or I'll let the fairy do ... things to you."

For the first time Zachariah's eyes widened and the angry crease left his forehead. "Lau-mer ... meir," he said through a bloody mouth. A moment later he started to laugh.

"Police," Foster said. I heard the sirens and the flashing lights followed the sound down the street. "Take him with us."

I nodded and started dragging Zachariah toward the entrance ramp. It was the most likely place for Carter to show up with the rental, and he didn't disappoint. The black SUV flipped on its hazard lights and came to a screeching halt a few feet away. Carter had the window down and yelled at us. "Get in!"

Zachariah stopped laughing and started struggling again when he saw the werewolf. Before I could even think much about it, the dark necromancer raised his hand with a clenched fist and said, "*Inimicus averto!*"

A dome of rippling force blasted out from Zachariah's hand and hammered me backwards. Son of a bitch, I thought, he could use ley line arts too. "*Impadda!*" I said as I bounced and rolled into oncoming traffic. My shield snapped up just in time as I hit the side of a stopped bus. Metal gave and two of the windows shattered. I dropped the shield too early, cursed, and tried to roll out of the path of an incoming police cruiser. I closed my eyes and gritted my teeth when the tires started screeching, waiting for the impact as bits of gravel and debris pelted my face.

"Get up, Damian!"

I glanced up to find a wide-eyed officer standing beside his cruiser. Foster was running at me. He scooped me up and leapt for the SUV in the span of a heartbeat. I almost giggled at the thought of what the officer must be seeing, a scraped up Renaissance vagrant bouncing merrily through the air. Foster ripped open the back door, threw me inside, and followed. Carter had his foot down before we even had the door closed.

I pushed on my ribs and was relieved to find them sore, but not broken. "Where'd Zachariah go?"

"He vanished," Carter said.

"No, he ran for the mall," Foster said. "We can still kill him."

I looked out the back window at the growing mass of police and fire vehicles. "No way, we already made a big enough mess. We know where to find Philip. That's enough. Carter, take us to the Pit. We need Zola."

Carter pulled his cell phone out and hit redial. "Hugh, meet us at the vampire lair." He paused and listened to Hugh for a moment. "Two dead here. Someone else's wolf and one necromancer. Zachariah escaped. We know where the others are going: Laumeier Sculpture Park. We'll see you soon."

"Thanks, Carter," I said.

"For what? I just drove the car." Carter's hands flexed around the wheel and he took a deep breath. "Why did he tell us anything if he could have escaped?"

"Zachariah?" Foster said.

Carter nodded.

"That's simple enough," I said. "It's a trap."

CHAPTER 15

Foster was sitting on the dashboard by the time we left Manchester Road. The Pit was only a few minutes away. I pulled out my cell phone anyway.

"Wow, my phone survived," I said. "It's supposed to be ruggedized, but damn, I'm impressed." I went to unlock it and the face of the phone fell off, dangling by a few wires, mocking me. "Son of a bitch."

Carter and Foster exploded into laughter.

I laughed too and slipped the remains back in my pocket. Maybe the store would be able to transfer my contacts. "Can I borrow your phone, Carter?"

He tossed me his brick of a phone and said, "Get a better phone. Trust me, those cheap ones break way too often."

I punched in Sam's phone number and smiled when she answered. "Hey Sam."

"Damian? I haven't heard from you in *days*, so I'm just going to take a wild guess and say you need something. What do you want?"

"Hey sis, it's good to hear your voice."

"Cut the bullshit."

I laughed. "Okay. Are you at the Pit?"

"Yeah, I've only been awake for an hour or so."

"Is Frank with you?"

"No, he's visiting his brother this weekend in Springfield."

"Illinois or Missouri?" I said.

"Does it *matter*?"

Carter pulled onto the outer road, separated from the highway by a chain-link fence on one side and a row of evergreens on the other, and cruised down to the Pit's subdivision while Sam and I talked.

"No, I just don't want him involved. The proverbial shit is about to hit a very big fan. Are any of the Pit's enforcers in town?"

"Umm," Sam said as she tapped the phone with her fingernail. "Maybe Dominic, but the others are on vacation with Mary and Jessica and the rest. Don't you remember me telling you about that? You freaked out about me going to Chicago, for god's sake. It's *Chicago*."

"Oh," I said. I did remember that, I was not a huge fan of Mary and Jessica, but I should have had more faith in Sam's decision-making skills. "Sorry Sam, I shouldn't have done that." Especially since Mary was the vampire I'd done some very, ah, inappropriate things with. "Alright, see if Dominic's home. And if Vik's around, we could use his help too. FYI, I'm bringing some wolves, so make sure no one tries to kill them in the driveway."

Sam snorted and said, "Demon, sometimes I could kill *you*."

"Well, tonight there are better people for killing. See you soon."

Sam hung up and a minute later the Pit's home loomed into the view through the windshield.

Carter put the SUV into park at the peak of the U-shaped drive. I picked my staff up from between the seats. Foster flew out ahead of me before Carter and I hopped out and walked to the front door. I rang the bell and Carter shifted back and forth on his feet.

"Nervous?" I said.

He pointed at the door. "It's a Pit. I'm walking into a vampire Pit. What do you think?"

I waved my hand in a dismissive motion. "They're good people."

Carter laughed despite himself.

Foster flew up to the small window at the peak of the huge double doors. "Someone's coming."

I changed my grip on the staff as the deadbolts shifted and the right door swung into the entryway. I blinked a few times when I realized Zola had opened the door, a frown etched across her face. "Um, hi!" I said.

She stepped forward and belted me across the face with an open hand. The smack was loud enough to hurt my ears. I heard Carter and

Foster curse at the same time. I rubbed my face and winced at the sting.

"Idiot, boy! Why didn't you get me first? Zachariah? You faced one of Philip's assassins without me?"

She smacked me again. "What manner of idiocy possessed you to do that?" She didn't wait for me to answer. "Tonight," Zola said. "We have to go to Laumeier tonight. Together."

"How did you know about Zachari ..." Hugh walked into my line of sight. "Oh, never mind. Sorry Zola."

She glared at me and stepped inside as Hugh walked toward us. "Alan's with Maggie," he said. "She's healing well, but Jimmy ... Jimmy's dead, Carter."

"Son of a bitch." Carter kicked one of the nearby pillars.

My hand tightened around the raised silver inlays on my staff. I hadn't liked Jimmy and his teenage smattering of acne, but I had never wanted the kid to die. "Sorry Carter."

Carter nodded and took a deep breath. "We need to concentrate on tonight. If they know we're coming ... it's going to be bad."

"Bad?" Zola said. "It's going to be an unholy shit storm, wolf. Get inside. We need to talk."

The Alpha bowed his head and walked past Zola in silence. I cocked an eyebrow as I walked by her and her stern glare slipped a little. She glanced at the Alpha's back, shrugged, and ushered me forward. Foster darted in before Hugh closed the door behind us.

"The vampires are in the kitchen," Hugh said.

"They're not in the spiffy conference room downstairs?"

Zola cursed and shook her head. "No, Ah suppose they're afraid of the wolves gathering intelligence."

"Oh good god, let's just go to the kitchen. Bloody vampires." I shook my head as we walked off to the right through the entry hall. The grand staircase loomed above us to the left. We came to another hallway and followed it to the left, past the edge of the living room and into the kitchen. Sam, Dominic, and Vik were all camped out around the enormous walnut kitchen table. The wall behind the table was covered with a projected map of Laumeier Sculpture Park. Sam's fingers were a blur over her laptop's keyboard. She stopped typing and all three vampires looked up at the same time. It kind of creeped me out.

"Damian, I miss the days when the worst thing I had to worry about was you feeding my Barbie dolls to Jasper." Sam glanced back at the computer screen, hit a few keys, and brought up a satellite overlay of the sculpture park. She hopped out of her chair and hugged me. "What the hell are you wearing?" Before I could answer, she said, "Hey Carter!"

"Samantha," Carter said. "Thank you for letting us meet here."

"Oh, don't thank me, thank Dominic here. He's the enforcer on, umm, on call?" She glanced at Dominic. "On duty?"

Dominic held his hand up and shook his head. "It doesn't matter, Sam. It doesn't matter. The necromancers are a threat, the wolves can help. It wasn't a difficult decision to make." Dominic stood up and extended his hand to Carter. I could see Carter fight his instincts to run as the vampire straightened his back. Dominic was a monster with an ultra-short blond crew cut and eyes such a dark brown they looked black in the kitchen's light. He made Hugh look small and me look scrawny. Carter, well, he made Carter look like lunch. "Alpha, I am pleased to meet you in peace."

"Please, call me Carter."

Dominic's expression softened and he looked the Alpha over again. "Very well, Carter. I believe you know Vik, yes?"

Carter nodded and Vik returned his nod. Dominic sat down again and some of the tension left Carter's shoulders.

"Hey Vik," I said.

He gave me a two finger salute off his eyebrow. "Damian, you know the most interesting villagers."

"Villagers?" I asked as my eyes trailed down to the Renaissance outfit I was still wearing. "Oh, you're funny."

Vik's face cracked a small smile as I sat down beside Sam, with Hugh and Carter between me and Zola.

"So, what do you have for us, Sam?"

"Zola's research turned up the location for a soulstone. It's in this exhibit." She zoomed in on the screen and it showed a sculpture I recognized, even from above.

I knew what it would look like when we were standing beside it. The narrow stone steps crawled up the edge of the steep angled walls surrounding the outside of the earthwork amphitheater known as Cromlech Glen.

"Shit, that's back in the nature trails," I said.

"Far back," Foster said. "It's some pretty thick woods between the glen and the rest of the park. Hard to be quiet."

Dominic nodded. "It's a prime place to set up an ambush."

"Come on, Dominic, you know we're not the ones setting up an ambush. We're the ones walking into it," I said.

"Maybe we are," Sam said. "But we know we're probably walking into a trap. We can surprise them. There's no way they'll know you're going to have three vampires with you."

"Sam, this is Philip," Zola said in a placating tone. "He knows about you and Damian. He may plan for vampires."

"Even if he does, do you really think he'll plan for three of us?"

"It is possible, but perhaps not," Zola said. "Perhaps, even more than that, he will not expect the wolves and the vampires to be united."

"We'll come in from the forest to the east, just outside the park," Vik said. "Zola, Aeros will help. Just ask him." We all stared at Vik when he spoke.

Dominic looked back to the map on the wall. "You may be on to something." He stepped up to the wall and pointed to the eastern woods. "If we come through here, the glen may have a lighter guard than the more obvious ways in. If Aeros can cover the southern trail ... I think we should try it."

"Very well," Zola said. "Ah will ask Aeros for his help." She stared at me for a moment. "Talk to Happy. The bear may help too."

Foster grinned as he sat down beside Sam's keyboard. "Oh yeah."

"Really?" I asked.

"Yes," Zola said. "Ah'm concerned about what waits for us, especially since *we* will be the bait."

I fought a shiver and nodded. "We'll hit Forest Park, then come back out Highway 44 to Laumeier."

"I like the vampires' plan," Hugh said.

Vik smiled.

Dominic shook his head. "I'm worried about the wolves."

"For what reason?" Hugh said.

"Not you, or Carter," Dominic said. "Adannaya told us you were attacked at home by these necromancers. What if this, all this," he said as he gestured at the wall, "is a diversion to expose the pack?"

"Dammit," Carter said. "It could be, but there's no way to know."

"We do know there's a soulstone in Cromlech Glen. We have to go there," Zola said. Foster flitted by the map, and then glided to the counter beside the stove.

"Yes, you are right," Dominic said as he turned to Carter. "But you shouldn't leave your wife unguarded. They could use her to get to you. It's a strategy our own Pit has discussed in the past."

"*What?!*" Sam said.

Carter laughed. "Sam, it's fine. It's fine. We haven't always been friends, so to speak."

Sam glared at Dominic long enough the large vampire started to fidget. "The hell is wrong with you people?"

Dominic slunk back to his chair and sat down.

"My baby sister can be a firecracker." I grinned when Sam turned her glare on me. Zola failed to hide her laugh behind a cough.

"Mom and Aideen can help the wolves." Dominic jumped when Foster spoke directly behind the vampire. "I bet Nixie will help too. They could be at your house in no time, Carter."

Sam elbowed Dominic in the ribs. "Aw, did the wittle fairy scare the big bad vampire?"

Dominic's sulky expression cracked into a rumbling laugh.

"I would appreciate that, Foster," Carter said as he shook his head with a smile.

"Consider it done."

"I will send Haka, as well, Alpha," Hugh said.

Carter nodded his thanks. "Get Alan to join us at the park. We need him."

Dominic glanced at the large watch on his left wrist. "The sun will be fully down in an hour. Let's move on the park at nine o'clock. That gives you time to get to Forest Park and back out to Laumeier. Do any of you have a watch?"

"Pfff," Foster said. "The day I need a watch, just toss me into a bug zapper."

Carter laughed. "I don't need a watch either. I have Hugh."

The bigger wolf shrugged his shoulders and nodded. "With the sun and the stars, I haven't felt the need for a timepiece."

"What if it's cloudy?" Dominic said.

"It won't be," Hugh said.

"But–"

"Good god man," I said. "They'll be fine, stop worrying."

Dominic crossed his arms and leaned back in his chair as his face took on a distinct scowl.

"The vampires' plan ..." Carter said, "it's very good." Dominic's scowl softened a little as the Alpha spoke. "The vampires coming in from behind, with Aeros on the south, and everyone else to the north-east." Carter stared at the map and nodded. "Without knowing what's waiting for us, I think it's a good place to start."

Zola slapped the table. "Good, very good. Ah will go with the vampires. Ah want to be sure Philip hasn't set traps for them."

My gut tightened at the thought. Philip's traps were merciless. Last year we'd been in Pilot Knob. Philip had killed everyone and turned it into a warded city. When the trap was sprung, it raised a zombie horde. I didn't even want to think about what Philip could do to a vampire, especially Sam.

"Ah have something for you all, Dominic." Zola said as she reached into an inner pocket in her cloak. She pulled out a handful of bronze amulets attached to black silk cords. I recognized the discs. There were a series of runes etched on either side and I knew if I looked at it with the Sight I'd see deep red, yellow, and violet lines twisting around the runes.

"Zola," Sam said as her fingers ran over the amulet my master had given her just a few months ago. "Are those what I think they are?"

"Yes, Ah suspect so." Zola handed one to Dominic and then to Vik. "There are two more." She handed the extras to Vik. "Ah trust you will give them to those who can help us."

"Zola ... thank you," Vik said. His eyes were wide as he rubbed one of the amulets between his thumb and forefinger.

Dominic flipped the disk and looked at Sam. "What are these?"

"They'll protect you from necromancers," Sam said. "Even if you haven't fed on them."

"They're wards," Zola said. "Ah only know two other people who can make them, but Philip doesn't know how to break them."

"Wards?" Dominic said. "I thought wards could only be created by a powerful Fae."

"Or a very old woman," Zola said with a smile.

Dominic laughed and tied the ward around his neck. "Very well. I thank you for your gift."

Zola nodded.

"Nine o'clock. We'll see you all there," Dominic said.

Carter and Hugh stood up, and I followed. I squeezed Sam's shoulder and looked her in the eye. "Be careful, will you? I don't want to *make* you be careful."

She grinned and punched me in the arm as her hand moved to her amulet. "That's not even funny, Demon."

I frowned and rubbed my arm. "Ow, I may need that later."

"One thing," Zola said. Her voice was low and it grated with her accent. "Remember, Cromlech Glen is built over the meeting place of several dozen ley lines."

"It's a nexus," Foster said.

Zola nodded. "Think before you channel any power. Everything will be more powerful in the glen, and if you forget," she pointed at me, "you'll end up looking like burnt bacon."

"Mmm, bacon is an underrated food," Vik said.

I raised my eyebrows and looked at him. He was wearing a smile. "Better than a ferret?"

"Well, let us not be hasty."

The wolves both wore baffled expressions while everyone else laughed.

"Enough," Zola said, "we must prepare." A sense of pride swelled in my chest as I watched my master. There she was, with an Alpha werewolf and a vampire enforcer following her order without question.

CHAPTER 16

It felt good to be back in jeans and a black t-shirt. Before we left, Vik slapped my emergency clothes into my arms and told me to change because I was making him feel old. That got a laugh. Carter called Maggie to let her know who, and what, was coming. Apparently she was excited about meeting the cu siths. I was pretty sure that sentiment would pass the first time they playfully punched holes in her legs. We were on the road a minute later, getting drenched by a nighttime thunderstorm.

"I'm so glad you punched the sunroof out," Carter said as he glanced toward the gray sky. "I thought you said it wouldn't be cloudy?" His hair was plastered to the right side of his face where a torrent of rain was coming through the roof.

Foster laughed and tucked himself closer to the middle vent at the front of the dashboard. "Don't look at me. Hugh said that. But I think he's right, this is going to clear up fast."

"Great, that's helpful," Carter muttered.

I smiled and stared out the passenger window. I tried really hard not to laugh at Carter but my brain mouth filter slipped as I said, "Do I smell wet dog?"

Even Carter burst into laughter as we cruised down Highway 40.

With the storm, it took about a half hour for us to arrive in Forest Park. The rain stopped as we neared the exit. I directed Carter to the birdcage. It was one of Happy's favorite haunts, next to the red pandas. By the time Carter pulled to the curb and we both stepped out of the mobile swimming pool, I could feel another presence.

I didn't even have to focus my Sight to see Happy. He came bounding through the bars of the birdcage, headed straight for us. I saw Carter stiffen as he caught a glimpse of the bear.

"You can see him?" I said.

Carter nodded.

"Huh, that's new. Commoners still can't see him, but I guess werewolves go with his new guardian duties." My skin started to buzz as Happy's aura came close enough to brush my own. "Hey boy," I said as I rubbed him behind both ears. There was a time I couldn't touch Happy without feeding power into his aura. Ever since he'd adopted the little ghost we'd met the year before, that wasn't the case. I caught a shimmer out of the corner of my eye and the little ghost appeared beside the panda bear. I waved to her. She smiled and then buried her face in Happy's fur. "Well buddy, we need your help. I think Aeros is coming, so you'd like that, wouldn't you?"

The bear snorted and poked me in the face with his nose.

"Holy shit," Carter whispered.

I could hear Foster laughing as I took a step away from Happy. The little ghost girl looked up at Foster's laugh and smiled when she saw the fairy fluttering above Happy. She waved by opening and closing her hand as Foster swooped closer to her.

I'd only heard Happy speak twice before, and the third time wasn't any less disturbing. The bear's mouth rippled, but it didn't open. His words burned behind my eyes and were suddenly *there*, an ancient bass timpani vibrating across my mind.

I will help. I will bring the child.

Happy snorted and tossed his head. The little ghost climbed onto his back an instant before their forms and auras collapsed into each other and they vanished in silence.

"What happened?" Carter said. "Who was the little girl?"

My eyes widened. "You could see her?"

"Yes."

"But she's a ghost," Foster said. "Werewolves can't see ghosts."

Carter's eyes widened too. "What?"

I shook my head. "Not important now. They're going to help, that's what's important."

"Is he meeting us at the park?" Foster said.

I scratched my head and started walking toward the car. "I guess. He said he'll help and he's bringing the little ghost."

"But why?" Foster said.

I shrugged. "Let's just get down to the park."

Carter shook his head in a slow and deliberate manner as he climbed back into the rental. "That was weird."

Foster laughed. "You're driving a necromancer and a fairy around with no roof in a thunderstorm."

Carter stared at Foster for a moment. "You make a good argument." He started the SUV and we took the long way through the park to Kingshighway. It took us past the History Museum and I wondered how Cassie was doing. I frowned when I thought of Sam attacking me on those steps last year. A few minutes later we were back on Highway 44 and headed to Laumeier.

Carter's hands flexed around the steering wheel hard enough to make the leather creak.

"You alright?" I said.

He ran his left hand through his hair. "I don't know. I just, I hope we're doing the right thing here."

"Yeah, so do I."

"Look on the bright side," Foster said. "If it's not the right thing, you'll be too dead to worry about it."

Carter grimaced. "Thanks, I feel much better now."

"There is no better way to die, than to die with your enemies' entrails in your fist."

Carter pulled a disgusted face and glanced at Foster. "What?"

"There is no better-"

"Stop, never mind. I heard you the first time."

"What's up with the wolf?" Foster said as he looked at me.

"Gee, I have no clue."

"Was it the entrails?"

I burst into laughter. I even caught a hint of a smile on Carter's face. Foster and I had learned a long time ago to laugh in the face of adversity and atrocities. It was that or endure a psychotic break that would make a dark necromancer proud. Or go over the falls in a barrel, whichever you prefer.

The mood sobered as we pulled off the highway and wrapped around to the entrance of Laumeier Sculpture Park. I couldn't hide a grin when Carter backed out of the parking space and straightened the SUV.

He glanced at me and said, "What?"

"I didn't say a word."

He turned off the car and got out. I did the same, and Foster fluttered past my head before I closed the door.

Something hammered against my senses as soon as my feet hit the asphalt. "Shit, there are more dead here than there should be."

"What do you mean?" Carter said.

I could feel them. I pointed to the path we were about to take. "We're going to be walking right over them."

"A trap?"

I nodded.

Carter jumped as a seven-foot fairy suddenly appeared beside him. Foster drew his sword and held it in reverse, against the length of his right forearm as we moved forward.

"I'm impressed, Carter," I said. "I think most people would have run screaming from this mess by now."

He laughed without humor. "I am the Alpha of my pack. And they shouldn't have screwed with Maggie. I don't run screaming from anything." He glanced at Foster. "Not even a crazy fairy."

Foster flashed his teeth and took the lead.

"I've never been here at night," I said.

"I've never been here at all," Carter said. "It feels homey."

"I think you mean creepy," I said as I looked around at the encroaching trees. I tried to walk in silence, but the gravel paths were a little uneven and crunched beneath my boots. I leaned into Carter and whispered, "Everyone should be in position already, right?"

He glanced at his watch and nodded as Foster looked skyward at the crystal clear night and nodded. Carter grabbed my arm and placed his index finger to his mouth. Foster and I stood stock still. Carter stripped out of his clothes, stepped off the path, and tucked them inside a wooden structure that reminded me of a small Aztec temple. He didn't even break stride, only released a muffled grunt, as his body began to shimmer and pop and a covering of khaki fur flowed over him in the moonlight. The wave of power his transformation pulled in was warm against my aura.

"Are those boxer briefs?" I said.

The wolf-man grinned and snapped the waistband lightly against his thigh with a carefully controlled claw.

Foster slapped his hand over his mouth and I could see he was losing the battle not to laugh. I couldn't wipe the grin off my face either until a darker wave of power brushed my aura. I shivered and we all fell silent again in the darkness.

"They're here," I whispered.

There was a rustling on the path behind us and the cricket song abruptly died. My head snapped around. My eyes scanned the shadowy edge of the woods to either side, but nothing was there. I took a deep breath to calm my pounding heart and started down the path behind Foster and beside the werewolf.

Every instinct screamed at me to get off the path, but we were the bait. Instincts be damned. It wasn't much longer before the dark, looming visage of Cromlech Glen came into view. The circular earthworks were covered in grass, split with a narrow access point in the northwest. The woods surrounding Cromlech Glen were unbroken but for our path and one other. The rim of the structure was lit with an orange glow from the inside, turning the trees around us to dense black shadows. My eyes had already adjusted to the darkness, so the two burning torches at the center of the glen looked bright as the sun. I could see shadowy figures moving past our limited view into the circle of the glen. A man at the far side was pointing to the southeast and my heart pounded in my ears as I thought I heard the word 'vampires.' One of the silhouettes closest to us screamed. Two figures started running at us from the interior of the glen.

Carter's ears swiveled back and forth, pausing and twitching. His right ear locked its position and he tapped me on the arm. He pointed to the edge of the earthworks to our right. I could barely make out a pale green glow when it suddenly spiked into brilliant blue flames.

The wolf's ears flattened. I shook my head and gave him a thumbs up. I knew the green glow and the blue fire. Zola was summoning Aeros. It was time to move.

Carter was two steps ahead of me. I heard him growl, "Alpha," as he dove at the first incoming man, planting his front claws in the dirt and then exploding from his crouch. It took me a moment to realize the man in back was a werewolf. He was coming fast with a confident smirk on his dark face. I realized then I was looking at the Alpha who'd been causing Carter so much grief. By the time I finished thinking about it, Carter's clawed fist smashed through the first man's ribcage and tore out bits and pieces I was sure were vital.

"Son of a bitch," I said. Two more shadows came tearing out of the woods to our left, along the north side of the glen. The figure in back was a huge, fully-formed werewolf. I drew my pepperbox from the holster beneath my left arm and leveled it at the wolf.

I hadn't noticed Foster leave, but he came down from above with a swift strike across the front werewolf's shoulder as the wolf started to shift. A bloody arm twirled away as the werewolf howled and stumbled to the side. Foster struck again. He went low, removed a leg at the knee, spun with an obscene grace, and cleaved the wolf's head in two. Another wolf appeared at the edge of the northern woods. Foster charged the wolf and followed him into the dense tree line.

The two surviving attackers stopped dead as a figure of rock rose from the earthworks beside us in a circle of blue flames. Aeros pounded the ground as he materialized, and roared with the voice of a god as he was born once more into our world. He smacked his fist into his granite chest. Carter fell back beside me as the impact rattled the entire area like an earthquake. Aeros's voice was a booming, gravelly, grind. "You dare assault my followers, dog?"

The Alpha's confidence broke as a line of worry etched itself across his forehead an instant before he shifted forms. He was smart enough to retreat into the glen. The other werewolf, the fully formed hulk, just watched as Aeros picked up a paving stone from the crest of the earthworks and threw it hard enough to turn the wolf's head into a fine mist.

A beam of deep red light flashed from inside the glen and my jaw slackened as the light hit Aeros. He stumbled and fell backwards in a flailing avalanche of granite. I cursed and hoped Zola had gotten out of the way. I couldn't see her.

I changed the grip on my staff, placing my left hand just below the shield rune so I could have it up in a heartbeat. "Move it," I said as I led Carter toward the break in the earthworks.

I heard a voice before I saw the attack. *"Incursotto!"* My hand slid over the shield rune on my staff and tightened in a death grip on it. The flowing glassy sphere of the shield flared around me a heartbeat before a jagged bolt of power tore across it. Sparks of energy flared in yellow-orange fireworks. The bastard was in the woods to the south and I couldn't see him.

"Damian!"

"Sam!" I said. "Watch yourself!"

The necromancer who attacked me never had a chance. Sam leapt out of a nearby tree and came down in the shadows. I saw the hooded body of the necromancer as Sam forced him toward the light. His face was shadowed, but his screams were clear as day. Sam tore out his throat with one savage bite, dug her hands beneath his ribcage, and bared his heart to the world with a horrific series of snaps.

Two more cloaks came out of the woods behind Sam. Vik and Dominic were a split second behind her. They flowed over the earthworks in a visceral display of carnage.

"Damian!" Dominic said. "Carter! It's a huge trap! We're not prepared for this!"

"Just keep your wards on," I said as I dropped my shield. "Keep your fucking wards on, Dominic."

He came to a halt beside me and nodded once before his eyes went wide. "Get down!"

Dominic slapped me to the ground just before he dove in the other direction. The impact with the ground knocked the wind out of me. I was gasping as a wave of force tore through the earth between us, sending a cascade of dirt and rock into the air. The next thing I heard was the angry bark of a panda bear. Something screamed and died with a gurgle a moment before Happy came tearing down the path behind us with another necromancer's head caught in his jaws. Happy didn't even pause. He headed straight for Aeros.

The ground shook as something exploded on the other side of the glen. A fireball lit the skies deeper in the eastern woods, near where Hugh and Alan should have been. Enormous branches spun through the air and crashed down on top of the earthworks and trees groaned as they shattered and collapsed in the woods.

I heard Carter yell and I found him further down the northeastern side of the glen. I ran at him and could hear him better as I got closer.

"– wrong with you, Emily?" He had a werewolf by the throat. "Why are you *doing* this?"

The small, black wolf laughed as it scratched at Carter's arms. The wolf must have been Emily. "Weak little *Carter*," she said between snarls. "We'll kill you and eat your bitch."

Carter looked away as he snapped Emily's neck, tore off her head in one vicious strike, and let the body drop to the ground. He released a howl so full of agony my eyes burned. Fighting started deeper in the woods. I could hear the vampires tearing something apart in grunts and screams. The noise was growing and Carter didn't see the first zombie shambling out of the woods.

"*Carter!*" I screamed as the rotten corpse fell on him. It had its teeth in his arm before I could even think. All hesitation left me, and I sent my aura forward, searching for the strands keeping that godforsaken zombie alive. I found dozens of sickly orange bonds and severed them all as I found them. No matter how many I severed, Carter was still struggling beneath the zombie. I cursed, focused my necromancy, grabbed onto the unnatural thing with my aura and tore the body apart with its own cursed life force.

Pieces exploded across the grass as I came to know Jack Summers to an intimate degree. I knew what a good man he'd been, a school teacher, a loving father. The worst thing he'd ever done was drive away from the scene of an accident after he hit a parked minivan. He'd died trying to save his wife in a fire, died with her name on his lips. And I tore him to bloody bits. I ground my teeth and turned my attention to the werewolf.

Carter gasped and rolled onto his knees. He was cradling his left arm. I knew he'd heal fast, but he was going to be prey for a little while.

The earth shook again as Aeros regained his feet. I heard the rocky figure laugh as two zombies fell on his legs. He punched toward the ground and the first disappeared in a spray of gore. I didn't wait to see what happened to the next one. I was too busy trying to figure out what the hell to do about the new werewolf bearing down on us from the east. I put myself between it and Carter as it raced across the steep grassy wall of the earthworks, galloping on all fours.

I turned the pepperbox toward the wolf a second before Carter growled, "Damian, it's Hugh."

"Son of a bitch." My finger flashed off the trigger and I took a deep breath.

Hugh's voice sounded even more like a growl than Carter, "Zombies, dozens. How did they do this?"

"I don't know," I said. "They could've been burying them for months and we wouldn't know it."

Another wolf ran up behind Hugh, low to the ground. He was huge with dark brown and black fur and traces of white around his feet and claws. His voice was deeper than Hugh's. "They're herding us toward the glen."

"Alan?" I said.

The wolf nodded. His ears rotated to the right and then flicked forward. "They're here. I'll slow them down."

I glanced toward the opening on the earthworks. "Fine by me. Kill the necromancers and the zombies go away. This wasn't a warded trap. The power is tied to someone nearby."

"Then they die," Sam said. I turned to find my sister flanked by Dominic and a very bloody Vik. The smile on Vik's face almost curdled my blood.

My heart tripped over itself as I felt the air rush by my head and power was dragged across my aura, all to the roar of a distant tornado. "Zola?" I said as I looked back toward Aeros. "Bloody hell, get the fuck *down!*" The sound alone triggered my memory, like a god taking a deep breath, as the incantation gathered power from every dead thing in a mile radius. If the vampires didn't have their amulets, they would have been used up like so much kindling. A few figures dropped out of the shadows behind us. Zombies were caught in the unholy tidal wave, the meager life force torn from their bodies.

The thunderclap felt like it shook the world as Zola unleashed hell. I'll never know how many creatures died in that instant. The west wall of the earthworks shattered and erupted a hundred feet into the air as the trees nearby splintered and burned in an enormous flash fire. The fire roared forward in a spiraling cyclone, and then dispersed so fast debris was still falling when the flames went out. Zola would be hiding. That incantation would have wiped her out. I could just barely see the peak of an enormous glassy shield inside the glen. It was too big, far too big to be powered by any necromancer, even a gifted one.

"Philip's here," Aeros said. Before anyone else spoke, Aeros roared and charged through the new opening in the glen's western wall. I could see a glowing panda behind him with streaks of red and brown across his face and paws. I swear I saw a little girl giggling on his back.

"Move, now!" Dominic said.

Our group ran up the earthworks as something crashed through the woods nearby. I glanced toward the trees behind us as we came up the incline. More zombies. Dozens of them. I cursed again and my brain raced to figure out how that was possible. Either Zola's incantation hadn't killed them all, or one of our enemies had shielded some of them.

I vaulted over the peak of the earthworks behind the vampires. The boulders forming Aeros's feet were covered with a thin gore, destruction and carnage on vulgar display all around him. The rock god laughed as a werewolf launched itself at his face. His huge fists slammed together on the top of the wolf. Legs fell to the ground with nothing but mush attached to them.

A black-cloaked figure stepped toward us from the opposite side of the glen, stopping at the edge of the blackened earth. The figure threw back his hood and revealed himself. Philip Pinkerton. It was still odd, seeing someone you'd only seen in old yellowed photographs up until that very week. His round face contorted as he took another step toward Aeros and the rage continued poisoning his aura. I caught a smirk above a strong chin as he moved through the torchlight glittering from the silver highlights of his cloak. Philip's eyes stayed hidden in the shadows of a prominent, sloped forehead. His hands were gloved and his voice was deep as he held his right arm toward Aeros and said, "*Inimicus Deleotto!*"

A thick white beam, two feet in diameter, burned across the field and hit Aeros on the left side of his chest. It spun the monolith around and he crashed face first into the collapsed earthworks with a monstrous grunt. Aeros didn't move much and I almost laughed at the fact I was worried about a demigod.

I'd been distracted too long. I heard another incantation behind me. I turned fast enough to see Zachariah come out of the woods with more zombies. His face was covered in scabs and his nose was swollen. I didn't even get a shield up before a wave of force smacked me in the gut and sent me tumbling down the hill, into the glen. I kept a death grip on my staff and my pepperbox until I came to a stop at the feet of another necromancer. I could see his eyes in the weak light, a pale gray like my own. He raised a dagger and opened his mouth. I shot him in the head before he could do anything else.

There was another flash of white light and I turned to find the vampires battling a group of werewolves near the peak of the northeastern earthworks. Shadows snarled and rolled and died in the silvery moonlight. Philip turned toward them and watched. His face curled into a sneer as he turned back to me.

"Vampires, Vesik?" He laughed. "You bring vampires to fight necromancers? It would have been quicker to shoot yourself in the head."

Philip's sneer faltered as he raised his hand toward Vik and nothing happened. "No, *no*." He turned in a circle and the red-black rage rippling off his aura burned my senses. His scream tore through the night like a ragged wound, *"Adannaya!"*

I heard Zola's laugh before I saw her. She was standing rigid as a centurion at the peak of the southern wall. The zombies crested the hill behind me with Zachariah in the lead. Zola held her knobby cane out toward them and said, *"Modus Ignatto."* Flames scorched the air over my head. I saw Zachariah dive outside the glen once more as the wall of fire ate through a huge number of zombies. My head swung back to Zola in time to see her shoulders slump after the massive effort. Her cane was smoking from the energy she'd pulled through it. Zola laughed and turned back to Philip. "Ah've been studying, love." She spat the last word. "Ah've been studying since we ran into your horde, you bastard."

Vik broke away from the werewolves as Carter and Hugh joined them. Vik dove at Philip with his fangs extended and a snarl disfiguring his face. Philip barely moved a finger and Vik's body looked like it hit an invisible wall. Philip waved his hand again and whispered something. Vik shot backwards like he'd been hit by a car. "Your wards can't stop everything, Adannaya." Philip's face was stone, but the rage in his aura still flooded the glen.

I raised my gun and shot Philip just for the hell of it. It careened harmlessly off his cloak. "You're an asshole," I said.

He turned to me and laughed. He started to speak, but he screamed instead. His eyes widened as two translucent arms burst through his thigh. My skin crawled with pins and needles when I saw the little ghost running away from the dark necromancer with blood all over her arms. What the hell?

Zola didn't miss a beat. She leveled the head of her knobby cane at Philip. "*Magnus Eversiotto!*" The cane shook and blackened and she screamed as the nearby ley lines tore through her body. A thick white beam erupted from the cane and lanced into the earth a few feet from Philip. The grass laid flat as the incantation surged above it. Truckloads of dirt and debris rocketed into the air an instant later. I saw a glimpse of a shield flash around Philip at the center of the explosion. The shield was almost lost in the roaring debris cloud, pummeled by rock and dirt and bodies. The force was enough to lift the shield and Philip off the ground and slam them into the edge of the earthworks behind him.

Zola was on her knees and holding her stomach as the cloud dispersed in a rain of dirt and rocks. I caught a glimpse of Happy tearing through a line of zombies near the entrance to the glen before the body parts were flung out of my narrow view.

Philip dragged himself to one knee at the top edge of the earthworks and I stared at the necromancer with a mixture of disappointment and appreciation for how durable he was. Philip's hands were shaking and his eyes were wide with shock. He fumbled for something in his cloak. I saw his mouth move and he vanished from the glen with a crack.

"No!" Zola screamed. She tried to stand up, but fell to her knees and vomited.

"Hi Damian," said a small, airy voice.

A surge of adrenaline wracked my body as I turned around with my hand sliding to my shield. I blew out a breath when I found the small ghost we'd left with Happy the year before, and the panda himself. Blood was dripping from her hands and vanishing before it hit the ground. I noticed it didn't stick to Happy when she touched him. My eyes widened as the panda bear nudged her back with his nose and she giggled. The ghost rubbed Happy's snout, and looked back to me with a huge smile. It was so very out of place in that field of carnage.

"Ah," I said eloquently, "You're talking now?" My eyes trailed back to the edge of the earthworks. More zombies were cresting the top. Further down, a flurry of vampires and werewolves flickered in and out of shadows. Aeros was on his feet again, watching over Zola as blood flew and wolves roared across the glen. I turned back to the little ghost and she was nodding in a sage-like fashion.

"I used to be Elizabeth, but now I'm Vicky, like your car." She smiled and ran her hand through Happy's fur.

Bloody hell, I thought as I rubbed my face. She knows who she is. She probably knows who her family is. I need to tell them. I wanted to tell them last year, but how? Where do I even start? Do I ever not want to make that house call.

Vicky giggled and climbed up onto Happy's back. She pointed behind me and I turned to find three werewolves stalking us in a semicircle. Happy tossed his head and roared at the line of wolves. The sound shook the ground as I watched Happy pull in ley line energy to fuel his roar with power. Two of the wolves took a step backwards. Shit, I was tempted to take a step backwards. Happy was anything but.

One stupid wolf stood his ground. I shot him in the gut. Happy leapt forward with Vicky's fists wrapped in his fur and dismembered the wolf with a snarl. I don't care how fast you can heal, being reduced to your component parts is unhealthy.

There was another flash of light from the woods beyond the vampires and werewolves. Zachariah came over the northern hill near the battle, but he never saw Hugh coming. The wolf tackled him and I thought it was over. A flash of red light sent Hugh tumbling down the side of the earthworks with a howl. I cursed and ran at Zachariah. I worried about Hugh for a second before my mind regained its focus. It was time to end him. As I concentrated on the necromancer, I realized all the sickly orange lines of power were tied to him. "It's Zacha-riah!" I said. "The zombies are tied to *him!*"

Hugh righted himself and went for the kill with a vicious leaping uppercut. Zachariah shifted his body enough that Hugh only put three deep slashes into the necromancer's face. Zachariah didn't even scream. He summoned a shield as Hugh leapt again, knocking the werewolf senseless.

The necromancer's face pulled into a twisted smile as he dropped the shield and drew a wavy Kris dagger from his belt. I gritted my teeth, aimed, and fired at Zachariah's chest. I missed. The dagger came down fast at Hugh's neck. I was still further away than I would have liked, but I curled my hand into a fist and screamed, "*Pulsatto!*"

Zachariah dropped the dagger as he doubled over from the force hitting him in the gut. He started to limp away and fell to a knee. I glanced at the vampires. Carter was with them now, battling the coal-black Alpha. Zombies were closing on them from three sides. Alan's dark form took two down in a flurry of dismemberment. I sucked in a breath to yell a warning to Carter. It was the last thing I did before another necromancer came over the hill and blasted me fifteen feet across the glen with god knows what. I saw the night sky, then the grass, then felt the hard earth as I spiraled across it, rolling as best I could. I saw stars dancing in my vision before I saw the huge rocky face.

"You appear injured," Aeros said.

"Thanks for that," I muttered as I came up onto my knees. The smell of dirt and grass was ground into my face and I could feel blood mingling with the mess.

"*Inimicus Letum Phocanen!*" I heard Zola's voice before I even real-ized she was up again. The incantation flowed across the battlefield in a haze of sparkling white dust.

My eyes whipped back to Zachariah. He stiffened as the haze moved around him and the orange lines of power evaporated. Zom-bies fell all across the glen, no more animate than fallen logs, as Zola's incantation sealed Zachariah's necromancy.

"Witch!" Zachariah said. "You can't–"

Vik tore the throat out of the werewolf he was battling and threw the mass of cartilage and blood into Zachariah's face. Zachariah screamed and clawed at his eyes as the sack of flesh hit him, but Vik was on the necromancer before anything else could happen. The bones in Zachariah's arm snapped.

"Vik! Don't kill him!" Zola's voice was shaky, but it carried well enough for the vampire to hear. He nodded, held one hand at Zachariah's neck, and then wrapped Zachariah's good arm behind his back. Vik looked around, placed his leg across Zachariah's, and smashed his face into the dirt.

With the zombies down, all that was left were three wolves. Hugh was groggy, but at least he was moving. If there were more necromancers in the woods, they weren't anxious to join the fight. Dominic picked up a zombie by the ankles and swung it into the side of a wolf. The rotting corpse exploded as it sent the werewolf tumbling down to rest beside the last remaining torch.

Sam pounced and rammed her fist through the wolf's neck before it could get up. She flashed back to the other earthworks to help Dominic and Carter with the last two wolves. One of the wolves was a darker khaki than Carter and the other was the coal-black Alpha. They were all upright now, facing each other down on bent hind legs and primed claws. Their fur was just as matted and bloodied as Carter's, but they were still almost too fast to follow.

Carter's hand snapped out and caught the other khaki wolf by the ankle. That was all it took. Dominic fell on the wolf the instant it slowed. I didn't even know what he did to kill the wolf, but gore flew from the wolf's back and Dominic attached himself to the furry neck.

When Dominic started to feed, the last wolf, the Alpha, darted over the earthworks and disappeared into the woods. Carter bounded after him with a roar.

Silence fell over the remains of Cromlech Glen as the werewolves raced deeper into the trees. Hugh was gone. I could only assume he was with Carter. I heard the necromancer beneath Vik struggle again and heard a slurp from Dominic's direction. Sam started toward me and the smile beneath the blood on her face startled me. She squeezed my arm and turned to Zola.

"You take me to the most interesting places," she said.

Zola snorted a laugh and rubbed the head of her cane. "Ah would prefer to blame your brother for that. Are you well?"

"Yes, actually. I feel good." Sam smiled and I wasn't sure if I should be happy she was okay or very, very, disturbed. She looked around and her smile cracked. "Where's Foster?"

"Shit, I saw him go into the woods when we started fighting. I haven't seen him since." I shook my head. "Don't worry, it's Foster. He'll be okay."

Sam started chewing on a bloody fingernail. "I hope so."

CHAPTER 17

"Vik," Zola said. "Bring us the necromancer." She hobbled into the light of the flickering torch at the center of the glen. The crackles of the flame were fireworks in the silence. Zola held up her hand to stop Vik where she wanted him.

Dominic dropped the body he'd been feeding on and looked toward the woods. Vik put Zachariah between him and the sounds of screaming rolling over the eastern earthworks.

I smiled when Hugh came over the crest and into the glen. His fur was bloody and matted with dirt and twigs, but his stride was effortless. There was a dirty bundle of clothes wrapped up in his arms. A battle-worn Foster and Alan walked behind him. Alan had a black-cloaked figure in tow.

"We found one alive," Hugh said as Alan dragged the screaming man close to the torchlight and left him on the ground. One glance showed me his legs were broken. The man started to talk, but Alan knocked him out with a quick punch.

Sam ran up to Foster and hugged him. The hard lines etched in Foster's face softened and he returned the gesture with one arm. "You're hurt," she said.

"It's not bad."

Sam reached out and touched a tear in his right wing. Blood poured from the wound in rivulets. "Dammit, Foster. It *is* bad."

He shook his head. "Aideen will fix it, don't worry."

"Yeah, after she kills you," Sam muttered.

Hugh stopped beside Foster and unwrapped the bundle of cloth he was carrying. His body began to shimmer and pop while he was still working with the bundle. A now familiar burning brushed against my aura as Hugh shifted back into human form. His exaggerated muscles vibrated and flattened out over his arms as his posture straightened and his fur fell off. He stared at the contents of the bundle as it fell open.

"May I help?" he said.

Foster nodded.

Hugh crouched down in all his naked glory and pulled out a small mortar and pestle, some herbs, and what looked like a sports bottle of water.

I elbowed Sam in the ribs when I noticed her staring. She blushed under her drying mask of blood. A deep rumbling shook the earth beneath our feet and I turned to find Aeros staring at us. His craggy granite face wore a jagged grin as he laughed. I smiled at him and turned back to Hugh and Foster.

Hugh was mixing something with the mortar and pestle. He lifted it to his nose and took a deep breath. He nodded and scooped out a pasty green mixture. Hugh rubbed his hands together and then smeared the concoction over both sides of Foster's wings. "It won't do much, but it should stop the bleeding." By the time he finished talking, the flow of blood was greatly diminished.

"Thanks, Hugh," Foster said.

"One good turn deserves another, my friend. I might have been killed if you hadn't caught the necromancer." Hugh tilted his head to the side to indicate the cloaked figure on the ground. He rubbed his hands off on the bundle of clothes and stood up.

"Hugh, clothes," Zola said.

The werewolf glanced down at himself and a wide grin spread across his face. "Indeed, I suppose that would be appropriate now, yes?"

Sam continued staring at Hugh's backside as he pulled on a pair of jeans. I heard Dominic and Vik laughing behind her.

Zola's smile died as she turned to the necromancer on the ground. He was waking up. "Now, where is Philip? What's he planning?"

"Go crawl in a hole and die."

Zola clubbed the man's broken legs with her cane. When the screaming died down, she asked again. "Where is Philip and what is he planning?"

"Stones River," he said in a tiny voice. The man gasped and stiffened. "Stones River. I don't know what else. Don't know what he's doing. He wants to kill the wolves." His eyes unfocused and he started rambling. "Wolves have to die, vampires have to die, the humans, everyone has to die, demons, die ..."

Zola cracked him in the face with her cane. I was surprised when the man's eyes focused again behind the stream of blood.

"What the *hell* you old bitch!"

Hugh turned around and pounded the necromancer's face with a quick jab. "Respect," he said.

The necromancer spat out a tooth and glared at Hugh. I watched his aura darken and a flare trailed toward the vampires.

"You can't touch them," I said.

The necromancer cursed and stared at me. "There's dozens of us, dozens, you dumb fuck."

I heard Zachariah mutter something along the lines of "Shut up."

The man spit out blood and another tooth across the trampled grass and dirt. His eyes moved back to Zola. "You'll die. You'll all die, you stupid bitch."

I glanced at my master. She nodded.

"You first," I said as I pulled the trigger on my pepperbox. The smell of gunpowder was a relief over the scent of blood and rot in the air. I watched the body twitch as I pondered the man's last words and cleaned his blood off my arm.

"Damian, point your gun at Zachariah," Zola said. "Ah think he's aware we have no issue killing him." She pointed her staff in his general direction and said, "If you run, we will kill you. Do you understand?"

The necromancer nodded once as his eyes flashed between me and the dead man.

"Vik, let him go."

"You sure?" Vik said.

Zola nodded.

Vik shrugged and walked over to stand beside Dominic, a short distance away from Zachariah.

"Why do you follow him, Zachariah? You were a good man."

"Adannaya ..." Zachariah laughed in a slow rhythm. "Philip is going to change the world. He's going to cleanse the evil from the earth—the Fae, the wolves, even the humans—they'll all be gone. Only the necromancers will be left in a glorious world of the dead." His hand moved by degrees, creeping toward the seam in his robes. If I saw it, I knew Zola did too.

"He's at Stones River?" Zola said.

Zachariah didn't answer.

"Damn him." Zola ran her fingers over the ashen knobs on her cane. "You were a good man." Zola's eyes widened slightly as she said, "*Modus Fustisatto!*"

Zachariah raised an arm and his mouth formed an O. His arm crumpled and burst into bloody strips of meat as the force of Zola's incantation hit him. I didn't hear him call a shield, but one flashed up before the force of the blow could kill him. The shield caught the worst of it and sent him backwards, bouncing off the tip of the earthworks, and tumbling about forty feet into the tree line with a shout.

The vampires and I ran after him. Before we cleared the glen, there was a burst of light like a flash grenade. By the time I could see again, Zachariah was gone. I looked back at Foster. "Can you track him?"

He closed his eyes for a moment and then shook his head. "He's masked, or teleported, or something, like Philip was. I've never felt anything like it before. They're just *gone*."

Hugh slipped into the woods and looked around. "He's right. No tracks. The man is gone."

"It is an old magic," Aeros said. We all turned to look at the battered demigod. He rubbed his forehead to the sound of crashing boulders. "Those spells were demonic. Only the old ones were disturbed enough to use them."

"Shit," Zola said.

Foster turned to her at the same time she looked at him.

"It can't be," he said.

"It has to be," Zola said. "Someone has the arts."

"No, there's no path," Foster said as he gestured at the tree line. "There's nothing left behind. When the old king used the arts that started the Wandering War, he created permanent wormholes. Yes, they could be sealed, but we can still tell where they are."

"It wasn't always so," Aeros said. "There were others, before the Fae king."

"Nudd be damned!" Foster kicked a nearby werewolf corpse. "How the hell are we going to counter something like that?"

"You just need to know someone fluent in demonic arts." My lips pulled up in a devilish grin.

Foster cocked an eyebrow and flexed his wings. He winced and patted the tear in his wing gently before his eyes widened and snapped back to me. "Mike the Demon!"

"Huho!" Aeros said. "You know the fallen smith?" His rocky face smiled.

"We've met," Zola said.

"Quiet!" Hugh said. I followed his gaze to the vampires. All three were tensed in a defensive posture. A minute later I could hear it. Pounding footsteps and heavy breathing in the woods.

A bloody body clothed in boxer briefs crested the hill a moment later. Everyone let out a sigh of relief as Carter came into view. "Look what I found!" he said as he held up the decapitated head of the other Alpha.

I grimaced and said, "Carter, you don't know where that's been."

Zola laughed and a humorless smile crossed Foster's face as Carter let the head bounce down the embankment. Dominic kicked it like a soccer ball and I suddenly had visions of vampires in shiny shorts. Hugh jogged over to Carter and started looking his Alpha over.

"Enough, we need to find the soulstone," Zola said. She looked around the piles of earth and dead and frowned. "It's the whole reason for this ... mess." She glanced at Aeros. "Can you tell if there's a soulstone here?"

"I am sorry, Adannaya, but I cannot. They are not of my realm."

Zola nodded and turned to the vampires. "Dominic, help me dig."

Sam looked at Dominic and cocked an eyebrow. "Are you going to take that?"

Dominic smiled. "She's the most powerful necromancer I've ever seen in a fight. I'll pretty much take whatever she wants to give."

Vik laughed and dragged Sam toward the torch. All three vampires got down on their knees and started tearing up handfuls of earth.

Happy and Vicky came running into the glen. The ghost was giggling and I was glad to see the blood was gone from her arms, though I was still worried what it could mean. Happy ran straight to me and nosed the side of my face.

I smiled and scratched the panda's chin before turning back to Aeros. "How do you know Mike the Demon? Why did you trust him with the hammer?"

The rocky head ground across his shoulders until he was looking at me. "Ah, that is a story I rather like. Would you like to hear it?" His voice grated together like stones beneath the soil.

I nodded and put my arm over Happy's neck. I could see Zola in the middle of the vampires, digging with a small spade. I wondered where she'd gotten it until I noticed Hugh digging around in his bundle before he pulled out two more. I laughed and shook my head.

Aeros sat down and I was surprised when the little ghost climbed up to sit on the boulder forming his knee. "I met Mike a fairly long time ago, during the Civil War. Near the time I met your master, in fact. Mike was a very bad man." Aeros paused and rubbed his stony hand across his chin. "Well, demon, I suppose."

"From what I know of it, Mike was travelling with a young necromancer in Tennessee. She was just a teenager. She told the army she was a boy and cut her hair short so she could fight in the war. Volunteered with one of Sheridan's brigades. Seems it was mostly troops from Illinois if memory serves." He paused and his eyes seemed to unfocus slightly before he looked down at me again. "She was a crafty one, that. She would have to have been to win Mike's affection. The demon forged a cursed bayonet for her. Even a nick on the skin would kill anything it touched.

"Well, the battle went bad there at Stones River. Many people died in the cornfields, which was not unusual of course, and not something Mike would care about, but ... his little necromancer took a bullet in the chest." Aeros shook his head and his rocky face frowned. "Something broke inside that demon, boy. In a good way mind you, but he was broken nonetheless. He fought claw and tail to keep the soldiers away from that poor girl. He dragged her into the broken stone trenches they named the Slaughter Pen. In enough numbers though, not even a demon can keep the humans away forever.

"Ah remember," Zola said as she ran her fingers across the braided rope belt at her waist.

"It is not something I expect to forget," Aeros said as his gaze shifted from Zola back to me. "Mike's little necromancer was already dying when two more shots hit her in the thigh." Aeros looked up at the sky and then down at the circle of torchlight. "She told him he was her friend and made him promise to stop hurting good people." Aeros laughed and shook his head. "A demon, promising not to hurt people. No matter how long I live, there is always something new.

"Mike held her while she died. I heard him swear the oath. I had seen the demon fall. I gave him back the hammer so he could swear that unbreakable oath. Mike is bound to the hammer now. It gives him power to fight the darker beings in the world, but if he ever kills an innocent, his own hammer will destroy him."

I watched Aeros for a while as I scratched Happy's ears. The panda stretched out and laid his chin on his paws.

"That's so sad," Sam said. "Did she always fight with the North?"

"Does it matter?" Aeros said. "War is war."

I yelped as something cold wrapped its arms around my head and said, "Guess who!"

She felt so solid it was hard to believe. I pulled her arm away and turned to find Vicky grinning from ear to ear. She giggled and dove over Happy.

"Zola, what's going on with Vicky?" I said.

My master stood and brushed her hands together. Her lips curled up into a small smile. "Vicky has become a demigod, Damian."

"What?" I turned my head toward Happy and stared at the little ghost hugging his neck.

Zola smiled at the small ghost, and then glared at Aeros. "I wonder how *that* happened? Hmm?" I swear Aeros looked nervous and was fighting not fidget. My master can make a pile of rocks nervous. That ... is just ... wrong.

"Yes, well, I think I'll take my leave, and let you discuss your next adventure," Aeros said as he stood and bowed goodbye. Vicky waved as a swirl of bluish light rose around Aeros and he sank into the ground in a flash.

"Wow, was he in a hurry?" I said.

Vicky giggled and tugged on Zola's cloak.

"Yes, dear?"

"My bear wants to go home."

I thought Foster and the vampires were going to go into hysterics they were laughing so hard. I snorted a laugh of my own and laid down on the grass. Happy nosed the side of my head and I scratched him again. "Now you're a pet bear, huh?"

Happy lumbered over to Zola and Vicky and nosed the little girl until she climbed up his fur and sat across his back.

"Damian?" Vicky said.

"What's up, kiddo?"

"I ..." she started, but stopped and stared at her fingers, wrapped up in Happy's fur.

I stood up and brushed my ass off before I walked over and touched her arm. She felt as real as a living being. It made me fight back a shiver. "You can tell us, we're all friends here."

"The bad man with the van."

My teeth ground together and my fist turned white on my staff. We'd killed a murderer last year. Her murderer. Foster had torn him to pieces and trapped his soul in a dark bottle, a fairy bottle capable of trapping the soul and the aura. We'd come too late for Vicky. She'd been dead long before we found the killer.

"He wasn't the only one. Elizabeth told me so."

My arm shook and I tried to stay calm. Vicky didn't need to see me explode. I heard Foster curse and he started pacing.

Vicky's face glazed over and her expression was more haunted than any child's should ever be, living or dead. "I want to kill him." Her voice had gone black and her aura swirled in a twisted mixture of red and darkness.

"No, Vicky." I grabbed her chin and held her until she met my eyes. "You're better than them."

"Maybe," she said simply.

Foster stepped up beside Happy and put his hand on Vicky's leg. "Show me."

The preteen demigod didn't even hesitate. She turned to Foster and put her small hands on either side of his face. Her aura brightened, and the darkness recoiled as she touched Foster. His eyes widened and his wings flared, with no hint of pain as his wounds stretched. It would be years before Foster would talk about what he saw in that vision. He gagged and his body shook as Vicky flooded his mind with images that defined horror. When she let go, Foster fell to the ground and took heaving breaths. He looked like he was fighting not to curl up into a ball.

"I ... I know him." His voice was a quiet whisper.

"Kill him for me," Vicky said.

Happy barked as their forms and auras collapsed onto each other and they were gone; back home.

Foster was on all fours with his head hanging between his arms. His wings looked limp across his back as he raised his eyes to me. "I know him, Damian. I've seen him near the Goth clubs downtown that Colin used to go to. He was one of Colin's *friends*." Foster closed his eyes and grimaced. "Colin stopped him from beating a prostitute once. Colin never thought, he always looked after the bastard. I never thought ..." Foster punched the ground and the ground lost.

"Stop," Zola said. "You cannot save everyone."

"But Zola," he said.

She held up her hand. "No. You cannot save everyone. Live with it. Correct what you can, but do not dwell on it."

Foster sighed as he stood up. "Then he dies."

"Why did Vicky talk about Elizabeth like it wasn't her?" I asked. "Like it wasn't her old name?"

"Because Vicky isn't Elizabeth anymore, Damian." Zola rubbed her hands on her face. "Ah think Aeros gave her the power to become a demigod."

"I thought only a god could grant power to a demigod?"

"We'll talk about it later." Zola gave me a meaningful look and I nodded.

Aeros was a god, and a lot of the people around us didn't know it. A god that apparently still had a few tricks up his sleeve.

I watched Carter push himself off the ground with a grunt. He was still clad in his boxer briefs and I couldn't suppress a smile. He flexed his right arm, nodded to himself, and looked around at the carnage. He eventually noticed me watching and waved. "Who's going to clean this up?" he said.

As if on cue, "Oh my *god!*" sounded from the stars above us.

I glanced up to find Edgar and two other suits descending into the wreckage of the glen. I'd love to know how they were able to fly. It was always good for an entrance.

I grinned and looked at Carter. "Cleanup's here."

"Vesik! Zeus's balls, what the fuck happened here!" Edgar's eyes swept from one end of the glen to the other. I could only imagine what it looked like from above. The entire area was coated in zombies, dead werewolves, dismembered necromancers, with enough blood to feed the vampires for a decade, splintered and burned trees, and literal tons of earth displaced from the battle. I scratched the back of my head and shrugged.

Carter casually walked over to the vampires and Hugh. I wondered if Edgar realized an Alpha had just placed himself within striking distance. Dominic looked up from his digging and pointed at Edgar. I heard Vik mutter something before Hugh and all three vampires burst into laughter. They went back to digging like the fuzz hadn't shown up.

I threw my arms wide and smiled. "You missed the party, Eddie."

Edgar's cohorts, an older blonde woman and a young Japanese woman, glanced at each other and then back to their leader. Edgar shook his head and held his hands open as he gestured at the destruction. I was pretty sure he was begging for an explanation.

"Edgar Amon," Zola said. The slow cadence and tone in her voice brought the attention of all three Watchers. "This is the work of Philip Pinkerton, a dark necromancer." She looked pained as she finished the sentence.

Edgar's eyes narrowed. "Again with this nonsense?"

Zola cocked an eyebrow and swept her gaze across the carnage-filled horizon.

Edgar closed his eyes and took a deep breath. "Check the perimeter. I want to speak with the group alone." The other two suits disappeared into the woods at opposite ends of the glen. My eyes widened when Edgar's professional façade vanished. Anger creased his face when he turned back to Zola. "Adannaya, Pinkerton is dead. What are you talking about?"

I almost crapped myself when Zola reached out and put a hand on Edgar's shoulder. "Amon, it's true, and he has followers. A lot of followers."

Edgar shook his head. "No, impossible. The Watchers would know. Something would have come up."

"No, this is *Philip*. He knows your system. He helped bring the Watchers out of the Stone Age. If anyone knows how to evade you–"

"It's him." Edgar's face soured and he turned away from Zola. He looked nauseous. "Someone has to be held responsible for this mess. I'd rather prefer it be Vesik."

"What?" I said. "What'd I ever do to you?"

Edgar leveled a glare at me.

"Ah, fair enough," I said.

"Edgar, Ah don't have time for this right now." Zola gently pushed him aside with her scorched cane. Zola bent down and started digging beside the vampires and Hugh. Vik handed her a spade and she nodded her thanks.

"You may cite me if you wish," Hugh said. He didn't look up from the furrow he was digging in the dirt. "I have no issues with the Watchers' duty."

"That is kind, wolf," Zola said. "She glanced at Edgar. "Ah think we should play a game, Edgar. If you can spell this wolf's name, you can issue him a citation.

Edgar blew out a breath. "You haven't changed a bit, Adannaya." He actually cracked a tiny smile and I thought my world was ending. "What is your name, wolf?"

"Hohnihohkaiyohos," Hugh said.

Edgar glared at Zola for almost a minute. His mouth was open and his eyebrows were raised. I was waiting for him to break down crying or laughing. Instead he just shook his head.

"You get used to it Eddie," I said as Foster snickered.

"All clear." The voice came from the tree line.

I glanced up to see the fortysomething blonde woman hovering out of the woods. Edgar's posture was rigid and his face stone by the time I turned around.

"No, I don't think I'll ever get used to you people," Edgar said.

"Goodness," Zola said. She was digging in one of the deeper gouges the vampires had dug up. With the vampires' and the werewolves' help, the center of the glen had been dug into a trench almost a foot and a half deep. Zola worked the spade around in a careful circle and then dug her fingers into the earth. "Got it." She smiled as she stood up and started picking pieces of dirt out of the small object in the palm of her hand. A few seconds later I recognized it. I'd seen one before.

"Zola, what is that?" I said. The vampires and the wolves gathered around us. I squeezed Sam's hand when she put it on my shoulder.

"It's a soulstone, a rather large one. It's not a major stone, but Ah suppose it's why Philip and the wolves led us here. Zachariah used it to power their trap."

"Fucking hell, Ashley has at least two of those things in her house."

Zola's head jerked back and her mouth moved without making any sound. "What? Philip can detect the soulstones at a distance ... no ... now that we have this one ..."

My heart sank. "They're going to go after her."

Zola grimaced and nodded before she spoke. "Any dark necromancer can detect a soulstone at distance, even a small stone. But Philip is a very good bastard."

"Yeah, and Ashley has one the size of a goddamned softball."

"What?"

"She has one a little smaller than that one, but she was holding one in a photo at least the size of a softball."

"How in the hell?" Zola said. "Where could she even? Shit. Call her, she is in danger." Zola looked up and said, "Carter, do you have anyone near the shop? Ashley is in trouble."

"Give me a phone. Mine got smashed." He pulled some electronic remnants out of a small pocket on his boxer briefs. I tossed the durable chunk of plastic Sam used for a phone to Carter. He dialed and his face hardened as the phone rang. "Maggie? No, I'm fine. Ashley, the Wiccan priestess, is in trouble. Get anyone you can over there. It's going to be bad."

Zola's hand clamped down on Edgar's arm. "Amon, you are a good man, help us. Our friend is in danger."

Edgar's face closed down when Zola called him Amon. I don't know what he was thinking, but his hand shook as he pried Zola's arm away. "For what I owe you, Adannaya." His head snapped to the side. "Agatha, Nomiki, get started on the cleanup. I have to follow-up on a lead." Edgar started to float away.

The suits nodded and disappeared over the earthworks.

"We'll meet you there," Zola said. Edgar held up his hand and drifted to the northwest.

CHAPTER 18

"Let's move befo–" Zola squeaked as Vik picked her up.

"We will be faster," Vik said. "Carter, are you okay to run?" The Alpha nodded.

"Come on, Demon," Sam scooped me up like she was carrying me over the threshold and I didn't even have time to blink before we were tearing through the woods. Gravel and shadows blurred by in a nauseating blend of gray. We were at the rental in a minute.

Carter and Dominic climbed into the front seats. Everyone else crammed into the back. The SUV lurched as Carter pushed it to its absolute limits.

"Can you do something about the police?" Carter said.

"Yes, a little." Foster fluttered from Dominic's shoulder to the dashboard and sat down with his legs crossed. "It's only a little misdirection, so if you run into someone, chances are good people will notice."

"Do it."

Foster nodded and closed his eyes. I watched him, something to keep my mind off Ashley, but I couldn't see any shift in his aura or the nearby ley lines.

The air roared over the missing sunroof as we hit the highway. My stomach churned with angst as my mind crawled back to Ashley. I liked her. She did good things, was always friendly, even when I knew shit was bothering her. I gritted my teeth and tried to be optimistic. The wolves were going over there. Nixie and Cara and Aideen would be with them. A Watcher would be there. I needed to keep my mind off the less optimistic scenarios.

I bowed my head and turned slightly toward Zola. "Tell me about Aeros."

She nodded and dug in her cloak. Her hand came out with a small charm that looked strikingly like a severed ear. I didn't want to know if it really was. Zola saw my apprehension and rolled her eyes. She slapped her hand, with the ear charm, onto my palm and held it tight.

A thin wave of power wrapped around us and the excited voices in the car grew muffled. We could just barely make out what they were saying.

"They won't hear you now, boy. The less people know about Aeros, the better."

"So, how did Aeros give Vicky demigod-hood?" I paused and tapped my chin with my free hand. "Is that a word?"

Zola smiled and shook her head. "Ah want you to understand, this is not something you can repeat." Her voice turned into a quick whisper despite the sound barrier. "Ah trust you Damian, don't think that Ah don't, but Ah'm only telling you so you won't pester me with questions at the wrong time and have someone overhear us. Understand?"

"Yes."

"Good. What you said before is true. Only a god can grant a demigod its power."

"So Aeros is really a god?"

Zola rubbed her face and blew out a breath. "Damian, Aeros is not just a god. He is an *Old* God, a true child of the Old Ones."

I blinked at Zola and raised my eyebrows. "What? The Old Ones?" I shook my head. "No, I mean, yes, he's old and he's a god, but I didn't realize that's what you've hinted at. Bloody hell." I'd always thought the Old Gods were scary stories to tell on Halloween until Zola had shown me a photo of one, locked deep within the arctic ice after a war with another god. I'd had nightmares of the blasted thing for weeks. Beings so vast and powerful we puny humans could scarcely hope to understand them. Some masqueraded as supermassive black holes, devouring galaxies that wandered too close, while others thought on a smaller scale. Some hid in the oceans and dragged sailors to their doom using masses of tentacles the size of redwoods. Others hid in the shadows and fed on the lost and the homeless, while a few stormed across the worlds of the living and the dead in an unbiased plague upon reality itself.

Zola laughed. "Yes, do you understand? He is careful, but if someone of ill intention gained that knowledge ..."

"Goodbye world."

"Simply put, but yes." Zola pulled her hand away and tucked the creepy ear charm into her cloak. The muffled sounds of the vampires, the werewolves, and the wind tearing across the hole in the roof returned to sharp definition.

I felt a hand on my shoulder before I heard Alan's cavernous voice. "Your sister's alright for a vampire, Vesik."

"That's just because you don't know her yet," I said with a sideways grin.

Sam was far less gentle as she smacked the side of my head.

"Ow."

We laughed and joked, but the tension was palpable. I don't think the rental ran below ninety five except for a few turns that would have rolled us. Everyone fell silent when we reached Fifth Street and Carter took a hard left. In another minute we were driving into the small cul-de-sac Ashley called home.

The front door of her ranch-style home was obliterated. A good chunk of wall was missing between the door and the front window, and scorch marks still smoked across the brickwork. There was a trail of churned earth and smoldering grass leading back behind the house. The fight had come outside.

"Foster," Carter said. "You and Damian check the house. Everyone else follow me. We're going hunting."

No one said a word.

Carter barely had the rental in park when I jumped out and ran to the door.

"God damn it!" I screamed and punched what was left of the door frame. The wolves and the fairies were nowhere to be seen. They'd probably left in pursuit of whoever had torn up the house. The front room was destroyed. The couch and the coffee table were splintered and coated in gore. Ashley was on the ground. Her leg was obviously shattered and looked like so much bloody rubber. She coughed. It was wet, and pain savaged her face as a stream of red ran from her mouth. Her right hand clutched an athame. She was still conscious. Tremors wracked her body as she tried to breath and her eyes begged me for help through a flood of tears.

"I came too late," Maggie whispered. I glanced at the wolf for the first time. She was in the corner near the window. Her left hand was mangled. The living room around her was a mass of blood and dismembered limbs. I recognized the severed head of the necromancer, Michael, who I'd seen with Zachariah. Terror was etched across his dead face. There were at least two torsos amongst the gore. Good riddance.

"No." Foster's voice was stern. "Get her shirt off. Nudd be damned, it's not too late. I need contact with her skin."

I didn't hesitate. I pried the athame out of Ashley's grip and sliced through her shirt and her bra. She whimpered as I lifted the cloth to avoid cutting the skin below and more blood ran from her mouth. Ashley's entire chest was red and swollen and I felt tears running down my face. I jumped out of the way as Foster pushed in beside me. I put my hand on her cheek. "It's okay, we're here. It's okay." I felt a horrible guilt twist in my gut for lying to her like that.

Foster placed his left hand just below Ashley's right breast. Her body trembled as he made contact with the wounds and her flesh gave much further than it should have, her ribs not supporting the pressure. Foster's right hand went over her heart and I'll never forget the set of his face and the steel in his voice when he said, "*Socius Magnus Sanation!*"

The room went completely white and silent but for the high pitched whine of a massive flash of power. I was still blind when Ashley's screams tore at my eardrums. Foster's incantation started pulling her body back together, and she felt it. All of it. When I regained some of my vision I could see the veins in Foster's face pumping visibly beneath his skin. He shook with the power he was channeling into Ashley.

"*Foster!*" Aideen screamed as she and Cara barged back into the house with bloody swords drawn. "*Foster!* Stop, you did it. She'll live. Stop it or you'll die!"

The spell died like someone threw a light switch and Foster collapsed on top of Ashley. Ashley was crying hysterically. She wrapped her arms around Foster's neck and squeezed the fairy as she cried herself out.

I looked up to find Nixie standing wide-eyed in the doorway. "Is that ... do I cause that kind of pain?" Her face crumpled and she stepped back outside the house.

I put my hand on Ashley's forehead. "It's okay, they're gone. You'll be okay."

Ashley's sobs turned to hiccups and she nodded. Foster tried to stand up, but Ashley wouldn't let go.

"I'm too tired to argue," he said and his wings went limp around the priestess.

I smiled and looked at Maggie. Aideen was already stepping through the body parts to get closer. "Let me see your arm," she said. Maggie held out her mangled hand and winced as Aideen gently laid her fingers on it.

Nixie was next. I needed to find her. I didn't have to look far — she was outside by Ashley's little frog fountain. Her knees were drawn up to her chest and tears were running down her face.

I sat down beside her and put my arm around her shoulders.

Her voice was choked. "How could I have ever killed people without a reason, Damian?"

A white flash of power flashed through the broken door. I was sure Aideen was healing Maggie.

"That is horrible, Damian. I saw how much Ashley's wounds hurt you, and she's only a friend. I killed men with families, fathers. It's just ..." Her voice cracked and she buried her head in her knees. Her voice was muffled when she said, "It never bothered me before ... What made us like this?"

Gravel crunched behind us before a deep voice said, "Vesik."

I looked up to find Alan standing with one foot in Ashley's landscaping rocks. "Bad timing," I said. He was back in the Saint Louis Rams sweatpants I was beginning to think of as the wolves' street clothes. "What is it?"

"Carter wanted me to tell you we're checking the perimeter. He was hoping you could stay here with the fairies and watch over Maggie."

"And Ashley?"

The whites of Alan's eyes were an intense contrast to his dark skin as he opened them wide. "She's alive?" He glanced at the doorway. "The Fae?"

I pointed my index finger at him like a gun. "You got it."

"That's good." Alan nodded to himself. "That's very good. Scream if you need us." The werewolf smiled and walked to the edge of the house.

"Aren't you the funny one?"

He laughed as he disappeared around the corner.

"He's gone, Nix."

She nodded her head a little.

"Nixie, you don't have to kill if you don't want to."

"You don't understand. With you, with you Damian, I don't want to, but it's our way. What the Queen declares, it's our *law*." Nixie's eyes widened and she buried her head between her knees again.

I laughed and squeezed her tighter. "Not supposed to talk about the Queen, huh?"

She shook her head.

"So, what happens if you don't do what the Queen says, Nix?"

"She'll kill me." Nixie raised her head and met my eyes. "Or have me killed."

"There has to be some way around it."

"No, there's not. Even if she dies, a new queen could just reinstate the same laws."

"Could?" I said.

"There are other beings above the Queen. I can't tell you anything else, I'm sorry." Nixie piled her hair into her lap and started picking bits of leaves and grass out.

"I don't give a shit about your Queen."

Nixie paused in her grooming. "It doesn't matter, she is still my Queen."

"What a bitch."

A small smile showed itself across her lips. "Yes, actually, she is."

I heard two quick raps of wood on concrete and turned my head to find Zola. "Maggie is fine."

"Good, glad to hear it."

"Nixie is not," she said.

I glanced at Nixie and then back to Zola. "There has to be some way get her away from that *law*."

"Oh, there is," Zola said as she sat down and leaned against the side of the tree trunk. "We've fought them before."

Nixie stopped picking through her hair and stared at Zola. Her face had a look I'd never seen before, and I was afraid it was desperation.

"Where?" I said.

"Lake Okeechobee in Florida. September 17th, 1928. There are some dates you will never forget. The water witches moved in behind a hurricane. They helped power the storm surge. Thousands died, from Puerto Rico to Florida. Philip found out they were planning to invade us. An old grudge against Gwynn ap Nudd." Zola laughed. "He had cast them out for their senseless killing several years before. They found he was living in the States."

"Yeah, unlike that Wild Hunt thing. No senseless killing there," I muttered.

"No one ever claimed Glenn was the most consistent ruler."

"What happened?" Nixie said.

"We fought the witches. It was a hard battle, well fought on both sides in the remnants of the hurricane. What was left of the area was destroyed by the battle. Eventually the Queen joined the fighting when enough of the water witches were dead."

"Dead? How?" Nixie said.

"With help from below." Zola's smile was empty. "Ah didn't know it then, but now Ah'm sure Philip was channeling a demon. When the Queen arrived, he struck her down like a stalk of wheat."

"Some water witches stayed in the States in the aftermath. Only a handful abandoned the old ways. But, as Nixie said, it is not only the Queen you must worry about."

"What else do we need to worry about?" I asked.

Zola looked at me and frowned slightly. "You must worry about what you may unleash by killing royalty."

Nixie shook her head slowly. "This is not the time."

I ran my fingers through my hair and looked between Zola and Nixie as an idea took hold. "Mike!" I said. "Mike the demon could help us."

"Perhaps," Zola said. "Remember, Mike can't kill innocents. While we may consider the Queen an abomination, she may be an innocent. Ah cannot ask Mike to risk that." Zola held her hand up when I started to speak. "But, it is possible Mike would be willing to teach you how to kill a water witch."

"And then?" I said.

"And then we kill the Queen," Nixie said.

"I thought that might be where we were going." I rubbed my face and set my hand on Nixie's thigh. "I guess we'll have to talk to Mike before we can decide anything else."

"Yes," Nixie said, "but even if you succeed in killing a Queen, the next could be worse."

"Super."

Zola smiled a moment before her face turned into frown. "Edgar's here."

Nixie looked up as the Watcher came down on cue. He spared us a glance from the small front porch. "Adannaya, did you see the devastation behind the house?"

Zola shook her head.

Edgar gave her a slight nod in acknowledgement. "We need to talk. Come inside."

Zola laughed a little. "Let us humor the man." She stood up and offered Nixie her hand. Once we were all standing, Zola walked into the house.

Nixie started after her, but I grabbed her arm and turned her around. The moonlight reflected across her eyes. I kissed her briefly and pulled her close. "This will all turn out, Nix. We'll get you away from the Queen."

Nixie sank into me as she wrapped her arms around my back. "Thank you Damian. Even if it doesn't work out, it's nice to know you care."

My heart rate sped up with a surge of adrenaline. I could feel the pulse in my neck and waves of warm fear coursing through my body. I don't know why I decided to say it then, it just felt right, even though it scared the hell out of me. "I love you, Nixie."

She jerked in my arms and leaned back to meet my eyes. "Damian, you don't know me that well, but ... and ..." She buried her head in my shoulder and I heard her whisper, "I love you too."

I pulled her head back with a hand on either of her cheeks and kissed her hard. She pressed her body against mine. Her lips were a soft brush of relief after a night of hell. When I pulled away I just stared at her and smiled.

"We should go in," she said.

I nodded and we started toward the door with my arm around her shoulders and her head leaning on my chest.

CHAPTER 19

"Where's Ashley?" I said.

"We put her to bed," Cara said. "She didn't need anymore excitement."

"I can relate." I glanced around the room. Foster, Aideen, and Cara were all back to their usual size and camped out on one of the padded chairs in Ashley's living room. Their armor was still covered in dried blood, but their skin looked clean. Foster was sprawled across Aideen's lap and snoring like a model freight train. Aideen ran her fingers through his hair and smiled.

I had my arm around Nixie at the mouth of the hallway. My staff was leaning against Zola's chair. The vampires and wolves were still outside except for Maggie, who was getting a drink in the kitchen.

Edgar leaned against the sliding door to the patio. "We need to talk, Adannaya." We all looked at him. Edgar stood there with an amulet hanging from his right hand. "You're the only person I know who can make these."

"No, Edgar, I am not. You know who the other person is."

Edgar's face reddened and he threw the amulet onto the ground. "Philip Pinkerton is *dead!*" The calm rationale I'd always seen on Edgar's face vanished and he snarled, "*I killed him!*"

The shock on Zola's face was plain.

Edgar started to pace in front of the patio door. "I can see it your eyes, Adannaya. You never thought I'd do it. You thought I'd sit back and *watch*. That's all the *Watchers* ever do. Are you really that naïve?" Edgar held up his hands and flexed them into fists. "You who has lived so long? We keep the balance. We destroy what we have to. Pinkerton *can't* be alive. I tore him to *pieces*."

179

"You did that?" Zola looked away and closed her eyes. "Ah saw him, after he died, or at least Ah thought he was dead too. But he's not, Amon. Philip is alive. We fought him tonight."

Edgar stormed over to the fairies' chair. "Cara, *Sanatio* of the Sidhe, by word and ward, is what this woman says true?"

The glare on Zola's face could have lit Edgar's pants on fire.

"Edgar Amon," Cara said. She paused and waited until Edgar started to fidget. "Philip Pinkerton lives. My sons have faced him, the Alpha has faced him, and even the vampires have faced him. You should take care to question my friends lest we put your immortality to the test on my blades." She paused and stared at the Watcher before she said, "By word and ward."

Edgar took a step back and stared at Cara like she'd grown horns.

Foster took the opportunity to let loose a ragged and impeccably-timed snore.

I smiled despite the tension overpowering the room. "Edgar, Philip's not dead. Get over it. You didn't kill him. Whatever you did kill was enough to fool Zola, but Philip's still alive."

Edgar leaned back against the kitchen counter at the edge of the room. "No, he can't be. One of us would have known. How could he have fooled us?"

"Ah don't know," Zola said.

Edgar slid the back door open. "I don't want to believe you, Adannaya. I don't want to believe any of you, but after seeing the wreckage at Cromlech Glen and hearing the word of the *Sanatio* ... I don't know what to think." He stepped outside and started to close the door.

"He's after something, Edgar. He came after Ashley for her soulstones. No good can come of the dark ones with soulstones."

"No, Adannaya, you're right about that. If that devil is still alive, gods help us." Edgar slid the door closed behind him without another word. We all watched him float away and I wondered when we'd see him again. I had a feeling it would be soon.

"I take it you know our illustrious Watcher," Maggie said as she walked into the room with the rest of us.

"Yes," Zola said. "Ah know Edgar. Ah have known Edgar for almost a hundred years."

"Has he always been such a prick?" Maggie said.

Zola laughed. "Yes, he has. Good at taking orders, not so good at improvising." She sighed and rubbed the side of her face. "If Edgar fought Philip, Ah don't think Edgar could actually kill him. He never had that kind of power."

"Perhaps," Cara said. "Philip is powerful, but do not underestimate Edgar. What about a simulacrum?"

"Strong enough to fool me?" Zola said. "No, you'd have to use another soul and ... and ..." Zola's face fell. She put her hands over her eyes. "Oh god, Philip, that's it. That's what he did. That wasn't his body." She looked up with bloodshot eyes. "The traces of soul Ah felt by that body. It wasn't an old ghost at all. It was the souls he tore to pieces to make a simulacrum." Zola's expression was so sour I was worried she was going to vomit.

Nixie shifted under my arm and put her arms around me. "We should all get some rest."

The front door creaked open and I glanced over my shoulder to find Carter in the lead of a mixed pack of bloody, dirty, vampires and wolves. "Nixie's right. We all need rest."

Nixie and I stepped out of the way so Carter could get to Maggie. He wrapped his arms around her and she almost collapsed against him. "I'm so glad you're here." I could barely hear her whisper.

"The door's ruined," Hugh said.

"Where's Haka?" I said.

Hugh smiled. "He's outside taking in the night air. I think he's a little shaken up from the experience. He's never fought a true enemy before." Hugh's smile widened and I swear his chest swelled. I almost missed the tremor of concern that crossed his face. "I put some drop cloths over the bodies in front. The Watchers should take care of the rest later. Someone needs to stay with Ashley tonight."

"I'll do it," I said without hesitation. "You want to stay too, Nixie?"

"Yes, please."

"Good, Ashley's got a guest bedroom. I don't think she'll mind if we stay."

"We're staying too," Aideen said. "I don't think Foster's going anywhere tonight."

"Count me in," Sam said.

I smiled and nodded. "You're not stealing the bed."

"No need." She plopped down in the recliner beside the fairies and leaned back. "Oh yeah, no need at all." Sam laced her fingers over her stomach and took a deep breath.

Carter peeled himself away from Maggie and extended his hand to Zola. "Thank you." He shook her hand and turned to me. "Hugh said he had a good feeling about you, Vesik. I've never been a big fan of necromancers, or vampires for that matter." He cracked a sly grin at Vik who gave a flourish in return. "Consider me pleasantly surprised."

"Thanks, Carter. I never knew how bad werewolves shed."

Carter blinked a few times and then broke into a deep laugh with Hugh and the rest of the room.

We found a plastic tarp in Ashley's hall closet. Sam and I tied it over the missing door after she washed her face and arms off in the kitchen sink. We also added a blanket to help insulate the air conditioning. The Watchers still hadn't shown up and I didn't want the gory front room to start smelling any worse than it already did. I gave one last yank on the twine looped around the porch light and nodded. When I ducked back inside, Sam was staring at the bloody carpet.

"Hungry?" I said.

Her irises were almost gone when she turned to me.

"I'll take that as a yes."

She closed her eyes and took a deep breath. "No, I'm fine. The smell just makes me a little munchy. Nothing I can't put off until tomorrow."

"Well, if you need to kill something, I can always call Frank."

Sam laughed and punched me in the arm. "Stop it. You know you like him."

I held my finger across my lips. "Shhh, that's a secret." We both laughed. I put my arm around Sam's shoulders and walked her to the kitchen. "I'm hungry. Let's raid Ashley's fridge." My voice turned into a whisper as we got back to the living room. Zola was already asleep on one of the recliners. Aideen and Cara were both out cold on top of a throw pillow. Foster had one arm dangling over the edge of the chair, still snoring like a train.

Sam giggled as we tiptoed into the kitchen. "Where's Nixie?"

"She said she was going to take a bath." I could hear the water running on the other side of the house and the quiet tick of an old cuckoo clock on the wall across from the kitchen sink.

"Oh, that sounds like a fantastic idea. You think Ashley will mind?"

I almost laughed. "No, no I don't think she will, but I'm taking a shower first, dammit. You always were a hot water hog." I opened the fridge and was flabbergasted at the selection of fresh fruit and vegetables mixed in with steaks and bundles of herbs. "I think Ashley's just going to be happy to be alive, Sam."

Sam made an excited squeak when she opened the pantry. "Oreos!" she hissed.

"Sweet. I'll get the milk." I pulled the glass bottle of milk out and set it on the kitchen table.

Sam pulled one of the straight legged chairs out and sat down. I dug out a glass and poured the milk. I started to sit down when Sam said, "Put the milk away. It's one thing to ruin your own milk, but–"

I held up my hands in surrender and put the bottle of milk away. I pulled two colas out of the fridge and sat one by Sam. She punched the can open with her fangs and grinned when I raised my eyebrows. "Dominic showed me how to do it. Cool, huh?"

"It's, well, it's different."

"You're just jealous." Another Oreo met its doom. She spoke through a full mouth of chocolate and cream. "It's even better with beer bottles."

I shook my head and held a cookie in the milk until it started to dissolve. "And if you break your fangs off?"

"They grow back pretty quick."

"So you'll just drink blood through a crazy straw in the meantime."

Sam's eyes widened and she swallowed her mouthful of cookie. "That's a *brilliant* idea!"

I heard the water shut off as I shook my head. "I think Nixie's done. I'm going to hop in the shower real quick. You mind?"

Sam waved her hand. "Not at all. I have Oreos."

I smiled and tiptoed past the fairies to the back hallway. I tapped on the bathroom door.

"It's open," Nixie said.

A wall of steam met me when I cracked the door open. Nixie was wrapped in a towel and was working another through her hair.

"How you feeling?" I said.

"Better. Water always helps, even though you humans like to put a lot of chemicals in it." Nixie reached behind me and closed the door. "Go ahead and hop in. I won't look." Her lips quivered while she tried to hide a grin.

She did, of course, and I felt a ridiculous blush run over my face. Thankfully I was well hidden in the water by then. I stuck my dirty clothes in the bottom of the shower in the hopes of getting some of the grime off. I sighed and scrubbed the dirt and blood off of my body in the hot water.

"What happened tonight, Nix?"

"Philip and Zachariah. They tricked us, got Cara, me, and Aideen to chase them into the woods. We killed a few in the trees. But that's all the time they needed. When we got back to the house you were already there, Maggie was hurt, and Ashley. You know. It was bad." I heard the towels rub together in rapid bursts.

"It wasn't your fault, Nix."

"I know. I just wanted to help. I should have seen the lie before Ashley got hurt. Guess I'm losing my edge on dry land."

I laughed and rinsed the soap out of my hair. "You're not losing your edge, and you did help. Everyone's alive, we should be extremely happy about that."

"Yes, but the dark ones are alive too."

"Not all of them," I said.

Nixie laughed. "That's true. It was invigorating."

I peeked around the shower curtain. "Invigorating, eh?" I said in the deepest voice I could muster.

Nixie grinned and hung the dripping towel back on the chrome rack. "You should hurry to bed."

"Oh really?" I said.

"Oh really," she said as she opened her towel and arched her back.

I was very thankful for the little traction ducks Ashley had stuck all over the tub. I gaped at Nixie's porcelain body.

"I'll be waiting." She smiled, wrapped a drier towel around herself, and slipped out the door.

"Oh god, I'm too tired for this," I said to myself. Other parts of myself disagreed. I rinsed off and wrapped a couple towels around me so I wouldn't drip too much water across Ashley's house. I turned the exhaust fan on as I left the bathroom and went to tell Sam the bathroom was open.

I found her in the kitchen with half a bag of Oreos demolished. "Shower's open," I said.

"Great, thanks. Is there any hot water left?"

"Yeah, I made it a pretty quick one. You still alright? You did some serious Oreo damage there."

She nodded as she stood up. "I'm fine. Sleep well, Demon."

"Thanks. You too."

She disappeared into the back hallway. I got a glass of water and headed back to the guest bedroom. Nixie was tucked firmly beneath the comforter until I closed the door behind me. When she threw the covers back she was completely nude and crooked her finger at me. I smiled, dropped my own towel, and joined her.

CHAPTER 20

I heard the quiet knock at the door. I glanced at the alarm clock's green face. Green? For a moment, I'd forgotten I wasn't home. I expected to see the blood red face of my own clock. The horror of the previous evening was blessedly distant, but it all came rushing back in a second.

"*Damian.*"

I smiled when I recognized Sam's loud whisper.

"What's up?" I glanced at the alarm clock again. "It's 8:00 in the morning. Good lord."

"The Watchers came. You have to see this."

I sat up on the edge of the bed and rubbed my hair. I wrapped a cold, wet towel around me and joined Sam in the hall. "Let me grab my clothes real quick."

She rolled her eyes as I turned down the hall to the bathroom. My clothes were still damp, slung over the towel rack, but wearable. I came back to Sam and followed her through the living room and into the hallway. It didn't look like Foster had moved all night. He was going to have a stiff neck when he got up. Zola didn't even budge as I walked out the other side of the living room. She must have been wiped out. I remembered when I was training with her, I couldn't even tiptoe to the outhouse without waking her up. I'd always had a healthy respect for modern plumbing after having to use an outhouse in three feet of snow.

"Holy shit," I said as my eyes took in the renovations. It didn't even look like the same house. The front room was completely cleaned out, and the splinters of the coffee table were gone, along with the bloody carpet and the broken couch. The tarp and blanket we'd hung over the doorway were gone too. Instead there was a slick black six-panel door, a fully intact wall, new carpeting, a new coffee table, and a new low-profile leather couch. "They even replaced her furniture?"

"I know. It's crazy," Sam said. "They even upgraded her furniture. Normally they just get rid of the bodies."

"I'll have to thank Eddie next time I see him. I wonder if this has something to do with Zola being here, or if it was that little argument they had." I could smell the fresh paint. "This is crazy."

"Yeah, I already said that."

I glanced at Sam and smiled. "Well, whatever the reason, I'm glad. It'll help Ashley out a lot."

Sam sat down on the couch and crossed her legs on the coffee table. "What now?"

"We have other things to take care of too."

Sam raised an eyebrow.

"You remember the little ghost Foster and I, um, inherited last year?"

Sam nodded.

"Well, she's a demigod now."

"*What?* How? She was human."

I told Sam everything. I told her about Vicky's old name, Elizabeth, and her detachment from it. I told her about Elizabeth's murderer, and about the vision she'd given Foster of another abuser. I told her everything except who granted Vicky her powers. Even though I wanted to tell her, Zola's warning stayed strong in the back of my mind.

"Christ, you have to tell her parents, Damian."

I sighed and ran my hand through my hair. "I've thought about it. Where do I even start?"

"You let them talk to their daughter. She's still Elizabeth too."

I nodded and let my eyes trail over Ashley's snow globes, most of which had been spared destruction.

"Are you going to go after him?"

I didn't have to ask her who she meant. "I'm sure we will. It'll probably be pretty high on Foster's to do list when he wakes up. Apparently he's met the guy before — one of Colin's friends."

A small frown crossed Sam's face. "Colin ... he seemed like a good guy."

"Yeah, he did. I would have died last year if it wasn't for him."

"I remember. You got royally pounded by one of those demon puppets. I know the fairies are great healers, but it still scared the hell out of me."

"*You?*" I laughed a little. "Scared the hell out of me too. It didn't feel too good either." I dropped down on the couch opposite Sam and put my feet up on the table beside hers. "I see your feet are still freakishly large."

She tucked her feet under the coffee table before smacking me in the face with a throw pillow. "You're an ass."

"Only on Tuesdays."

"It's not Tuesday."

"Oh," I said as my eyes wandered over the rebuilt room. I had a hard time reconciling it with the disaster from the previous night. "So, are you staying for breakfast?" I pointed at the window and said, "The sun's coming up."

"Yeah, I'll stay until Ashley's up at least." Sam laid her head back on the couch and smiled. "They haven't completely broken me. I'm not as paranoid as all the old vamps yet."

"Mmm, *yet*."

We both laughed and relaxed on the couch until we heard footsteps in the kitchen fifteen minutes later. I heard the fridge open and close and the quiet crack of a pan on the glass stovetop.

"Who's up?"

I shrugged and stood. "Let's find out." I saw Zola first, she was staring into the kitchen with wide eyes and a small smile. She glanced at me and then pointed into the kitchen.

When I stepped around the corner I found Ashley bedecked in flannel duck pajamas. Her mass of strawberry blonde hair was pulled back with a duck hair clip and she was cracking eggs into a yellow mixing bowl.

"Ashley?" Sam said.

The priestess glanced over her shoulder and smiled. "Hi. I thought I'd make breakfast so maybe I could talk everyone into helping me clean up the ... the ... front room." Her eyes closed and she put both hands on the sandstone countertop. I could see a tremor run through her body as she bowed her head.

Sam moved forward and put her arm around Ashley's shoulders. "There's no need, honey. It's all cleaned up."

Ashley's head snapped up. "What do you mean? It was … my home is wrecked!"

"You might want to go look," I said.

Ashley sped by and I noticed she was wearing duck-themed slippers. I smiled as she came to a halt at the entryway into the front room.

Her hands came up and covered her mouth. "But how?" she said, slightly muffled. She turned back to us. "How?"

"Edgar," Zola said as she shifted on her recliner.

Ashley's eyes were wide as she shuffled back into the kitchen. "I need to thank him. That's just … how did he do that? My home was utterly wrecked."

A half asleep fairy bobbed and weaved into the kitchen and crashed onto the counter in front of Ashley. "Yeah?" Foster said. "If you don't start cooking that bacon, maybe it'll get wrecked again."

Zola snorted a laugh from the other room.

"You're so considerate," Sam said as she sat down at the back of the kitchen table.

Ashley cracked another egg into the mixing bowl along with a weak smile.

I recognized the look Sam gave Ashley. Her eyebrows were pulled together and she looked mad, but she was really just worried.

I heard the bathroom door close in the back hallway.

"Sounds like Nixie's awake," Zola said. She righted the recliner she was in, walked across the floor in her dirty socks, and took a seat at the kitchen table a moment later. "How are you, priestess?"

A small smile etched itself onto Ashley's face. "Thanks to you all, I'm alive. And that's more than I expected." She stared at Foster while he rubbed his eyes. "Thank you."

He waved his hand in a dismissive gesture. "You'd do the same for me." He paused and moved his eyes to the ceiling for a moment. "Well, maybe not *exactly* the same, but you know what I mean."

Ashley nodded as she pulled a wire whisk out of the drawer beside the refrigerator. I heard Aideen and Cara talking before they landed on either of Ashley's shoulders.

"How are you?" Cara said.

"Better, thank you." Ashley didn't even twitch when the fairies landed on her, but when Aideen stepped to the side, Ashley winced.

"Are you hurt?" Aideen asked.

"My shoulder, where I was stabbed."

Aideen pulled the edge of Ashley's collar back. "It's not bleeding, but it looks a little rough. Foster must have missed it." A small glow of white light flashed from Aideen's hands before she let the collar go and glided down to Foster. She settled in beside him.

I thought I heard him say, "Bacon." At that point, I was pretty sure he'd made a full recovery.

Zola moved around Ashley and started laying the bacon in the skillet.

"Tell us what happened," I said.

"Thank you for that," Ashley said as she rubbed her shoulder. She didn't stop whisking the eggs while she talked. "The necromancers came here." Her eyes locked on the swirl of yellow in the mixing bowl. "They broke the door down. Cara and Aideen and Nixie attacked them. When they ran, the fairies followed. Nixie was right behind them."

"I drowned the first one in the front yard." I glanced up to find Nixie with the most fantastic bed head I'd ever imagined, like the spray of Niagara Falls modeled in hair. I was admiring her jeans and t-shirt when what she'd said registered.

"You drowned one?" I said.

"With the water in the frog fountain, yes." She pulled out the chair between me and Sam and sat down.

"That fountain isn't even big enough to fit a head in," I said.

"I used the water. I didn't say how." She leaned over and kissed my cheek. "Let Ashley finish her story."

I shook my head and looked back to Ashley. "Sorry, go on."

She picked up like we hadn't interrupted her. "As soon as they were gone, another man appeared at the front door. He wasn't very tall, I just remember thinking he had a round head and it was weird how his forehead kept his eyes in shadows all the time. I don't remember much else about him."

"You don't need to," Zola said. "It was Philip." She slapped the last two strips of bacon into the skillet with a vicious flick of her wrist. The room started to smell fantastic as the meat sizzled and popped.

Ashley glanced at Zola and went back to her whisking. "Okay, well, while I was talking to Philip, someone else grabbed me from behind. I never saw him. I don't know how he got in the house. I just felt my shoulder burn. I didn't realize I'd been stabbed at first. They wanted the soulstones." Ashley made a hollow sound I almost didn't recognize as a laugh. "I didn't even *know* they were soulstones. The guy I didn't see hit me again and I saw him. His right arm was a mass of red scars, like he'd been glued together. Then two more came in ... and then my leg." She started to shake. "They got the smaller stone."

Zola took the mixing bowl out of Ashley's hands and set it to the side. She patted Ashley on the back. "Sit down, girl. There's no reason for you to cook for us. Sit down."

Ashley sat as she wiped tears out of her eyes. "The other soulstone is hidden. We have an old witch who keeps some of the older traditions alive. She lights a protection candle for the stone every day and whispers something else from her book of shadows. I don't think she knows it's a soulstone, but she knows it's special."

"A curse of keeping," Zola said. "You have to have a very pure soul to cast such a spell over a soulstone. Not even a dark necromancer would be able to sense it."

Ashley nodded. "I was barely conscious when Maggie showed up. I just remember thinking, 'Is that a werewolf? *Really?*'"

"I know that feeling," I said.

"Maggie saved me. You all saved me, but she tore the last two guys to pieces. I remember a rush in my tummy, like a rollercoaster. I was so happy to see them die before I had to die. Then another wolf came in."

"Ah think that was Haka," Zola said. She dumped the eggs into another pan. I saw her toss some spices in, but I couldn't tell what they were.

Ashley nodded. "He got his hands on Philip. I saw him wrestle the bastard through the door. The other necromancer followed Haka and

Philip. Maggie chased them both outside. She came back a little later with her arm all mangled. I couldn't really breathe then. I heard crackling sounds in my chest and it felt like sucking air through a straw. And then you were here. And Foster saved me." Tears ran down her cheeks. "Thank you, again. I can't say it enough."

"Yes, you can," Foster said. "You already did."

Ashley laughed and wiped her eyes.

"Where're your plates, Ash?" Sam said.

"Up here." She stood up and opened one of the arched cabinets to reveal an unnaturally large selection of Fiesta ware.

Sam pulled down six plates and set them around the table. She opened the pantry in the corner and grabbed a loaf of bread, some peanut butter, and napkins. Ashley dug around in the fridge for some jelly, shredded cheese, orange juice, and a huge bottle of Crystal Hot Sauce.

Zola saw her pull the hot sauce out of the fridge and her eyes widened. "Oh, bless you girl. Bless you."

Sam laughed as she set glasses out for everyone.

Zola grabbed a large plate and slid the bacon onto it, grease and all. The eggs came off next. A hint of cloves and paprika hit me as she put a huge bowl on the table along with the bacon. Sam slid back into her chair as Zola sat down. Ashley finished filling the glasses with orange juice before she joined us.

"Baconbaconbacon!" Foster clapped his hands together when Sam pulled a strip of thick-sliced bacon over to a small plate for the fairies.

"Damian, be a dear and pass us a small piece of potato bread, would you?" Cara said.

"Mmmph," I said through a mouthful of buttered bread and put a piece beside the bacon for them.

Zola dropped her bread into the bacon grease before she built a sandwich on it. She scooped up some eggs and dropped them into a bowl.

"Here comes the soup," I said.

Sam started to laugh and almost sprayed a mouthful of orange juice across the table as Zola picked up the bottle of Crystal Hot Sauce and proceeded to drown her eggs with it.

"I want to try that," Nixie said as she piled her hair behind her back.

Ashley just stared as Zola held the bowl out to Nixie and Nixie scooped up a spoonful of eggs and hot sauce. I never really thought Crystal sauce was hot, but my nose curled up at the sheer volume of it in Zola's bowl.

Nixie apparently had no issue with it. She closed her eyes and practically moaned as she devoured the soupy eggs.

Sam laughed and slapped the table. The wood groaned. She gave Ashley an apologetic look as she said, "Wow, that reminds me of our mom and chocolate."

The vision of Nixie moaning was suddenly replaced by our mother and I twitched. "Oh, dammit, Sam! Never, never, *never* compare anything my girlfriend does to Mom. That's just *wrong*." I shivered and grimaced.

Everyone laughed. Aideen was hiccupping in hysterics. I didn't realize why until I looked at Nixie. Her eyebrows were stretching for the sky. "Girlfriend?"

"Ah ... that is ... I ..." A blush warmed my face and I hunched down over my eggs and bacon. "Gee, Ashley, these sure are good eggs."

Everyone laughed at me again.

"I have a question, Zola," Sam said as she bobbed her fork up and down between her fingers. "Why did the Watchers fix up Ashley's house so well?"

"Ah can only guess that was Edgar. He has trouble admitting he's wrong, but usually makes up for it in interesting ways."

"You think he fixed my house out of guilt?" Ashley said.

"Perhaps. Edgar is hard to know. Ah never would have suspected him of trying to kill Philip. Edgar is the Watcher that decided to let Philip and I live, despite our pasts. He gave us a second chance, and Ah will always give Edgar the benefit of the doubt, as he did for me."

"Why is he so hard to read?" I said.

"He is very old. His full name is Edgar Amon." Zola smiled. "He was worshipped as a god in ancient Egypt." Zola's smile turned into a laugh before I could even say anything. "Before you ask, no, he is not a god, but an immortal mage."

"Immortal?" I said.

"Well, so far, yes. He stopped aging on his fortieth birthday. No one knows why. There are a few immortals Ah have known, but none as long lived as Ed." She shrugged. "It's possible he'll age again one day, but it hasn't happened in three millennia."

I patted a stream of bacon grease off my chin and said, "Damn, and I thought *you* were old."

Zola frowned and smacked me with the back of her hand as she leaned against the back of her chair. "You'll be old one day too, boy, if you're lucky." Her lips curled into a thin smile.

"No, I'm pretty sure one of us will kill him well before he's old," Sam said.

Foster cackled like a witch out of a cliché, and then proceeded to choke on a piece of bacon. Aideen slapped him on the back.

"See, you laugh at me and you choke to death. That's not so funny, is it?"

"Yeah, actually it is," Foster said. He coughed a couple times and then took down another mouthful of bacon.

Cara rolled her eyes and took a bite of the small sandwich she'd made for herself.

"What are we going to do now?" I said.

"Oh, that's easy," Foster said. "We're going to find the guy that molested and murdered Vicky and cut his fucking balls off."

Ashley's fork clattered against her plate and she stared at Foster.

The fairy continued to take bite after bite out of the bacon slice that was bigger than he was. Perfectly normal breakfast conversation.

"Okay, and after, um, that little task?" I said.

"Then we go to Stones River, full chisel and loaded with forty dead men," Zola said. "We go ready for war."

"Forty dead men?" Ashley said.

"That's Zola-speak for armed to the teeth," Sam said.

"War?" I'd never heard her use the term about any of the battles we'd been in.

"Philip is going to try to resurrect Prosperine," Zola said. "He can do it without you if he has the soulstones."

"What?" Ashley said. "Prosperine? The Destroyer?"

Zola nodded. "We have to stop him."

"What kind of maniac would want to resurrect a god of destruction?"

"I thought Prosperine was just another demon," I said. "A badass demon, yes, but we just killed a demon last year. Permanent like."

"Not permanent, necessarily." Zola sighed and rubbed her forehead. "Some days Ah'm ashamed to call you my student." She cracked a small smile.

"Yeah, Prosperine's just a demon," Foster said. "Like a tsunami's just a wave."

"Watch it, *bug*. I didn't know that either," Sam said.

Aideen laughed and elbowed Foster in the ribs. Foster's chewing slowed and his swallow was deliberate. He glared at Sam for almost ten whole seconds before he burst into laughter.

"She's real?" Ashley said.

"Prosperine?" Zola said. "Yes. She is as real as any of us. Ah've seen enough to think there are many more demons than we have names for."

"So what makes Prosperine so great?" I said.

"She is an arch demon," Ashley said. "Every terrible story you've ever heard about demons can't add up to the terror and brutality of a single arch demon."

I pursed my lips and frowned.

"She's right, of course," Cara said. "Arch demons are said to have killed the old gods. And the ones they couldn't kill, they dragged off into other dimensions, other circles of hell."

"Not all of them," I muttered.

Zola flashed me a grimace, then shrugged.

"What was that?" Sam said as her eyes roamed from me to Zola.

"Nothing, nothing," I said. "So, how do we keep Philip from resurrecting, reviving, or whatever, Prosperine?"

"Cut his balls off," Foster said.

I set my fork down and stared at the fairy. "Good god man, you're on a serious ball cutting kick."

Ashley laughed as she was taking a gulp of orange juice. It sprayed over her plate, soaking her eggs, and Sam.

"Oh, I'm so sorry!"

The rest of us burst into laughter.

"Hey, Sam, you got a little something," I rubbed my finger on my cheek, "right there." Nixie jumped when Sam growled at me.

"Enough," Zola said. "How do we stop Philip's cult? We know where he is. Ah don't think he'll have enough soulstones to bring Prosperine onto our plane, but Ah could be wrong. We need to act fast. Ah'll talk to the wolves. Sam, can you talk to Dominic today? And get some volunteers together for an attack tomorrow night?"

Sam nodded.

"Tonight, we should rest. Ah'm still weary from last night, but Philip and his survivors likely are too. If luck is on our side, they'll still be exhausted tomorrow."

"And if there actually are dozens of them?" I said.

"Then we have a war on our hands."

"Super."

Nixie squeezed my leg and polished off her eggs in two quick bites. "I want to help."

"It may be more dangerous than anything you're used to," Aideen said.

Nixie's eyes darkened and the creepiest laugh I'd ever heard came out of her thin smile. "I doubt that very much."

Foster raised his eyebrows as he shoved another piece of bacon in his face.

"Okay, let's get breakfast cleaned up and get moving. I want to run by the store today and spend some quality time with my girlfriend."

"Who? Frank?" Nixie said.

Sam held her hand out and high-fived Nixie, instigating a round of chuckles.

I blew out a long breath and said, "I don't know why I put up with you people." I tapped my chin as another thought occurred to me. "Say, Ashley, I don't think we have a car. You mind driving us back to the shop?"

For some reason, everyone found that rather amusing.

CHAPTER 21

W e dropped Zola off at Carter's house before we went back to the shop. It was a lot more comfortable in Ashley's Prius once there were only four adult-sized people in the car.

"I call couch," Sam said as she stumbled over a cobblestone. She'd been dragging her feet as we walked the short distance from the car to the shop.

"Didn't get much sleep, huh?" I said as I turned the key in the deadbolt and waved to Ashley. The lower deadbolt whined as it saw my boot headed for its face. I pushed the door open and stood to the side. Sam still had her eyes on the sidewalk when Bubbles leapt. Sam squeaked when the cu sith hit her mid-chest and took her to the ground with a thud. Bubbles's ears were draped over the side of Sam's head and the cu sith's tongue was a bright pink weed whacker on Sam's face.

Peanut sauntered to the door and sat his butt down right in the doorway.

"Hey boy," Foster said. Peanut's face vibrated as he growled. Foster landed by the cu sith's paw anyway. "Hungry?" Peanut jumped to his feet and shot back into the shop.

"I'll get him some food," Nixie said. She scratched Bubbles's head and slid in through the back door.

I heard Sam groan and I laughed. I leaned over and picked Bubbles up before staggering under the weight. "Gah! How much do you weigh now, girl?" A sloppy tongue bath was the only response I got. I waddled into the shop with Bubbles in tow and set her down beside Peanut. Both pups stared at Nixie while she dug through the fridge.

Sam was still on the ground when I walked back outside. I grinned and offered my hand. "All your vampire friends are going to think you're weird, lying out in the sun like that."

She raised both her hands up like a B movie zombie. "Just drag me to the couch." She started laughing when I grabbed her wrists, dragged her across the asphalt, up the step, and into the back room of the shop.

"Alright, you have to get on the couch yourself. I think Bubbles threw my back out."

Sam pulled herself up to one knee and then flopped across the old couch. "Ah, the green monster. I haven't slept on this in a while." She yawned and rubbed her eyes. "Wake me when it's over."

I checked the time on the grandfather clock as the fairies disappeared into it. "You know Frank should be here in like an hour."

"Mmm, wake me when Frank gets here," she said as a small smile curled her lips. "I need a snack."

I left Sam and Nixie in the back with the cu sith feeding frenzy. The sound of giant tongues slurping up everything that came within striking distance followed me to the front of the shop. I unlocked the door and flipped the sign to open before heading to the register. There was a knock at the back door and then a crack of light when Nixie opened it. I was surprised to see Ashley there. She crouched down and scratched the cu siths' ears while Nixie slapped more food in front of the garbage disposals.

Ashley came up front and whispered, "Do you mind if I pick up a few things?"

"You don't have to whisper. A freight train wouldn't wake Sam up."

I heard a snort from the back room.

"It's all yours for the browsing," I said. I watched Ashley walk to the other side of the register and pick up a small wicker basket. "What's that?"

"Oh, you haven't seen them?" She smiled and held it up higher. "I told Frank he should get some shopping baskets. They've been here for a week or so."

I walked behind the counter and leaned over the side of the display cases. Sure enough, there was a small stack of five wicker baskets. "Cool, I never thought about that. I guess most of my customers only buy a handful of stuff."

"Not me," she said as she piled in a bundle of bramble leaves, bramble thorns, dried figs, and damiana. I cocked an eyebrow at the damiana.

"Got a hot date?"

Ashley grinned. "Maybe. That's none of your business."

I gestured at the basket. "Actually, it does seem to be my business."

She rolled her eyes and moved down the aisle. I laughed and turned my attention to the laptop beside the register. Frank had replaced our ancient cash register with a real-live inventory system. My eyes widened when I looked at the month's totals.

"Go Frank," I said. I'd made Frank my gemstone buyer last year. It was probably the best business decision I'd ever made. I could actually afford Frank's salary now.

I glanced into the glass display case below the laptop and smiled. A few more of the old obsidian arrowheads had sold. I wondered if Hugh had told someone about them. Frank had a new piece of metal in the case too. It took me a moment to realize it was Magrasnetto, as the sharp edges and oblong shape were far from the norm.

A thump caught my attention when Ashley dropped a candlestick on the hardwood floor. She blushed and set it back on the shelf. Her basket was almost full as she made her way to the gemstone display.

"Frank said he was getting some more moss agate. Do you know if it came in?"

"Should be in the third drawer down on the right if it did."

I heard one of the dark wood drawers slide open. "Perfect!" Ashley said. "Maybe just one more piece of amber too." Ashley was our best amber customer by far.

"You still making jewelry out of that stuff?"

She sighed. "If you mean *protection charms*, yes."

"It does make nice jewelry."

Ashley shot me a look and I gave her a wide smile.

The front door jingled and we both looked up when Frank walked in and waved to Ashley. He was wearing a fabulous brown bowler that I recognized from one of our previous ... adventures. It was an excellent mask for his graying baldness. Sam thought it looked dignified. I kind of thought it looked funny, especially with the plaid shirt. I watched him walk, his usual bouncing gait making him look peppy, and shook my head.

"Hey Damian, what are you doing here so early?"

"I've been up since eight this morning."

Frank's bushy eyebrows crawled up his forehead. "*You?*"

I nodded.

"The world is ending."

"Frank, you look even thinner than the last time I saw you," Ashley said.

Frank grinned and his arm ran down his stomach to his belt. "Thanks Ash. I've been trying."

"Well, it's working."

I tapped the top of the laptop. "I saw the numbers Frank. They're fantastic. I don't think the shop has ever done this well."

"I don't want the place to go out of business," Frank said. "I'm out, and want to stay out, of my–" his eyes flashed to Ashley and back to me "– you know."

"Yep," I said. Frank used to run with a very bad crowd before he tried to adopt the retail life. He was, more or less, a small time arms dealer with his father until the whole thing went south. His dad didn't make it out alive. I knew it, he knew it, and even Sam knew it. Frank wanted out of his old life and he'd been enough of a friend to me that I wanted to help him out. Although giving him a job hadn't been my first choice. "Oh yeah, Sam's waiting for you in the back."

"Really? It's daylight."

"She's weird like that."

He smiled and almost skipped into the back room. I heard a muffled cry before I made out, "Ugh, wet!"

I heard Nixie laugh and was pretty sure Frank had just gotten a faceful of Bubbles. Nixie came up front and set her butt on the counter beside me. "Sam's snacking. I think I'll stay up here for a while."

"Out in the open?" I said. "Good god, I guess she was hungry."

Ashley set her basket beside the register. "Okay, I think I'm done."

I tried to be delicate, but just threw the question out there. "You going to be alright going back home?"

Ashley paused and frowned for a bit. "I think so. Some of the coven is coming over. Plus, I mean, I don't have any more soulstones, so you don't think they'll come back, right?"

"That's Zola's assessment." I unloaded everything and started ringing up her treasure trove. "I'm sure she's spot on about the necromancers, but I don't really know about the werewolves."

"It's the wolves that are trying to take Carter's pack, right?" Nixie said.

"Yeah," I said.

"I doubt they'd come back for a priestess," Nixie said.

"If that didn't make me so happy, I think I'd be offended," Ashley said with a weak smile.

When I was almost done ringing up the pile, Nixie hopped off the counter.

"Damiana?" she said.

Ashley blushed. "Yes, I'm buying damiana, okay? You people sure are nosy."

I grinned as Ashley paid and hustled to the back door with her brown paper bag in tow. I heard her gasp when she walked into the back room. "Oh, oh god." I could only imagine what she'd walked in on. "That is just *wrong*."

I heard something like a slurp and someone talking with an entire chicken stuffed in their mouth. The back door slammed closed a moment later.

Nixie walked to the doorway and started laughing. She glanced back at me and said, "They still have their clothes on. I've seen worse."

"Don't tell me. Just don't tell me."

***

Nixie and I worked the shop, handling the few tourists that came in before Sam and Frank finally showed themselves. Frank was stumbling around with a ridiculous grin on his face and his bowler cockeyed on his head. Sam had her hand on his shoulder and guided him to the stool behind the register when I stood up. She smiled, her teeth still glazed in red.

I just shook my head. "Vampires. I'll be right back. Frank looks like he's going to pass out." I walked to the back room and dug a bag of Oreos out of the closet and a cola out of the fridge. When I got back up front I said, "Eat these. You'll feel better."

"Nice. Thanks Damian," is what I think Frank said, but it could have been, "Nnnn, thnnn Dmmmn."

"Ooo, dessert!" Sam said. She took down an Oreo in one bite and started feeding them to Frank. When he was looking a bit more coordinated, he took a drink of cola.

"What a rush," Frank said.

"Whatever," I said. "My assistant manager is a vampire whore."

"Hey, he's *my* vampire whore," Sam said.

"Yes I am," Frank said as he put his arm around Sam.

Nixie laughed and put her arm around Sam's shoulders, peeling her away from Frank. "You would have made an excellent water witch, Samantha Vesik."

Sam grinned. "Thanks."

"What?" I said. "Did I just witness that? I will have a ceremony to mark this day in history. Sam, you used to threaten people with death for calling you Samantha."

"That's only because they were *your* friends, Demon."

"Nixie's my friend too," I said.

"Ah, no, you're *her* friend. I'd have to say there's a *distinct* difference."

My jaw hung slack and I held my finger out to Sam, speechless.

Nixie laughed, squeezed Sam's shoulder, and put a terrifying smile on display.

"I'm not sure how I feel about you two getting along."

"Just drive me home before your little brain starts smoking from the effort, okay?"

Nixie, Frank, and the newly arrived fairies burst into laughter.

I sighed and turned to Foster. "God help me, what's up?"

"We're putting the word out today. I want to find that son of a bitch."

"The guy Vicky told us about?" I said.

Foster nodded.

"Oh, we'll do more than find him," I said with a growl. I don't know what expression was on my face, but everyone fell silent. Sam frowned a little and her forehead creased, revealing the concern she didn't voice.

I closed my eyes and took a deep breath. "Foster, you mind looking after Frank? He may be a little low on blood. Nixie and I are going to run Sam home to rally some troops. Or guilt them into helping, whichever comes first."

"He'll be happy to help," Aideen said.

Foster shot his wife a look and then laughed. "Yeah, no problem."

"Thanks, both of you."

We drove Sam to the Pit to take care of business — business being getting some crazy vampires to come with us to Stones River. I was surprised when we pulled up to the old Town and Country home and Zola was sitting on the front steps with Carter and Vik. He gave me his standard two-finger salute as I stepped out of the car.

"Vik, you look like a dead man," I said as I shook his hand.

"Funny as always. Nothing worse than a necromancer thinking he's a comedian."

Zola laughed and leaned against Vik briefly.

"What are you all doing here?" I said.

"I wanted to talk to Vik and Dominic about tomorrow night," Carter said. "Zola, here, is the only one that knows anything about Stones River. Alan's been there, but he doesn't remember much. Too young. Unfortunately, Dominic's out like the dead, so we're not really getting anything done."

"Except enjoying the sun," Vik said with blatant sarcasm.

Nixie laughed and sat down on the other side of Vik. "You enjoy the sun like I enjoy the desert."

"As sure as a man loves wenches and mead."

Zola chuckled. "That's a bit old, even for me Vik."

Vik flashed a smile and leaned back against one of the pillars on the porch.

"Is anyone awake?" Sam said. "I want to talk to them about tomorrow."

"Good luck," Vik said. "I brought it up and half the Pit," he paused and considered his words, "'freaked out' about it not being our business."

"And I'm sure you were all panache when you asked," Sam said.

"Of course, milady."

Sam laughed and shook her head. "Well, I'll give it a whirl anyway. It'll be dark soon enough. I'll talk to Vassili."

Vik's eyes widened. "You mean to ask Vassili? He is, well, I do not wish to criticize our illustrious leader, but he is a bit unstable."

Sam shook her head. "It's an act Vik. It's all an act."

"Some men will kill to sustain an illusion," Zola said. She settled herself beside Nixie on the wide porch and turned to look at Vik.

Vik's gaze lingered on Zola and he nodded before shifting his eyes to me. "You heard your sister. This is her idea. Do not come after me if she ends up in pieces."

"Just don't be here when I get here if she ends up in pieces."

Vik glanced between Sam and me and back again before he sighed. "You are both insane. I have known many unbalanced people, but you are truly insane."

"We try," Sam and I both said at the same time. I stared at my sister and burst into laughter.

"Any luck with the pack, Carter?" Sam said.

"Some," he said. "I was worried Hugh wouldn't want any part of this, but he wants to help. We'll have at least five wolves between me, Hugh, Haka, Alan, and Maggie. The rest of the pack is settling in at Howell Island. I want them entrenched in case things go bad and another pack tries to move in again."

"That's great," I said. "I can't even tell you how much I appreciate it."

"Well, if it helps, and especially if it helps Aideen and Foster, we'll be there. I can't thank them enough for helping Maggie and Ashley. Maggie's quite fond of the Wiccan."

"Yeah, she can grow on you."

Carter smiled and patted Vik on the shoulder as he stood. "I think I'm going to run. Let me know how the recruitment turns out. I'll pick you all up tomorrow morning before we meet at the Double D."

"We're meeting at the shop?" I said.

Carter nodded as he walked to the end of the driveway. "I'll get a van. It should be big enough for twelve or more if we pack in."

Zola and Sam waved to Carter as he drove off in a small blue sedan.

"I like Carter," Nixie said.

I held out my hand and pulled her off of the concrete steps. "Me too. You coming with, Zola?"

"No, Ah have work to do in the archives." She fished a small bundle of blank bronze amulets out of her pocket. "And Ah'm going to help Sam with some bribery."

"How?" I asked.

"By offering them protection against necromancers," she said.

"What would your master say?" I said as I shook my head slowly.

Zola grinned as she stepped toward the door.

"Can we get out of the sun now?" Vik asked. "We are not all as strange as Sam."

"Yeah, come on you wuss," Sam said as she yanked Vik to his feet. "See you later, Damian."

I hugged Sam and then wrapped my arm around Nixie's waist as we turned to leave. "Call me if anything comes up."

"Will do."

CHAPTER 22

"I'm hungry," Nixie said as she propped her feet up on Vicky's dashboard while we drove past Earth City. I couldn't even think of my car's nickname now without thinking about our little ghost—now demigod—and her family.

I took a deep breath. "Yeah, me too. Let's stop and grab something on the way home."

"Some place with beer."

"You're a *great* girlfriend."

Nixie kicked me as I pulled off the highway and onto Fifth Street. We parked across from Trailhead Brewery and walked over the cobblestones on Main Street. We had burgers, beer, and a pile of brewhouse onion rings before we set out for the car again. It only took about ten minutes to make it home from there.

I threw the car into park and we clattered up the bare wood stairs. Nixie and I walked into the apartment and were greeted by my answering machine's flashing red light. I hit the button and listened to the playback while Nixie headed straight for the couch.

"Damian, pick up if you're there. It's Mom."

"No shit, Mom," I said.

She must have waited a good minute before she said, "I guess you're not there. Call me when you get home."

I hit the delete button and the next message started. "Damian, I tried your cell and no one answered. Where are you? Have you talked to Sam? I can't get a hold of Sam either. Call me." Delete. "Damian? Where are-?" Delete. "Dami-?" Delete all. I pounded the button a few times until the answering machine let out a final, agonized, beep.

"Maybe you should call your mom," Nixie said.

I rubbed my forehead and smiled at her. "Maybe you're right. You mind?"

She shook her head and flipped the television on. I watched her melt into the leather and prop her feet up on the coffee table. "How did I ever live without a couch and a television?" The channels started flipping by faster than I could follow.

I laughed, picked up the phone, and dialed my parents' number.

"Hello? Damian?"

"Hey Mom, what'd you need?"

"I couldn't get a hold of Sam. I must've left her fifteen messages and I haven't heard a thing."

Fifteen. I was glad I pounded the delete button on my answering machine into submission. "Sam's fine. Things have just been ... interesting, lately."

"Who died, Damian? You know I hate it when I can't get a hold of you two. Why didn't you call me?"

"Was that one question or two?"

My mom puffed into the phone and the burst of static reminded me of Sam.

"No one you know, Mom. No one you know. We're fine, don't worry." I flopped down on the couch beside Nixie.

"Hi Mom!" she said.

"Who was that?"

"Ah, just a ... *friend?*"

"Damian Valdis Vesik, you need to keep your pants on. Samantha told us all about you and that vampire, Martha."

I groaned and Nixie burst into laughter. "You heard that?" I said, mortified as I looked at Nixie with my eyes wide.

Nixie nodded between hysterical gasps for air. She leaned up against the arm of the couch and threw her legs over my lap while she was still laughing.

"That was *Mary*, Mom, but please, can you never, ever, *ever*, say anything to me about that again? Let's try to avoid further emotional scarring."

"You're mad, I can tell by your tone of voice. Don't you remember anything your father taught you?"

I smacked my hand over my face and took a deep breath. "Yes, Mom, I remember all about tone of voice, and body language, and no, I'm not mad. I swear. Are you feeling okay?" I glanced at Nixie and her lips were pressed into a thin, trembling line.

"You're sure you're not mad?" she said, completely ignoring my question.

"Yes, is Dad around?"

"I think he's painting your room."

"Mom, it's not my room. I never even lived with you guys when you were in Florida, much less when you moved back."

"You know what I mean. The second bedroom's always yours and the third is Samantha's. And speaking of Samantha, have her call me, will you? If she's not too busy biting people?"

"Alright Mom. Can you get Dad for me?"

I heard her walking down the hall and knocking on the wall like it was a door. "Honey, it's Damian. Can you talk?"

"Sure." There was a rattle and static as my dad took the phone. "Hello?"

"Hey Dad, what's up with mom? She sounds, ah, a little strung out."

He laughed and took a deep breath before his deep voice took on a slow, steady rhythm. "Yeah, the doctor's got her on some new medication for her reflux. I think it's ranitidine." I heard a door close on the other end of the phone and my dad whispered, "She's driving me nuts this week. I can take a lot, lord knows, but I think I have my limits."

"Glad it's you and not me."

"Thanks, son. That means a lot."

I laughed and squeezed Nixie's ankle. "That's what I'm here for."

"So, your mother tells me you have a lady friend."

I raised my eyebrows. "Already? She *already* told you that?"

"Yes, she's holding up a piece of paper as we speak."

I heard a door open and slam on the other end of the line.

"I don't think your mother appreciated me relaying that. Anyway, Damian, I hope things go well for you and ..."

"Nixie."

"For you and Nixie. Nixie ... that's an interesting name. She's not a commoner, is she?"

"You're too sharp for your own good old man. Don't tell Mom until she's sane again, alright? I don't want Sam to have to listen to it."

"Not a problem. And don't worry about your mother. I'm taking her to the doctor tomorrow."

"Thanks, Dad."

"So maybe we'll come visit you soon? We're almost done remodeling this old house."

"And Sam?"

"Of course. Of course. I'll talk to you soon, Damian."

"I can't believe you guys bought the same house we grew up in." I shook my head. "I love you Dad."

Nixie's leg stopped bouncing and the phone fell silent.

"What's wrong, Damian?" My dad's voice was darker and the urgency filled me with guilt because all I could say was, "Nothing."

He sighed and said, "I love you too, son. Be careful with your *nothing*."

"I will, and tell Mom too," I said as I hung up the phone and let it clatter to the coffee table.

"You're worried," Nixie said.

"Yeah, I am."

She swung her legs off my lap and scooted up beside me. "Even if the worst happens, you'll be with friends. There's not much more to ask for in the world." She leaned over and kissed me.

I couldn't help but smile.

"Let's watch a movie," she said.

"Really?"

She slapped my thigh and said, "Yes, we never watch movies."

"Alright, I've got a few movies. What do you feel like?"

"Your pick. I'm up for anything."

A few hours later we'd plowed through *Spirited Away*, *Howl's Moving Castle*, and two bags of microwave popcorn. My eyelids felt heavy. The credits started to roll and Nixie clapped her hands together.

"Those were amazing!"

I smiled and put my arm around her. "Two of my favorites, for sure. Sam actually got me hooked on Miyazaki films. She's been watching them since she was like four years old."

"It's getting late. We should get some sleep. You have to get up early tomorrow."

"Yeah, that's going to hurt. You going to keep me up all night again?"

"I think not. And I would like to remind you of the fact Sam kept you awake much longer than I did last night."

I laughed. "True enough. True enough."

Nixie grabbed my hand, pulled me off the couch and led me to the shower. "You need to wash up. You're starting to smell like the dead."

"Ouch."

She kissed me on the cheek and hopped onto the bed. "Hurry back."

After the shower I lay down with the water witch and fell asleep in about four seconds. No nightmares woke me, no dreams at all. Something tickled my nose a few hours later. I rubbed my face and rolled over. I heard a whisper and cracked my eyes open. Nixie's face was about two inches from mine. She was wearing a grin and shaking my shoulder.

I groaned, pulled the covers tighter and rolled over. I could hear her laughing.

"Damian, I have to leave."

I flopped onto my back and looked up at her crystalline eyes. "Where are you going?"

"I have to report back to the Queen."

My eyes shot open and I sat up, almost head-butting her in the process. "What? Why? Where do you have to go?"

"I can't ..." She put her hand on my shoulder. "I'm sorry. I can't tell you."

I grabbed Nixie's hand and kissed it. "Can't we just kill the Queen and be done with it?"

"No, and that is something you have to understand. I'll never truly be done with it. There will always be a Queen, always be the laws."

"Dammit. How long will you be gone?"

"Not long. I can take the rivers to the oceans. I won't be back before you leave for the battle, but I will join you there. I hope to have help when I return."

"Help?" I waited. "You're not going to tell me are you?"

She smiled and kissed me. "No, I'm not." She kissed me again. "Come down to the river with me."

I looked at the alarm clock and groaned. "It's four in the morning."

"Yes it is, so no one will see us. Now come down to the river with me."

"Alright, alright, let me grab some clothes." I threw on a pair of jeans to go with my stylishly wrinkled Totoro t-shirt and hiking boots. I pointed at the ceiling and said, "To the river!"

Nixie laughed and pulled me off the bed. The river wasn't far from my apartment. We walked across the street and down a gentle slope. Nixie led me down the riverbank until we were below one of the bridges. My mind flashed back to the night Foster and I fought Lewis Hood. He was buried under a bridge much like this one. Or was it the very same bridge? I tried not to think about it.

"You have a fabulous apartment, Damian."

"Um, really? I always kind of thought it was a dump. A convenient dump, yes, but still a dump."

Nixie shook her head. "It's so close to the river. I love it."

"You're not biased about that though, right?" I cocked an eyebrow. She laughed and elbowed me.

"Come on." She pulled on my wrist as she waded into the shallows. I watched as her legs grew translucent and the lower half of her body and even her clothes started to look like water.

"That's just cool," I said.

She smiled. "Come in with me."

"I don't really make it a habit to get in the river."

"Are you scared?" Her lips puckered as she let go of my hand and sank further into the river. "I'll keep you safe."

I rolled my jeans up and stepped into the river. "It's warm," I said.

"That's because you're standing in me."

I cocked an eyebrow and looked at the water. "It just looks like water." The warm river rose around me, up to my chest. I felt a pressure on my back like an embrace and then the water receded to my shins, leaving me perfectly dry. "Oh, that's new."

Nixie wrapped translucent arms around me and I could feel her presence press against my consciousness. I caught flashes and pictures of what she was planning on doing.

"You still have clothes on," she whispered.

"So do you," I said.

"Really?" Her clothes shimmered and vanished. Her lower body was translucent and lost in the waters. Her upper body shimmered and faded into a clear, glimmering perfection. I could still see her nipples in the faint light and reached out to caress her waist. My hand slid through her and she moaned.

Nixie melted into the water. I felt a tug on my jeans and I slid into the water as Nixie ripped them and my boxers off before throwing them onto the shore. The waters stayed warm. My shirt followed a moment later as the river grew warmer. Nixie's head surfaced again and she wrapped her arms around me. Her kiss was heavy and I stepped into her shimmering form. She shifted in my arms and I gasped when I felt something hot and slick slide over my groin.

"Is that?"

"Don't talk," she said.

Her body shimmered again and I could see myself inside her as she moved. The alien presence of her mind strengthened and I shivered as she flowed around me. She licked my lips and I couldn't help but return the gesture on her neck and breasts and her own lips, her body formless and firm at once.

We stayed locked together in the moonlight as long as we could. Nixie's face solidified again and I could see the curtain of hair I'd grown so fond of so fast. She smiled and kissed me again.

"I'll miss you Damian Valdis Vesik." She kissed my cheek.

I brushed a thick lock of her hair away from her face. "It's just one day. We'll survive."

Her smile shone in the moonlight as Nixie grew translucent and slid away, into the river. As she disappeared beneath the gentle ripples, the cold water hit me like a brick wall.

"Holy shit!" The passion-filled starlit night suddenly decayed into a freezing cold, somewhat fishy river. I took huge, exaggerated steps toward the shore, sending torrents of river water into the air. I was halfway out of the river when I realized I was still naked. "Holy shit, where're my pants?" I found my jeans a few feet away. There was a series of sucking sounds as I pulled them out of the mud. I cursed again as I pulled the freezing, wet denim over my legs. I found my shirt a few feet from that beside my shoes, but didn't bother to put the mud caked thing back on. God only knows what happened to my boxers.

I climbed back into bed about twenty minutes later, dripping wet from a warm shower and already missing Nixie.

CHAPTER 23

I pried my eyes open at the roar of my alarm clock less than two hours later. I didn't fight it. I just turned the infernal buzzing off and headed for the kitchen. After bouncing my shoulder off the doorframe and grunting in a bleary-eyed haze, I made it to the fridge. I pulled out two Frappuccinos, chugged the first one, and took the second to the couch. The news was on, depressing as hell. I changed the channel and an even more depressing movie was on, then another depressing newscast, and finally a true crime special. "Good god," I said as I turned the television off. I took the Frappuccino to the bathroom and took another shower to get the river water out of my hair. "Going to need to do laundry again," I said to the shampoo bottle. I finished my shower, got dressed in black jeans and a grey t-shirt, and headed to the bookshelves at the back of my living room.

I pulled out the first tome to catch my eye and spent part of the morning reading the old Book of Shadows Frank had gotten his hands on. I'm not normally all that interested in the ramblings of would-be witches, but this book was from a survivor of the Salem witch trials. Toward the middle it began to resemble a diary more than anything else. One passage really stuck with me.

> *I felt terrible placing the blame on Sarah, but it's kept them away from me. We'll leave tomorrow and this place will be no more than an awful memory. I don't dare write John's true name here. I don't want my fate to be his if they discover my secret. He has the horses tied up beneath the covered bridge. If I don't write here again, I will be one with the earth.*

Luckily for the unknown author, there were several more pages with writing, so I'm guessing she made it. I don't know if the Sarah she mentioned was one that died in the trials, but I did remembering hearing the name repeatedly. I'd have to ask somebody. The phone rang a few minutes later.

"Hello?"

"Damian, come to the shop. Foster found him." Zola hung up the phone without saying goodbye.

I didn't have much doubt about who it was that Foster had found. I strapped on the holster for my pepperbox and pulled a black button-down shirt over it. Payback's a motherfucker.

***

Five minutes later the car rattled across the cobblestones on Main Street. I pulled around to the lot in back, hopped out of the car, and slammed the door. I had my keys in the top deadbolt, kicked the bottom deadbolt, and had the door halfway open when Foster shot out through the gap.

"What's in the bag?" he said as I opened the door fully.

"Change of clothes, just in case." I hoisted the small duffel bag over my shoulder and slid my staff through the handles. "How'd you find him?"

"Sent a message out to some of Colin's old friends. They knew who the guy was. They were surprised too. I had to convince Dillon not to kill the guy himself."

"Well, I don't think I'd have been too disappointed if he was already dead."

Foster frowned. "Oh no? You remember that van? You remember what we saw in that thing? What he did to those people? Those kids?"

My brain screamed at me not to think about it even as my memories bubbled to the surface. Bloody pieces of bodies hung from the roof on meat hooks. They were moving slightly from Foster violently breaking open the door. The ceiling and walls were layered with limbs and heads, and I cringed at the memory of saggy intestines draped around the windows. Foster had found her there, pieces of a little girl beneath the detritus of a dozen bodies.

"Yes, I remember." I said as my teeth ground together and my hands curled into fists. After taking a few deep breaths, I saw Carter pull up in a huge, cherry red van. It took a violent bounce as he clipped the curb.

He waved and rolled down the window.

"Is that another rental?" I said.

"Yep, sure is."

"I can't believe they gave you another one," I said, happy for the change in conversation.

"I always buy the insurance, so there's not much they can say when I just tell them I have no idea what happened to the sun roof."

I laughed and shook my head. "Foster and I have some business to take care of."

Carter nodded and hooked his thumb toward the back seats. "Zola told me. How long will you be gone?"

"I'm not sure. Foster didn't tell me where we're going."

"Chicago," The fairy said. "We shouldn't be gone more than a few hours." My eyes widened. "Say, you'll have room in there for a couple dogs, won't you?"

"Sure," Carter said as he glanced at the clock on the dashboard. He froze and then looked at Foster. "What did I just agree to?"

Foster smiled and fluttered to my shoulder.

"Never mind. Just surprise me."

Foster grinned.

"You know, even if you're only gone a few hours, that's no good. We need to leave now if we're going to get to Stones River at nightfall." He tapped the steering wheel and said, "Meet us in Paducah. We'll stop there for a while. Do you know where it's at? Right on the Kentucky side of the river? It's off of, uh, Highway 24, I think."

"I know it," Cara said as she swooped past me and landed on one of the van's mirrors. "I'll be sure we get there on time. There's a passage near the river."

"Good. Meet us at Denny's."

"A passage?" I said.

The rear door slid open to show me Zola, four werewolves, and five unhappy vampires. Actually four unhappy vampires. Sam looked just fine. I didn't recognize the white-haired vampire in the far back, but Mary flashed me smile. Bring on the awkwardness.

"Boy, suck it up," Zola said. "You're taking the Warded Ways."

I started to protest until she held out the hilt of a bladeless sword with dime-sized holes spiraling up the grip at regular intervals. I grinned and stuck the focus under my belt. "You know me too well."

"My friend appreciated the loan very much. He'll be sending you something in the mail."

"Alright, but it's really not necessary," I said.

"Let me take your staff. You won't need it in Chicago."

I shrugged and pulled the staff out of the handles on the duffel bag.

"We'll see you in a few hours."

I nodded and handed the staff over.

"Bye, Demon!" Sam said. Aideen glided into the van, fully armored and golden in the early light. The cu siths bounded in after her and started clawing their way over vampires and werewolves to get to Sam in a chaotic mass of flailing limbs, growls, curses, and barks. Zola closed the door with a laugh. Aideen waved to us from the front window and Foster held the hilt of his sword to his forehead.

I waved back as they started to drive away, tapped the hilt in my belt, and looked at Cara. "So, we really have to take the Warded Ways?"

"Of course, Damian."

I shivered. "Hell, is there no other way?"

Cara shook her head. "Even if you take a flight, you're looking at four hours, with travel to the airports and back. He'll be gone."

"Son of a bitch," I muttered. "If it wasn't ... if it wasn't for Vicky ..."

"But it is."

I nodded once, broke the pepperbox open to be sure it was loaded, grabbed my duffel bag, and followed Cara and Foster. We walked into the back room of the shop and the fairies landed on the grandfather clock.

"We're going through from here," Cara said.

"Here?" I said as my eyes looked around for an invisible power source.

"Through the nexus, dumbass," Foster said.

"The clock?"

"Of course," Cara said. "We can open one of many ways from here, though some destinations would kill you instantly." With her words of encouragement out of the way, she turned to Foster and said, "Do you have the bottle?"

He squeezed the leather pouch on his waist and nodded.

Cara launched herself into the air and looped around to face the clock. She held out her hands, palms flat, and made a triangle with her index fingers and thumbs. I could feel the flare of ley line energy and the electric blue glow edged its way into my sight. I didn't know what she did, but the shimmering rainbow of an oil spill formed an oval before the clock. I stepped to the side and my eyes widened. The oval wasn't in front of the clock, it *was* the clock.

"It's ready," Cara said.

Foster didn't even hesitate. His armor rippled with color as he jumped from the top of the glowing clock and swooped back through the shimmering surface.

"You next, Damian."

I took a deep breath and stepped into the Warded Ways.

It felt like the drop of a big roller coaster at first. My stomach rose up into my throat and my body shook as it was enveloped in the raw Fae energies. Then it started to hurt. It hurt like my feet were being pulled up into my stomach *through* my legs and my entire body was being smashed into my brain. Every pore felt warm and wet and clammy as my head ruptured and turned inside out. Then it was over in a flash of light and crunch of wet pavement. My head was a mass of pain. I managed to roll over and puke onto the ground instead of myself.

Cara came through a beat later and the shimmering glow of the portal snapped out of existence as soon as she was clear.

"Gee, and we get to do that again today." I groaned and sat up. "Don't you ever worry about someone coming through the other way? Showing up in your clock? Showing up in the Double D?"

Cara shook her head. "No, the nexus paths are one way. The only path in the Warded Ways that comes near your shop is down by the river."

The L train rolled by overhead in a rumble of thunder and steel as rain began to beat against the pavement around us. I squinted my eyes while a ferocious headache fought for control of my head. It receded a minute later and I almost managed to stand up. The old black street lamps, mounted two on a pole, were cold in the shade of the elevated tracks.

"Oh god, that sucked. Where are we?"

"Van Buren and Wells. Now get up before someone notices," Cara said.

"Are you alright?"

I looked up to find an elderly man with a crease of concern on his forehead. "Yeah, thanks. I must have tripped."

"Okay, just wanted to be sure," he said with a small smile.

"Thanks, I appreciate it."

The man tipped his hat and walked off beneath the rumble of another train.

"Sometimes I love Chicago," I said. "The people up here are almost always nice." A series of car horns blared out from the intersection. "As long as they aren't driving," I muttered as I rubbed my neck. "Okay, where to."

"It's close. Maybe two blocks. Follow us," Foster said.

Cara and Foster took off fast and I followed after them at a jog. We left the shadow of the L and ran down Van Buren until we came to an overpass. Foster and Cara swooped over the edge and disappeared. I ran up to the guard rail and looked down. Then I cursed. I ran down the entrance ramp to the sounds of more horns and leapt the barrier where the drop was much more manageable. My knees still screamed when I hit the pavement.

I heard the smack of a fist on meat before we saw him in the shadows of the overpass. It was almost a tunnel beneath Van Buren. The deeper parts were hidden from the street. I caught a glimpse of the bastard through a passage that led closer to the river. Foster's wings flared in front of me. The seven-foot fairy punched the weasel-faced man in the throat and he made a horrible, choking sound. I could see a prostitute in the corner where the man had been beating her. The shadows moved in around us, hiding the scene completely, waiting for blood. I glanced at the prostitute again and my stomach churned. I didn't even have to check to know she was dead. Her head hung off the threads of her neck like a dead chicken. She couldn't have been more than sixteen. More rasping sounds came from the man on the street, down on all fours, gasping for breath in a pile of refuse. He never saw us coming.

In my mind I saw his beady eyes and sweaty palms all over Vicky before he helped tear her to pieces ... and I snapped. I grabbed his hair and wrenched his head back, hammering all six barrels of my pepperbox into his eye socket in one savage motion. His body jerked and I almost lost my grip on his hair. He tried to scream. Foster punched him in the throat again, and I could hear a gristly crunch. I watched the terror wash over Elizabeth's killer and wished I could make it last forever.

"Are we silent?" I said.

Cara nodded and flexed her fingers. I could feel the power of her working rolling across the ley lines and swelling up to soundproof our little event.

"Elizabeth sends her regards," I snarled into his ear.

His good eye went wide and there was a brief moment of silence before his head exploded in a thunder of gore. He probably thought it was over, peace in death, but Foster pulled the cork out of the small bottle in his hand and slid the lip into the bastard's remains. It was the sister of the bottle we'd trapped Elizabeth's other murderer in, the last of the dark bottles Cara had made. For the second time in my life, I watched as the aura was pulled out of a body, torn away from the soul which itself was torn asunder and twisted back inside the killer's aura. The golden and blackened mass was shredded and swirled together as the entirety of soul and aura spiraled into the dark bottle.

Foster jammed the cork home and said, "Rest in hell you piece of shit."

I looked around at the blood and chunks strewn over the garbage pile. "Can you bury him here?" I asked.

"No," Cara said. "There's just too much concrete."

"Shit, then what do we do?"

"Leave him," Foster said. "They'll never find a trace of evidence." He turned to Cara and said, "Burn it."

There was a flash of light from Cara's hands as tiny fires took hold in the garbage. "That fire will burn flesh and bone to oblivion. No one will ever know where this man died or who he was. It is as it should be."

I wiped as much gore off my pepperbox as I could, then started stripping out of my clothes. I had them off in seconds and tossed them into the pile of burning garbage. "And that would be why I brought a change of clothes."

"You still have something in your hair," Foster said.

I started to reach for it and caught myself just in time. "I'll stop at a bathroom."

"You didn't need to burn your clothes," Cara said. "When we take the next path the flesh and blood will be absorbed in the transition."

"Now you tell me," I muttered. "Let's get out of here."

I heard a grisly crack and glanced back to find Foster's foot had completely caved in the remnants of the murderer's head. I grimaced, but I didn't say a word. There was *nothing* that bastard didn't deserve.

Foster and Cara stayed in their battle forms for our walk through the city. Cara kept up a misdirection spell so no one would think twice about the blood and nuggets on my arms and in my hair. Foster's hand alternated between flexing on his sword hilt and checking the flap on the leather pouch at his waist.

I didn't pay much attention to how far or how long we walked, thinking instead of Vicky's family—Elizabeth's family—but when I looked up and found the Field Museum I said, "Shit. That was a walk."

"We're almost there," Foster said. "The way is outside Adler Planetarium."

"You know, we really need to come up here for pizza sometime."

"Hell yes," Foster said.

A few minutes later we were standing in front of a tall, silver spiral sculpture, a mad swirl of metal waves and clean curves. Cara ran her hand along the edges and nodded. "This is it. This trip shouldn't be as hard on you as the trip through the Nexus."

"Uh huh," I said. "I'll believe that when I'm not puking my toes out."

Foster laughed and sailed through the shimmering portal once Cara had it open. The misdirection spell faded and two kids pointed at me.

I sighed and stepped through after Foster before anyone else noticed me. My eyes widened, or at least I think that's what widened, when the path didn't feel like I was being turned inside out. I barely even felt nauseous. And then I fell out the other end of the Warded Ways and performed a screaming belly flop from about twenty feet above the Ohio River.

By the time I swam to shore I was dripping water from every fiber of my being. I pulled out my pepperbox and poured water from the barrels. The focus drained through the dime-sized holes in the hilt like a water fountain. Foster and Cara were laughing so hard it didn't look like they were breathing, just twitching.

"Well, I'm glad someone found that amusing," I said as I ran my hand through my hair and whipped the water at the ground. "Oh, look. It's Denny's." I struck out for the restaurant.

"Did you see his face? It was like AHHH!" Foster said as he widened his arms and his eyes, and moved his jaw back and forth.

"I know. It was great. It was *great!*" Cara burst into laughter again as I walked toward the restaurant's parking lot.

CHAPTER 24

I held the door open long enough for Foster and Cara to follow me into the restaurant. It wasn't hard to find Zola. She was pretty obvious with the cluster of werewolves and vampires around her. I couldn't help but chuckle at the mixed up bunch. We didn't even make it to the table before Aideen crashed into Foster and tried to hug him to death. Surprise choked my laugh into silence when I recognized Mike the Demon at the table. He looked up and a wide grin split his face.

"Well, well, if it isn't my favorite necromancer. Where's your water witch? It looks like she exploded all over you."

I smiled, shook my head, and then shook Mike's hand. "She's not mine."

"Yes, the devil's in the details, so I hear."

I wasn't sure if I should laugh, but Zola thought it was hilarious.

A huge, dark hand belonging to an equally huge werewolf came up to greet me as I said, "Hey Alan, thanks for coming."

"You couldn't keep me away. Carter told us what's going on. If this cult gets a bigger foothold in the country, we'll be looking at war. I don't want my kids to see something like that."

"I don't want your kids to see that either. I didn't know you had kids."

Alan nodded. "A boy and a girl. They both have the gift. I have a new understanding of the terrible twos."

"Yeah, I bet," I said. "I guess it's pretty hard to wolf-proof the house."

"You have no idea."

I smiled, nodded to the rest of the table, and pulled up a chair. Sam was arguing with Vik in the corner of the booth. The other vampires were looking around nervously, as if a slayer might to materialize, complete with stake-firing bazooka. I could tell Dominic was trying to be calm, but his eyes flashed around the room every minute or so. I laughed to myself as Zola slid a plate of nachos toward me. "Thanks," I said, and I shamelessly buried my face in them.

Foster skewered a jalapeno with his sword and dragged it through the cheese. "Oh, I love these things."

"Demon Sword," said an unfamiliar voice. "I have not seen a warrior such as you in many years." The voice was thick and Russian.

Foster's cheeks were puffed out, full of jalapeno as he looked up at the newcomer. My eyes followed his and I saw something new.

It was a vampire, the white-haired vampire from the van, but he wasn't like any vampire I'd ever met. He was dead still, entirely unnatural, entirely other. His round features reminded me of my grandfather, like a pure-blooded Russian bear, but just looking at the long, stark white hair framing his pale flesh and black eyes made my aura try to crawl inside me and hide. The man leaked power.

"Vassili!" Sam said. "The wet one is my brother, Damian."

Vik's apprehension of Vassili suddenly made a world of sense and I was baffled as to why Sam had none. I held my hand out and didn't even cringe when the vampire took it. Go me.

"*Privet,* Vesik, ah, it's a good name, yes." Vassili's cold visage fractured into a huge smile and he shook my hand with vigor. I was so shocked I just stared at him.

"I am not as bad as you have been hearing, I am sure."

"No, it's just, ah, it's nice to meet you too."

"Come now, I am certain there is more on your mind. Speak your questions, I am patient."

I saw Vik's head twitch to the side in a tiny warning. I decided to be polite. "Why, that is, why are you here ... sir?"

"I will tell you, so long as you do not call me sir." Vassili smiled and I tried not to stare at his bright white eyebrows. "Do we have an accord?"

"A what?" I said.

"An agreement."

"Oh, sure."

"Good, then I will tell you why I am here. Your master, I have spoken with her on occasion, has promised us an immunity from the necromancers. Such an opportunity, well, I could not pass." He held his hand out and closed it into a fist.

I glanced at Zola. "You're a master of bribery."

She grinned and pointed back to Vassili.

"So, your master, clever as she is, will only grant this gift to those of us helping to kill the dark necromancers. That is why I am here. I wish to have this immunity. You understand, *da*?"

I nodded.

"Excellent!" He crossed his arms and nodded.

The server came by, a small brunette with huge eyes and a thin nose. She stared up at Vassili with a vacant smile. "Can I get you anything else, sir?"

"No, my beauty, but please see to my friends," Vassili said.

The server turned to us and said, "Do you need anything?"

"I could go for a cola."

"Get some chicken strips," Foster said.

"And chicken strips," I said.

She scribbled something on her little pad of paper and said, "I'll be right back with that."

The vampires squished together to give Vassili room to sit down. There was still tension as the wolves and the undead exchanged meaningful glances. That's about as nice as I can put it, but really it was a bit more hostile. Alan's face was wired tight and his eyes were fixed on Vassili.

"Peace, wolf. I do not bite." He paused and frowned before a smile lightened his face. "Well, that is not exactly true, *da*?"

Everyone laughed, even Dominic and Alan. I relaxed more and more as the meal wrapped up. Haka's shoulders deflated and he began talking to Mary. Mary was laughing and kept putting her hand on Haka's forearm. I caught Hugh glancing at the pair at regular intervals and could only imagine what he was thinking. Foster was lying beside a half-eaten chicken strip, groaning with his face smeared in honey mustard.

"We need to leave," Carter said. "If we want to make it to Stones River at nightfall, we need to be on the road soon."

Vassili held two fingers up in the air and beckoned for the server. She almost fell down, she came running so fast. He reached into his pocket and pulled out a money clip. It was stuffed, and the bill on the outside was a hundred. He peeled off two, handed them to the server, and said, "I do not need change, my beauty."

The server didn't even seem to register how much money Vassili had just given her. She just stood there and stared at him with that same vacant smile. I looked. I had to. I raised my Sight and was awed by the control Vassili had of his aura. It didn't flare out and chase everything in the room that was a potential meal like Sam's did. It was focused on the girl, reds and deep blues caressing her aura. I could see the colors shiver along the lines of contact. I shook my head and rid myself of the vision.

"Get some ham steaks, Damian," Cara said.

"What for?"

"Do you want hungry cu siths getting grumpy in a small, enclosed space?"

"Ah, no. Miss? Could we get a few ham steaks to go?"

The server glanced at me and nodded her head. She kept looking back at Vassili as she wandered into the kitchen. She came back out almost instantly with To Go boxes in her hands.

"There is no way they cooked those that fast," I said.

"You think she took someone else's?" Aideen said.

I shrugged and smiled as the server held out the boxes.

"*Dasvidaniya.*" Vassili leaned over to kiss the server's hand and the poor girl looked like she was about to melt.

We all got up and filed toward the front door. Almost every patron in the restaurant stared at us on the way.

"You're quite a charmer, Vassili," Maggie said.

Vassili wore a flat expression as he turned to Maggie. A small smile lifted his cheeks. "Thank you, wolf mother."

Maggie blinked a few times and almost stumbled. Wolf mother was a term of endearment, almost respect, that vampires generally did *not* use.

Vassili scared the hell out of me.

I piled into the van with the werewolves, and the fairies, and the vampires, and the cu siths. I was scrunched between Maggie and Zola. I heard Haka laugh in the far back with Vik, Sam, and Mary. I'm sure Hugh was thrilled. Bubbles laid her claim to Alan's lap. Her green paws were hooked over the back of the second seat and her black nose sniffed at me as we started down the highway.

"Hey, Bubbles. Look what I got you." I held out a small pile of ham steaks. Bubbles's tongue shot out and tested the meat a second before her head followed and snatched the steaks out of my hand. She spun, ham steaks swinging from her jaw, and smacked Alan in the face with them. He grunted as she wriggled up to the front seats and started eating between Carter and Vassili. Dominic held his hand over his face, but belted out a laugh despite his best efforts. Alan shook his head and I caught the edge of a smile.

"You were right, Cara. Good thing I got a lot of ham." I pulled another pile of ham steaks out of a To Go box. Peanut materialized from beneath the seat in front of us, grabbed the steaks, and dragged them to their doom beneath the bench.

Some of the tension seemed to be leaving the group. Enough that I started to doze off as the rhythm of the highway sank in. My eyes shot open when the entire van started laughing.

"What'd I miss?" I said as I rubbed my eyes.

"Nixie, apparently," Mary said. "You kept saying her name."

I think my blush probably came close to turning me purple. "No, that can't be–"

Even Vassili laughed at me from the front seat. "I am impressed, Vesik. Sleeping on the cusp of a battle? You have strong guts."

"Or a weak brain," Sam said, eliciting another round of laughter.

"Face it, D. You've got it bad," Foster said.

"You know what a mess it would be?" Maggie said. "Dating a water witch? The girl is born to kill." This from a werewolf.

"What am I supposed to do about that?" I said. "I can tell her she doesn't have to, but she says there are rules, laws even."

"Nothing," Hugh said. "You do nothing. You can only accept her ... but I have seen her change much in recent days."

Zola's laugh caught my attention. "Damian," she said. "Damian, Hugh is right. Nixie's bloodlust is almost lost. Do you know why? Do you know what can break an undine's nature?"

I shook my head.

"Nixie doesn't want to kill anymore because she's falling in love with you," Cara said. "I think it started when she saved Haka."

Haka didn't comment. Mired in a conversation with Mary, I doubt he'd heard Cara.

"You aren't a weekend fling for her," Cara said. "Her nature is being fundamentally torn apart. She is questioning everything she knows. To be honest, I don't know if *you* can come out of it unchanged, never mind her."

"You really think she loves him?" Maggie said, leaning forward to glance between Zola and the fairies.

"Oh god, can we talk about something else?" I said.

Zola chuckled. "For some strange reason, yes. She seems quite attached to the boy."

"She's not even *human*," Sam said.

"Neither are *you, da*?"

Sam glared at Vassili and he just laughed.

"Neither are most of the people in this van," Carter said.

Zola smiled. "There was a time we couldn't have been in this van together."

"Hell, three days ago we couldn't have been in this van together without killing each other," Alan muttered.

"Ah mean more than that," Zola said. "Not just werewolves and vampires, fairies and necromancers, but black skin, white skin, red, brown."

"What does it matter?" Mike said. "Human. Fae. The difference is not so great. Everyone bleeds. Everyone dies."

"*Da*, I remember Zola," Vassili said. "My first Pit, they said you were dirtying your fangs if you feasted on more ... exotic fare."

"Ah remember too," Zola said. "But now, this is a better world. An open world, not like the one Philip wants to bring about. Ah will stand against him until Ah'm dead, or he is."

"We all will, Zola," Sam said. Even Vassili nodded in agreement.

"Once Ah would have let it burn, let everyone die, and it wouldn't have mattered to me. Ah would have felt nothing." She wrung her hands around her knobby cane. "Now ... now Ah would die to stop him."

"So would everyone here," Carter said.

"*Da*," Vassili said. "Undoubtedly."

***

We'd been on the road for almost an hour when Mike the Demon broke the silence.

"I always was a sucker for a love story," he said.

We all stared at him. The van drifted in the lane a bit as Carter's eyes locked onto the rearview mirror. His eyebrows were almost raised to his hairline.

"Really?" I said with half a snort before Aeros's story came back to me. Mike had sworn an unbreakable oath on the Smith's Hammer to never kill an innocent. If he did, the power in the hammer would destroy him. And he'd done it all for the love of a necromancer. "Really?" I said in a much more subdued tone.

"Yes, and I think I know something that can help you," he said. "I'm sure Nixie told you fire demons used to kill undines on sight."

I nodded.

"There are ... arts ... that can kill any undine. Even the Queen of the water witches. You already have the tools you need."

"What do you mean? I don't use fallen arts."

"Perhaps, but you see Damian, you already have the *tools* you need," Mike said again. "I know who wrote the Book of Shadows you've been reading."

"What?" I said, unable to keep the surprise from my voice.

Mike nodded. "I sold it to Frank because I knew it would end up in your hands. It's safer in your hands than mine. Hold the book upside down and speak the incantation, *Aperio tectus veneficium*."

"What is that?" Zola said. "It is not a fallen art."

"No," Mike said, "It will reveal a fallen art, though not one as dark a one as you think. One capable of killing an undine. One that does not require you to harm an innocent to kill the corrupt."

"How do you know that?" I said.

"Because I wrote it."

Zola and I both almost gasped in surprise.

"I wrote it as a last resort. In case the undines came for me. The first half of the book, which I'm sure you've read by now, was written by a necromancer I knew long ago. She was a witch for several years before she realized her true potential. The hidden text was written by my hand. Didn't you wonder how a book hundreds of years old looked new?"

I grimaced and Mike laughed.

"I'll take that as a no," he said. "The only question I see now is: do you really love Nixie? Enough to use a fallen art to kill her queen? When you don't even know if killing her queen will really free her?"

I looked out the window. I didn't have an answer.

"I wouldn't know either," Mike said.

Zola squeezed my arm. "You should not tempt him so thoroughly Mike. What happens if he uses *your* art to kill an innocent? What then? Will it be enough to break your vow?"

"I don't know, but the Queen of the undines is no innocent."

"What happens to me?" I said. "What happens if I use it?"

"Damian, you can't!" Sam said.

"Just, hypothetically, you know."

"Right, sure, like when you *hypothetically* stole dad's car and drove into the neighbor's garage, while the garage door was closed." Everyone laughed, even me. "You don't even know what hypothetically means."

"Harsh Sam, harsh," I said.

"The truth hurts, Demon."

Mike scratched his ear and said, "I always thought I had a bad nickname. Congratulations, yours sucks."

I grinned and bobbed my head.

"What happens to the practitioner?" Zola asked. She stared at the demon, a mixture of apprehension and interest on her face.

"If your intentions are pure, and your target is not, nothing will be unbalanced. No sacrifice will be made." Mike looked down at his hands. "If your intentions are misguided, or the target is innocent, you will become the sacrifice. You will find yourself dead and imprisoned so far into the depths of hell not even the bravest harrower would dare to seek you out. Your soul will rot in flames until the end of days."

"Oh," I said. "At least it's not something bad."

Mike let out a low laugh.

***

Another hour passed and the monotony started to take its toll. Everyone started to fidget or sigh or polish their sword, or tap on their bloody cane with their fingernails. I stared at Zola's hands as they hammered out a steady rhythm. I cringed and rubbed my face.

"Hey, Vassili," I said.

The old vampire craned his neck to look at me. "*Da?*"

"I'm sorry if this isn't phrased respectfully, but, what are you exactly? Are you a lord or a duke or ..." I moved my hand in useless circles.

Vassili smiled and turned back to the road. "No, my friend. I am only a luminary for my Pit, though I do like the title of duke. Perhaps I can convince the lords to grant me the name, *da?*"

"Vassili is our leader," Vik said. "We don't really have a formal title for him."

Dominic nodded and glanced back at Vik. "Only the lords have titles, I don't know why though."

Vassili chuckled. "None do, and some have been around a very long time."

"Are there a lot of lords?" I said.

Dominic shook his head.

"There is one lord for each time zone," Zola said.

"You are full of surprises," Vassili said. "Not many outside our race know of that fact."

"Are you serious?" I said to Zola. "I've never heard that. Are they named after the time zones? Like the Central Standard Lord?" I laughed at my own wit. Sam didn't.

She smacked me in the back of the head. "It's not funny, Damian."

"Oh god, there's not really a Central Standard Lord is there?" I said.

"No, you ass, there's not. They just use their real names."

Zola chuckled. "One per time zone per country. Camazotz is the only lord in Guatemala because they only have one time zone. Formally, another vampire may call him Lord Camazotz, but it's unusual."

"You are a funny man, Vesik," Vassili said. "You should know these things, being such a reputable necromancer, *da*?"

"That's what Zola keeps telling me."

Vassili laughed and slapped the armrest on his seat. "Always the master knows what is best."

"She tells me that too."

The entire van burst into laughter again.

CHAPTER 25

"We're getting close now," Carter said.

"Yes, we are," Zola said. She fished around in her cloak and pulled out four bronze amulets. "Ah think it's time you all had these." She leaned up and handed two over to Dominic and two to Vik in the back. After the battle at Cromlech Glen, Vik and Dominic had given theirs back without prompting. I guess watching a necromancer devastate the landscape gives you some extra motivation not to cause trouble.

Dominic tapped Vassili's arm and the old vampire took the amulet with a smile.

"Ah, a fantastic payment Zola. Truly fantastic," he said as the black silk cord slipped over his neck. "Now, I must insist, try to touch my aura. I want to see your wards in action."

Zola elbowed me and said, "Go on. Try it. These are a bit different from Sam's."

I glanced back at Sam and then up to Vassili. "Alright," I said. I focused and sent my own power coursing over Hugh and the cu siths until it rolled across Vassili's aura. I watched as my necromancy passed through the old vampire's aura like it was a living aura, almost as if it wasn't even there. "It's not ... I can't even grab it."

Vassili clapped and rubbed his hands together. "It's perfect, Zola. I can tell something is touching me, *da*, but it is powerless against the ward." He held up the amulet and said, "*Spasibo*."

I broke my concentration and let the flux of power dissipate.

"It does not render all magic impotent, Vassili," Zola said. "Be wary of the mages, for the powerful have the knowledge to break wards."

"True words, my friend. True words."

I looked out the windows at the sky's fading light as we closed in on Stones River. An all-too-familiar heaviness pressed on my chest and I took a few deep breaths to calm my nerves.

"Carter," Zola said. "Take Wilkinson Pike. Ah want to avoid the front door."

"We're over a mile out from the river," Carter said. "I doubt Philip will be watching this part of the park." He glanced at us in the rearview mirror. "We're better off being overly cautious."

Zola nodded as she resumed tapping her fingernails on her cane. It made me think of my own chunk of wood.

"Hey Zola, where's my staff?"

"In back, behind the seats."

"Oh, good."

"Is your pepperbox dry?"

I pulled the gun out of the holster and looked it over. "Yeah, it looks alright."

"May I?" Vassili said.

"Sure," I said as I checked to make sure it was unloaded. I passed the gun to Alan, and he passed it to Vassili.

He turned the gun over in his hands and ran his fingers down the creases between the barrels. "Magnificent." Vassili shook his head. "Hmm, a modified 1837 Allen and Thurber." He cracked open the center of the gun and raised his eyebrows. "The entire mechanism is changed! I see you added rifling and a firing pin as well, but what is the second trigger for?"

Aideen jumped down to the console. "I can tell you that."

"Ah, fairy work, *da?*"

She nodded. "It will fire all six barrels at once, or whichever ones are loaded."

"Magnificent." Vassili ran his hand over the butt of the gun and the etchings above either side of the triggers. I heard the hiss of a steak frying and Vassili frowned. He rubbed his fingertips together and then smiled.

"Oh, shit. I'm sorry!" I said. "The silver is blessed."

"Da, I noticed." He held his hand up and he was already healed. Vampires shouldn't heal that fast. I was torn between being glad he wasn't hurt and being worried the silver hadn't done more damage.

He closed the gun and handed it to Alan again.

"It's silver!" I said as Alan grabbed the butt of the gun.

"Blessed silver," The werewolf said as he looked the gun over, broke it open, snapped it closed and handed it back. "It won't hurt us unless it cuts us. That's a hell of a gun." I holstered it once Alan passed it back.

"Sorry about that, Vassili" I said.

"Think nothing of it. I am quite fine."

Zola was staring at the back of Vassili's seat. She wasn't smiling, or frowning, just staring. I would have loved to have known what she was thinking.

Carter glanced up at the rearview mirror and said, "We're here."

***

I caught a glimpse of an entryway flanked by two large, stone signs in the distance as Carter shot through a yellow light at Wilkinson Pike. I didn't need to see the words to know what they would say, "Stones River National Battlefield." I took a few deep breaths, but my chest tightened up again as Carter cut the lights. Tires crunched on gravel as we bounced up to a closed gate.

"Allow me," Vassili said as he vanished from the front seat. I could see his hair moving in the shadows as he leaned over the chain locking the aluminum gate. His head turned to the wooden post. There was a quiet crack of wood as Vassili tore one half of the metal blockade from its mount and laid the gate wide open. The van fell silent when Vassili closed his door and we continued into the park. Darkness was rolling across the area as Carter pulled the wheel to the right and drove into a field of vegetation as high as the van. He slowed to a stop near a copse of trees.

"We'll leave the car here," Carter said. "No one's coming through here this late."

Waves of horror and desperation chewed at the back of my brain and I couldn't shake the feelings. Hugh slid the door to the van open and hopped out, flattening tall grasses as he made his way over to the gravel drive. I let everyone else get out ahead of me until Maggie finally patted my shoulder in a not-so-subtle effort to get me moving.

My feet touched the ground and I swayed. Sam grabbed my arm and steadied me.

"You okay?" she said.

"The dead, bloody hell, there're so many." I closed my eyes and hundreds, thousands of dead battered my senses. "It's horrible. This is an awful place."

"Concentrate, boy," Zola said. "You can handle this. Think of them as fuel, weapons."

"They were people," I said.

"Past tense. Worry about it later. For now you have to focus."

I nodded and pulled Sam's hand away from my arm. "Let me try." I took a few deep breaths, steadily pulling air through my nose, holding it for a second, and releasing it through my mouth. The damp smell of freshly burned grass filled my nostrils and grew sharp. In my next breath I smelled gunpowder, and blood, screams and cries filled my head. I took another breath and pushed back against the restless dead. Silence and the scent of the evening air returned. I opened my eyes and found Sam's frowning face about two inches from my own.

"Are you okay?"

I smiled. "Yeah, I'll be alright. Thanks." I followed Sam a few steps to the back of the van. The werewolves and the vampires were in a semicircle around Carter and Vassili. Carter stomped a stubborn clump of yellow flowers to the ground before he pulled the van's back door open. He tossed my staff and a bandolier full of speed loaders for the pepperbox to me. I caught the black nylon straps in mid-air and stared at them. "What's this?"

"A gift, from Vassili," Carter said.

"*Da*, Zola told me about your gun," Vassili said. "I don't really know much about guns." He winked and turned back to the gathered group.

I glanced at Zola and she just shrugged.

"Thank you," I said.

Vassili nodded.

The bandolier crisscrossed over my chest. It didn't limit my movement and it was still easy to get to my holster. I pulled out a speed loader experimentally. It was a tight fit. It wasn't going to fall out, but with adrenaline pumping I wouldn't even notice the resistance.

Mike the Demon tugged on one of the bandoliers and smirked. "Not bad, and it's not even cursed."

I raised an eyebrow. "What?"

"Last time I saw a vampire as old as Vassili give a gift, it was saturated with one hell of a curse."

Vassili laughed. "Yes, the demon is right Damian. You should always be wary of the old vampires. But today your master gave me a great gift. I only reciprocate." He gave a small bow and Mike shook his head.

"This is a long way from McFadden's Ford," Mike said.

"Ah know," Zola said. "Philip will not be watching the woods. He will watch the roads."

"Alright, let's stick to the plan," Carter said. Everyone's attention turned back to the Alpha. "Zola, Damian, you're going straight in. Philip's going to be expecting you. The vampires will fan out behind you and move in through the woods. One wolf for every vampire. The necromancers may not be able to manipulate you while you wear those wards, but they'll still know something's out there. They'll never expect you all to be with werewolves." Carter laced his fingers under the edge of his shirt and pulled it off. The other wolves followed suit and stripped down to nothing. I tried not to stare at Maggie, but she, was just, *ripped*.

"Oh, this is a good trip," Mary said as she clapped her hands together.

Sam blushed as her eyes flashed between Hugh and Alan. Alan grinned and raised his eyebrows in quick succession before he shifted. Sam snorted a laugh as the wolves began to shimmer and fur flowed in a surge of power. Their muscles popped and expanded as the fur covered their skin, claws replaced fingernails, backs swelled and hunched, and the human sheen to their sunburst eyes was lost. Not a single wolf so much as grunted during the shift, and I was just guessing it was because the vampires were with them.

If Maggie caught my eye when she was nude, she was a work of art as a wolf. Her fur was a fine silver covering, flashing in the moonlight as she moved. She crouched onto all fours and almost could have passed for a wolf. The front of her body was too wide, but seen in the shadows, the extra width would be a very slight detail.

"You?" Vassili said. "*You* are the silver wolf?"

A sound like a chuckle mixed with a growl came from Maggie's chest.

Vassili's face turned into a snarl. "If we were not here as allies against a greater foe, I-"

Carter laid a khaki-colored claw on Vassili's chest. "Old battles, Vassili. Put them behind you for now. There are worse things in the woods than us tonight."

The old vampire nodded and turned away from Maggie. The group moved toward the tree line and the path into it.

Zola sped her pace and came up beside Dominic. "Stay to the west edge of the Slaughter Pen," she said. "Keep their attention divided."

"Where is the Slaughter Pen, exactly?" Dominic said.

"Look for the rocks. You'll know it. The place will feel wrong, even to a wolf." Her hand locked around Dominic's wrist until he looked at her. "The eyes of the dead are never closed. This was a terrible battlefield. There may be more here than we know. Watch yourselves."

"Sometimes you really creep me out," Vik said as Zola let go of Dominic's wrist.

Zola smiled and turned away, toward the demon. "Mike, well, do whatever it is you do."

"Don't worry, I will." The smile that crawled over Mike's face curled my toes. "There aren't any innocents among our enemies."

We left the van behind and walked together to the north. Our footsteps were quiet, but noticeable in the still air. A gentle breeze carried the smell of burnt grass. Something groaned in the woods and the black wolf beside me shivered.

"I heard this place is haunted," Haka said, his voice a throaty growl as we all headed toward the path and the woods beyond.

I let out a slow laugh. "Everyplace is haunted."

"No, I mean by something dark, something evil. It's supposed have like, bright green eyes or something."

"No, son," Hugh said. "You are thinking of Chickamauga, Old Green Eyes. We won't see him here."

"Nope, the only scary thing here is Sam," I said.

"I heard that!" Her voice was a fierce whisper from the shadows.

Hugh and Haka both muffled their laughter.

"What is Old Green Eyes?" I said to Hugh.

"There are a few theories, but I believe him to be an overly active gravemaker. It would have to be a powerful gravemaker to be seen by humans and be able to hide itself from the Fae."

"Hide from the Fae?" I said as I passed around the low-hanging branch of an old tree.

"It's only a story, Damian. Supposedly the creature can hide himself. If you ask me, it's just a convenient cover-up for an urban legend. A very old urban legend."

"Quiet," Zola said. "We're at the trail. It's time to spread out."

And so we did.

CHAPTER 26

I walked beside my master on the wooded trail. The trees were dense enough to drop a thick covering of leaves across the forest floor, but the gravel still crunched beneath our feet. The moon was at a sharp angle in the sky and shadows breathed around us in silence. The last of the daylight faded away to the quiet song of a few cicadas. I couldn't hear the vampires or werewolves moving through the woods. They were either far enough away I couldn't hear the crunch of leaves, or they were much, much better than me at being quiet.

We hadn't been walking long when I took a step forward and it felt as though the world began screaming at me. Zola's gaze trailed off to the west, beyond a cannon set along the path. I took a few deep breaths and began walking again, unable to stop gritting my teeth.

"The Slaughter Pen," she said. "This was a sad place, Damian. You can still see the rocks." She pointed into the shadows. I could just make out the nearest of the shallow valleys and trenches formed of natural stone. My vision flickered, and the wall of dead soldiers standing in that place made me gasp. So many souls. So many dead.

Our pace quickened. I wasn't sure if Zola wanted to get away from there as badly as I did, or if adrenaline just pushed us faster. My breath came easier as we distanced ourselves from that wall of watching eyes. We followed the path for another ten minutes, gravel becoming asphalt, before Zola put her hand on my arm and stopped me. I glanced at her and she held her index finger to her lips. She tilted her head and then smiled.

"Ah thought Ah heard something." She turned toward the trail behind us and then back to me. "Damian, use your staff and your gun as much as you can. Philip's going to be waiting for us. Ah can feel a strong knot of ley line power, but Ah can't find its purpose."

"Neither can I," Cara said from behind Zola's shoulder. Her sudden appearance made me jump. "Something's out there, toward the river. We're getting closer to it."

Zola nodded as Cara fluttered back into the trees and another breeze rustled the branches.

It felt like we were walking through a tunnel made of tree branches. The darkness seemed ever closer, or perhaps it was only the dread of what was coming. We walked for a while longer before the trees dropped away on either side. Fields of what seemed to be tall grass flanked us in the darkness. I thought I could see a shadow moving far off to the west, and then it was gone.

A fence closed around us on either side. The uneven, layered edges of the posts seemed more like fingers, grasping for anything they could reach. I started to feel trapped.

"We need to get out of here," I hissed.

"We're safe," Zola said. "No one could hope to detect us here.

"Why not?" I asked, sounding less panicked than I would have thought.

"How's your concentration?"

"It's alright," I said. "The shock wore off a few minutes ago. I can think over the static again."

"Good, that's good, boy. We're close to a cemetery," she said as she pointed to the northwest. She moved her hand toward the east and said, "That's Hell's Half-Acre. Don't look."

But I was already looking. I closed my eyes and swallowed hard, forcing the vision into the back of my mind. As bad as the Slaughter Pen was, this was no better. The unblinking eyes of the dead swarmed the fields around us and seemed ever more dense to the east. It was only as the vision faded that I realized they hadn't been looking at us.

"They're not watching us," I said.

"Ah know," Zola said. "Ah think there are louder things to watch."

"The ley line energy?"

She nodded as we approached a modern road. "If you're okay here, you should be alright by the river. A long time ago, this crumbled old road was McFadden's Lane." Zola rubbed the scars on her wrists before we rushed to the other side. Trees replaced the fields on our right, but the fence still followed us on the left. "Don't worry about being quiet. We want them to focus on us. Maybe they'll miss the wolves and the demon."

My foot immediately caught on an uneven slab of pavement. I let out a muffled shout as I did a face plant onto a patch of overgrown grass.

"You don't have to be *that* loud," Zola said in a whisper.

I heard a snicker from the woods to my right as I spit out a clump of dead leaves. I was pretty sure it was Cara, or a ghost with a good sense of humor. I groaned, stood up, and started following Zola again, taking a bit more caution with my footing.

"Some things never change," Zola said.

I grinned and followed her gray cloak in the darkness for another ten minutes. The trees and the fence fell away and we were suddenly standing outside the protection of the forest. We climbed a gravel rise over some old railroad tracks before scrambling through more tall grass and out onto another stretch of the decaying street.

We came to a newer, wider road that cut across our path. I could see headlights in the distance. The rest of the world remained still. The wooden fence on the opposite side of the street worked its way into my view as we jogged closer. Another set of railroad tracks was left behind before a second fence closed us in on the west as well.

A strong breeze rushed by. It was faint, but when I breathed deeply I caught a hint of the river I knew laid beyond the hill. Something pulled on the ley lines in the distance, and I could see the electric blue streams around us flux and shift in response.

I bit my lips and glanced at the road in front of us. It vanished around a curve to the east about twenty feet ahead.

I laid a hand on Zola's shoulder. She stopped and leaned toward me.

"Should we leave the road?"

She shook her head, the tinkling of the metal in her braids a silent whisper. "Be quiet so we don't raise alarm or suspicion, but remember we go in as a distraction."

I nodded and followed her around the bend. A bright white obelisk cut the darkness of the northern night sky as we reached the top of a short incline. I couldn't make out the plaque fastened to the obelisk's face as we started down a narrower path. The fences that lined the battlefield continued with us. Our left was flanked by boulders and a shorter fence while our right was smothered by a tall wooden barrier that looked reinforced.

Only a few sparse trees separated us from the vast field that led to the river. There was another knot of woods a bit south, and even a sparse covering of trees to the north, but Zola led us straight into the field. Three necromancers became visible off to the east as we passed through the shallow tree line. My eyes swept the area from left to right. I could see the river in the distance now, a ways north, but nothing else moved. The only sounds were the call of a few cicadas, the faint rush of the water, and the intermittent breeze ruffling the branches behind us, sending a handful of dead leaves swirling between us and the necromancers. I could smell the dampness of the river, but by the sound and scent, I knew it was smaller than the Missouri River.

My hand moved up beside the shield rune on my staff when two of the necromancers moved. They stepped forward and threw back their hoods. I saw Zola's body jerk when the moonlight fell across their faces. Her knobby cane whipped up in front of her and she held it diagonally across her body. I did the same, resting my right hand on the butt of my pepperbox.

"Volund, Jamin ... why?" Zola's voice turned brittle and hard.

The hooded necromancer dropped away from the other two. Something rippled on the ground, and then stabilized. I wasn't sure if Zola had noticed it.

She pounded her cane into the ground and shook her head. "Why do you side with *him!*"

A short, dark laugh rolled across the field. I turned my head slightly to the left and watched Philip Pinkerton appear in a slowly expanding orb of sickly red light. When the light faded he tucked an object into his robes. I didn't catch what it was, but for a second I thought I saw a finger.

"Adannaya ... so good of you to bring friends," he said. "I've brought friends too." Philip closed his eyes and murmured something. When his eyes opened, the illusion across the field collapsed. My heart lurched as at least fifteen necromancers came into view. Not all of them were draped in robes. Two at the edge of the line behind Philip wore tactical gear and had some vicious looking rifles leveled at us. I doubted the hybrid shield from the staff would be able to stop a bullet. Maybe a deflection, if I got lucky. I realized what Philip had done as I stared down the barrel of a monstrous weapon and my heart sank. The guns didn't matter, they were a distraction. My head whipped back toward Philip and he was already in motion. He held his hand out like a claw.

"*Stanasatto!*"

"Zola!" My shield sprang from my staff as I moved toward her. Philip's blade of force stabbed through her cloak. She hadn't even raised a shield to try and stop it. A moment later the cloak fell to the ground, empty. I hadn't seen her move. I had no idea where she'd gone.

Philip let out a slow breath. "So resourceful, Adannaya. Come, face me!"

The pepperbox hissed as I drew it. I dropped the shield and fired two quick shots at the nearest rifleman. I heard the dull thud of an impact and the figure barely took a step backwards from the force. "Not more puppets ..." Last year we'd fought puppets. They were zombies, except different in every way that mattered. They were vampiric zombies, fast as hell and able to absorb obscene amounts of damage. Only a dark necromancer or a demon could create them. Philip was so far out of his mind that it made me hopeful Zola wouldn't be too broken up by his death.

The field stayed quiet except for a handful of cicadas and the distant hoot of an owl. No one moved. I could feel the vampires nearby. I wouldn't have noticed them if it wasn't for our little test in the van, and even they stayed still as the muscles tightened in my shoulders. Philip's head cocked to the side and a tiny smile split his face.

"Welcome to your death." He dropped to a knee and slammed his palm against a deep furrow in the earth. A surge of electric blue energy poured into the figures he'd carved into the circle. The birds and insects fell utterly silent when the flux of ley line energy suddenly erupted. Even the rustle of leaves was deafening in the stillness that followed.

It didn't take long for my brain to register what he was doing. "Shit, *runes!*" My hand shifted to my own shield rune and the glassy sphere flashed up around me.

Philip stood and laughed. He looked behind him and it was only then I noticed the string of necromancers all along the river side at his back. My god, how many were there? They all stood at the same time and stepped away from their own glowing runes before they retreated behind Philip. Most of them clustered in the east, but a few stayed spread across the field.

Philip turned his attention back to me, cocked his head to the side again, and said, "*Seditiotto mergo incoleggra.*"

Power lanced out from Philip's circle and burned through the grasses until it met up with all the other circles between him, the river, and the far edges of the field. There was a burst of light at one of the furthest circles and I saw the power dissipate into the air as the necromancer beside it fell over dead.

Philip wore a flat expression as his head turned toward the downed man. "You only stopped one, Adannaya. Can you stop a hundred?"

There was a flash of steel and wings and the puppet I'd shot at fell to pieces. Foster leapt into the air as Aideen and Cara came down on the other puppet. Their swords cleaved through the tactical gear with unnerving ease. I saw several of the necromancers in the circles take a step backwards. Fear. The rest of them weren't puppets.

Philip turned toward the pile of limbs on the ground and snarled. "God damned Fae, show yourselves!"

A flash of light caught my eyes. It rose and fell behind the line necromancers closest to the river as they searched the scrub for Zola. Something was moving in the water. The surface rippled and swelled, before it receded and swelled again in an ever-increasing roil. Shallow waters began to surge up and over the sheer riverbank. Some of the necromancers turned to stare at the river. I watched as they broke into a run. They started in my direction and a surge of adrenaline pumped through my body, my hand tightening on the shield rune. I could hear some of them laughing as they slowed and stopped in a cluster behind Philip.

A scream tore from the woods off to the east. A white and red demon sprang from the cover of leaves and landed beside the stragglers. It took me a moment to realize it was Vassili, hidden behind a curtain of bloody hair. He punched through two necromancers in quick succession and vanished back into the tree line before the corpses hit the ground.

Another voice thundered across the field from the southeast. "Move in." It was Carter. Maggie was behind him, her silver fur flashing in the moonlight. Vik and Dominic were a step behind them.

I caught a smirk on Philip's face as his hand rose and closed into a fist, bringing a massive shield up around his entire group. Carter careened off the edge of it, but Maggie hit head on. She bounced off, fell onto her back, and leapt to her feet. Both of the wolves snarled and swiped at the incandescent dome of force. A tiny ripple and a small burst of sparks were the only response to their attacks.

"You'll never get through this shield," Philip said as he nodded toward the river. Why don't you show me what you plan to do about them?"

"Oh fuck, what are they?" Alan said from right behind me. I only just kept myself from turning around and smacking him for sneaking up on me. Vassili was with him, which meant Sam was still with Hugh, Mary, and Haka.

I glanced toward the river and cringed. "Wights," I said flatly.

Skeletons were rising in decayed uniforms. Some still had skin hanging from their emaciated bodies. They were armed with swords and bayonets. They pulled their ruined bodies up onto the bank and marched toward us in silence. A few carried the remains of rifles, the wood long rotted from the river water.

Sam would be coming from the west with no idea what was in front of her. She'd be walking right into those things. Dominic and Vik were both engaging the Wights. Bits of bone and flesh and cloth were torn away by the vampires, but no blood seeped from the long-dead men. They continued marching forward, getting further and further from the swollen river.

I ran toward the line of wights, firing a shot at Philip's shield just for the hell of it. It ricocheted harmlessly into the air. I leveled the gun at the nearest wight and pulled the trigger. Fragments of its skull fell to the ground but the body kept coming. I pulled the second trigger at point blank range and the thing's spine splintered and collapsed. My hands moved without thought, cracking open the pepperbox and slamming a speed loader home.

The last of the wolves and vampires hit the water-logged skeletons from behind. Armor and pieces flew into the air as strike after strike found its mark. Claws and fangs flashed in the moonlight, but still more of the damned things crawled out of the water.

I held out my staff and said, *"Pulsatto!"* Two of the creatures shattered at the waist, but as soon as they toppled to the ground, their bony fingers found purchase in the grass and crawled toward me.

A pale blur landed on top of them and tore the remnants into unidentifiable pieces. Sam looked at me with her fangs fully extended. Her eyes were as black as the sky. "What are they? Zombies?"

An auburn werewolf grunted, leapt over Sam, and tore another skeleton to pieces. The arms clattered off a tree in the distance. "I think they're wights." Blood ran down Hugh's leg as he stood up from a crouch. Something had gotten a grip on him. "There are more of them to the northeast."

"Foster?" I asked.

Hugh nodded. "Aideen is with him, and the the cu siths." His eyes strafed across the shambling dead. "Wights."

"I think so," I said. "Zombies wear flesh, these don't have much." I vaporized another wight with six quick shots from the pepperbox. Its body jerked and stumbled from the impact before the last bullet took its head off at the neck.

Sam screamed and doubled over as a sword ripped through her back and almost caught my arm.

"Sam!" I bent down to help her before taking out the wight. It reached out with a bayonet and would have clipped me, except for the roar of a black werewolf that landed on its skull and scattered its body to the winds. As fast as Haka had come, he vanished into the horde of wights.

"Pull it out." Sam shuddered as I grabbed the hilt and tore the blade out of her back. She was standing again a second later, demolishing another skeleton.

I heard screams from the other end of the army of undead and saw Alan's massive form stumble backwards and fall. A huge ball of light erupted around him and the four wights closing on his fallen form were blasted into the air. I caught a glimpse of Zola, her cloak settled around her shoulders once more, before I turned and crushed another skeleton with an overhead smash from my staff.

I cursed as the wall of undead surged forward again. I saw Dominic pick up one of the larger wights and hurl it back into the river. Mary's bloody form plowed through the front row of the dead. Something tripped her and she landed beside me in a heap.

"Getting faster, Damian, they're faster ..."

I spared Philip a look. He was standing with his arms crossed behind his shield, a smirk twisting his face.

"Why in the hell isn't he attacking us?" I said as I turned my gaze back to the vampire. "Get behind them, Mary. Find Vassili. Get behind the necromancers and take them out. Philip can't shield them all."

She nodded and ran to the south.

"Sam!" I said. "Hugh! On me, now!" I pulled the focus out of my belt and started carving a rune into the ground. I drew two quick circles around it and smashed the ferrule of my staff into the center.

Haka got to me first with Hugh on his tail. Sam leapt over a group of wights that were almost breaking into a run. I marveled at how well she could move with her wounds. As soon as she was clear, I moved my hand over the shield rune on my staff. With the extra circles I'd carved into the ground, a torrent of ley line energy flooded my being. I held my hand out as my skin started to blister and my vision narrowed to a gray tunnel. I'd underestimated how fast the power would build and now I was paying for it. "*Incidatto!*"

I let my staff fall and broke the circle as soon as the incantation obliterated the closest wights. Pieces of severed swords and bone and armor fell to the ground as a rippling scythe of electric blue power swept through them. I grunted and fell to a knee as the energy left me. "Too much. Shit ..." I felt a hand on my back and my face was pulled up. I almost smiled at the line of worry etched across Sam's face. Exhaustion felt like it was gnawing at my bones. I could see through the line of wights now. Their ranks were thinning near the river.

As the last of the skeletal creatures cleared the waters, the river surged forward and then receded again. The line of wights thickened around us and I didn't have a clear view of the river until it rose up high enough to tower above them.

"God dammit, what now?" I said.

The murky water swept forward and covered at least two dozen wights at once. I felt my eyes widen as a translucent arm shot out of a wave and pulled two more wights into the raging waters. The waves receded, revealing the shattered pieces of the swallowed wights.

The river surged again. Only this time, instead of wights, the river bore three screaming water witches into the fray. Nixie held her arms forward with a massive, rotating orb of water between them. I saw her lips move as the orb swept through the ranks of wights like a wrecking ball. Pieces of bodies and armor exploded in the force of each impact. The other water witches followed suit, leveling dozens of wights in the space of a heartbeat.

Nixie launched herself out of the water and smashed her wrecking ball down on the wights near Zola. The ground shook as the bones were ground into it. Nixie's translucent form turned toward us and called a flood of water to push the entire line of the dead back toward the river. She flowed over the earth and solidified into her alabaster skin a few feet away.

"Is Sam okay?" she said.

"I'm fine," Sam said from behind me.

"Good, don't lose your concentration. Wights are not so easy to kill." Nixie's eyes locked on my hands and she frowned. "What did you do?"

"It's nothing. Later. I'm fine." The blisters on my hands and arms hurt to move, but I didn't want Nixie or anyone else distracted by the injury.

Hugh laid a claw on Nixie's shoulder. "The wolves and the water witches. What would my grandfather say?"

Nixie smiled as she slashed through another wight with a casual flick of her wrist. "He'd probably tell you you're as crazy as the necromancer."

Hugh's laugh rumbled out of his chest. "He would at that."

"They're pulling themselves back together," Sam said. The bones were vibrating across the ground. Skeletal fingers clawed at the dirt and rejoined with arms and legs and tiny chips reformed into entire skeletons as we watched.

"Wights are not so easy to kill," Nixie said as she launched herself into the mass of undead once again. She punched through a tight group of skeletons and ran toward the other water witches. They were battling a larger group of wights where the ground fell away into the river.

"Adannaya!" I heard the yell before I saw who it was. "Adannaya, throw me the hammer!"

I spun to find Mike the Demon bolting from the southern tree line. He smashed through the fence with hardly a pause, dragging the bodies of two necromancers behind him like they weighed nothing. Mike launched himself into the air and slammed the corpses against Philip's shield. Philip's other followers stared at the exploded remains sliding down the shield. The demon leap-frogged off the shimmering wall of power and paused for a split second as he hit the ground and then took off toward the wights.

All the necromancers' attention was on the demon. Vassili and Mary followed behind Mike. The unshielded necromancers never knew what killed them. Three bodies fell to the ground in pieces before the vampires vanished into the shadows once more.

Zola drew the Smith's Hammer from her belt and didn't so much as hesitate as she whipped it across the short distance to Mike. The demon caught it at a dead sprint. I saw his mouth move and deep red flames leapt from the hammer. The handle elongated as Mike turned to the side with a two-handed grip and obliterated a wight with an overhead smash. Bits of charred bone and armor pattered away from the now-enormous flaming head of the Smith's Hammer.

"They're coming!" Mike said as he spiraled with the flaming hammer and destroyed two more wights. The hammer hissed and a burst of steam shot into the air as the fiery head hit the damp ground closer to the river.

"Who?" I said as Mike brought the hammer down on the wights fighting with the water witches. Bodies and bones erupted into the air on an explosion of water. I slammed another speed loader into the pepperbox and blew another skeleton apart. I grabbed the sword it dropped and hurled it into the woods to disarm the thing before it could rebuild itself. Nixie rode a wave over the wights as I moved toward her and Mike. She stumbled as she hit the grass. I grunted as something grabbed my arm and a sharp pain seared my skin. My hand opened and my staff fell to the ground.

Something hot and thick ran down to my hand as I jerked it away from the skeletal fingers. There was a ragged wound on the back of my wrist and a bloody bayonet in the wight's hand. The wight still had strips of decayed flesh clinging to its bones beneath its tattered Union uniform. It was coming too fast to aim my pepperbox so I grabbed it with my necromancy, bracing myself for that terrible moment of *knowing*.

James Anderson. Fifteen years old, he screamed when his brother died beside him. Face covered in his sibling's blood, he lost his mind. He didn't know how he'd be able to tell his mother that his brother was dead. Then something stung him in the back. A cold acceptance of death came to him as the light left his world.

I screamed and dismantled James Anderson to dust. I knew him like he was my own brother. His body left in a cloud and I hoped it would find peace as I turned, tears in my eyes, and unloaded my pepperbox into another wight's spine.

"Damian!" I turned to see Nixie backpedaling as she screamed, *"Gravemakers!"*

I fell to a knee and grabbed my staff as two of them seeped out of the ground between us like ink through water. Their bodies materialized in a blackened brown nightmare of deep cracks and crevices that looked like thick tree bark. The sound of a thousand snapping bones echoed across the field as the gravemakers straightened their hunched forms and opened their milky white, dead men's eyes. They stepped forward together as their hands began to twitch. One finger jumped, and then relaxed as another did the same, in a nauseating rolling motion.

The wights closest to the monstrosities stopped moving. Their bony skulls turned toward the gravemakers. Each gravemaker waved its arm in a rippling motion ending in a snap, its palms facing the wights. The skeletal bodies jerked and stumbled and fell into bony piles before their bones vanished into the earth.

There was a blur of motion between the wights as a vampire closed on the gravemakers. I recognized Mary's lithe body as she pulled her feet up in mid-air with her claws reaching for the nearest monster. I didn't even have time to shout a warning.

The gravemaker's gaze locked on Mary and it swatted her away like an insect. She tried to scream before her body smashed through a small tree and it joined her in a tumble toward the river. The tree fell slowly as Mary came to a stop. I heard it splash down in the water, but my attention came back to Mike when I heard him swear.

Mike reached into the pocket of his jeans and pulled out a tiny cluster of crystals. My eyes widened and my gut twisted as I realized he was holding a soulstone. Mike threw the stone with a sidearm flick of his wrist. It broke through the gravemaker's skin and lodged in its head, cutting through the fractured face with a crack. Steam rose from the wound as the gravemaker clawed at the opening. The creature released a horrific moan. The fire demon charged and screamed as he leapt into the air. It happened so fast I barely even registered what he'd done. Mike brought the Smith's Hammer down on the gravemaker's head and the body exploded in a hail of fire and a fine cloud of white soul fragments. As fast as it had come, the gravemaker dispersed in tendrils of black and gray smoke.

Mike didn't have a chance to move before the second creature came at him. I was already charging the gravemaker, hammering wights to the side with my staff. The muddy ground sucked at my boots as I leveled the pepperbox and unloaded all six barrels into the thing's face. Fire and gunpowder scorched my lungs as I took ragged breaths. I holstered the gun as my grip slid to the blade rune on my staff and my other hand wrapped around the sword hilt at my waist. I stiffened as power was ripped from the nearby ley lines and blended with my own aura to form the aural blade.

"Damian! Don't!"

I heard my master's scream over the buzz of power, but I wasn't going to let Mike die at the hands of a gravemaker. I wasn't going to let any of us die at the hands of a bloody gravemaker. I brought the pulsing blade of blue, gold, and silver filaments down and cut through its neck. The world stopped as my necromancy flared and was dragged up through the blade until it bit into the creature's being. And in the heartbeat it took for the power to decapitate the god-forsaken gravemaker, my soul burned. I saw the first death and the second, the tenth, the forty-second, the seventy-fifth, the swarm of men and women and children that died in terror and rage to give birth to a devil. I tried to scream, but no sound left my throat. My body seized as it felt the gunfire and the cannons tearing it apart—as if I had been the one to die, and not the hundreds of souls before me. The scents of ruptured bodies and voided bowels grabbed my lungs and squeezed the air out of them. I died screaming a hundred times in a heartbeat before my world went black.

CHAPTER 27

" **–U**ck up Vesik!"
Something felt like an anvil as it cracked against my face. The slap was deafening in my throbbing head. I raised my hand to ward off any more blows. "Up, I'm up," I mumbled. I opened my eyes to find Hugh and a circle of vampires and Fae around me. Hugh had his arm pulled back ready to smack me again until I raised my voice and said, "I'm up!"

"Good, get yourself together. Zola thinks we can stop the wights if we break all the circles."

"All?" I said.

Hugh nodded.

My eyes roamed the circle and I didn't see Zola. "Where's Zola?"

"She ran to help Aideen," Hugh said. "She chased some of the necromancers to the southeast." As if in confirmation, something exploded in a thunderclap of sound off to the south. "Haka and I cleared the field through the northwestern trees with help from the vampires, but these men ... they are like roaches."

I sat up slowly and found Mike on his knees just outside the circle. He had the head of the hammer planted in the ground. The demon was breathing hard, with his hands on the skyward handle and his head bowed between his elbows. He looked at me and one corner of his lips quirked up. "I hate those things." The cloud of black and gray tendrils was the only remnant of the second gravemaker. "There's more of the damned things here. I can feel them. Break the circles quickly. I don't have enough soulstones to keep killing gravemakers."

I put my hand out to steady myself and bumped into a still form. It was wet and bloody and it took me a second to realize it was Mary. My eyes widened. "Is she?"

"No," Sam said as she squeezed my shoulder from behind. "But if you don't get moving we're all dead."

I nodded, but didn't look away from Mary's battered body. The clash of steel on steel and the more muted sound of steel on bone echoed over the field as the wights continued battling Foster and Cara and the wolves. I caught a glimpse of Sam's face as she charged into the fray once more. Blood was pouring down her right cheek.

"Foster!" I said, and the authority in my voice surprised me. "Haka! On me." I launched myself forward and didn't speak another word.

Foster swept in from my left and Haka's matted black fur was a mountain on my right. The werewolf's breath whistled through a deep gash in his snout as he threw himself forward on all fours. Foster's sword slid through wights left and right with ferocious precision while Haka handled them with vicious brutality.

We hit the first circle in less than a minute. I wrapped my hand around my focus and started to shift my grip on my staff to form a blade.

Foster's hand clamped down on my staff hand. "Don't risk anything with necromancy, Zola's order. Break them with ley lines."

I nodded and slid the hilt beneath my belt as Foster turned back to the wights. A khaki werewolf bounded past us and snarled as it bowled through a cluster of skeletons. As soon as he was clear I saw one of the other water witches toss the bones back into the river with an eruption of water.

I knelt beside the radiant green glow of runes and circles and cursed. There was enough power pouring out of that single circle to crumble a house. I glanced back at Philip. He was watching me. His arms were crossed in front of him and his face looked calm, interested. The shield around him rippled as a vampire bounced off of it and tumbled into the distance.

The shield. A shield tied to a circle would stop every kind of energy I knew of.

"Foster! Dagger!"

He took down another wight, reached to his calf with his left hand and flicked the dagger into the grass between my feet without even looking. I grabbed the hilt and started dragging it around the circle of power. Foster and Haka beat the wights away from me as I finished the rough circle of my own. I glimpsed one of the necromancers in that mass of pale flesh before he was swept away in a rogue wave of water. My eyes shifted back to the raw wound I'd carved into the earth as I placed my fingers into the furrow.

"Orbis tego!"

The instant the shield snapped into place the energy in the runes slammed against it and the recoil of power burned across my already blistered hands. I gritted my teeth and held the shield until the line of power running from Philip's circle shot into the air like lightning. The runes died. I cut a line through them with Foster's dagger to be sure it wouldn't be easy to reactivate the circle.

"Next one, on me!" I said.

I glanced across the field as we hammered through the wights. There was fighting in the woods now. I couldn't see half of our people, but I could hear them yelling and grunting among the constant clatter of bones. I saw Dominic briefly as he tossed a wight into the unnaturally roiling river. Translucent arms reached forward and dragged more of the undead back into the water. The mass of dead flesh continuing to march out of the river despite the efforts of the water witches was terrifying. I spared a glance over my shoulder but could no longer see the cluster of vampires and werewolves we'd left with Mary's still form.

We carved through another ten of the circles without too much trouble. As we closed on the eleventh, Haka roared and stumbled backwards. There was a bayonet stuck through his hamstring. He went down hard. I moved to help him.

"No," he snarled. "Finish the circles! I can still fight."

"Shut up, Haka," I said as I pulled the bayonet out of his leg. He growled and pounded his fist on the ground. Foster circled us, slashing through bones and armor as fast as he could.

"Foster, close his wound."

The fairy nodded and knelt as I stood up and swung my staff into the closest wight. The metal and wood slammed the decayed body into the ground, collapsing in a clatter of dry bones. It started to get up again immediately. I blew the wight apart with two quick shots from the pepperbox. Four more shots pushed the closest wights back. The recoil from the gun felt like knife blades on my blistered hands.

"*Socius Sanation*," Foster said.

By the time I blinked the flash of power away and fought off the next three wights, Foster was beside me with his sword flickering through the bones. Haka jumped back into the fray with renewed vigor, his massive claws raining immediate and brutal destruction.

"He's not fully healed," Foster said. "You need to be healed too, D. He's a wolf. He should be fine. You won't."

"Good, I'm going for the circle."

Foster didn't answer. He just moved in front of me and collapsed two wights in one strike. Some piece of metal sparked against his sword as the blade moved through the second wight. We moved forward, collapsing Philip's circles as we were all battered senseless by the release of power at each one.

"This is stupid," Haka said between gasps for air as we moved toward the last green glow. "The wights are faster, but they're still no match."

"I know," I said. "Philip's up to something."

"Trying to tire us out?" Foster said as he kicked another skeleton away. Nixie laughed as she caught the bones and pulled them back to the river.

"Could be," I said. "It's sure as hell working." I fell to my knees and plunged the dagger into the earth. The river was louder near the last circles and it added a constant background noise to the clatter of swords, claws, and bones. With the circle done, I dug my fingers in and said, "*Orbis tego!*"

The last bolt of power shot into the skies and the entire cadre of wights collapsed onto the earth, leaving a handful of necromancers exposed across the field of remains. The water witches moved in with the river and started dragging the bones and armor back into the water. One of them managed to catch a necromancer, and he screamed as he vanished beneath the wave. His grasping hand was the last thing to disappear.

"Give me your hand," Foster said. I held it up and he grabbed it. "*Socius Sanation.*"

I could have kissed him when the burning suddenly vanished from my wrist in a burst of power and light. I could see the survivors now. Hugh and Sam were still standing beside Mary's crumpled form. They'd pulled back a little from their earlier station, but I could see two other forms on the ground beside them. One was Dominic, but at least he was still moving. Alan was on his hands and knees, and I wished we were close enough to see how bad they were hurt. Mike the Demon was near the river with Nixie and the other water witches as he gestured toward the southeast. At the other end of the field, Carter was on the ground, leaning against a tree beside Cara and Zola. I couldn't see anyone else, but an explosion of light drew my attention to the south once more.

"Where's Aideen?" I asked.

"With the others," Foster said. "To the south. Bubbles and Peanut are with her too."

My gaze flashed between Philip's group behind the shield and the southern tree line.

"No," Foster said. "We're here for Philip."

It was almost as though Philip had heard the fairy. He dropped the shield. The pop of dissipating power drew my attention. I watched as the necromancers spread out from him and they all started backing toward the southeastern trees, away from the deadly water of the river.

Vassili struck. The old vampire came out of the woods like a streak of lightning, but it didn't matter. Philip smiled as he turned to the bloody vampire, made a complicated gesture with his hands, and then blasted Vassili with a wave of force when the vampire was about a foot from him. The pale form crashed through the thin line of trees along the riverbank with a grunt before he slid off the edge into the river.

"Still giving wards out to vampires, hmm?" Philip said. "Did you think that would stop me?"

Zola stepped away from Carter. She walked toward Philip and glared at the one time love of her life. "Where are the soulstones, Philip?"

"So you did know what I was after." He wiped a thin line of blood off his temple, and I didn't think it was his. "I wasn't sure you'd figure it out."

"You were always easy to figure out."

Philip frowned and reached into his pocket. He held his fist out and opened it. A small soulstone rested on his palm. "You have no idea what I'm after."

"Prosperine," Zola said as she shifted her cane across her body.

Philip laughed without humor. "Prosperine. *Prosperine?*" A terrible smile raised his lips. "Prosperine is just a taste, a tiny taste. Necromancers will be supreme when the world is dead. Imagine it."

"And our friends?" Zola asked as her voice rose. "Our families? All dead. The world will be a corpse you *idiot.*"

"You never saw the bigger picture." He tossed the soulstone into the air at Zola. My eyes tracked it, her eyes tracked it. I'm pretty sure everyone's eyes tracked it, except Philip's.

He blurred into motion and had his arm wrapped around Zola's neck and a wicked blade against her chest before any of us could react. Even the vampires stared at our worsening situation with something like confusion. Philip shouldn't have been that fast.

He dragged the blade up her cloak and onto her neck. "Did you forget about the grave, Adannaya?"

The expression that rolled across her face and the weakness in her voice sent chills coursing down my arms. "Oh, god, you can't."

"A prehistoric mass grave Adannaya, with thousands buried there, and thousands of years later the Confederates. You're right next to them and you didn't even notice." He dragged out the first syllable of the word, sweet, nauseating.

Foster shrank and shot into the air faster than I could follow.

I sent my power coursing through the area. I found nothing until it butted up against the old cemetery. "There isn't a mass grave here," I said. "Let her go."

Philip's laugh was low and dark. "It's not the bodies, boy. It's the souls. Drop it, Zachariah."

My eyes widened as Philip's assassin released a misdirection art he must have been holding in place since we'd gotten there. The tiny hills of grass in the eastern field shimmered and became piles of dirt behind a narrow, twisted stone inlet. Stacks of thin, wide stone were set a few feet into the earth and formed a winding channel leading out to the river. What looked like stone steps led into the strange channel, and then a pale light drew my eyes beyond that out-of-place structure.

In one horrible moment I *saw* the open wound in the earth. It was a churning mass of restless souls. I'd seen things over the years, horrible things. Hell, I'd seen horrible things earlier that night, but looking into that wound in the earth … it was the first time I felt like I was looking straight into hell. Some souls were so old they were nothing but floating bits of luminescence, their human forms long forgotten. Some were more humanlike, clawing at the sides of the grave with silent screams as others stepped over them, crushed them into the ground, and repeated the process in a constant, churning, flow.

"You're insane," I said.

Philip's arm tightened around Zola's neck as he backed closer to the grave. "Insane? Hardly, boy. Besides … you and me, Vesik? We're the same."

"Hell we are."

I saw Foster glide smoothly in behind Philip, pausing between the trees at the edge of the river. He leapt again and moved forward in total silence. Keeping Philip talking was my only thought. Foster would finish this.

"Oh, we're the same, boy. We are. You're just as much a liar as I am. You want power and domination. You're just too scared to admit it. Too distracted by the maggots you surround yourself with."

Zola choked and Philip jerked her neck hard, drawing blood with the tip of the dagger on her neck. Foster surged forward, exploding into his seven-foot form as he pulled his sword back for a killing blow.

"All I need now is a dark bottle," Philip said.

My heart stuttered. "No, Foster, get back!"

Everything went to hell, or, perhaps, hell came to us.

Philip released his grip on Zola and kicked her in the small of the back. She went down hard. Philip turned and dropped to one knee as he said, "*Modus Pulsatto!*"

A torrent of force hammered Foster backwards.

"No!" Aideen cried as she broke through the southern tree line.

Foster's wings tore as he screamed and slammed into one of ancient trees before he fell to the ground in silence. The monstrous tree shuddered and leaves showered all around the limp fairy. Philip made another gesture with his hand and the small pouch at Foster's side was torn away. The bottle came out of the pouch and I heard it smack into Philip's hand as the incantation died.

"Philip! Don't!" Zola was on her knees with one hand extended. "Please, *don't* ..."

The dark necromancer glared at Zola as he tossed the bottle into the center of the ancient mass grave. The souls cringed away from it. "*Minas Opprimotto.*"

The bottle splintered like glass. Just a quiet tinkling of metal shards. A detached part of me remembered the assault on Azzazoth. Silence washed over the world before the amalgamation of soul and aura came screaming out of the dark bottle and shot to the edges of the mass grave. I watched in horror as the souls of the dead were broken and reassembled, only to be broken again. A blood red pinpoint began to pulse near the center of the grave. It grew and distended into a thin disc as the entire mass began to spin. It picked up speed and started to roar like a tornado. The earth rippled and reality screamed as an impossibly thin arm shot out of the distortion.

Vik and Sam moved toward Philip. Vik wore a film of gore across his face.

"Don't attack him!" Zola said. "It will draw you in."

Philip laughed and stepped into the middle of the maelstrom. His surviving men were scattered around the grave. Some looked terrified. Others seemed to be having a religious epiphany. Philip reached out for the hand and I stared in sick fascination as he started pulling on the emaciated limb. The flesh was red and worn like a rotted leather saddlebag. Philip dragged more of the creature into our world. Its head was bowed with a thin mass of tangled, matted black hair covering its scalp. It was clothed, but visions of decay flashed through the rotted blue robe adorning its body. Its legs weren't much thicker than its arms and Philip laughed as the swirling disc of power dissipated.

We all watched, impotent, as the world gave birth to a demon.

Philip smiled at me with the proud eyes of a father. "And just think, Vesik, I couldn't have raised her without the twin souls of child killers. I owe you my thanks for sending one with Azzazoth."

I choked back a cry when his words hit home. Vicky's killers were inside that thing. They were part of it. "Oh, god no."

Philip touched the filthy, matted hair. "Arise, child, and claim your rightful place as the Destroyer, Prosperine."

The demon raised its head. It had no eyes, just the faint silver glow of starlight in its vacant sockets. It stared at me and I stared back. My skin started to crawl but I didn't look away as the creature straightened its form and stood beside Philip.

I barely even registered the fact that another battle had begun. Sam and Vik launched themselves at the demon. Agonized screams filled the night when Prosperine flicked her wrists and four parallel slashes tore into Vik and my sister. I saw a huge wolf charge, it had to be Alan, and he suffered the same fate. The necromancers were laughing as they scattered, moving to strike my fallen friends.

I tore my gaze away from the demon and leveled my pepperbox. Three shots. Three dead necromancers. By the time I aimed at the fourth, he saw me coming.

"*Impadda!*" he said and my shot careened off the edge of his shield. The shield may not have been able to take a direct hit, but I had bigger problems than one necromancer. Power, lightning, fire, and screams tore through the air as the battle erupted into absolute chaos.

I saw Vassili at the edge of the river. A necromancer made the mistake of attacking the old vampire. Vassili charged him, his amulet deflecting the necromancy. The vampire's left hand grabbed the necromancer's black cloak as his right hand blurred into motion. Blood and tissue erupted from the necromancer's chest and he fell to the earth a moment later.

A massive bolt of power shot towards me, and I threw myself backwards, afraid I didn't have the time to raise a shield. The incantation sent a thin wave of earth into the air as it cut into the field. I caught a glimpse of Aideen as she deflected another necromancer's attack. She chased him to the south. Bubbles and Peanut melted through the shadows behind her.

I pushed myself up and ran toward Zola as I took two sloppy shots at my attacker. He called a shield, and then retreated closer to Philip. Blood was trickling down Zola's neck when I got to her. I glanced toward Sam and Vik. They were still down, but the area around them was relatively clear. They were both moving, but not quickly. Alan was back in the fray. "What do we do?"

Zola shook her head and raised a shield of her own. "Kill Philip. Maybe it will banish the demon, but Ah don't know for sure."

I nodded and ran toward the river. One of the water witches was on the edge. "Try to kill Philip. It may get rid of the demon."

The translucent head nodded and said, "I will tell my sisters." She vanished into the water. I didn't even make it back to Mary and Hugh before the water witches rose up and slaughtered two more necromancers. Without Philip's shield, their own shields were useless. Nixie lunged at Philip, but he backed away, raised his hand, and blasted her with a surge of power.

She was already getting up again before I could think to yell her name. The demon took a step toward Sam and Vik. I cursed and changed course. I was at Sam's side in fifteen paces, dragging her back toward the trees. She cringed and grabbed the bloody gashes on her chest as her heels bounced over clumps of grass. Prosperine was almost to Vik when Philip called her name. The demon paused and turned toward the necromancer. Mary was a short distance away. Haka and Alan were close by, staring at the demon. I took the opportunity to grab Vik and drag him back to the woods beside Sam. He grunted and cursed at me, but was otherwise silent.

"Damian?" Sam said as I laid Vik down.

"Yeah, it's me."

"Are we gonna make it through this?" Her voice was a whisper.

"Yeah, we are. I'll be back for you."

"Okay ..."

I clenched my fist and turned back to the battle. Foster was gone. I hoped that meant he was alright. Prosperine was striking out at a black wolf and Vassili. They were both too fast for the demon, for now. Philip used the distraction to stumble into his circle and raise his shield again. There were three other cloaks inside the circle and I recognized the three bloodied necromancers. Zachariah, Jamin, and the man Zola called Volund.

Another line of necromancers oozed out of the woods to the south, forming a line between me and the risen demon. They should have been watching their own asses.

Aideen walked out of the woods behind them. Her right wing was frayed and her left arm hung uselessly at her side, coated in a ribbon of blood. My skin crawled as she bellowed a high-pitched war cry and slammed her sword into the dirt. "Bubbles, Peanut, kill them all!"

Bubbles and Peanut charged, smashing through parts of the wooden fence that were still standing. Their long ears were plastered against their rippling backs as they pounded toward the necromancers between us and the demon. Their green bodies glowed with a white light and I could see them pulling tiny bits of life force in from everything around them. It flowed in tiny green streams from the trees and the earth and even the necromancers they were about to assault. The cu siths grew in an explosion of light and green fire, and when the now pony-sized Bubbles and Peanut fell upon the necromancers, I finally understood why they made good guard dogs.

The first necromancer was still blinking furiously after the flash of power when Bubbles's jaws closed around his head and snapped it off. Peanut landed on the next victim claws first. Blood and entrails exploded from the body. Another tried to raise her hand and throw something. Bubble's tongue lashed out and wrapped around the hand while Peanut knocked the necromancer to the ground and crushed her head with two vicious rabbit thumps of his hind legs.

"*Cu siths?*" Philip said as he dropped his shield, stepped forward, and raised his arm. "You underestimate me. *Inimicus deiciotto!*"

The wave of force hit Bubbles and Peanut mid-stride. There was a horrible crunch as they ran headlong into it and were thrown about fifty feet through the air. I didn't see where they came down. I'd learned my lesson from the soulstone distraction, but I could have sworn I heard Zola laugh.

"You shouldn't have left the circle," she said. I found her at the tree line, wearing an awful smile behind the line of surviving necromancers.

Philip's eyes widened as he looked down and tried to take a step back into the circle of power, but Zola was too fast. Her cane whipped forward

"Tyranno Eversiotto!"

Philip screamed as the torrent of devastation sent bodies and earth into the air and blasted him twenty feet away from his precious shield. He fell somewhere behind Prosperine and Vassili. The demon finally caught up with the vampire. Vassili grunted as he took another airborne trip across the field. He bounced off the ground near Sam and Vik and rolled into the northwestern woods beyond them.

I raised my gun and shot the demon in the head. It spared me a glance before turning away, heading toward Sam again. Dammit. The lights in its eye sockets flared and pulsed. I charged it. I didn't get there before Carter.

The khaki wolf came from the southern line of trees, near Aideen. Carter leapt and his jaws closed on Prosperine's shoulder. His muzzle and forearms were thick with blood and viscera. I heard him growl as Prosperine pulled him off her shoulder, leaving ragged wounds in the demon's red flesh.

The lights in Prosperine's eye sockets flared before she punched through Carter's chest. Her hand came back with a bloody, beating heart as the wolf jerked once and dropped to the cold ground, dead.

"Carter!" I heard Maggie's scream before I saw the silver wolf, following the same trail her husband had carved. She leapt over her fallen mate and the sound that came out of her mouth sent shivers down my spine.

"Maggie, stop!" Zola was running after the wolf. There was nothing she could do.

Prosperine caught the silver wolf in mid-leap and tore her arm off. The wolf howled and writhed in the demon's grip, biting the demon's arm again and again. The world slowed as Prosperine pulled her arm back and punched through Maggie's chest with a crack. The demon pulled out Maggie's heart and swallowed it before the dead wolf even hit the ground.

My body shook as I stared at the unmoving bodies of the wolves. My friends. Rage swelled. Rage powered a step forward. Rage flared my necromancy. I lost control of it. The dead came to me and I went to them. Some of them had been priests, some were children, some were murderers, some were mothers, and then I lit upon something else. Something distant, and vast, and terrible. I began to see flashes, a woman tied on top of my back, a girl, my daughter, she screamed as the men cut her. Soldiers, ancient soldiers. The vision cut off. *Don't go there son, you don't want to see that. Take this power, save your master, save Adannaya.* Another flood of power washed back through the ley lines until I thought my body would ignite. The last soul I touched, I knew. I knew her and she knew me. She showed me the cursed bayonet the fallen smith had made for her. She showed me Mike the Demon in the Civil War, the Union uniform he wore, the hammer he carried, the love she carried for him. Mike's little necromancer. She was a practitioner of the fallen arts and her knowledge came to my mind like a series of photographs. What changed Mike the Demon? What was changing Nixie? What did Maggie die for? The love and protection flowing through Carter and Maggie's auras still hung in the air. I didn't think. I didn't think about the consequences. I didn't think about how it would work. I just *knew* it would. It would kill me, but the demon would be dead. And that's all that fucking mattered.

I screamed and my necromancy flashed out to Carter and Maggie. Their bodies stood as I ordered them to and their souls wound back around the corpses as a needle of my power stitched them back together. The images of their lives and love and past flooded my brain until I was blinded in a hysterical rage.

And as I felt their loss, and their fear of death, their fear at what I was doing, they saw *exactly* what I intended to do. Both of their lifeless bodies turned gaping chest cavities to me and said, "Do it."

I pulled the focus from my belt and ran between my two dead friends. They grabbed my legs and hurled me at Prosperine with ungodly strength. As Carter and Maggie released their grip, I pulled their auras and their souls into my own with a soulart and channeled it all through the focus. My arms strained as I pulled back and swung a soulsword, the blade of a dark necromancer, in a vicious arc. It passed through Prosperine like she wasn't even there. I smashed into the left side of the demon's body and it fell away in a spray of black tar and gore. I thought the impact would kill me, but my body still moved. I stood up and struck again, cleaving her head in two between the fading lights of her eye sockets before I struck again, and again. There was nothing left by the time I felt the sting on my back. I didn't even know what hit me, but blood was coursing out of a wound below my right shoulder. I ran my hand though the warm flow and rubbed my fingers together. Rage took hold again and I turned toward the line of necromancers.

I felt something coming before the inky cloud oozed out of the ground in front of me and congealed into another gravemaker. A grin twisted my face and I raised the soulsword in my hand to strike it down.

Use it.

I heard Carter's voice in my head and I screamed.

Use the gravemaker.

Maggie's voice vibrated through my blasted mind.

Right and wrong didn't matter anymore. Only revenge. Only death. I reached out for the gravemaker with my necromancy. Some-one screamed and distantly I thought it was Sam. The blood loss was taking its toll, but Maggie and Carter pushed me on. They stayed with me in that sea of insanity. Carter told me he was proud. He'd been watching me a long time. His father had known my grandfather, knew Zola. He'd been ordered by the Watchers to keep an eye on me. Maggie was glad she'd known me. *Kill Philip, any way you can.* Maggie wanted him dead. I wanted him dead too. I didn't flinch as the flood of screaming souls and death and horror flooded my body when my necromancy tore into the gravemaker. A single thought could have dismantled the monster, but I had worse things to do that night. I turned my hand over into a claw and sent the gravemaker after the other necromancers.

They didn't realize what had happened until it was far, far too late.

The gravemaker's rough hand closed over a necromancer's hood and the crack of his skull echoed across the field. Some tried to run. A few disappeared into the woods, only to be chased by enormous green blurs. The rest just died.

My voice sounded like the dead as I turned on Philip. "*PINKERTON!*"

Philip's astonishment cracked into a laugh. It was a dark, twisted thing. He held up a shield as he backed away. "Just like me, Vesik.

Just like me. You'll never see it coming, just like this." Philip pulled a hand of glory out of his cloak and waved it through the air. Reality screamed as a portal formed into the Warded Ways. Philip backed into it after Volund, Jamin, and Zachariah fled before him. The oily wound vanished from mid-air with a snap.

Sobs wracked my body as I fell to the ground in a heap. I let go of Carter and Maggie. I didn't want to. I wanted to put them back together. Bring them back. Make things right. I heard their ghostly whispers as they said goodbye.

Mike the Demon stood over me with the Smith's Hammer. The flames still rippled across it as he said, "She spoke to you." I looked up at the demon and then lowered my head. He blew out a breath before he said, "What are you?"

And for the first time, I worried that Philip Pinkerton could be right.

CHAPTER 28

I hear the aftermath of the battle at Stones River was eventually added to the Watchers' handbook as an example of how to clean up a really, really, really big mess. As for our little group, Nixie and her fellow water witches left to report to their Queen. I didn't even get to hear their names before Nixie kissed me and disappeared into the shallow river. Aideen healed Foster and Cara as soon as the area was clear before healing the worst of my injuries. Foster healed the wolves and I was surprised when Hugh offered his blood to help heal the vampires. The other wolves followed suit, albeit less enthusiastically. It was left to Cara to heal the wolves again once the vampires had finished.

"I thought Philip used a hand of glory," Mary said as we walked through the trails of Stones River battlefield. We'd been slow to leave the area. I don't think anyone fully grasped what the hell had just happened. The sun was barely starting to peek above the horizon.

"No, it wasn't a hand of glory," Zola said. "It was the hand of a dead king."

Cara cursed and kicked a chunk of a demolished necromancer off the side of the trail. "Nameless King, still you haunt us."

Hugh was in front of me, carrying Carter in his arms and Vik walked beside him with Maggie. We found a quiet tree in the cemetery along the northern wall. Hugh laid the bodies side by side with their arms around each other. He was shaking when he stood up.

"I'll miss them," Hugh said. "He was a good Alpha."

"The best," Alan said.

Foster held out his hand and I gave him my staff. He dragged the ferrule in a circle around the bodies. "*Somes reverto terra*," he said and brought the ferrule of the staff down in the center of the circle. A murky grayish light flashed around the bodies before the earth churned and swallowed Carter and Maggie. We left them there, buried together on the battlefield at Stones River.

"Rest well, silver wolf," Vassili said.

A small smile quirked Hugh's lips as he turned away with his arm around Haka's shoulder.

We piled into the van a while later and headed back to the highway. Peanut stuffed himself between the front seats. The cu siths shrank a little, but not much. Bubbles was sprawled across Alan, Dominic, and an empty seat. No one talked much between the stops for gas and fast food. I stared at my hands and struggled to smile when Sam or Zola tapped my arm every now and again.

"You killed a demon," Zola said. "Aside from us, no one knows what you used to do it, and no one ever needs to know. You're not like him."

A thin smile cracked my lips. "That easy to read, huh?"

"Yep," Sam said.

"Damian, you are a spirit warrior unlike any I have ever heard of," Hugh said as he glanced at me in the rearview. "I know Carter would understand what you did, and I think the rest of us should follow his example."

I knew Carter understood. I don't think I could have gone through with it if he and Maggie hadn't told me to. The shadows of the highway rolled by as I looked out the window and contemplated why that didn't make me feel better about doing it.

"Get over it, *da*?" Vassili said. "It is miracle so many of us are alive." He was huddled in the back of the van beside Vik and Mary and Haka. He looked miserable.

Mike pushed Peanut's huge furry head down between the front seats so he could turn and meet my eyes. "This may not mean much, coming from a demon, but you did the right thing. I don't care whose rules you broke. If Prosperine was loosed on this world ..." He shook his head. "Carter and Maggie died for the good of their pack and even the good of this entire world. I can't think of a more noble death."

Hugh was nodding his head from the driver's seat.

"Thanks, Mike. It means a lot."

The fallen smith smiled and turned back to the road. His head snapped back to me and he said, "Oh, and if I catch you talking to my little necromancer again, I'll cut your balls off."

Everyone laughed. It wasn't loud, it wasn't joyous, but it was laughter.

***

Ashley cried for almost an hour when Hugh and I told her about Carter and Maggie. Hugh wanted me, Sam, and the fairies to be there when he told Ashley. I wasn't sure why until he hugged her, stepped away, and opened his mouth.

"Priestess of the River Wiccans, I, Hohnihohkaiyohos, would formally request you preside over the induction of the new River Pack Alpha this evening."

Ashley blinked a few times and nodded her head with wide, wet eyes.

"There's a new Alpha already?" Sam said.

"And a new name?" I said.

"Oh yes," Cara said. "Hugh is the new Alpha. He has passed on the honor two times before."

Hugh smiled. "Yes, I did. I cannot let my brothers die in my place any longer."

Ashley sniffed and said, "What do I need to do?"

"Come with me to Howell Island. The ceremony will be in the woods at twilight. I will teach you the few words you need to know."

"Cara, Aideen, Foster, I would like you to give your blessing at the ceremony."

The fairies bowed as one.

"Damian, Sam, I would like you to be our witnesses," Hugh said. "We always have an outside witness, but we've never had a vampire or a necromancer. I want to use this as an example of Carter's influence, an example of peace between the wolves, the vampires, and the necromancers."

"Of course, thank you," Sam said as she bowed her head.

"Is this a formal thing?" I said.

"Yep," Foster said.

I sighed. "I need a tux."

"Damian, you really don't need–" Hugh said.

I held my hand up. "No, we'll do this right. I'll just go by the mall."

Hugh nodded and said, "Buy the insurance."

I cocked an eyebrow but no one said anything else.

It was only two hours before we were standing in the woods of Howell Island with the whisper of the Missouri River and dozens of naked werewolves. I felt a little ridiculous in my loose-fitting tux, but it's all they had on such short notice.

Hugh was on his knees below Ashley, and the priestess was in full regalia. We were arranged in a formation that reminded me of a wedding, except for the fact everyone was standing up, oh, and did I mention they were all naked?

"Do you give your blessings to this wolf, *Sanatio* of the Sidhe?" Ashley said.

"We do," Cara said.

Ashley nodded and drew a scimitar from the sheath on her hip. It was an ancient blade with the stamp of a wolf's paw near the hilt. "Do you accept this mantle, Hohnihohkaiyohos?"

"For my friend, and for the good of the pack, I accept."

I cringed as Ashley sliced open Hugh's shoulder with two quick slashes of the scimitar. The wounds healed as we watched in silence. Legend says an unworthy wolf would not heal from a cut by that blade.

"It is done. I give you Hohnihohkaiyohos, the Alpha and the Shield of your pack."

The wolves erupted in applause and shouts. As Hugh stood, he shifted into his monstrous, auburn wolf form. He threw back his arms and howled. The wolves in the small clearing all shifted at once, blasting my senses with a surge of power. The air shook as Hugh's howl was joined by dozens.

Ashley wore an enormous grin and the howling went on. Goosebumps marched up and down my spine and I shivered at the cacophony of sound.

"Silence!" Hugh growled. Quiet followed immediately, though the mass of werewolves shifted and sniffed with impatience. "Damian Valdis Vesik, come forward."

I raised my eyebrows and stepped toward the hulking werewolf. I walked at a slow, wary pace past the front row of wolves.

"Give me your left arm."

I did and cringed when Hugh tore the sleeve off my tux. Thank god for tux insurance.

"Damian Valdis Vesik, I deliver unto you the decision of the River Pack. For your help and friendship of our Alpha past, we mark you pack."

I didn't have time to register what was happening as Hugh lifted my arm and bit down on it in one quick snap. My eyes widened and I stared at the bloody rows of puncture wounds on my arm.

"Let it be known, Damian Valdis Vesik is our *brother!* His sister Samantha is *our* sister! His family is ours and ours is his!"

The wolves roared and howled and my entire body shivered.

I leaned over to Hugh and said, "Does this mean I'm going to turn furry?"

His wolfish features peeled back in a grin. "That only happens in the movies. Usually."

Sam, Foster, Cara, and Aideen were laughing when I looked up. Cara shook her head and wiped her eyes as she held her other hand over the bite and whispered, "*Socius sanation cicatrixia.*"

I watched the wounds close, but they didn't heal completely. A dozen shiny scars decorated the front and back of my arm. And with that, I was pack.

ABOUT THE AUTHOR

Eric is a former bookseller, guitarist, and comic seller currently living in Saint Louis, Missouri. A lifelong enthusiast of books, music, toys, and games, he discovered a love for the written word after being dragged to the library by his parents at a young age. When he is not writing, you can usually find him reading, gaming, or buried beneath a small avalanche of Transformers. For more about Eric, see www.daysgonebad.com.

VESIK, THE SERIES

Days Gone Bad
Wolves and the River of Stone

Available in paperback and ebook from www.daysgonebad.com and
all major book sellers.

Made in the USA
San Bernardino, CA
01 July 2014